Toby Guise

THE GOLD SANDS

'Had I been rich, ah me, how deep had been my delight in matters of the soul...'

Flecker, *Hassan*, Act 1

Principal Characters

Nicholas Paget	*a former resource prospector*
Charlotte Falk	*his sister*
Daniel Falk	*her husband, a banker*
Dominic Bannerman	*a lawyer*
Imogen Somerville	*his girlfriend, a financial analyst*
Roger Curtis	*a retired pop star*
Irina Ivanova	*his girlfriend, a drama student*
Dinah Laughlin	*a painter*
Sir David McAllister	*chairman of United Minerals*
Conrad de Salis	*a Mayfair club-owner*

MAY

Nicholas Paget stood in the Serpentine. Morning sun glinted on the water and two British flags fluttered above the treetops on the other side of the lake. Spring had arrived late, and his calves were wrapped in deep winter cold. He had come the day before but lingered back and not changed into his swimming trunks. Now a jogger had stopped further along the shore and was watching him with her arms crossed. Nick thought of his pale body rising from the green water, and launched himself in.

For a moment, the shock felt like freedom. He turned onto his back and kicked away from the shore, where other swimmers were already leaving for work. He was starting to envy them their three holidays a year, even if the very word made him shrink. The months without travel were turning into a living death, and Nick grimaced at the thought of himself.

He flipped over and attacked the still water with a crawl. This wasn't even a real lake, just an underground river pumped up and spread across this concrete basin. Not even a real river! Not like the great Panjshir, roaring through northern Afghanistan; or the Indus, fault-line of empires; or the Zervashan, spraying its golden sands along the valleys of Uzbekistan.

Spraying them, above all, along *his* valley. He remembered pale dust hanging in the evening light, the only time he had been there. For a decade, the secret had taunted him like a djinn. It could still skip away in an instant; even now, when it was so close to hatching into gold.

The thought made his chest tighten in the cold water. No! Soon ore would tumble out of the earth, glistening like the water around him. One strike and you're *in*! So what if today would only bring lunch with his sister, then another date with her friend? And if the month would only bring a cheque for his *Sufi Journal* article on Prince Dimitrie Cantemir? By the end of the year he would be able to travel anywhere; buy a house in Greece; even start a family. This life was just a waiting room, telescoping closer to the moment when everything became new.

Nick was no longer cold as he turned for the bank, and he hauled himself up the handrail with vigour. Timur stood and stretched with a yawn, the short tail oscillating as he placed two paws on Nick's leg. Nick stood under the outside shower and the cold water wrapped itself around his taut sides. The moment of depression was gone and the words of Rumi came to him: 'Many ways lead to God, I have chosen that of music and dance'. And he clapped twice into the sun.

*

Dominic Bannerman sat at his desk in a dressing gown. Sun spilled into the room from the terrace, where the remains of breakfast lay. He watched a fly land on the flecked rim of the orange juice glass and silently rub its front legs together.

Dominic always started the working week at home. It held back the attentions of his partner and staff, who could not see that Monday was a quiet day. He placed a bare foot on the edge of the desk and tilted back his chair, the finger and thumb of one hand turning slow circles on each cheek. An item had caught his eye from the curt list prepared by his secretary each Friday afternoon.

It was nearly a year since Nick Paget had first asked for a meeting. The following week, Dominic had watched from his office window as Nick crossed St James Square with the same riding gait and long, straight steps which he remembered from school. The sight reminded him of Nick's odd superiority; his conversation peppered with half-seen opportunities, yet disdaining the success they might bring.

The hour was almost up before Nick inched around to the secret which he so obviously hoarded. With quiet intensity, he said that he had evidence of an untouched gold seam in Central Asia. The mineral rights kept slipping through his hands and now he wanted help. If Dominic could get an option on the concession, he would find an investor to let them take ownership. Nick sat back with a grave look, and Dominic inclined his head respectfully. Nick's past was written in his tanned forehead and loose summer shirt. He had been on the ground in these countries but had never returned rich. And what will be different this time?

When Nick reverently produced the results of a seismographic survey, Dominic asked the obvious question. If the rights had passed through so many hands, why had the deposit not already been found? Nick gave him a pregnant look. The seam is an anomaly, he said. It is too far from the original mine for anyone to have looked. Dominic had nodded neutrally, wondering how little was fantasy.

The reminder now on his screen told him that the rights were about to lapse. He clicked on it, smiling when he saw in which country the concession lay. Something surfaced in his memory; a news item glimpsed the previous year, which he should have noted at the time. He opened another window and started searching the newswires. Yes, there was the man who could quietly help him get the option. And here, opening another window, was his number.

Dominic sat back, finger and thumb returning to circle his cheeks. What had he missed? What was there to miss? There was hardly any information, just a thread of hearsay and an illegible graph. All the legal work would remain in his hands and Nick didn't look like a man who read the small print. That was interesting, and ideas about how to structure the deal started coming to him. He had seen life-changing information come from stranger sources than Nick Paget before. And something in the very fantastical nature of the story attracting him. It might be fun.

He exhaled lightly and entered the long number into his telephone. He heard the sound of an overseas ringtone, then the call was answered with a short

Russian syllable.

'Mikhail?' he said. 'Dominic Bannerman here... No, *Bannerman.*' His face hung at the uncertainty then relaxed into a smile, and he replaced a foot on the edge of the desk. It was lunchtime in Moscow and Mikhail was feeling loquacious, yet his jolting accent and the background noise of the restaurant gave Dominic an uneasy nostalgia. When he was sure that Mikhail had understood the request, he declined the invitation to say hello to someone called Ekaterina and excused himself from the conversation.

The flat seemed too quiet after that window into his old life. Antiques supported thickets of photographs and walls were crowded with prints and oil paintings, most of which were crooked. The asymmetry tortured him but asking his downstairs neighbours not to slam their doors would be worse. After all, he had chosen Pimlico for its anonymity as well as its good postcode. And the light was beautiful, reflecting over a low skyline from the River Thames.

He took a sip of tepid coffee and looked back to his diary. The week was too crowded and would need to be thinned out. He could see which appointments to prune as clearly as if each name glowed like a falling or rising stock. Was it wrong to accept meetings with the intention of cancelling them? It hardly mattered, as people always asked for another. At least he was seeing Imogen that evening. He closed his eyes for a moment, then went back to his list.

2

Charlotte Falk stood in her white drawing room. The new painting lay against a sofa, bubble-wrap gathered like melting ice cream around its base. The picture's blue and gold pigments glowed in the room, just as she had imagined when she first saw it through a gallery window. She smiled.

She kicked off her shoes and lifted the piece to the wall, its frame weighing nicely on her gym-toned arms. She loved her walls: they felt like the only part of the house she really owned. Even so, the picture rail would have no dust on it, just as there was none beneath the cream leather sofas. She had not known such cleanliness until she married. Daniel had given her the decoration, but she could hardly have recreated the multi-coloured, dog-strewn madness of her childhood. It had to be white, like his sisters' houses. The work had been finished four years ago; and now it felt like they were too rich to live in anything other than a house like this. The previous year, the basement had been excavated for a gym and a cinema. Daniel liked new releases and held movie nights for his colleagues. On winter weekdays, Charlotte would go down and lose herself in long hours of Bergman and Tarkovsky.

She laid down the painting and went through to the

kitchen, where a superabundance of packaging greeted her inside the fridge. In a series of unannounced visits, Daniel's mother had made it clear that empty shelves were not looked upon well. Every Sunday, he now drove their donation to the food bank. She had been with him once but not gone back. It was the ease that unnerved her; the sheer lack of embarrassment or incongruity as the long car drew up. He had not opened the boot remotely, but stepped out and handed an armful directly to the waiting woman, some silent energy passing between them. Whatever the source of Daniel's adjustment, she knew her son Adam would inherit it; and be a stranger too, came the unwelcome thought. Her daughter Rachael was different. Charlotte saw a softness in the child which she thought had come from her.

She moved into the last space before the garden, where a studio photograph of the children looked down on their play area. All of Daniel's sisters had ones of their children, so it had been a fait accompli that they should have one too. But the frozen physical detail had scared her when the picture arrived, seeming more dead than alive. She still wanted to have a proper portrait commissioned, and thought of asking Nick if he knew anyone. Her brother had an attraction to bohemians.

She pressed a button and the French doors slid open with an unwilling creak. Too loud: she must have it looked at before the garden party. The watering system had just stopped and droplets hung trembling on the wisteria. She knew what it meant. The silent expectation; the weight upon the body. Babies. She linked her arms across her front and started gently blowing the drops from a leaf.

*

Timur began barking before drawing breath, so the first sounds came out high-pitched and strangled. He careered around a corner, drifting like a racing car on the metal surface of the houseboat. It amazed Charlotte that he had never fallen into the river.

'Timur, for God's sake!' she said. The dog stood with a front paw raised, growling and wagging its tail as if it had only half-recognised her. She put her head around the cabin door and Nick looked up from the piano apprehensively. Manuscripts were scattered across its walnut top.

'Oh, it's you,' he said, sliding some documents into a folder.

'Yes, it's me,' she said, then indicated the terrier. 'Doesn't family count for anything around here?'

'Apparently not,' said Nick, and played an unresolved chord.

'Am I disturbing you?' she said, and Nick smiled. It was one of their rituals.

'Of course you're disturbing me,' he said. 'I would hardly be sitting here doing nothing!'

'I see,' she said. 'Then may I ask if you *mind* that I'm disturbing you?'

'Ah,' said Nick, standing up from the piano. 'The answer to that, my dear, is not at all!'

Charlotte smiled delightedly, her chin pulling back

towards her neck. They embraced and her shopping bags made a necklace around Nick's back. She dropped them by the piano and pointed to an animal skin lying on the sofa.

'How long has that thing been dead for?' she said, and Nick looked at it appraisingly.

'About a century,' he said.

'Should be long enough,' said Charlotte. She settled on it, her white chiffon dress billowing on the coarse brown hair.

'I'm lying, of course,' said Nick, and her eyes narrowed. He had spent their childhood convincing her of unlikely things then encouraging her to share them with people. 'I only shot it last week,' he said. 'In Putney.'

'I shot a bear in Putney / With the hope of making chutney,' she recited. Nick sprung back to the keyboard and played a music-hall chord.

'Not a bear, madam!' He improvised a crescendo and left it hanging in the air. 'A Himalayan *go-al!*'

They both burst out laughing.

'Shall we have a drink?' he said.

'Oh, let's!' she cried, clasping her hands together.

*

They sat down to a cold lunch and a bottle of Sauvignon. Charlotte talked about his date that evening, and Nick assented neutrally. She already knew he wasn't interested in Samantha, so there was little for him to say. They discussed their mother, whose energy pulsated as far as London from her cottage in East Sussex. Charlotte shouldered most of it, at her husband's insistence taking the children down every few weeks. They moved on to discuss their summer plans, of which Charlotte's were more populated; and the party that she and Daniel were giving the following month.

As the conversation followed these familiar channels, Nick's real thoughts were pulled inwards to the message he had received from Dominic Bannerman. It had contained nothing more than a date for dinner, yet Nick knew the man didn't give out his time for nothing. His excitement had tingled all morning but there was no point in telling Charlotte yet. He stood instead and suggested they finish the wine outside.

They sat in two deck chairs and Timur curled into a silent ball between them. Clouds hung high in the still air and the River Thames lay before them, flanked by plane trees and brick-red glimpses of Chelsea. A pending silence settled.

'So, Nicky,' said Charlotte. 'How are things going?'

The muscles of Nick's jaw tightened. Forty-two may be too old to be broke, but it was certainly too old be asked about it. His biography of Fitzroy Maclean had neatly sold its print run and no more. Then the royalties from his guide book to Turkey had also glimmered and died. The publishers had even brought his replacement to one of the meetings; a boy barely into his twenties who grinned at him as if they knew each other. The letters from people using Nick's old edition still arrived, and he hated himself for appreciating them so much.

Now he had seen no new money for a year. Charlotte

had remained silent when his plan to teach Persian at a London college had collapsed in acrimony, and only now was asking what he would do instead. But there was nothing instead, except to gnaw at the money which he needed for Dominic to buy the option; the money which would alchemically turn into millions, if only he could keep it intact for long enough. Until then, every expense was a decision. Even today's bottle of Pouilly Fumé had cost minutes of hesitation. Buying decent wine was one of the reasons he invited people onto the boat in the first place. Being family, Charlotte came then asked the questions that no-one else does; the ones that cannot be answered.

'I've been asked to become a Knight of the Garter,' he said, draining his glass.

'Seriously,' said Charlotte, smiling. 'You still writing about that composer, Canterloube?'

'Cante*mir*,' he said, remembering his overdue article. 'Canteloube is French. Yes, I am.' He continued quickly: 'How are Rachael and Abraham?'

She shot him a dark look.

'Adam, you mean,' she said. 'They're fine. They're all fine.' She paused. 'Life goes on.'

'And how are you?' he said, needing to equal the score even as he sensed the danger. She looked at him.

'It's so easy for you, isn't it?' she said. 'Living this Peter Pan life on your stupid boat, writing books about people no-one's ever heard of. You can barely afford to feed your fucking *dog!*'

Nick felt his eyes widen, yet there was truth in what she said. He complained that he couldn't travel but he was infinitely more free. Charlotte could leave the children with an army of nannies, but she had to come back. His kinder intuition had lost out to cruelty when the opportunity had come to needle her, so he had really brought it on himself. Yet her undertow of sadness was getting stronger, and this new outburst scared him. She was already starting to blush and he wanted to reach out and touch her, but that would be such a terrible overstatement.

'I'm sorry, Nicky,' she said. 'I didn't mean that.'

'It's ok,' he said.

His sister was staring at the other bank, her eyes fixed on Battersea Power Station.

*

Nick walked to the edge of the water, taking controlled breaths. Across the river, the Savoy Hotel was painted in quiet stripes by its floodlights, and a single pale flagpole rose against the night sky.

His evening with Samantha Allerton had followed predictable lines; dinner preceded by a concert of Romantic cacophony at the South Bank. Listening to the jumbled noises, he had silently railed against these European composers who trampled the listener's spirit under their own. He imagined the whispering flutes of a Dervish ceremony and thought: meet me out *there*, where we are equals; for inside your head I am nothing.

Samantha had booked a table in a chain restaurant beneath the concert hall, where they drank Chianti and ate simple pasta. They spoke about his sister, and Nick thought privately how much she had changed. The grain of darkness which used to set off her personality now seemed to be consuming her. Her humour had used to be a rebellion against the world; now it seemed it to be a rebellion against herself, caustic and grudging. Most of all, he could not have imagined her pushing Samantha on him before she herself had married. When Samantha picked up the bill with swift finality, he felt coals of anger at what Charlotte must have said to her. They parted company in early night and she reached up to kiss him goodbye. But his face had set like cold lava, and she left with a rueful smile.

Drinking in the cool air, Nick felt low at what he had done. Samantha's generosity was not an insult, nor was it only directed at him. Much of dinner had been given over to the charity project she managed in East Africa. The pictures on her phone showed her moving through crowds of children, drunk with sun and affection. He too knew the draw of Africa: the smell of dust and blossom blown over a thousand miles; the unbearable pathos of their choirs; the faces of the children like a hundred suns. Yet for all the time Samantha had spent out of England, something in her frank mouth and steady look made him think that she had never really left.

He turned and walked upstream into a breeze that carried the promise of summer. Somewhere on the opposite bank was the candle-lit cellar bar where he had used to meet his controller during trips back to London. The conspiratorial setting had been lost on the quiet civil servant, and it had disappointed him to find that most spies were so boring. He had little to tell them anyway. 'They are going to shut the casinos in Baku because the president is addicted to gambling.' The man would nod professionally and Nick move on to another topic. There was no point in explaining how little any of it meant if they were determined to take these things seriously.

Emerging from beneath the railway bridge, he saw the National Liberal Club across the water. It was on the terrace there that he and his father had shared their last bottle of wine. Roddy Paget had not gone gently as the illness took hold, and a month later he was dead. Nick smiled, thinking that his father had faced death as quixotically as he had faced politics.

Arriving at his dinghy, he found the bow held high out of the water by the mooring rope. He swore as he climbed over the railings. He often forgot about the tide tables when he was in a hurry, and could not afford to lose his runabout on something as stupid as this. Something had made him think there was a public mooring here; probably the way Samantha had said 'just along the river' when she called to invite him. He had skiffed around angrily looking for it before tying up illegally on some old stone loading steps. Now the knot was tight and he had to take the weight of the boat with one arm while levering it apart. It gave and he vaulted down into the small hull, then fired the outboard as quietly as he could. It took him out into the stream and he relaxed again as the banks of the great city slipped by. The motor whined back from the underside of Westminster Bridge and he emerged before the glowing amber front of the Houses of Parliament. Again he thought that his father would not have been happy as an MP, in spite of all the money he had spent trying to get elected. Only later did Nick realise that it had been the unscrupulousness of his father's friends, as they led a political party in its death throes, which had also cost the family so much. The long decades and endless replaying were usually enough for him to have stopped caring about the loss. But now that ownership of his mine was finally in sight, it hurt not to be able to finance more of the deal himself. He would get rich but some outside backer would get richer. And he didn't even know who yet.

If only John Streeter were still alive. He remembered the day which had led to their first prospecting trip together; the day, he now realised, when his separation from England had first begun. He had joined his father and John for lunch during his first summer at university, thinking the conversation would be an antidote to student life. He was right, and John was soon regaling them about Kyrgyzstan and the mineral rights he was going to extract there. Nick's face must have betrayed him, as John's eyes settled suggestively in his.

'Come with me!' he said, and dismissed the idea of a visa with a flutter of his hand. A week later they were lifting off from Bishkek airport in an old Sikorsky helicopter. Two bearded men sat by the open door, the downdraft beating their robes around their Kalashnikovs. John leant over and shouted in his ear: 'The Great Game is happening *now*'. Nick was breathless. He never saw Cambridge again.

Remembering John's winged eyebrows and Puckish smile, Nick felt a sharp longing for his company. The old man had eventually given up chasing mineral deposits and retreated to a monastery on Mount Athos. When an unexpected bequest happened, Nick assumed it meant that John had died.

And now, finally, he needed to tap into the diaphanous webs of money which had floated around his old friend. Instead he was naked in the face of this moment for which he had waited so long. The dinner with Dominic was only days away and had started to scare him. What if Dominic already had the option, while he lacked not only an investor but even any ideas? Bannerman would simply pick up his address book and call someone else for the money. They would push out him and tear the land apart themselves until they found the seam. Mixing with the cheap wine and the slapping of the boat, the problem was starting to make him feel sick. He found himself hoping that Dominic had failed even to secure the option, so the vice of responsibility would open and he could go back to simple evenings of wine and music with Timur.

The wind was cold now, cutting through his jacket and dusting his face with spray. The grand peaks of Albert Bridge finally came into view and he nosed the dinghy into Cadogan Pier beside the *Roxanne*. Only when John had left him the houseboat did he give some credence to the smiles which their friendship had raised in his father's circle. But the idea still seemed a shallow one, and Nick preferred to think that John had done it out of sympathy for the family's destitution; the very destitution which those same smirking men had encouraged. John had named the *Roxanne* after Alexander the Great's mountain bride, the most beautiful woman in Asia. Now most people connected the name with a pop song; and Nick didn't know if it was worse to correct them or just to let it go.

Stepping onto the deck, he heard Timur jump down inside the cabin and run to the door. He opened it and swept the dog up to eye level.

'Timmy!' he said. 'Timmy Timmy Timmy! Nick heard some *very* strange music this evening!'

Timur's brown eyes narrowed and he flexed his shoulders, trying to get close enough to lick Nick's nose. Nick let him out onto the deck then quickly moved around the cabin, taking off his wet shirt and lighting the woodburner. He poured a glass of wine from the open bottle and put some Buxtehude on the stereo, then turned down the lights so the rugs and artefacts were lit by the gathering firelight. Once Timur had scratched and been let back in, Nick locked the door and settled on a rug to meditate. He soon opened his eyes to see Timur curled up by the stove, watching him.

'Our man is out there,' he said. 'I know he is.'

3

Nick looked across the table at Dominic Bannerman and thought: you never seem to age. When he tried to picture Dominic back at school, he saw the same double-breasted suit; the same crepuscular glimmer of candlelight on his silk tie; even the same grey around his temples. Probably the only real continuity was his host's relentless display of manners. Dominic would lean across the table attentively then sit back with an easy laugh, raising his glass as if toasting what had been said. Nick wondered if he was a chameleon, changing between countries and people; or if this suffocating charm was the only disguise he needed.

Dominic's main course had been cooked in sweet wine and was pulling uneasily on Nick's palate as he tried to enjoy his grilled lamb. They were in some kind of club, surrounded by its smooth orbits of activity. Waiters in fawn jackets moved between the flickering tables, replacing the coasters with each new round of drinks. A fireplace was lit in an inner courtyard, where strands of ivy fell over a carved stone lintel. Cocoons of greater privacy seemed to recede from the main spaces and he had half-recognised a face at an upper window. The air contained not a hint of age, just the ambient trace of incense. Nick rarely felt displaced, yet something in the lapidary warmth of the place reassured him. It was impossible to imagine a bluff failing in a place like this.

Cesare passed the table and looked with discreet interest at Mr Bannerman's guest. The man was sitting still and erect, neatly slicing the meat and lifting it to his mouth with quick movements. The suit was good but old and its seam had burst at the elbow. Up from the country, he thought.

Dominic was looking across the table with invisible attention. Nick's auburn hair was swept back over a round forehead, a permanent trace of worry now written across the brow. His curved nose sat between hollow cheeks and the front of his collar met away from his neck, like someone who was recovering from a tropical disease. The look was distant, flicking to the walls and table then making abrupt eye contact when he laughed. The humour itself was difficult and elliptical, and it annoyed Dominic having to fake so many laughs. Nick's tan extended up under his thinning hairline and Dominic thought: you are a lazy man, so you have made an easy life for yourself. Yet Nick was clearly proud of answering to no-one, and carried an air of ownership without seeming to own anything.

Well, thought Dominic, maybe you will own something one day. Earlier that day, he had got a call saying they had been offered an option on the mine. The problem of how to get himself a more respectable stake had come into focus, as Nick had offered him only ten percent. The solution he reached was some nice cheap options, lying quietly in the paperwork with Dominic's name on them.

'Now,' said Dominic, and Nick prepared himself. He had not much enjoyed leading the conversation and seeing even Dominic's polite interest begin to slip when he stayed onto Cantemir. Talking about the deal would be easier, even if it did mean lying about having found the money. He nodded readily.

'I've been working on the deal,' said Dominic. 'But I'm keen for it not to fall into the wrong hands.'

Nick nodded again. He was pleased to hear it. Dominic had worked in New York and Moscow before re-emerging as a partner in Bannerman Lloyd LLP, a small law firm which seemed to do everything but law. He knew a lot of people who could take the deal away from them in an instant.

'If we are offered the option, I'll form a company in Jersey to buy it,' said Dominic, deciding at the last minute not to tell Nick about the day's success until he had shown more of his hand. 'But it will need a flexible capital structure for follow-on rounds.'

Capital structure, thought Nick: ziggurat. Follow-on rounds: *duck!* He chuckled silently. His imagination always shied onto the wrong associations when people talked about finance, and his attention returned to the painting behind Dominic. A desert Arab stood tall in the wind, his head cloth painted in lead-white oils. A Martini-Henry rifle hung from his shoulder and the sandstorm blew behind him. Nick wondered if it had been painted out there in the desert, and if Europeans had carted their easels and classical training around Mesopotamia. The man's gaze looked out across the room. The most beautiful smell of all, Lawrence had written; the smell of the desert wind.

'Does that make sense?' said Dominic, and Nick's attention telescoped back to the table.

'Oh yes,' he said. 'That all sounds fine.'

'Now,' said Dominic, surprised at how easily the moment had passed. 'Tell me what you will need to do at your end.' Nick's eyes flickered with unease, and Dominic realised that he didn't have the money yet. It was strange to have been given the answer to a question that he hadn't even asked. 'Operationally, I mean,' he said, and Nick leant forwards with greater confidence.

'I'll buy some new satellite photos to see what surface activity has taken place,' he said. 'Then I'll need to go to Tashkent to organise core sampling. Drilling, I mean...' Dominic nodded. 'But finding a trustworthy sampling company in that part of the world is the difficult part.'

'Why?' said Dominic.

'Well,' said Nick expansively. 'All kinds of things can happen. They can falsify the results. Switch the samples. Even run gold rings around dud samples to overvalue a mine. In the old days, they used to load shotguns with gold dust and fire them down a mine shaft, then sell it on to some unsuspecting buyer. Shotgunning the mine they used to call it.'

Dominic chuckled.

'And who's the bad guy in all this?' he said, the long eyebrows floating upwards. 'Where does the risk lead?'

Nick smiled and gave his glass a confident swirl.

'Straight to the State Geological Committee!' he said. 'And they've no qualms about kicking out a multinational to keep their gold reserves for themselves. They did it to one of their own joint-venture partners the other day, and they were a lot bigger than us!'

Dominic's eyes were sparkling, and Nick stopped. Hadn't he had to leave Russia in a hurry then look over his shoulder for years? Nick felt a flush of embarrassment at having lectured him on foreign governments, and was annoyed he didn't think of these things first.

'You get the picture,' he said, rearranging the knife and fork on his plate.

'Well, you should know,' said Dominic with a sly smile.

'Now, now...' said Nick. They looked each other in the eye and laughed. Dominic privately found it alarming that someone like Nick had used to be a stringer for the intelligence services. Yet he had enjoyed the moment of familiarity, and leant back casually.

'So,' he said. 'How about this investor then?'

'Well,' said Nick, lifting his wine glass. 'It's best to do that once the option is in place, so the investor can't bypass us. But I'm working on a few leads.'

The flicker crossed his eyes again, and Dominic felt strangely moved that there were still people who couldn't lie.

'Good for you,' he said.

Nick nodded contentedly and looked down at the dessert menu. His pate was mottled from the sun, yet Dominic thought how little he had really aged. He had a vision of Nick as an old man, aloof and unchanging, never having communicated what he thought he had discovered about life; still yearning for an enlightenment that would never come. It made him regret not saying that they had already secured the option, so Nick could go home happy for the evening. And Dominic searched for one thing he could delegate; just one decision that would make Nick feel like the man he wanted to be.

'One more thing,' he said, and Nick looked up. 'What would you like me to call the company?'

Nick pursed his lips, looking past Dominic.

'Call it Cantemir Resources,' he said.

*

Sir David McAllister stepped back from the upper window of the courtyard. Nick Paget, of all people! Their time in Baku came back to him; trying to keep the boat upright in the Caspian wind, followed by an evening feast of shrimps. Dear Nick, he thought. Always talking about the wrong thing and looking in the wrong direction. But he did it with such love, such enthusiasm! It was odd how affection and respect could be such strangers, and he guiltily remembered the words of his mentor Franz Rosenheim: friends count. Nick was nothing if not a friend; or rather, that's all he was. David would have liked to go down and say hello, but then he would have to listen to Nick's latest scheme. And once David had started, he would have to greet half the people in the Club. No, it was better to stay back in the owner's apartment with its little window overlooking the courtyard.

Conrad de Salis sat with his long ankles crossed and a cigar slumbering in a round oyster shell. His Saluki slept on the sofa, sand-coloured save for its black eyebrows and ear-tips. The dog raised its head when David returned to his armchair then replaced it between the cushions with a long sigh.

David liked de Salis's company. The man was worldly enough to pass the time, yet disclaimed any corporate interests of his own. David knew it was an act, as the Club itself was a big an interest as anyone could have; but it was an act to which he enjoyed succumbing.

Conrad's club was much more than just the building it occupied. It was a membership list chosen to span London and the world; a list which the man opposite him knew intimately. At a stroke, de Salis could facilitate powerful alliances or the end of dangerous enmities. He could pass information a hundred ways or simply let it mature in his pocket, watching the dance of those who needed it. Without seeming to move from his chair, Conrad always knew who was in the building. David wondered if he wore an earpiece connected to a camera room, or if the building was wired for sound as well as the usual closed-circuit cameras. He had thought of asking his own head of security to find out. But it seemed wrong to ask Kobus to spy on a friend, so instead he just assumed that it was.

When Conrad did circulate through the club, it was with a bemused air that made him hard to approach. He would ignore a developing drama only to swoop down on an overlooked detail. The nearest member of staff would receive an account of how painful he found it to see lilies going thirsty, or how demoralising to see food going out on cold plates. Conrad would then quickly sink back into anonymity as if he was just another member, or even a guest. Newcomers would sometimes take refuge with him on that basis, and Conrad seemed to like passing the time of day with them. But as soon as someone realised who he was, he would look through them with a quizzical smile and move on. The ability to cut people without being rude fascinated David: it was the skill of the English which he would most like to acquire.

David paid his way with occasional pieces of information from his own pocket, and by sending over the visiting ministers of countries where he owned mines. He never came with them or else it would be his thousands going into the tills; but the dignitaries believed coming through the door was a favour enough. They often sent him little trinkets the following day, which he would donate to the Catholic hospice for resale. It was a nice, zero-cost set of arrangements and David felt an urge to pay tribute to their friendship; but Conrad pre-empted him.

'It's not a bad place,' said Conrad excusingly. He seemed to have a sixth sense for a compliment coming over the horizon, always heading it off with a quick shower of indifference. David too easily forgot how for men of Conrad's background, emotion was the most embarrassing bodily function of all.

'Aye,' he said. Seeing Nick Paget was a good opportunity to test his theory about the Club being wired, although Conrad might sense an ulterior motive behind the question. What the hell, he thought: Conrad's a grown up.

'Just saw an old mate of mine, Nick Paget,' said Sir David, swirling the tumbler of whisky meditatively. 'I wonder who he's seeing?'

Conrad made a helpless gesture.

'Perhaps he's taking his mother out?' he said.

David smiled. There was no chance Nick was a member here, which meant he wasn't taking anyone out. Someone had bought him here. David wondered who and why, as Conrad was clearly not going to tell him.

'How are things at United Minerals?' said Conrad. 'Your lord and master Alexander Rosenheim was here the other day.'

The lazy change of subject was typical, yet David felt Conrad was also needling him by referring to one of his main shareholders like that. He wondered if he had annoyed him with the leading question.

'United's doing what it always does,' he said. 'Digging things out of the ground.'

'And burying them?' said Conrad, his green eyes momentarily playful. A compressed smile crossed Sir David's lips, then he threw the dice and they both leaned forwards to see the roll.

*

Charlotte looked at her husband. Daniel's strong eyebrows and saturnine face were lit by candlelight, the winter white of his shirt glowing in the light of a single flame. He kept clean ones at the office to change into for the evening, and she knew how much it meant to him to be a member here. She couldn't tell him how stressful she found it. It was the most sought-after place in London and influence swirled in every room, eddying around large groups and pooling in quiet corner conversations. When they met people, Charlotte was quickly appraised as a plus one. She would be happy to be one and would have loved to join these ethereal women drawing from their bottomless wells of small talk. But no-one had given her the keys, so instead she stood dumbly. Neither a one nor a plus one, she thought; and probably pitied by both.

Once a precious beam of intelligence had reached her from one of the other members. Within moments, they had covered Chagall, Paul Klee, even Klimt. The Paris School. Gertrude Stein and her mad unilateralism. Kiefer's cityscapes. Laughing at German Expressionism and mimicking its poses. Daniel had noted it happily but a look from the other man's wife soon ended the conversation. That awful correction had made her feel like a whore. Never again had she risked breaking the great rule, the same rule to which she could not conform: that the wives only get on with each other. She had little more in common with the power women; so instead just lingered near Daniel, exchanging the odd empty syllable with one of her peers.

Daniel was talking with quiet seriousness about the children's future education. She had met him the year after her father died, and he soon became the best man to have taken her out. His quiet competence was so unlike the fragile pride of the artists and quasi-musicians who had gone before him; the real achievements of his career seeming instead to be a source of humility. His family had shown her such warmth, with no trace of the scepticism which she had been led to expect. Her mother too had been loved by them; a task which she had been preparing to face alone with Nick so often out of the country.

Who wouldn't have said yes when Daniel proposed? Yet she hadn't realised the mechanism would start so soon and so uncontrollably; an engagement party, the wedding, the pregnancy, the house. Only her hen party had broken the momentum, throwing her back into an earlier life, and through that crack an odd doubt had begun to seep. But she never told her friends and the twinge was soon subsumed beneath the machinery of life. Since then, the forward motion had been relentless. Even his lovemaking left her with the sense that it was just another part of his day. Why don't you just tie me up in that gym of yours? she thought. Because he would probably ask how she wanted it done first.

Charlotte wiped the corner of her eye and Daniel's face lit up with concern.

'Everything ok?' he said.

'Nothing darling,' she said. 'Just make up.'

'You're too beautiful for make-up,' said Daniel.

Charlotte smiled to hide her embarrassment and took more of the velvety wine. He had made himself into an amateur expert on Australian wine and liked explaining how it was overtaking French wine on a number of measures. She found herself missing tart red wine from a plastic cup, the lifeblood of her art school. But she knew Daniel's wine hobby made him happy and she was hardly in a position to order herself. And it was wine. He was asking about the house now, and the preparations for the garden party; and she knew each answer almost before the question came. I do know how to make small talk, she thought. This is small talk.

She looked guiltily around the magnificent surroundings. Most of the paintings were of Middle Eastern subjects but painted in a European style. She wanted to touch their surfaces and see if they were originals or turned out in a warehouse in Battersea. The pictures reminded her of Nick. They looked like scenes from inside his head: dhows under sail, Ottoman seraglios, and tribesmen men carrying weapons. It was a shame they had never bought him here... But here he was! She broke into a smile, and Daniel smiled back at her.

'Darling,' she said to Daniel. 'Look who it is!' Her brother had appeared behind him with a mischievous smile. 'I was *just* thinking of you!' she said.

Nick loved his sister's look of incomprehension, because it exactly mirrored how he had felt when he saw her. He realised how little he knew of her life with Daniel; even so, what better claim could he have on this place than running into a sibling? He had felt a small tide of gratitude, and enjoyed Dominic's surprise when he announced that he should go and say hello to his sister. Now he hoped that her surprise didn't betray *him* and he thought: yes, we are both interlopers here.

When his brother-in-law rose to greet him, Nick's

thoughts earthed like lightning. Daniel was a banker: he could easily put together a syndicate to buy the mine! But the man's dark suit and perfect hair made him uneasy, speaking of a scrutiny which the deal might never pass. When Daniel asked him to join them, Nick turned to look for his host.

Dominic had seen Charlotte from other side of the room and was already walking over to the table.

'Join us,' said Daniel with an open gesture.

'What a nice idea,' said Dominic, settling into the banquette.

Charlotte noticed the newcomer's strong head and sharp features, his lithe frame neatly encased in a double-breasted suit. She didn't catch his name from her brother, so the grey eyes rested on her anonymously as she took a soft hand. When they flicked on to Daniel, the narrow lips seemed to hang with impatience, curling like Lord Byron's in his portraits. She saw a similarity too in the square forehead and puckered brow, although the straight, flared nose was his own. His long arms implied strength in the shoulders and ended in clean, square cuffs. The jaw was still smooth at the end of the day and the wavy hair might have been gelled to sit back so cleanly from his forehead. She thought he would make a good artist's model, then that few heterosexual men still groomed themselves like that. The miasma of wealth and success made him an unusual associate for Nick. She remembered lunch on the boat, when her brother's thoughts had so obviously been elsewhere, and wondered what the two of them were up to. Daniel had recognised the man's name and was pouring him a drink before Nick, so she turned to talk to her brother in solidarity.

Dominic saw the banker's eager look and resented for a moment the intrusion of being recognized, even though it was a recognition which he had cultivated for years. When Daniel said where he worked, Dominic interrupted him.

'Yes,' he said swiftly. And with a few strokes, he made it clear that there was little Daniel could tell him about the bank that he did not already know. Instead, he himself began to offer glimpses of the company's future, reflected from a world Daniel couldn't see. As the man started to search for the one card that he could use to impress, a dull familiarly settled on Dominic. Pulling out information like this used to be fun because it had been a challenge. Now it was too easy, and he found himself hoping that Nick really would make him rich enough to leave the dance forever.

'Well,' said Daniel. 'You know about...' And he named a huge deal. Jesus, thought Dominic. Your little bank has got *that*?

'Yes,' he said with a familiar smile. 'I had heard. Apparently there were a few snags at the end though?' When weren't there?

'There were,' said Daniel. 'But it's signed now.'

'Exclusively?' he said.

'Exclusively,' said Daniel firmly.

'Congratulations,' said Dominic, sitting back. He would tell the rivals to stop working on their pitches; maybe say Daniel's bank was planning to sit on the information for even longer. As his boss in Russia used to say: a little bad blood never hurt anyone, if it comes from the right place. He let Daniel carry on talking and concentrated what attention he could on Nick's sister. He picked up large, disbelieving eyes set in a soft face, the features strong but restrained. Either her complexion or her make-up was perfect, and he thought it must be natural as she was wearing hardly any jewelry. A small pendant hung around her neck and the two rings spoke drearily from her hand. Her husband's wedding ring was already buzzing like a gnat as the man gesticulated in front of him. Her hair had received an expensive cut and a cursory brush. He wondered if there were earrings behind it and what sort of ears they would grace. She was playing some cryptic game with her brother, and he saw love and disappointment mingling in her look. It was the look of all siblings, which his own brother and sister used liberally on him. Yet there was something more than impatience behind her eyes, something almost caustic. He had seen the look before; an unexpressed sensitivity, curbing in on itself and becoming depression.

Dominic refocused his attention on Daniel Falk, who was spreading his conversational wings opposite, and felt a new flush of irritation.

'How interesting,' he said, then addressed himself to the table at large. 'I feel like having a dance. Would anyone care to join me?'

Charlotte had been playing an old game with her brother, striking expressions with tiny modulations of their faces to make the other laugh. She had survived The Bat and The Gerbil, but at The Blowfish had almost succumbed. Now she felt her eyes light up at the idea of dancing, but thought she should let someone else answer first.

'Great idea,' said Daniel.

They have a dance floor here? thought Nick.

Waiters appeared and lifted the table out at a shallow angle. Charlotte led the way although didn't know where she was going. She felt a hand on her elbow, guiding her lightly towards a heavy curtain. It was parted and she heard music, then stepped down a shallow staircase which curved into the centre of a wide space. The conversation was louder and the atmosphere closer. She turned to find that Daniel had run into a client and stayed upstairs, and she felt a guilty rush of gratitude. He hated dancing and had only briefly showed her the basement on their first visit, which had left her with a gnawing curiosity about it. Now she took it in properly. Zulu shields lined the ceiling, cellars like varnished wombs gave off the sides, and the people seemed younger. She looked at the other two expectantly. Her brother's eyes were travelling slowly across the rich walls, while his friend's glimmered in the low light.

'Great song this,' said Dominic. 'No time to lose!' He clapped Nick lightly on the back, pointing him towards a beaten copper bar in one of the side cellars. 'Can't expect Nick to dance,' he said. 'He's far too serious!'

Charlotte laughed but Nick was relieved. Dominic was right: he did find it difficult to dance to pop music. He would automatically try to reproduce the slow movements of the Dervishes and end up swaying like an anemone among the fast-moving figures. It was an embarrassment he could do without, and he left gratefully for the bar. Around him, people lent into each other with quick repartee; their laughter sudden and hard. He knew the crowd contained many times over the money he needed to buy the mine. He stood in the crowd by the bar, still and tall in his suit, and tried for a moment not to think about how he could find an investor. Behind the chatter, music floated through from the dance floor.

'It's a living thing...' he heard. 'Such a terrible thing to lose.' I used to know this song, he thought. When he reached the front, the barman lent across to him with smooth expectation. He had been going to order three drinks, but then thought of the difficulty of getting them to the others and decided to make it one. When a woman started talking to him, he quickly doubled the order. The drinks were set down on their delicate coasters, and he turned to speak to his new friend.

4

Roger Curtis trailed his girlfriend along the pavement. Irina's attention was taken by the shop windows, her eyes darting like a searchlight between them. Roger had begun to dread these trips. His phone rang.

'Dad? For fuck's sake! Where are you?' said Lily.

'On Bond Street, sweetie. Just outside...' Irina had stopped in front of a shop and was eyeing him warily. He looked up and saw its unpronounceable name. A sign on the nearest side street was too far away for him to read, and he beckoned to Irina.

'Sweetie, could you tell me what that says?' he said.

'Dad, I'm on the fucking phone!' said his daughter.

'Not you darling,' said Roger. 'Irina.'

'What the fuck is that bitch doing there?' said Lily.

'Who is?' said Irina, jabbing a finger at the phone.

'It's Lily, sweetie,' said Roger. 'She's coming shopping with us.' Irina's eyes rolled. 'Sweetie,' he said to her. 'Could you just read that sign to me?'

Irina shrugged and thrust her head around.

'Maddox,' she said. 'Maddox Street!' The flat first vowel made it sound like a medical treatment.

'Hey sweetie,' said Roger into his phone. 'We're on the corner of Maddox St!'

'Bond and Maddox?' said Lily. 'I don't live here! That

means nothing to me! I'm calling a fucking cab.'

The line went dead. Irina was looking at him with narrowed eyes.

'*Bezobrazniza!*' she said. 'Why she come?'

'Come on, sweetie. She's over from Paris. You guys get on!' Roger let out a gurgling laugh.

'Come!' said Irina, and pulled him into the shop.

When Lily arrived, they were at the checkout with a small number of things. The two girls kissed the air around each other, and Lily gave her father a contemptuous peck.

'Hey,' she said. 'This is great stuff! You guys wait, I've got to check out this stuff!'

After twenty minutes, they left. In the next shop, Lily circled Irina, launching compliments. Roger knew she was trying to read the price tag of the dress Irina was trying on, if only to bid her higher on the next round. He sat in the corner glumly, looking for an excuse to phone someone. He saw Fabrice's number and thought Bond Street was a good place from which to explain that he couldn't share the boat charter this year. But he still didn't have an excuse. Roger scrolled on and saw The Centre for Human Consciousness. He stood up by the window, and dialled the number.

'Hey,' he said loudly. 'Do you guys have a meditation course coming up?' He listened for a moment. 'Can I book myself on?' he said, giving his name with a lift at the end. He thought of it as a little runway for people's recognition to come into land. But it didn't work, and the other person just asked how many places he wanted. He looked at the girls making their stony way back to the dressing room. 'Just two,' he said.

By lunch, he was feeling queasy. Their outside table on Mount Street was heaped below with shopping bags and above with shellfish. Compound spending, his therapist called it. The less money you have, the more you spend just to feel you have any at all. Irina was eating hungrily while Lily picked without enthusiasm. The slim neck of a bottle of white wine poked from its cooler. No, he thought. Keep to the path. No meat, no drugs, and certainly no booze.

Lily was discussing her career as a fashion photographer.

'Hey sweetie,' said Roger. 'I thought you were going to be an actress?'

She gave him a withering look.

'Are you kidding, Dad?' she said. 'Actresses are fucking whores!'

'I study acting!' Irina burst out, and Lily smiled at her.

Roger reached for a prawn, glad the shopping bags were at least out of sight. Every stage of a relationship seemed to demand its payload of shopping. First to win them; then to show them you loved them; then to keep them or make them go. After eight months, he had lost track of where he was with Irina. She was studying in Moscow and flew in to see him. But who knew what went on at the other end? No girl under thirty had just one boyfriend, not one! What would be the point, when they could double up so easily? All he had to do was give them his business card; then one call, one dinner, and then the next thing! Why should he lose out to Irina's other life in Russia? She may be the best girl around at the moment, she was certainly the only one who was studying. But how could he trust her? He imagined proposing. Will you be my next wife? Will you be my *ex*-wife? Ha! He had one of those already and could hear her in Lily. Someone had said that every man of substance should have at least two ex-wives. Substance? Not for long, they were like piranhas! No, maybe it wouldn't be so wise to marry Irina.

'Excuse me,' said a voice. He looked around to find a couple standing by their table. They had stopped walking along the pavement and were holding a cluster of shopping bags from Oxford Street.

'Hi!' said Roger.

'Are you from The Ice Machine?' said the man.

'Might be...' said Roger, smiling broadly beneath the black sunglasses. Lily had crossed her arms and was looking away. Irina smiled at the couple, her eyes flicking back to Roger. The man's wife was looking on uncertainly.

'Roger Curtis,' said Roger, extending a hand across the rope barrier.

'I love your stuff,' said the man, untangling himself from the shopping. 'We ran a night in Sheffield, used to play it all the time.'

'Hey...' said Roger, extending his arms outwards. It had been years since he last carried photos of himself. Now he wished he had some and looked for a pen instead.

'Don't worry,' said the man, whose wife had put her arm through his. 'Thanks for the music,' he said, and they walked on. Roger could sense the doorman and some of the other tables looking over. He leant back and his smile swept the table.

'You're such a dork,' said Lily.

'Hey!' said Irina, reaching out to cover Roger's hand.

*

When Irina left for her yoga class that afternoon, Roger went out into Primrose Hill. He took a seat on Regents Park Road and looked at the waitress through his large sunglasses. She was small, tanned and impatient.

'Hi sweetie,' he said. 'Could I have a cappuccino?' The girl nodded and left with quick steps.

Roger loved his neighbourhood. The Island, they called it, and days went by without him leaving. He loved sitting out like this, spotting old faces from the music business and trading the odd wave. Often he stayed still and just watched from behind his shades. He didn't need to be recognised to know he was one of them; and it avoided the question to which they all seemed to have an answer. 'Working.' 'Collaborating with...' 'The new project.' What's the point in making music no-one wants to hear? he wanted to ask. Plus if you weren't working, it meant you had to be big. He hadn't put anything out for fifteen years; by his reckoning, that made him pretty big.

The man at lunch had left him with a glow, reminding him of the tens of thousands who had been touched by their music. It was still so real how he and Neil had bathed the charts in the warmth of their synthesizers. He remembered when they first started building a studio in his father's garage in Oxford, Roger buying the equipment while Neil laboured endlessly over the details. But Roger wasn't interested in the details; the Germans with their long nouns or what was happening in Detroit. Or the politics. He was interested in the – what was the word? – the *aesthetic*. The look! Yes, there would have been no Ice Machine without him. And who was to blame him for having a better lawyer than Neil. Who didn't have a good lawyer? Apparently Neil had gone off to become a music teacher afterwards.

Roger brushed some foam from his stubble. Yes, music was important. But there was more. There was Truth. He was sure its strands lay in a hundred different books and beliefs. But how to pick out the right ones? Wasn't there a movement that had done it? The word perennial came to him, then he remembered that was a kind of plant. Anyway, he hadn't wanted someone else's movement: he had wanted to find out for himself. So he had hired someone and they criss-crossed the world for a year, visiting the headquarters of great spiritual organisations. His researcher compiled pages of notes, cross referencing the similarities and striking out things that didn't fit. He liked what he heard about Gnosticism; the idea of knowledge, something concrete. But no-one could tell him what the knowledge was, and he was put off by the name. He couldn't introduce himself as a Gnostic. Not everyone was as well read as him: they might think he believed in gnomes!

He grinned. The summer was coming up. He opened

his diary and the usual dates were in. Some music festivals in the UK; the villa in Ibiza, lent by a more famous contemporary; sailing in Croatia. He wasn't sure Croatia was very safe but everyone seemed to do it now. Yet still the diary was lighter than usual. St Tropez was missing. The yacht charter company had turned him down and his secretary couldn't find another. Fabrice would already know and would soon be calling to find out why. His brow tightened. The ripples must have spread from the court case in New York. But how? Was it the bank in Monaco? The lawyers in New York? His own accountants in London? What was the point of different jurisdictions if information could just do this? Anyway, he had sold the loft fair and square: no-one could prove he knew about the redevelopment. He hadn't even sold it because of that: he had sold it because he was bored and he wanted the money. That was two years ago, when he had first touched his last million.

Roger hunched into the table, the black jacket stretching across his shoulders. He hated it when people talked about royalties trickling in because, in his case, that is exactly what they did. Winning the lawsuit in New York wouldn't be enough to survive and the lawyers were already asking for payment upfront. Worse, Lily's mother had become hungrier just when he had hoped she would go away, hiring a new law firm and putting them on a percentage of the kill. First Roger's lawyers didn't return his calls, now he didn't return theirs. Even his bank in Monaco had lost its deferential tone. They could all smell blood, and it was the sort of blood that made them swim away. Something had to happen to pay for the next twenty years: something new. He closed his eyes and rocked.

5

Wind whipped around Nick's collar as his car flowed across the South Downs. *'In dreams,'* sung the stereo. *'I dream... Of you!'* A woman sat beside him, the wind catching her blond curls, and he could see Timur in his side mirror. The dog was standing on the rear seat with his front paws resting on the sill, the ears flush with his head and his small eyes narrowed against the speed. Nick pressed the accelerator and the old Mercedes rocked back on its springs as he overtook. He looked with love at the tame hills and thought: this England *exists.*

Ever since Dominic's call the morning after their dinner, the world had been singing to him. He had been pottering around his boat with an expensive-feeling hangover, making Turkish coffee then dragging some of his rugs out to brighten in the sun. The mining papers were too much and he felt that having dinner with Dominic had been work in itself. He sat at the piano instead and ran through Mozart's Rondo alla Turca, taking it fast and stamping on the wooden floor towards the end. He had finished with a flourish and was looking up having a real Turkish Stop fitted to the piano when the phone rang.

Seeing Dominic's name, the music was gone from his

mind. His first thought was that he had done something wrong the night before. He had talked to the woman at the bar for two more drinks, then handed over his number and lost track of her. He finally found Dominic and Charlotte at a back table covered in empty cocktail glasses. His sister looked up at him with glazed excitement and it seemed that Daniel had left. When the unnatural rhythms of the music and heaving, free-spending crowd became too much, Nick also said goodbye. He searched briefly for the girl, not knowing that she would actually call him, then argued with the cloakroom attendant about his bag before finding it under their dining table. He somehow assumed this altercation was the subject of Dominic's call.

'Dominic,' he said tentatively.

'Morning Nick,' said Dominic with a spring in his voice. 'I thought you'd like to know we've got the option.'

Nick formed a chord with his right hand and looked down the river. Finally.

'Dominic,' he said quietly. 'That's great. What next?'

'I'll need your money this week to buy it, then your investor's money within the next three months to exercise it,' said Dominic.

'It's all in hand,' said Nick, and continued before Dominic could probe him. 'Fun night, last night! Did you get home alright?' He had automatically accepted the taxi that was hailed for him, and its receipt was in the crumpled pile by his bed.

'Oh, fine,' said Dominic. 'My driver's a very patient man.'

Nick wondered if he had dropped Charlotte at home but there seemed no reason to ask. He took down the bank details then rang off and sat at his computer. The amount of money he would have left after the transfer was surreally small. He felt light afterwards yet his grip on the world soon tightened again: he knew he would find an investor soon. Without one, the name of the mine turned in his head like a dancer without a partner. It lay across the Sussex skyline now, its stuttering cadences sprawling like a city: Kattakurgan.

'Only in dreams,' he mouthed as the song came to an end. 'In beautiful dreams.'

'Sorry?' he said, leaning across in the wind.

'The Centre is an amazing place,' the woman was saying. 'It's really helped me. It could help everyone.'

Nick glanced sideways at the girl he had met that night. Her call had come the day after Dominic's, with the suggestion that they drive out to a meditation centre on Saturday. Sure, he had said. It was a weekend, when he couldn't work on the fundraising, and maybe meditation would help. Out there, we are all equal.

When she arrived on the pier that morning in a flurry of long clothing and bicycle bells, Nick had realised that the driving would be taking place in his car. She looked older than before, although her girlish figure was quite intact; and he thought how hippy women often aged faster above the neck. She cooed over Timur and the boat, but when he offered her a cup of tea she remembered the trip with sudden enthusiasm. He looked across again, seeing her lined, self-absorbed face among the fluttering curls, and for a terrible moment forgot her name. Lara.

They arrived in a village and she directed him to a car park, which was shaded by a silver birch tree. It was populated by an old van and a few generic modern cars. He found them unsettling in a place like this as they spoke of the beliefs held by normal people, their mantras repeated in traffic jams and on school runs. He saw a new black convertible hunched in a corner and parked next to it instead. They got out and Lara put her arm through his, her hips swaying as they walked towards the Centre for Human Consciousness. Its red and white architecture made it look like a public building, and a temporary sign with an astrological logo stood by the door.

'It looks like a school,' said Nick.

'It is a school,' she replied. 'The Centre moves around everywhere.' Nick blinked and his step broke, but she took his hand.

'Come on,' she said, pulling him through the door.

The gymnasium of the school was lined with stalls. A large number of crystals were on display, their lapidary colours making gentle rainbows on the trestles. Women with shoulder-length grey ringlets sold services mostly related to healing. Some of the stalls had chairs and massage tables on which the clients lay inert. Nick looked at the traders and thought: who heals the healers? Lara spoke to a woman whose stall had a pyramidal structure over it hung with dream catchers in plastic wrapping. Nick's jaw was tightening and his breath deepening. He gently released Lara's arm, replaced his sunglasses, and made his way around the room.

Their meditation class was taking place in a classroom with childish art pinned around the walls. The tables had been pushed to the edge and exercise mats dragged in from the gym. The teacher occupied a single one while her students sat in pairs. She greeted them with a beatific smile and Nick saw one empty mat waiting terribly in the corner. Lara took his hand and led him to it. They sat and she exhaled.

'Ok, everyone,' said the teacher. 'We're all *here.*' The huge, cloying fricative. 'We're just going to have some moments of quiet before we start.'

Nick closed his eyes and dived. Layers of stillness unwrapped themselves, then more. He used his technique and visualised his thoughts as a Highland stream, its valley growing bigger while dimensions glimmered at the edges. The centre of the dance. I shouldn't be able to think that, he thought. Then the stream was gone and he looked at the world. A voice spoke to him. *I am silence*, it said. *Everything is in me.* He waited. *I am love*, it said. *I am your gift.* He felt a gasp and his edges became the edges of the universe. But something was happening in the valley: it was pulling him back. He desperately wanted to stay but the stream was rushing towards him and becoming a river, in which he would drown. He opened his eyes with a start and saw the classroom. The woman was addressing him.

'Would you mind taking off your sunglasses?' she said.

Nick got to his feet and left.

Poor guy, thought Roger Curtis. But it was good to remember that other people had worse problems than him. What was money anyway? He was interested in Truth. And Consciousness! That's why he was here.

'Ok,' said the teacher, recovering from her umbrage. 'Now we're ready to start. Everybody, close your eyes and concentrate on your breathing.'

Roger did so. He liked the feeling of his rib cage pushing outwards against his jacket. His breathing was strong and healthy: an hour in the gym each morning! 'Now, let everything else go,' he heard. 'Just think about the breathing.' Roger breathed in and out, and smelled cleaning products. He remembered some of the amazing places where he had done this; that retreat in Nepal and on the beach in Goa. But he didn't find it easy. The problem was that in trying to push things from his mind, it ended up fuller than ever! Irina understood it better. Her breathing was as steady as the wash on a beach. Listening to her reminded him of the row they had on the way down, and that she had not let him into the cubicle when she changed into her yoga kit. But she had relaxed now, so maybe they could stop in a field on the way back to London. Roger smiled. The breathing thing must be working as he was starting to feel calmer.

At the end of the lesson, the woman gave them some Celtic meditation tips. 'Walk through nature and think about your relationship to it,' she said. 'Pick a plant or flower and think about your relationship to it. Then think about your other relationships, to your family or to your work, for example.'

I'm going to try that, thought Roger. But he wanted to use something big. That tree by the car park would do; and he became impatient to get there before anyone else. When the woman finished, he left Irina and hurried out to it. A cloud of spring leaves was gathered around its pale trunk, rustling lightly in the breeze. Roger looked at the tree and thought about his relationship with it, but found he could hear music. Very strange music too; plucked strings, flutes, and percussion all playing in rhythm. He looked around and saw it was coming from a car parked further along. The man who had left the meditation class was leaning against it, looking toward the hills.

Roger wondered what to do. When he had been researching his project to find the Truth, many of the beliefs said you had to help people. Maybe he could tell the man what he had missed in the class? He was sure it had helped him. But he had to be careful: you can't run around after people all day, and you can't help people who don't want to help themselves! He wandered over and unlocked his car, then spoke across the black canvas roof.

'Hi,' he said. 'Who's that by, then?'

Nick looked around. The man who had addressed him was short and dressed in black, with blonde hair hanging from a low forehead and striking blue eyes. A nervous smile played on his fleshy lips. *I am love*, he thought.

'Dimitrie Cantemir,' he said.

'Know much about them?' said Roger.

'A bit,' he said.

49

'Where are they from?' said Roger. The Sublime Porte, thought Nick; the greatest empire ever known.

'Turkey,' he said. 'Well... The music's from Turkey, the man's actually from Moldova, of course.'

Roger nodded thoughtfully.

'I'm a musician,' he said, and Nick raised his eyebrows politely. 'We had a band, The Ice Machine.' The upward inflection told Nick what to say next.

'I think I've heard of you,' he said, and Roger grinned.

'Yeah,' he said. 'Pretty big!' It had been easier than he expected. 'So,' he said. 'Do you want to hear what we learned in the class?'

Then Nick noticed the Porsche.

'Yes, I'd love to,' he said with a smile. 'In fact, if you're free, why don't we have a spot of lunch?'

*

They drove across the hills with both hoods down, the low black front of the Porsche keeping a steady distance in Nick's mirror. Its windscreen framed two pairs of sunglasses, the wind tousling Roger's hair and plucking at his girlfriend's headscarf. Nick was glad of Lara's presence beside him. She had been unquestioning of the decision to go out to lunch with Roger, and now the four of them made a perfect square. He put a hand on her thigh and she shifted accommodatingly.

Roger sat back with one hand on the wheel. He liked driving the car slowly and listening to the patient rumble of the engine behind him, as it showed restraint and made the bursts of speed more fun. He was thinking about the man in front; the distant look he wore and how they had been brought together. Irina was humming in the breeze. He leant over to her.

'I knew it,' he said. 'That man needs my help.' Irina's brown eyes gave him a sideways look.

'Maybe you need *his* help?' she said, her Slavonic accent skipping in amusement. The full lips were spread into a smile, then she looked serious and pointed through the windscreen.

'Roger,' she said slowly. 'Who is?'

Roger gave his laugh.

'He's a friend, sweetie,' he said. It was typical of these Russians to be so mistrustful! Someone had once told him that the people who couldn't trust were the ones who couldn't be trusted. Still, Irina would come to see that there was a bigger picture. After all, how long had it taken him?

'New friend,' she said dryly.

'Yes, sweetie,' said Roger, contentedly looking along the valley.

Irina drew up a knee and rested her elbow on it.

'*Nuzhno opasatsya...*' she said quietly, touching the cross around her neck.

They entered a village, where red-brick houses with low eaves sat behind wide grass verges. A cluster of parked cars marked out a long building as the pub. Nick pulled up onto the verge and the Porsche crawled up slowly beside him. The pub had changed a lot since he had last been there. The cars outside were all new and it was a Saturday: it would be a challenge to get a table.

'Lovely old place,' he said.

'Love getting out of town,' said Roger.

'I like your scarf,' said Lara to Irina.

'Thank you!' said Irina. 'Look...' She produced a Celtic Cross which she had bought earlier.

'Wow,' said Lara.

Nick led them into the pub. It was late in the service and the beams rung with the sound of young children and couples drinking. A woman with a pen behind her ear approached them and was about to speak.

'I wonder,' said Nick, cutting her off. 'If you could fit us in? In the garden?' The manager frowned and relented, leading them to a round table in the corner of the garden and removing its Reserved sign.

'Good table!' said Roger. He and Nick sat facing the sun and the girls sat facing into the ivy-covered wall. Timur jumped onto the edge of Irina's seat and his nose began moving delicately along the circumference of the wooden table.

'Would you like something to drink?' said a waitress.

'I don't drink!' said Roger, raising his hand like a traffic policeman, and the waitress moved on. 'On second thoughts,' said Roger. 'I'll have a large scotch!'

They all laughed, and Nick ordered a bottle of Sancerre.

'The kitchen's quite busy,' said the waitress, wearing the same annoyed look as the manager. Nick looked quickly at the menu and ordered salmon. Roger joined him, Lara ordered a salad, and Irina ordered a burger.

'Are you a vegetarian?' said Roger.

'Sometimes,' said Nick.

'I am,' said Roger.

Nick looked at his new acquaintance. A dry drunk, clearly; no amount of mineral water could wash away that lined face. The trophy girlfriend was looking at Nick sceptically and he thought: if she has something to protect, maybe Roger really is famous? He wondered what kind of guesses Roger was making about him and felt a prickle of annoyance at the false trail Lara would lay, making him look like some kind of New Age ingénue. But then again, Roger was probably one himself; and Nick's embarrassment at having met at a travelling amusement park lifted a little.

Roger must be in his early fifties, making him older by a decade. Nick started a conversation about music, asking him about his career. He had not thought about pop music for a long time; but Roger's era was also the era of his youth and he remembered more than he had expected. Charlotte had embraced electronic music more fully, and he wondered if she would have heard of Roger's band. He could ask her at her garden party the following week. If things went well, he could even invite Roger! Surely the amount of money they needed wouldn't be a lot for a man like him? And it would be good to share the opportunity with someone fun rather than a faceless investment firm. He felt a fraternal gravity and wished they could share a drink together.

Roger felt the day was turning out wonderfully. He liked Nick's class; the old-fashioned sunglasses and ancient car. I could never get away with driving that, he thought. He had seen how Nick mesmerised the staff into giving them a table, which something he himself had used to do in London. Most of all, he liked the fact that their meeting was rooted in something bigger: the search for Truth. It lent the day a special quality, a kind of shared humility which restrained his name dropping and made him listen. He looked at Lara and wondered if Irina's young perfection made him look shallow; then remembered the strange music that had been playing when they met, and asked about it.

Nick confessed to being an authority on Cantemir and saw a glow of respect pass over Roger's face. You didn't go to university, he thought. He manoeuvred the conversation eastwards and made a glancing reference to the intelligence services, which only Roger's girlfriend picked up. Her large eyes made a quick round trip to him, and he wondered if her English wasn't better than she pretended. Soon he and Roger were speaking about the world; Marrakesh, Hydra, the baths in Budapest. Nick couldn't follow the conversation to New York as he had never been to America. But he saw a touch of unease as Roger himself mentioned the city, and the subject was soon gone.

Everything Roger was saying seemed to mark him out as a potential backer: the house in New York, the summer plans, the references to well-known people. It was as if each new detail placed him in a smaller concentric circle, until Nick nearly had to bite his tongue. They were both wearing sunglasses and he wished he could see Roger's eyes. He pointedly removed his and Roger did the same. The eyes were blue and mobile, giving his face a preoccupied air; and met Nick's with a fleeting, self-conscious camaraderie.

Timur was standing with his front paws on the table,

avoiding Nick's eyes as he was fed chips from Irina's plate. Lara's interjections were becoming longer and more lilting. Irina was flushed but composed. Nick wanted another glass and wondered what would happen if he ordered another bottle. When the waitress returned, Roger did it for him. They ordered pudding too and Nick thought of the bill mounting, yet their conversation mingled well over the new bottle. Roger and Lara found they had read some of the same books on spirituality, and Nick spoke to Irina instead. He saw the discernment in her eyes and kept the conversation general to hide his dislike of Russia. Her pale looks didn't appeal to him; yet he found himself wondering what his own love life would look like when he too was rich.

By three o'clock, their table bore the signs of good use and afternoon drinkers had replaced the families around them. Nick insisted on paying the bill and Roger acquiesced, saying he would return the favour in London soon. As Lara and Irina bonded over their goodbyes, Nick drew him aside.

'I tell you what,' he said quietly. 'My sister's having a little drinks next week. Why don't you come along?'

Roger caught his eye again with the same tentative look of friendship.

'What a great idea!' he said. They shook hands and Nick lingered at the table to avoid a duplicate goodbye at the cars. He would call Roger early in the week to confirm, then ask Charlotte to add him to the guest list. He needed Dominic there too to add his patina of credibility but that should be easy as Charlotte had already met him. Nick stood still for a moment, closing his eyes into the sun.

When Roger and Irina reached the car, she held herself against him and he heard her wordless sound.

'Come, my sweetie,' he said, stroking under her ear.

Nick heard the Porsche accelerate away as Lara returned from inside the pub. A light sweat had broken on her brow and her eyes flashed as she looked at him.

'That was nice,' she said. Nick nodded, the wine just starting to play on the back of his head.

'I've got an idea,' he said.

'Hmm?' said Lara, half closing her eyes. They passed through the pub and settled back into the warm leather of the Mercedes. Nick turned it south, winding across the hills towards the bright space beyond. They rounded a final crest and the wide expanse of the English Channel opened below them. Lara murmured appreciatively and Nick followed a lane down to the deserted end of a long beach.

'Fancy a swim?' he said, swinging open the door. He left his clothes halfway to the tide line and walked steadily into the opaque water. He dived and the salt water jarred in his sinuses, washing the alcohol from his blood, then surfaced with a burst of realisation. Of course he hadn't found his man in London, or even by his own efforts! He had been led to him only when he stopped looking; and out here, in nature! He turned towards the sky and sent a cloud of spray into the air. A whoop reached him from the shore line and he felt a surge of affection for Lara, sent by the universe to lead him to Roger. He whooped back, and swam towards her.

JUNE

6

Dominic was alone at the bar of the Club, waiting. His first whiskey had narrowed to a thin slice at the bottom of the tumbler. He hated having two drinks before dinner but the courtship ritual made it all but unavoidable. Even after six months, Imogen still had to be late. And he still had to be on time, just in case *she* turned up on time to catch him out.

He had already mapped the other club members in the room, each one discreetly mooring a small group of guests and hangers-on. Three of them had exchanged nods with him when he arrived. Two others wouldn't return a greeting even if offered; but it was their choice, not his. He didn't understand grudges. They seemed to be nothing more than an advertisement that someone had lost. But the silent waves of enmity made him nervous, and in a moment the old panic was back.

His last night in Moscow, moving between bars as the threads of information reached him. Avoiding his flat; avoiding his girlfriend; finally driving to the airport through a grey dawn and leaving the car unlocked for someone to steal. The next flight to London on a non-Russian airline. Burningly self-conscious as he passed through security, his stubble and lack of luggage marking him out even among the irascible early-morning crowd. At passport control, he tried and failed to stop the blood draining from his face. When the guard slid his passport back, he tried harder not to believe they were really letting him go. Only as the gangway detached and the airliner started to reverse did he let the gulf of relief open beneath him. On the flight, he had tried not to think of his employer Arman Selikov; no better or worse than his peers but never to be free again, maybe not even to live. He had told himself that Natasha was a smart Moscow girl and would leave his flat when she heard the news; that the government could not want anything with her. It was only later, as his beard grew and he rode the roofs of Andean buses and the bows of Thai ferries, that he had started to ache for her quiet presence. He had not gone travelling to hide; they could find and extract him as easily on the hippy trails as they could in London, probably more so. It had instead been a mark of respect for the President for Dominic to put himself and his information beyond the reach of Selikov's defence lawyers.

Yet surely he now had little to fear? In the years since cautiously re-emerging, he had armed himself well in London. His telephone calls now rang in some of the most powerful offices in the city. He no longer had to look for clients; and had noticed that the less he spoke, the more people listened. They listened for the same reason that the powerful took his calls. People didn't know what he held in his hand, and they didn't want to miss out. He had once been the gatekeeper to Selikov; now he was the gatekeeper to a crossroads that led a hundred ways. He had once overheard himself being described as a necessary evil, and had turned his eyes on the speaker. Better, he had said, than an unnecessary one; and the man left.

Dominic looked down at the bar, oscillating the empty glass on its thick coaster, and felt calm returning. He felt that he was not a bad man. All he took from life were his pleasures and his dues. If that was enough for a bad reputation then the world was at fault, not him. Whereas how did people acquire good reputations? Invariably, by lies and hypocrisy. Reality itself was either too mundane or too unpopular, so Britain had instead been trained in the surreal dualism of the marketing men. He saw it everywhere, from a politician's speech to a food label. And so people were forced to look between the words, navigating them with an inner ear tuned to reality. If only the country could find its inner mouth, so the truth could once again be spoken.

Sometimes even Britain's elastic talent for self-deception couldn't cover the rift between word and deed. Dominic relished the moments when it snapped and daylight fell behind the stage, showing the wanton truth behind public life. But the scene was soon reset with a fallacious apology; the invincible appeal to groupthink, the readmission to the public life, the relining of the pockets. A man like Castlereagh once did a fine job and was hounded to suicide; and even Churchill was booed once the job was done. Whereas now politicians lie, apologise, then start again. Yes, he thought; I would rather go to my grave an honest man than a popular one.

Something in the idea brought him back to Nick

63

Paget and his gold project. It was probably the dull worry which had emerged since writing his little insurance policy into the paperwork. Was that dishonest? Surely not. The dishonesty he hated was lying about who you actually were; the lies of a culture which wrapped its desires in the language of equality. Anyway, nothing said he had to call in the option. It was just there in case Nick did something stupid. And Nick more than anyone would want the company in safe hands if things got rough, which could easily happen now he was lining up someone to provide the money.

Nick had said the person would be at Charlotte's drinks party later that week. Charlotte. The memory of the time they had spent alone here returned to nag him. It had passed so easily that it had pained him to release her into a cab afterwards. But he knew it was illusory; just a few fugitive moments blown into existence by the conditions of that evening.

Dominic looked at his watch, and pushed the glass an inch towards the barman.

*

Imogen Somerville walked out of her office building. A ball of golden haze squeezed itself into the end of Upper Brook Street from Hyde Park, and she could almost see the dust-mites dancing in it.

She turned into the sunset, passing the entrance canopy of a restaurant and the polite smile of its doorman. It was nice to be noticed, or not to be forgotten, and she loved Mayfair for its familiarity. She loved the epicurean tans of the men, and the way they wore their suits as if they had never worked. The mid-blue cloth of an Italian; the crisp, unbuttoned shirt of a Scandinavian playboy; the sight of a hammered silver cigar case glinting in the sun. She loved their difficult, deft decisions about how long to linger on her when she noticed them looking. A decisecond of difference could say everything about a man or what he meant, or both. The Europeans always stayed too long, like boys or old men; the English, almost always too little. Except for the few who got it right, snapping their eyes away just early enough to win.

She crossed onto the island in the middle of Park Lane, where a stone and bronze animal memorial made her think of home. The calves would be out and she should go back for a weekend soon. But it was dangerous for her to spend too much time there, not least as the place was out of phone signal. The previous Christmas, her director had decided he needed a report before the markets opened after Boxing Day. A motorbike courier had duly appeared on the lane to Kingacre Farm. She signed for a kilo of documents, locked herself in her father's office, and worked for the next thirty-six hours. Yes· if one place was to be unreal, it was better that it was home.

Sun dusted a low embankment on the edge of the park. She would have liked to lie in the rays for ten minutes but her clothes were too good for that now. Yes, London had changed her. Even more than the money, she would miss the sheer theatricality of working life. It took a lot of suspension of disbelief for Samartian Capital to manage over a billion pounds. Every day, the rocks slipped from their feet into a precarious valley of error. The fund had fallen in more than once and she had watched the millions disappearing as her colleagues screamed at their brokers to get them out. But as long as you didn't commit a lone stumble, you endured.

And so she carried on, tracing the minute contours of professional life. She was always armed for contingencies, and had become expert in the honeycomb of relationships which made up the place. So many of her university friends still seemed to think companies were monoliths, where employees were just slotted in like bricks. She knew they were really creatures, battling against the waywardness of their cells; the most organic things on earth, in fact! The mulching on the forest floor may be done by computers but the great canopies were always people, casting their shade on the saplings beneath.

As she did every hour, almost every minute, she thought of *her* stock; her one analyst's pick which had yet made it into the main fund. There it had been today, still beating its dogged path up the graph. She loved it like a child, willing for it not to stumble. She wanted more like that: she wanted her own fund. Yet even as that one ambition crystallized into a sharp, gleaming certainty, the rest of her life became more undecided. The more her diary overflowed, the more she was pained by the idea of what she was missing; until the only really dependable thing became the figure in her savings account.

Perhaps it was best only to do the things she couldn't imagine *not* doing and just leave the rest? It would certainly help the unthinkably large question of marriage only to chose someone she couldn't imagine being without. Fine in theory, yet impossible to apply to her current man. It was as difficult to imagine marrying him as it was to imagine splitting up with him. With him there was only the present, undefined and yet somehow infinite.

Two minutes later she reached the familiar doorway. It was opened and she stepped through into the polished air.

*

Dominic rose from the table and his fingertips cupped her elbow.

'You look beautiful,' he said.

'I've come from work,' said Imogen. Hearing his compliment extinguished, Dominic's eyebrows twitched above the gleaming grey eyes. She thought of him as a small big cat; a lynx, maybe. His movements were lazy and precise, and he paid the same undiluted attention to the world. But his energy could never been released in speed or violence. It pooled instead behind his eyes, lifting them in a moment from trenches of disdain to dance upon the waves. It escaped in the almost invisible tick on his hips when the right song was played, and the sexual grunt when he drew on a twenty-year-old cigar.

Only his hands betrayed him. They trembled slightly

and he would chew on a nail when distracted by his thoughts. Most of his life was invisible, and it seemed that between seeing or speaking to her, she did not even enter his head. She knew it was impossible as they saw each other every week, and sometimes spent whole weekends together. Yet no-one created the impression like he did. Perhaps this artifice of not needing her was what kept her with him? It fuelled her curiosity, and her hope that he would open up about the past.

She had nearly asked him so many times, but then pictured his eyes going colder than ever and imagined never hearing from him again. Yet each time the Russian government released a picture of his old boss, sitting skeletally in his prison cell, the question came back stronger.

What she did know was that his name generated serious heat in London. It effortlessly elevated her in a new work relationship, drawing her level with any other name-dropper. Best of all, it detonated an immediate bomb under the wrong romantic hopefuls. She would judge them by the look of fear, horror, or blankness that came to their faces. If the fumbling attempt at a warning came, she could not help the look of contempt which extinguished it. The hypocrisy of one man warning her off another! By warning me off him, you're warning me off yourself, she would think. And Dominic knew it.

The main courses were cleared and Dominic lightly discussed the food with their usual waiter. Watching the easy conversation of their bodies, Imogen realised it was not simply an option to be involved with him: it was a necessity after all.

The waiter was scraping the crumbs away with something like a small, silver snow-plough. She reached out to move her glass and Dominic's eyes flashed in disapproval, so she smoothly lifted it to her lips. The smaller the solecism, the more it hurt him; sinking in like a needle. They were asked if they would like something else.

'Yes,' said Dominic, looking at his girlfriend with a smile. 'I think Imogen would like a zabaglione.'

'Bello,' said Cesare quietly.

Imogen excused herself and rose. Even here at the Club, Dominic felt other eyes than his following her out of the room. It wasn't just her height or her figure which made her unmissable. It was something in the way her blonde hair was piled above a high chin, the strong jaw and small nose giving her face an almost pugilistic air; finished by round, seal-brown eyes which missed so little and learned so quickly. Most girls in the room were Aphrodites: she was an Artemis. People said he would be mad not to propose to her. When he saw her vacuuming the attention from a room like that, it was hard not to agree. But they didn't know that marriage would be another step towards him giving up his life; and not even to the living but to people who had been dead for centuries. To stem the claustrophobia, he looked over to the corner table where he had sat with Charlotte. Next time he saw her, she would be in the dreary role of hostess; hostess, wife and probably mother. It suddenly felt like a high price for meeting Nick's backer.

7

Roger danced in his bedroom. A balcony overlooked the long sweep of Primrose Hill and music played throughout the top floor. *'Talking loud and clear, saying just what we feel,'* he heard as he shuffled backwards. He turned and the towel fell, then drew the hairbrush across his head and followed with a hand. *'Promises, promises of vows we shall return,'* he sung. *'Talking loud and clear saying just what we feel today!'*

The song finished and he threw himself backwards onto the bed. Small lights gleamed from the ceiling and a hidden strip glowed in different colours around the edge. What should he wear? Black had served him for years but he felt too excited and it was summer. Hawaiian? Not with that lot; not yet anyway! He grinned and thought further through his wardrobe. A dark, electric-blue linen suit? Then he thought of his car, the sunglasses, Irina; the whole of Roger Curtis. Too much! Classic, the word came to him. Yes, he needed something classic. He rolled off the bed and jogged to the door.

'Irina! Irina!' he called. She appeared from the yoga studio, a sweatband propping back the red hair and her brown eyes open wide. 'Hello sweetie,' he said. He gave her a hug and buried her smile in his neck.

'*Moy Roger*', she mumbled.

'Sweetie,' he said and picked her up, her arms still hanging from his neck. 'Help me find something to wear.'

'What do we do?' said Irina. He told her and she raised an eyebrow comically. Roger hoisted her higher and carried her into the bedroom.

The car arrived an hour later, and they walked down from the house together. Roger was wearing a cream linen suit and buckled shoes. Irina wore a pale green, backless silk dress with her hair in tresses and Roman earrings hanging beside her long neck. The driver saw them and got out to open the door. Irina sat close, holding Roger's hand in her lap. Regents Park slipped by, its deep green foliage the colour of paint straight from the tube. As they passed the sandstone pillars of St John's Wood church, Irina lifted a hand and crossed herself. Roger leant forwards and asked the driver to switch off the music.

They passed through Little Venice, where lateral light weaved the tendrils of willow trees above the water. He felt Irina sigh and wondered if they had places like this in Moscow. It certainly looked more beautiful and seemed more safe. The very thought of Russia scared him. He stroked her hand and her grip tightened in his. The car took a wide parabola under a flyover then joined Westbourne Grove, soon drawing up by the gates of a garden square. The driver opened the door for them, dissipating the still atmosphere, and Roger handed him a large tip. By the gate stood a girl and a man with an earpiece, both dressed in black. Roger gave his name and the girl ruffled sheets of paper on a clipboard.

'Serkis?' she said.

'Curtis,' said Roger, feeling Irina beside him.

'Can't see it,' said the girl.

Roger blinked.

*

The staff moved around Charlotte's party like black points on a radar display. She watched as they tilted white-collared champagne bottles and carried little platoons of canapés on square plates. She couldn't remember whose recommendation they had used for a catering company: she had finally chosen one almost at random to keep Daniel happy. The choice was an illusion anyway, as they all did the same thing equally well or else they wouldn't be in business. Other hostesses probably worked their ways through tasting lists of canapés. But all she could think of was how the decision of which particular things were best simply obscured the bigger question of whether these things were necessary at all. She thought an outdoor party should have something simple like a hog roast.

A hog roast! She looked around guiltily. Still, it was her party and she remembered her grandmother's words: 'Don't let us down, Charlotte. Imagine there is a rod of iron down your back, always!' And so she wore her rod of iron, intuiting whether the guests were happy; keeping an eye on her neighbours' houses; and noting which of the staff were drinking, which were flirting, and which were doing their job.

'Thank you', she said, kissing some newcomers. 'It's from around the corner.' Her dress was white with a V neck and a gathered waist. Large blue flowers climbed from the hem, their stamens marked in red. She had bought it the week before, with money dedicated by Daniel. A wave of giggles reached her from the children's entertainer. She looked over and saw Adam joining in as assistant to one of the tricks. His eyes were wide beneath the curly black hair, and he held a wand in one hand with his sister's hand dangling forgotten in the other. The guests' children were spread out on the grass, each back tilted forward and each little head titled upward. On the other side of the party was a band, and she remembered her discussion with Daniel about it two months before.

'Something...' he had said.

'Fun but not too loud?' she suggested.

'Yes!' he said, looking at her proudly.

So music had been the one thing she set her mind to. It was not easy. A string quartet was 'not too loud', by which he meant smart; but it was hardly fun. A jazz band was the opposite. Yet in the corner of her mind she could picture the perfect thing; something old-fashioned, fun and just a little louche. She went to look for it but everything she found was slightly wrong. The bands were all either too anarchic, too old, too boring, or too gypsy-infused. Daniel would hate the last option more than anything. She finally found one that seemed right and sent them a message, trying to be polite without sounding old. When she heard nothing back, she sent another and received an unpunctuated reply saying they were busy. The rudeness frustrated her: how could she, a mother of two, march into the wilds of London and pluck out a band? And so like everything else it had slipped from her hands. One of Daniel's sisters had taken over, and the music which now seeped through the crowd was the kind played in American hotels. It was indeed not too loud.

But there was Nick! He was wearing a safari suit and a panama which looked like it had narrowly survived the Spanish Civil War. Did you have to? she thought. He could only be gatecrasher or a family member, and she wondered when her guests had become so unvaried. Yet he was also with some people she hadn't seen before... Charlotte froze. She hadn't put his new guests on the list! She laughed at something someone had said then gave them an appealing look and skipped across to her brother. When she arrived, his glint of annoyance grazed her heart.

Nick saw her notice and her eyes widening quickly in apology. On seeing Roger's blonde hair over the hedge ten minutes earlier, he had walked straight out of his conversation and to the gate.

'Roger!' he had said.

'Nick!' Roger answered, giving him a theatrical hug. Nick had kissed Irina and complimented her, then swept them back through the gate with his back to the door girl.

'Hello Charlotte!' he now said, for some reason greeting her as if he had just arrived. 'Let me introduce Roger and Irina.'

Roger took Charlotte's hand and bowed, and Irina

smiled brilliantly.

'Lovely to see you,' said Charlotte. See me, thought Roger. But we've just met?

'This is a great party!' he said. He had been relieved when Nick arrived outside and doubly pleased to see his outfit, although he couldn't help feeling it looked more as a linen suit should look.

'Oh it's Daniel's party really,' said Charlotte. 'I'm just here!' Seeing these newcomers made her wonder if Dominic was there. The end of their evening was hazy; she remembered a lot of cocktails and dancing, and thinking her impression of him had been very wrong. She decided to add him to the guest list when she found his card the following morning, thinking she must have mentioned it. But when she opened the folder, she found Daniel had already done it. Something stopped her from now asking Nick if he had seen him. It was clear from the two people he had just introduced that some new thing was happening in his life. Her brother's enthusiasms often bloomed in the spring. There had been the attempt to create a modern Dervish band which had left him trailing a group of students for a summer; then the Orthodox monk with a hat like a champagne cork who had stayed on his boat; then the rug-importing scheme which had lost him money.

What was it this time? She didn't think it was a religious thing, unless Nick was joining another new cult; and the man couldn't be a spy, not with those shoes. Like Dominic, he was out of character for Nick. Even more so was bringing him here, when her brother normally guarded his interests so closely. She guessed it was either music again or business, and hoped it was the former. She liked Irina very much. The girl was tall and baby-faced, with quick brown eyes and delicate white skin. She had noticed the children and was looking towards them.

'*Lapushki...*' said Irina.

Charlotte laid a hand on her arm.

'I love your earrings,' she said.

'Thank you!' said Irina, looking down with another brilliant smile.

'Let's get a drink,' said Nick, extending a hand behind Roger's back.

'Mine's a double scotch!' said Roger.

They all laughed, although Charlotte didn't know why.

*

What a horror show, thought Dominic. Nothing but endless bankers and their bossy wives trailing ice-cream smeared children. He had woken that morning not wanting to come at all and thinking he could take Charlotte out to lunch to apologise for missing it. But then Nick had called to confirm he was bringing his target investor. Not liking the idea of being summoned, Dominic had said he was already going.

Now his first instinct was being proved right. Daniel Falk had greeted him like an old friend and tried to introduce him to people, so he had quickly escaped to a quiet corner. The party didn't seem to bear the stamp of the girl he had met at all. Either she would be a different person from the one he remembered, or she would look on him distantly. Probably the best thing was to avoid her completely, just seeing Nick and his contact before leaving. The double claustrophobia was weighing on him and he wanted to light his cigar. A cigar had used to keep people at bay but these day they just used it as an excuse to come up and talk. So he stood alone with a glass, trying to look happily self-contained.

A girl was hovering nearby, sunburnt beneath her red dress. Perhaps a conversation was a better place to hide after all? He smiled at her and they met. She started talking about Africa and some undertaking there which concerned the future wellbeing of local children. It seemed to him that taking on any infinite problem was a way to lose yourself completely; a kind of suicide even. The frightening illogicality fascinated him and he found himself interrupting her cheerful monologue.

'How long do you expect it all to take?' he said. 'I mean, how do you know when the job's done?'

Samantha Allerton paused. He could see it was not a question she had been asked before.

'That's not the point,' she said. 'The job is each child's future.'

'And then there are more?' said Dominic.

'Yes, there are,' said Samantha tersely.

'You might be there for rather a long time,' said Dominic mildly, taking a sip from his glass. 'They might end up rather depending on you.'

'Well, what do you say?' said Samantha, opening her hands with a small shake of the head. 'Don't go there at all?'

'Oh, do go there,' he said quietly. He remembered being inside an African motorcade, breathing a thick suspension of aftershave as he looked out at the shanty towns. The faces of the children were distorted by the bullet-proof glass as they slid by. 'Any place run by a small number of people is worth a visit,' he said.

'Dictatorships, you mean?' said Samantha with a deepening frown. 'It's worth visiting dictatorships?'

'Isn't that what you do?' he said with a smile. He remembered what the minister had said when someone in the car ventured a question about the poor: 'Oh, the West looks after them.' The minister too had then looked thoughtfully out of the window.

'Well, I would rather they were democracies,' said Samantha.

Dominic let out a small breath. He had known it would be a mistake to enter into a real conversation with her. Now something was wearing thin and a voice was telling him to get out.

'Democracy,' he said. 'And where might you find one of those?'

'Well, here of course!' she said. Her laugh contained all the thoughtless assurance of her class, and Dominic's thread snapped.

'Don't you realise,' he said. 'That the entire purpose of government in every country, particularly here, is to take power *away* from the people? This democracy you're talking about is fictive! It's just a show, like religion or football! You think what we've got here is better because no-one gets killed? That's exactly what prevents it from being democracy! Your Africans with their wars, that is power being held by the people. When someone hands you a gun and says: we believe in the same thing, let us fight for it!'

These profitless diatribes were beginning to frighten him and his inner voice was begging him to stop. Moments of altruism, he called them; when he gave and got nothing back. His breathing was heavy beneath the suit and he hoped the sunglasses were dark enough to hide his eyes from her. There was more coming: truth rising like bile.

'Believe me, if they could get rid of the people, they would. But they need the people to crank out the money on your little hamster wheels.' Your, he thought: did I really say that? 'So instead they get rid of the *beliefs*; everything that bound the people and made them into something. How can you and your neighbour stand up to them any more, now that you are strangers? When you share nothing? And at the same time, the government is making more and more laws. Is that what you call democracy?' Dominic could feel his face flushing as the words came fast from his lips. He couldn't stop. 'Well, *is* it?'

'I don't know,' said Samantha in a small voice.

'Everything between you and them has gone,' he said, whipping his hand across the space between them. 'Everything that answered downwards has *gone*. The Parishes, the Counties, the Lords and the Commons have all been eradicated! They told you they were doing it to help you represent yourselves better; that the past was your enemy! Well how are you going to represent yourself better? Join one of the parties and be hated by the leadership? Form your own and be turned into a crank? Go crying to your MP? They are looking up, not down; they represent the government to *you*, not the other way round! Believe me, they took away all those things to help themselves govern *you* better. And then they killed all of your beliefs, all of your culture and all of your history to make it irreversible. Revolution in England? It's already happened, from the *top down.*'

The girl was looking at him like she had been slapped in the face. Dominic slumped inside, wishing he hadn't said any of it. He felt a sudden, painful tenderness and wanted her to continue delivering the world from itself, child by child.

'I'm sorry,' he said quietly. 'It's just...' He reached for a card and was about to offer her help for her project. Then he realised that her forgetting his name was even more important than her forgetting what he had said, and slipped it quietly back into his pocket.

'Good luck with your project,' he said and she nodded helplessly, her eyes searching him with a cracked look.

Further from the crowd, he found a bench and sat down. The depression was welling up like oil from a well. He remembered the full surreal truth sinking in during his first year back in London. Freedom had become a dirty word and the people made into cheerleaders of their own enslavement. He soon reached for de Tocqueville and now the words of the bedridden French philosopher came back to him. A government that excels in preventing not doing; the people kept as perpetual children, constantly circling for petty pleasures. He watched as the crowd in front of him softened. Voices and hands were raised as people forgot themselves and started to relax. He didn't hate them at all. If he hated them, he wouldn't care. But he did care and he didn't know why. He sighed, feeling too low to light his cigar. The gold mine had become a distant pantomime. He didn't care if it got financed or not: anything would be better than Nick emerging from the crowd with some stranger. At least Charlotte was out there somewhere, and he remembered the spark of rebellion which still seemed to linger in her eye.

He stood and skirted behind the service tent, passing piles of wine boxes and plastic pallets of glasses, then mounted the steps of the house. Inside, he leant in a corner of the living room and watched the flow of people. The walls were white, like his old flat in Moscow, and hung with bright-coloured art. Charlotte entered from the garden, her small body moving quickly under the dress. She was shorter than he remembered yet seemed more physical. The shoulders were flat and strong, and her face looked drawn. He recognised the look from his sister, and knew her surface layer of charm hid the engines which were making the party happen. It would be a bad time to see her, perhaps. He watched as she exchanged a few brisk words with the caterer, then her eyes swept the walls and softened for a moment before she disappeared into the kitchen. He looked back to the art collection. Daniel Falk had crossed the room earlier with more time to spare than Charlotte but ignored it. He let out a contented breath and felt his mood recover, then crossed the room and took a drink from the inside bar. A few moments later, Charlotte emerged in front of him.

'Hello Dominic,' she said.

*

Nick could see Samantha casting glances towards him from across the lawn. It was rude not to go and say hello, but he had a good excuse in not being able to leave Roger. He searched the crowd again for Dominic. Maybe he hadn't even come? It was impossible to know how much he actually cared about the mine and easy to imagine him being distracted by some other opportunity. Nick was on his third drink and the thought had begun to anger him.

Irina had left them and was dancing with a group of children. The sight made Roger think how much more personal the party felt than the hundreds of similar events he had attended. Thinking it was time to try a confidence, he leant over to Nick.

'This music's a bit...' he said, and made a doubtful face. 'We should have... Canteloupe instead!'

Nick looked at him with a wry smile.

'No...' he said. 'We should have The Ice Machine!' They laughed and clinked glasses.

'So,' said Nick, trying to avoid repeating any of their earlier conversations. 'What were you doing down in that Consciousness place?'

Roger's blue eyes rested on him for a moment and the lines in his face stilled.

'Ah...' he said. 'Meditation is really important. A few

years ago I went through everything.... Everything!' He swept his hand around an imaginary amphitheatre, then gestured to one part of it. 'To find The Truth.' He paused. 'I don't think it's in any of the religions. I think there's a bit in all of them. And if you can just find the right bits and put them together, then...' He gestured forward from his chest with both hands, and a drop of elderflower cordial fell on Nick's wrist. 'You can grow! You can get better... Become superhuman!'

Roger's face was intent. The Perennial Philosophy, thought Nick; you? He too had once ploughed through the long texts, only to conclude that words were meant for poetry not truth. Truth can only be expressed in silence. I am silence, he thought; but the memory slipped away.

'Superhuman?' he said with a smile. 'Or human?'

Roger's eyes widened and his lips set momentarily.

'No!' he said. 'Not just human. The thing is always to improve... To be improving yourself every day!'

'I think I know what you mean,' said Nick. The names came back to him, passing on their great wheel. The Examination of Conscience; The Struggle against the Self; The Denial of the Self; Self-Emptying. It was hard to fit the meanings onto Roger and they seemed distant even to Nick himself. How to say it? He started to speak and was grateful when Roger interrupted.

'Yes!' said Roger. He was excited to be converging with Nick already. 'To understand more! To be fuller! And then for the universe to...' He made the outward gesture again. 'Give you its gifts!'

Yes, thought Nick; the universe giveth and the

universe taketh away. Well, it certainly took away from your bandmate! He had found some old news articles on the controversy. The pictures showed a younger Roger stepping in and out of courtrooms with a retinue of lawyers or standing at parties with a taller wife. It wasn't difficult to reverse-engineer that voracious pop star from this ageing playboy. The philosophy he was hearing fitted Roger perfectly, being anything from a justification to an atonement for having left his school friend with nothing. Nick had heard it before; a kind of spiritual rat race which espoused the strong and trampled the weak. Yet there was something appealing about the animated figure with his pale suit and bright shirt, and it warmed Nick to see the lined face lit up by such boyish enthusiasm. Roger was mercurial and disingenuous, asking himself the right questions even as he fed himself the wrong answers. Nick found it hard not to like him.

'Well old man,' he said. 'I'm hoping the universe might have some gifts in store for both of us.'

Roger nodded automatically then noticed the change of tone and looked at him more closely. Nick looked around again and finally saw Dominic walking down from the house with an animated sweep. He stopped his niece Rachael who was running past after Timur.

'Hello Uncle Nick,' said Rachael, hugging his leg. Nick lifted her up and soft hands grabbed his face. He whispered in her ear then set her down and pointed towards Dominic.

Roger remembered when Lily had been like that; in those few short months before he lost custody. Unfit to be a parent, her mother's lawyers had said. Unfit, that was the word they had used. Lawyers... He stopped the thought and watched Rachael set off seriously towards the house.

'Kids...' he said, and was about to ask Nick if he had any but stopped himself. Nick had a kind of austerity which made it easy to imagine him being gay. Not austerity... Aestheticism? Asceticism? Roger's dyslexia had made music a welcome relief after school and he still ploughed through reading material with effort. Then he remembered the girl Nick had been with when they met. Why wasn't she here? He made a note to ask after her, then thought perhaps Irina should instead. The little girl reappeared like a miniature tugboat pulling a man in a tailored blue suit. His thick hair was swept back and it was not difficult to imagine him stepping out of an old film. Like Nick, in fact; and Roger had a vision of them rolling along a corniche in Nick's convertible.

'Roger,' said Nick, turning to him. 'Meet my friend Dominic Bannerman.'

Dominic's eyes flicked towards Roger's green shirt and Nick saw a cloud of boredom pass behind them. Then the smile appeared and he dropped into gear.

'Lovely to meet you,' said Dominic, taking Roger's hand. 'Nick's told me all about you.'

Feeling the soft hand and firm shake, Roger had the sense that a new life was opening up for him.

'Irina!' he called. 'Come and meet Dominic!'

*

Imogen walked into the sun along Notting Hill Gate, breathing deeply as she cut her way through the tourists. The sweat was drying on her brow and her tense muscles were cooling in the evening air. She had run across the two parks after work, dutifully changing into running gear and stuffing her blouse into a backpack. She had used to jog in her office shirt, until one of the directors asked in the lift: 'And which mythical creature are you?' His orotund tone was matched to a suggestive gleam and it was only later she realised what he meant: office worker above, runner below. So she had gone out and bought odd sexless Lycra instead, just to look like everyone else.

This drift towards conformity worried her. She had always told herself conformity was a matter of consent: *consentire*, she remembered; 'to feel something together'. But she didn't feel at home in Lycra, any more than she did being precious about her work clothes. She knew there were only two ways to be free; to go home or to rise to the top. One of the fund's big clients had even brought his dog to a meeting that afternoon. It had run around the office like a spaniel in a farmyard, being petted by men she knew would rather have kicked it across the room. Yes, it was the people who made money who became free; and she had to be one of them.

The sun was still above the buildings although it was well past seven. Midsummer must be approaching and she thought of the Solstice parties back at home, then of the parties which she would give when she was rich. Hopefully her flatmates weren't at home so she could have a drink on the roof terrace and read through her presentation for tomorrow. It had to be perfect if the fund was going to back another of her stocks picks.

She turned right off Notting Hill Gate, then peeled off left towards Ladbroke Grove. The sound of a party reached her from inside a garden square and she stopped to peer over the tall hedge. People in suits were knotted in conversation, seated children watched an entertainer, an insipid band played... Then Dominic, sitting alone on a bench.

She raised a hand and was about to call out, then ducked behind the hedge and felt the warm pavement radiating heat onto her thighs. What was she thinking? They hadn't planned to meet this evening! How could she wave at him? Then again, *why* exactly couldn't she? Yes, it wasn't 'right'. Yes, London had taught her that preparation was essential to enjoyment and spontaneity usually diluted it; and yes, three foot of bare leg would hardly be the right look. But there was something else too: a moment of power. She put on her sunglasses and slowly raised herself. Dominic was holding an unlit cigar and looking down at his phone with the distant curiosity that always made her smile. Would he even be pleased to see her? Who wouldn't be pleased to see their lover on an summer evening, especially dressed like Lolita? For that matter, why hadn't he invited her? She stopped herself in contempt.

She watched as Dominic sent a bored glance around the crowd. The very fact he was bored meant he must have a strong reason for being there, as he valued his time above gold. She knew the light blue suit and recognised the dark red brogues, which had turned out to have no label at all inside; and yet still he seemed a stranger. She could imagine him getting up and doing anything; dancing, disrobing, embracing someone. Maybe the impression that he didn't think about her when she was absent wasn't a bluff, and she had just second-guessed herself into overlooking the truth?

Imogen shivered in the warm air. Something in the flow of ideas had chimed. Of course: 'embrace someone'. She couldn't go in because he might be there with company. She could already picture the temperature of his eyes dropping as they blamed her for turning up. And even if he was on his own, he would still expect to have the *option* of having brought someone. For Dominic, getting caught doing nothing was the same as getting caught doing something. The unplanned imprint on his time; the jeopardy to things he might have been doing; the very claim on him would be enough.

She felt a surge of annoyance that she had let things come this far without a proper discussion. But how could the conversation even start? She knew perfectly the ironic smile with which he would bat away the subject. And so he had made himself unapproachable, even twenty yards away on a summer evening!

She sighed. Of course, it was her own fault too. If the situation was reversed she doubted he would call out to her. He left an exaggerated berth around the evenings she spent with people of her own age, saying he didn't want to impose. She suspected it was really because he was terrified of boredom. She was exactly the same, of course, preferring to drink alone on the roof terrace than with her flatmates, and taking her oblique decisions about what not to do. Many of her friends probably felt there was a black hole around her life, just as she felt there was one around Dominic's. Maybe her very frustration actually meant they were suited to each other? And it had not been difficult to let the other me go. They had all seemed so pointless by comparison, with their nervousness waiting to hatch into petulant ownership. But it had seemed gauche to mention it at the time, and doing so since would only hand Dominic a power which she preferred him not to have. And so here she was.

Dominic stood and disappeared behind a tent, then emerged again to mount the steps of the house with quick short strides.

Imogen walked on, her fast steps replaced by a slow, swaying gait. There were not many people she could talk to about it. She hated the conversations which consumed hours of her girlfriends' time as they luxuriated in the unknowable workings of the other sex. And she couldn't mention it at work without puncturing the halo of power around their relationship. On the Portobello Road, she took out her phone and called home.

'Hello?' bellowed John Somerville. Imogen smiled. She knew what was coming next.

'Hi Dad!' she said. 'It's Imogen.'

'Imogen who?' he said, and she giggled. 'Still managing fun?' said John. 'Managing to have fun, are you? Stocks and shears? You don't use shears for stocks, Immie! Use secateurs!'

She laughed again. Her father pretended to think that investment meant a buying a new bull. She caught up with him, hearing how terrible things were on the farm. Terrible! It was their last year for sure! She smiled. It had been their last year for as long as she could remember; yet still new milking machines were put in, the land grew, and the tractors got newer.

'Can I speak to mum?' she said.

'What?' said John. 'Want to speak to my first wife?' Imogen laughed again, and her mother came on the line.

'Imogen?' she said tartly. 'What on earth are you doing calling me now? Don't you know I'm busy?'

She smiled again. Her parents pretended to be far too busy to speak to their children but she knew what they were really doing. Her mother would have been watering the garden, her brow knotted intently as she inspected the plants; and her father reading the newspaper with occasional cries of outrage. They would both be drinking gin and tonic, and there was nothing either would rather have than a call from her.

'Mum,' she said. 'There's something I'd like to talk to you about.'

'Use a vet,' said Val Somerville. 'They're cheaper.' Imogen laughed, half-wondering if her mother was serious.

'It hasn't come to that yet,' she said, and slowly started telling her mother about Dominic. She hadn't planned what to say so it came out weak and unformed, and she hated hearing her words tumbling out with so little sense.

'Hang on a tick,' said Val. Imogen heard the clink of ice at the other end of the line. Her mother always went to the sideboard when she wanted to think mid-conversation, and her tone was sweetly ironic when she came back on the line.

'Darling,' she said. 'I don't know why you've called. It seems to be to tell me you don't know anything. Why don't you call me when you *do* know something?'

Imogen laughed self-consciously but was grateful that her wandering thoughts had been brought down to earth so quickly. No wonder the farm was doing well. It was run by two people who rarely left a twenty mile radius yet always had the right answer. Rule number one: never trade off poor data. She needed more information and better, and it was not going to come from Dominic. She signed off and returned to her former brisk pace, thinking of ways to fulfill her mother's commission.

*

'What do you think?' said Nick carefully. He and Dominic were walking back towards Notting Hill Gate. Night had fallen and loose crowds formed outside the pubs. He would have suggested a drink but Dominic seemed unusually self-absorbed.

'It's your deal,' said Dominic distantly. 'If you think he's the man, go for it!' He felt Nick silently absorb the deference. 'You've got some other options though?'

'Oh yes,' said Nick quickly. 'But I like Roger.'

'So do I,' said Dominic dutifully, stepping around

some broken glass. A soft partner like Roger suited them both perfectly.

'What next then?' said Nick.

'People like him don't invest on numbers or advice,' said Dominic, focusing in. 'They invest with people they respect and trust.' Nick nodded. 'So show him some love. Take him down to country; get to know him, listen, confide...'

Nick nodded again, and had the absurd image of them visiting his mother at her cottage in Sussex.

'Where though?' he said. 'What's the occasion?'

Dominic thought for a moment.

'Weekend after next, there's a cricket match at my sister's place,' said Dominic. 'Invite him and we'll mention it after dinner...'

Nick smiled and felt a thrill. Dominic had been worth his weight in gold. Gold! He chuckled and Dominic looked at him inquiringly.

'Sorry, just something else,' said Nick. 'Who'll be there?'

'My sister Caroline, her husband Giles, their kids,' said Dominic, then paused. 'One thing,' he said. 'The captain of the other team is Alexander Rosenheim. You know who he is?'

'Yes,' said Nick vaguely. The name was familiar.

'Big mining family,' said Dominic. 'For God's sake don't mention the deal in front of him.'

'Quite!' said Nick. 'But thanks for the tip.'

They shook hands. Pulling away in a cab, Dominic's mind shed the conversation and he was again filled with warm excitement.

8

Charlotte stood in the centre of the Tredegar Gallery. Conversation clattered from the white walls and wine bottles circulated through the crowd. She was talking to a tall lady with white hair and bright eyes which seemed to reflect everything Charlotte said back to her as a question. The woman was speaking loudly in an Irish brogue flecked with adenoids and seemed not to notice each time her glass was refilled. She appeared impossibly old for her energy. Charlotte thought she might be Jewish-Irish but it felt like too direct a question. The woman herself was outrageously direct and would probably relish the question whatever the answer. And Charlotte realised that manners are not about the other person after all: they are really about yourself.

'Artist? I'm not an artist!' said Dinah Laughlin. 'I'm a painter. All these people calling themselves artists: I've never heard anything more pathetic! I mean what have they got to hide?'

The dark eyes flashed at Charlotte and she smiled. It was indeed hard to get to the bottom of what many artists actually did, whereas what Dinah did was stained into her fingers.

You're a dear girl, thought Dinah. Look at you with

your two rings and your yellow dress; your hair all done up in a bow. Tell me everything: tell me about your house and your children. Tell me about the world that is in your heart.

'I buy paintings,' said Charlotte. Dinah threw up her hands and seemed about to grab her.

'Buy paintings!' she said. 'You can buy one of mine! You can buy all of them!' She burrowed in her bag and handed Charlotte a creased card which smelled of white spirit. *Dinah Laughlin, Painter,* it read. The house was called Toadsmoor Cottage and was somewhere in the Gloucestershire countryside.

'What do you paint?' said Charlotte.

'Paint? Paint!?' said Dinah as if the idea had just occurred to her. 'What would you like me to paint? You're paying!' She flashed a wicked smile. Charlotte was falling in love with her.

'Why don't you do the children?' she said.

'The children!' said Dinah. 'What colour would you like them? I always did mine nice and bright so I could keep an eye on them.' The smile broke out again and Charlotte laughed delightedly. The idea of paint in their house! She thought of Adam's single-mindedness: orange? Rachael's gentle curiosity: aquamarine?

'I don't know,' she said. 'You'll have to chose!'

'Well,' said Dinah with a warning raise of the eyebrow. 'You'll have to live with it!'

Charlotte laughed again. Why didn't she come to gallery openings more often? The owner Felix Tredegar had even known who she was when she arrived. Mrs Falk, he had said, how nice to see you. I'm the person they all want, she thought; the person who actually buys the stuff. The invitations came through the door every week but she could never imagine being there or what conversations she would have. So she stayed at home instead, telling herself that art was better in a quiet room. Yet hardly anyone around her was actually looking at the art. She remembered the same thing from the old days; drink and conversation clinging tenuously to the pretext of someone's work. She had another mouthful of wine and listened as Dinah began a mercilessly funny review of the exhibition.

Dominic watched her from a corner. Charlotte stood with a straight back and her glass held in both hands. She was wearing low heels and her dress was cut just above the knee. This is the way to do it, he thought; don't crowd her on her night off. But it was annoying that she had ended up speaking to that Irish woman, who seemed to hate him for no reason he had ever understood. No, he couldn't leave them together for too long. He went over and saw the other woman's eyes freeze. Dominic spoke first.

'Don't you live at my sister's place?' he said.

'Dominic,' said Dinah. Her eyes flicked to Charlotte then back to him.

'Yes,' said Dominic.

'Do you know each other?' said Charlotte.

'I'm so sorry, I've forgotten your name,' said Dominic.

'Dinah Laughlin,' she said, her lithe tone quite different from before.

'Dinah's going to do the children,' said Charlotte.

'How nice,' said Dominic. 'Shall we go?'

He guided her away and they found Felix Tredegar saying goodbye to people by the door.

'Goodbye Mrs Falk,' said Felix, holding onto Charlotte's hand for a moment too long. She smiled and Dominic felt a red flash of jealousy aimed at his second cousin. Felix was younger by three years, with a too-perfect tan and a waist as narrow as ever. After dutiful attempts at childhood friendship, they had just missed each other at school then faded from each other's lives. Dominic had returned from his decade overseas to find Felix entrenched in London, having started his gallery with an inheritance from which Dominic himself had expected something. Still, they had gone out to lunch and tried to make the wheels of friendship turn. But Dominic saw too much of himself in the other man and realised they could never be just friends; only sworn allies, if such a thing were possible. They settled instead for an uneasy truce, neither helping nor hindering each other. Felix turned his fine bones and large eyes on him, the smile widening a fraction. His face wore its usual clown-like detachment, feigning bemusement at the success which he so assiduously cultivated.

'Good to see you,' said Dominic, shaking his hand loosely. 'I hope this show does better.' Their eyes collided, and Dominic stepped past him out of the door.

The sky glowed in a turquoise strip above Dover St, washed white by the sinking sun. Charlotte could smell cigarette smoke from a neighbouring private view which had spilled onto the pavement. Her instinct was to go and crash it, bearing her art-buying credentials for another glass of wine. To be among those people had felt like coming home, and she had met the wonderful Dinah! She thought of the hundreds of galleries dispensing their hospitality across London and wanted to hop between them forever. Dominic appeared beside her. They hadn't spoken much, and now she felt a thrill of gratitude for his casual invitation the previous week.

'Let's have a bite to eat,' he said. Charlotte noticed the space above the white wine she had drunk, and thought uneasily of arriving in the hall at home.

'Ok,' she said. They began walking down towards Piccadilly. A taxi trawled slowly by with its light on and Dominic pictured them tumbling into it together. Charlotte stopped, as if she had heard his thought. She was holding a white shawl together over her dress, and the yellow ribbon had come loose from her hair. Dominic looked at her uncertainly. Surely they had earned some time alone with her? Her eyes met his then bounced away.

'Shall we go to the Club?' she said.

Dominic smiled to hide his confusion. She could hardly believe it was really possible for them to go there together? Maybe she was in denial, or wanted somewhere familiar, or just somewhere nearby to avoid being swept off into the unknown. He looked at her, standing flushed and hesitant in the evening light, and wanted to hug her. Dinner is alright, he would say. Except that it wasn't alright at all, and he wondered who was really in denial.

'I've been there rather a lot lately,' he said, clearing his throat. 'And it's a little far. Let's pop around the corner instead.'

Charlotte came back to life and started walking. The movement released a dam of anxiety which Dominic had barely noticed appear, and he fell in beside her feeling disproportionately grateful. They crossed Piccadilly and he turned them into Jermyn Street, stopping in front of a long restaurant. The manager greeted him and offered them the last table outside on the pavement. Dominic declined and they were shown to the back instead.

Charlotte sat gingerly in the wide leather chair and was handed a menu the size of a map. She tilted it upwards so it hid her face and studied the food intently. A creeping, unformed nervousness had started to take hold of her. This was more than the 'bite to eat' she had expected, although in retrospect it was hard to imagine Dominic doing anything less. Still, the food looked excellent, and it would be rude not to enjoy herself.

'I think I'll have the tagliata,' she said.

'Tagliata,' said Dominic vaguely, his delicate brow creasing as he studied the wine menu. His idea of keeping the evening informal was giving way to a dangerous euphoria. The urge to celebrate was pulling his eye ever further down the wine list, into territory which would probably stand out a mile to Charlotte. Fuck it, he thought, feeling the same elation which had shepherded him here from the gallery.

'A bottle of Brunello,' he said to the waiter. 'A tagliata di manzo, and a ragu di cingiale.'

The waiter nodded and lifted their menus, removing Charlotte's shield and the last distraction between them. She started talking about the exhibition and Dominic enjoyed her unselfconscious digressions, prolonging them with his questions. He realised that she was talking mainly to herself, just to breathe the air of the thing she loved, and was reminded of her brother before chasing the thought away. When the dark red cushions of meat arrived, covered by their choppy sea of rocket and parmesan, Charlotte sawed into them appreciatively. Dominic nursed his wild boar stew, adding little prows of creamed spinach to each forkful then following them with long sips of Montalcino.

Charlotte soon forgot the food and started to talk again, passing her glass from one hand to another over the half-finished plate. Art was not his language but he was enjoying having to do so little work. When she started talking about her thesis on Neo-Platonism and Botticelli, he was on firm ground with the philosophy at least. Yet it reminded him that his interest in metaphysics sat uneasily beside his lack of belief, and that in darker moments he thought one would have to go. When she asked about his degree, he gently steered the conversation away. University had left him with an odd gap where the world should have been, and soon after leaving he looked back on it with a chill. Trying to imagine Charlotte's student days, he thought the sardonic undertow of her conversation would suit an undergraduate. But it was hard to imagine her rigid bearing in a younger girl. Too much seemed to have happened since for him to draw a line connecting the woman with her younger self. Or maybe it was one big thing; a broken engagement, or a death? Or a breakdown? He sat back, picturing it all too easily.

'And you got a First?' he said.

'But of course,' she said theatrically, touching her chest like a diva. Dominic laughed.

'You know what,' he said, trimming his sails. 'You should come and have a look at my prints.'

Charlotte's eyes widened but she laughed too, feeling they knew each other well enough to share a joke. The wine was warm and unpretentious, and she felt light. She wondered why she had never met Dominic before. Nick had known him at school and they both knew several people in common. Yet she realised how many people in London must be able to say that of him. She could see that he made it his business to know people without being known, and to know things without saying them. Somehow the thought comforted her. He had invited her gracefully but discreetly, and his charm had unfurled with an almost surreal perfection all evening. She was reminded of her grandmother's stories of being a debutante, told only after her grandfather died; and thought this must be the type of man she had meant. He filled up her wineglass by precisely the right amount and so naturally that she hardy felt she was drinking. His navigation of the menu had been calm and serious, the thin lips pursing as he read each line. The understated cadences of his Italian reminded her that the country had remained there through her years of absence; and she thought of it with a sudden, panicked longing. A picture came to her of them crossing the Ponte Vecchio in the early evening. She blushed lightly and looked for something else to say, then remembered Dinah and the strange frisson with Dominic as they left.

'Tell me about Dinah,' she said carefully.

'Felix is my cousin and represents her,' said Dominic after a pause. 'She lives at my brother-in-law Giles' place.' He pictured Toadsmoor House with its honeyed stone gables hidden from the world in a Cotswold valley, and had to pull himself up before mentioning the upcoming cricket weekend. It was too easy to imagine her sketching on the boundary then being wordlessly drawn to him in a corner of the house. But he had already invited both Nick and Roger Curtis, and Imogen too. The impulse made him worry about his self-control; but the very thought of self-control only made him want to lean across the table and kiss her.

'And what's it like?' said Charlotte.

'The estate?' said Dominic. 'It's beautiful.'

Charlotte chuckled.

'I'm sure the estate is exactly like every other estate,' she said, shaking her head minutely. Dominic blinked: she had just articulated the fear that drove his whole life. 'I meant her work,' she said, and Dominic remembered who they were talking about.

'The work is quite good,' he said distantly, and Charlotte understood the tone. You might as well go ahead if you don't like her, she thought.

'And what's she like?' she said.

Dominic's head equivocated.

'A little batty,' he said. 'A widow, I think. But perfectly harmless.'

'I thought she was nice,' said Charlotte firmly.

'Oh, she is,' said Dominic. 'Perfectly nice.'

The plates were cleared and Charlotte excused

herself. She wrapped the shawl around her flat shoulders and Dominic was fearful she would turn to the door and leave without a word. But she found the narrow back stairs instead, peering down them as she steadied herself with a hand.

Thinking of the weekend made Dominic realise that he hadn't called his sister to tell her about the extra guests. Caroline would give her usual, almost silent exhalation of annoyance. But already having lost her approval so completely had given him a kind of freedom, while she was also helpless in the face of her husband Giles's willingness to forgive him anything. It had been nearly twenty five years since he had taken the train down from school for their wedding, febrile with anticipation of what the night might bring. Giles had been distant, overawed by the presence of his new father-in-law; and Dominic wished that he could remember the man better before his erosion by decades of marriage. The descent was now complete and Giles would wander down to lunch each day trailing a book from his library. When Dominic visited, it would assume a special relevance: Sun Tzu or Clausewitz. They would trade submerged jokes across the table, both relishing Caroline's disapproval. More than anything, it was Giles's life that confirmed his fears for his own future; the future which his sister and brother so urgently pushed upon him. All estates are the same, he thought: no-one had ever put it as well as Charlotte.

The waiter appeared, asking if they would like anything else. He didn't know what to say. If she came back upstairs in a hurry to leave, having ordered sweets and grappa would be an embarrassment. The time had passed perfectly and instinct told to order the bill: if it was premature, it would only give them more reason to go on somewhere else. The waiter nodded sympathetically, as if something must be dragging Dominic from the unfinished ceremony of dinner.

Charlotte leant on the marble rim of the basin and breathed in the scented air, then opened her eyes and looked at herself.

When she emerged back into the dining room, it was to see the waiter tearing off a receipt and handing it to Dominic. She approached the table, not knowing what to say. Dominic stood, smoothing the pockets of his jacket.

'How was your tagliata?' he said.

'Yes,' she said, realising she wasn't answering the question.

*

She accepted his arm as they walked back along Piccadilly. The warm breeze lifted the hair from her forehead and she smelled Green Park on the night air. She knew it was time to go home but it was difficult to imagine doing it.

The question spun faster in Dominic's mind; flashing and showing itself first one way then the other, spurred on by her warm touch. She seemed unhurried and her arm was relaxed. When he saw her again, the evening could easily be wiped from the slate. She would sink back into her responsibilities and this moment be inaccessible forever. He turned into a side street and stopped.

'Do you mind if we just pop in and see Gianfranco?' he said.

'Who's Gianfranco?' said Charlotte, looking at him and realising they were the same height.

'He looks after the bar in here,' said Dominic, indicating a door with a small awning.

Charlotte shrugged. She had been surprised to find their dinner cut short and thought it must be before ten. And it would be a change at least. Dominic pressed a bell and the door was opened to show a small desk and a narrow staircase lined in red satin. Charlotte went first, stepping carefully with one hand on a velvet-covered rail, and emerged into a type of club which she hardly knew still existed. The sight of white tablecloths beside a dancefloor seemed to belong to another era. Dominic guided her towards the back, where a large barman passed a cloth over the dark, uneven surface of a polished wooden bar. He had elasticated metal bands around the upper arms of his white shirt and greeted Dominic quietly.

'Good evening,' said Dominic. He turned to Charlotte and indicated the lines of bottles and suspended glasses behind the bar. 'Any preferences?' he said.

'You choose,' said Charlotte.

'Gianfranco,' said Dominic. 'Make us an Aviation and a White Lady please.'

Gianfranco nodded approvingly and they were shown to a good table, close to the dancing but not crowded by it. The music played just loud enough to dance but quiet enough for conversation. Older men moved easily with accommodating partners, as if the place had been designed for them to enjoy themselves unselfconsciously. It was as if they had stepped through a looking glass from the Club into its mirror image. The service cut across the decades in the same way and there was as much tension in the air, yet the members seemed different. The drinks arrived and she saw citrus fibres floating on the pale surface of hers. She took a sip and it painted a cold line inside her.

'Where are we?' she said.

Dominic's eyes swept the room and found the owner in a corner, marked out by his bald, pointed cranium and wide stance. Even in the half light, Dominic could see Eric Dodds' eyes darting among his guests to check their reactions to what he was saying. Dominic didn't let his look rest for more than a small fraction of a second: he was glad Dodds didn't have a reason to recognise him and he didn't want to give him one.

'I'm not sure it has a name,' he said, not wanting Charlotte to talk about it or come back without him. 'It belongs to Uncle Eric.'

'Who's he?' said Charlotte. Dominic looked at her unmarked face and wondered what to say.

'He is what you would call a legitimate businessman,' he said. 'And a colourful one at that. That bar you just saw is a piece of wood from one of Nelson's ships.'

'Really?' said Charlotte, remembering Gianfranco's cloth passing over the thick patina. 'How did it get here?'

A smile twitched Dominic's lips.

'Sometimes these things just grow legs, you know,' he said. When he had first heard the story, he found the local news reports and looked with admiration at the smashed front of the naval museum and its glum curator.

Charlotte's eyes narrowed. She started to speak then stopped and leant forwards, gesturing to the dance floor.

'Are these men...?' she whispered, and Dominic cut her off.

'No, of course not,' he said meaningfully.

Charlotte looked around the room with new eyes. It was not hard to imagine that the shift in energy she had felt belonged to the modern underworld, but she also wondered if he was teasing her like Nick did. She leant towards him again.

'Do you think any of them needs a moll?' she said, Americanising the vowel and dropping an eyelid theatrically.

He nearly kissed her. How had she been locked into the existence of a banker's housewife? It was as if she had fallen through a hole into someone else's life, even as this gravity pulled her back to her own. Why else would she be flirting with him? His confidence rose and when a new song came on he felt a start of recognition.

'Let's go and find out,' he said. 'I love this song.'

'You're on,' said Charlotte, taking a last long sip from the White Lady. Dominic took her hands at the back of the dancefloor, keeping an open position. Lyrics appeared over the slow beat of the song. 'I am the eye in the sky, I can read your mind.' He moved to a closed position and she stiffened momentarily, then looked down and laid a ḥand on the front of his shoulder.

'Don't leave false illusions behind...' he whispered with the song. Charlotte looked up at him, her face weak as a tear balanced in the corner of her eye. Dominic laid a hand on her cheek and caught the droplet on his outstretched thumb, and kissed her.

9

Alexander Rosenheim gave a last look over his shoulder before turning to start his run-up. Dominic didn't move. Rosenheim's steps stuttered and foreshortened as he reached the wicket, and then Dominic shifted. Alexander saw but it was too late. He released the ball and Dominic stepped into it, connecting with a clean off drive. He paused with his bat in the air and watched the ball punch along the ground, pulling fielders into its wake. It flicked into the air as it hit the boundary rope.

A cheer went up from the pavilion and a smile flitted over Imogen's lips. Rosenheim threw up his hands theatrically and Dominic's eyes rested on him for a moment. Rosenheim Group, read his shirt; probably the only German to have a company cricket team. Dominic wondered what the family owned. Twenty percent of United Minerals: that alone was enough. But there were also copper mines from Zambia to Indonesia; Bolivian lithium; one of the largest smelters in Europe; their own brokerage for good measure. Diamond holes in Western Australia larger than the towns that served them. But what else lurked in those trusts in Frankfurt? The tall figure's arm was extended as he rearranged the fielders, and Dominic thought they must get to know each other better at dinner.

'More Short Leg than Silly Mid!' called Rosenheim to a fielder. 'Wilf, go to Leg Slip!'

Rosenheim looked towards Nick, who had been lent to his team and was now standing on the outfield. During the previous over, Dominic had noticed him with his arms extended towards the sun like a rag doll.

'Hey! Hello!' shouted Rosenheim. Nick was still looking away across the valley. Dominic closed his eyes, then heard Rosenheim call to him down the wicket.

'What's he called again?' said Rosenheim.

'Rodney,' said Dominic.

'Rodney!' cried Alexander, and Nick looked around.

'Go to Fine Leg!' shouted Alexander.

Fourteen people were looking at Nick. He started moving tentatively along the boundary.

'No!' shouted Alexander. 'The other way! Clive, show him Fine Leg please!'

Nick waited in embarrassment as one of his teammates jogged over. Alexander turned back to the wicket. You can't be serious, thought Dominic. Switching to the leg side, are you? Why don't you just write it on a postcard? And leg spin? He had played against Rosenheim the previous year and was sure he didn't have it in him. The Germanic bluff was so obvious: and Rosenheim's last glance was still on the off side! Dominic took his position and picked another hole in the field for his next shot. Alexander's steps foreshortened again and he released the ball. Dominic stepped into it and drove harder. The leg stump clicked and a cheer went up from the field. A string plucked in Dominic's head and darkness crowded the edge of his vision. Then the sunlight was back and he was strolling from the crease. He raised his bat to salute the applause: he had made forty one, and it was as well to go to Rosenheim as anyone. Passing Nick on the outfield, he stopped.

'I've told Rosenheim you can bowl,' he said tersely. 'When Roger comes in to bat, get in and give him some easy balls.'

'Right,' said Nick, nodding slowly. He had been keen to move faster with Roger but Dominic insisted that they should wait until today, curtly repeating what he had said about friendship and trust. Nick had heard the cold voice of experience, daring to be contradicted, and quickly agreed. He had slept badly the previous night and driven down impatiently that morning, passing the twin cupolas of his old school chapel twenty miles out of London; then slowed and dropped the hood when he finally entered a network of country lanes. The golden silence of the Cotswold hills mellowed him and when he found an old sign to Toadsmoor Estate, the excitement of the day overcame him. The rutted drive passed through woods and skirted the cricket pitch before an old manor house appeared from a fold in the hills. Its roof seemed to have been draped between the three gables, and rows of leaded bay windows emerged unevenly from the yellow front. He cut the engine and let his eyes rest on the sight. The house must be at least five centuries old, and he had felt a moment of shame that they were using it to warm up Roger.

He watched Dominic jog off to where a tiny cricket pavilion sagged like a Hobbit hut in the space between two huge oaks. In the wash of shade, two benches rose from an island of rugs. The Toadsmoor side lay around with drinks hidden among the bats and pads. They were calling out guesses at the name of Alexander Rosenheim's longhaired pointer, which was stretched out under one of the benches. 'Fritz?' said one, and his teammates sniggered. The dog arched its neck towards them, its eyebrows gathered in confusion.

Dinah and Imogen sat chatting on two ancient deck chairs by the boundary rope. Dinah's terrier Punk was curled under the nylon cradle of her chair, his eyes half-closed. Timur was sitting upright in Imogen's lap, his nose and ears quivering as they pointed towards the match. Dinah had been sketching the cricket pitch until a large dragon took shape breathing fire on the batsman. Now she was covertly drawing Imogen on a corner of the page. You *are* a beauty, she thought. Do you know how special you are? Of course not, that's what makes you special! Beauty without knowledge, wasn't that the Garden of Eden? Then; religion, no thanks! And she remembered the struggle of her father's life: damned if he took her mother to Mass, damned if he didn't. She had an awful feeling that Imogen had come with Dominic, when she had seen him with someone else only days before. And not anyone, but that lovely girl in the bright dress; Charlotte, who had offered her a commission.

The memory of another weekend here was burning strongly, and the thought of Dominic's endless path of destruction pulled downwards in her chest. She took a long breath of the summer-scented air and looked towards the old beech tree from which Emily would be watching the match. She hoped the girl would come down for tea, then go and fetch her some gin and tonic. Sketching in Imogen's small nose and tracing her strong jaw, she wondered if she could make it into a real portrait. But Imogen was too young to afford paintings, and selling it to Dominic was out of the question. She sighed and started on the Medusian hair, remembering these were other people's lives.

'Don't you just hate Pimms?' she said. 'It's like having sex with an Englishman: all promise and no punch!' Imogen gave a low cackle. She was still grinning from Dominic's dismissal and took a contented sip of her drink as he walked off the field.

Away from the main group, Roger was being given a crash course in batting by one of Dominic's nephews. His back was bent over the bat in a perfect arc, and Hugh Ancaster squinted painfully at the sight.

'How do you fancy cheating instead?' said Hugh, and Roger's face showed cautious interest. Hugh lifted his bat off the ground and he straightened up like someone in an old-fashioned print, his bright shirt rippling lightly in a breeze.

'Good,' said Hugh. 'Now keep your eyes level and the bat straight. Just watch the ball, step towards where it lands, and swing through it. Ready?'

Roger repeated the steps in his head and Hugh's practice ball sailed off towards the beech tree.

'Careful!' shouted Dinah.

'Easy on, we're just practicing!' said Hugh, jogging off to retrieve it.

What a feeling! The bat had come alive in Roger's hands with a marvellous sound! He wanted Hugh to get back so he could do it again, and he took a few practice strokes.

Emily Ancaster watched her brother approach from the branches of the tree and wished she had something to drop on him. He had teased her all the previous day about Alexander Rosenheim's visit. She didn't understand the point of teasing someone about something that was true. She did like Alexander. She liked his neat hair, his just-appearing wrinkles, and his encouraging smile. He was kinder to her than anyone and he didn't sound German at all, so she didn't know why they all said he was. Of course she had imagined marrying him. The only problem was that she didn't want to go and live at his house. They had been over for dinner after last year's match and her mother had been very funny about the refurbishment. Why do that to a house? she had said on the way back. Why not just blow it up and start again?

Emily smiled and ran her palm over the smooth bark. No, she didn't want to go and live at Covington Manor; or anywhere else for that matter. She really wanted to stay at Toadsmoor and live in Dinah's cottage after her, or somewhere down on the farm. That was one problem: the other was that Alexander was already married. No-one had ever met his wife and Emily had started to hate her for being married to him without keeping him company. She heard cries of encouragement for the new batsman, and peered through the leaves to see who it was.

Sir Giles Ancaster leaned across to update the scoreboard from his shooting stick. Plus ça change, he thought: thirty years later and I'm still doing the scoring. His elder son Hugh organised the annual match against their neighbour Rosenheim, and 'Toadsmoor vs. Covington' was scrawled in a space at the top of the scorebook. Covington Manor was the house Rosenheim had bought a few years before, and it was just far enough away for the two families to know each other. Hugh had originally befriended him in London, apparently over a mutual need to play cricket. Giles didn't quite see how the desire to do something could outweigh with whom you did it. Yet he was grateful, as the more people knew that he entertained Rosenheim, the less he had to troop around the county just to show that he still existed. And at least scoring was better than actually having to play. He thought indulgently of his second son Charlie, holed up in some corner of the garden with a book. The boy had barely hid his relief when he was shunted off the team to make way for Dominic's guests.

Giles looked for the two men out on the field. Nicholas Paget was lingering near the boundary, performing oriental-looking stretches. Giles had heard that his father was involved in a nasty political scandal down in Devon; still, the sins of the father were his own. The other one was undergoing some impromptu cricket coaching from Hugh, and Giles realised that he had already forgotten the name. But he had arrived in a fancy car and it didn't hurt to have some money on show with Rosenheim's team visiting. He watched as

Hugh corrected the man's posture, his son's face wholly focused on the art of batting. At twenty four, the boy was already lost to him. Hugh talked about horses with his mother, sport with his friends, and had recently started panicking Giles with questions about the estate. Giles didn't have the heart to say that the house was attached to them like a giant mollusc, and that he felt the four hundred acres conspiring against him every day. He had gone over to the farm that morning and the sheep had glared at him with their usual baleful accusation. His family had never farmed yet when his father-in-law had used to visit them, the man had come alive when discussing livestock. At the time, Giles had been taken by the patrician touch. Only later did he realise it was the Conspiracy at work.

Each morning, he now awoke to more advanced fantasies about selling the place. It had only been bought by his grandfather but now each new generation made it more inescapable. Hugh would blanche at the idea, of course. Emily would be heartbroken; Charlie, probably vaguely excited. And his wife? Caroline would just give him a sideways look of disappointment, unadorned by words. Yet still she called it 'the farm'. England: the only country where the greater the slight, the more undetectable it is. He wondered again if she loved him, trying to stop the thought as it happened. These dives into bourgeois melancholy were turning into a sort of bulimia. Of course she didn't. English women only love animals; men, they tolerate and occasionally admire. The thought plunged sickeningly on: and it certainly wasn't the latter. He could never match the sheer *echtness* of her whole existence; the attention to detail and constant expectation of the best from everyone. Her smell was the smell of cordite when they had once made love after shooting. Yes, physicality was really the difference. Her truth was material whereas his lay between the pages of his library. Yet she believed in God and he didn't. That was strange. But in the country only the material commands respect: so the higher he climbed on his stepladder of first editions, the more of a fool he became. He marked another wicket, wondering when someone was going to offer him a drink.

Roger changed into the sweaty white shirt which Hugh had silently handed him, and strapped on his pads. This was it! That lovely feeling, it was going to happen out there! He wondered if he should wear his sunglasses, but his eyes weren't good and he needed to be able to see the pitch. Irina had flown back two days before and cried at the airport, and he thought how much she would love seeing this. He walked out to a smattering of applause, not sure if it was for him or the man coming out. Tom Evercreech, they had called him. Tom Evercreech of Toadsmoor Farm! What names! His heart was pumping and the blood buzzed in his ears. Which end should he be walking to? Evercreech walked past and touched gloves with him. Roger followed the path he had taken and ended up at the bowler's end. Here was Nick! Roger grinned and Nick acknowledged him minutely before looking down at the pitch. Of course, he thought; we're on opposing teams today. He looked seriously at the other batsman instead. Nick ran past him, cast the ball down the pitch and the other batsman hit it.

'Run!' the man shouted, and in a flurry of cricket equipment Roger was running towards the other end.

'Run! Stay! Run!' shouted different voices when he arrived. He decided to stay there, at the action end! The other man skidded and turned halfway down the pitch.

Nick looked down the wicket, to where Roger seemed unable to decide if he was going to bend down or stand up. His first balls had not been bad; too good perhaps, if he now had to ease off for their guest of honour. The fielders had been brought in around Roger and Rosenheim was looking at him expectantly. Nick took a last look then turned and walked slowly to the end of his run-up.

Words raced in Roger's mind: eyes level, watch the ball, straight bat, move your foot to where it lands! Would he be able to do it all at once? The sun was in his eyes and he wanted to wipe the sweat from his face but Nick was already running towards him. Nick released the ball and it bounced a few yards ahead of him. He kept his eyes level, moved his foot towards it, and swung his arms forwards as hard as he could. The bat sprang backwards with a crack and he started running furiously. He passed the other batsman then paRogered at the other end before starting to run back.

'Stop, stop!' called the other batsman with a smile. Roger stopped in the middle of the pitch. There were more cheers from the pavilion and he wondered if he was out. The other man jogged up to him.

'Well done, old man,' he said, pointing to where

white figures were hacking in the undergrowth. 'You hit a six!'

A six! Right here in a real match! The sound rung in Roger's ears and he could still feel the animated kick from the bat. Even Dominic hadn't hit a six! He raised his hands towards the pavilion and there was a new round of cheering. He could see Dominic and his girlfriend; and Sir Giles, changing the score with his runs; and everyone still clapping. He wished that Irina was there and decided to call her before dinner. Roger hurried back to the crease, sure that he could do it again.

Alexander Rosenheim was looking at Nick in disbelief. He froze. He was bowling at his own side! And someone almost certainly had money on this: probably Rosenheim and Hugh Ancaster, or Dominic himself. You fucking snake, he thought. The ball reappeared at his feet and he walked back to the end of the run-up, flushing deeply with his eyes to the ground. He turned, saw Roger's gleeful preparations, and started to run.

Emily's hand flew to her mouth. Imogen and Dinah fell silent. Sir Giles shook his head. Tom Evercreech smiled. Fury engulfed the two captains. Nick ran down the wicket and knelt beside Roger. The wicket keeper joined him and took off his gloves without looking at Nick.

'Jesus, Roger,' he said. 'I'm so sorry. Are you ok?' Roger's breath was light. The ball had hit him in the chest at full pace.

'Fine, fine,' said Roger. 'It's a man's game!' He smiled weakly and tried to stand using the bat and Nick's arm.

People started walking out from the pavilion.

'Hang on,' said Nick, feeling across Roger's chest. He reached the point of impact and Roger winced; and Nick felt the shaking as he helped him to his feet. The two captains appeared and the umpire offered Roger a retirement.

'No, no!' he said. 'No need!' He swung the bat gamely and Nick saw the pain cross his face again. It was explained to Roger that he could resume later but he waved away the idea. 'No need!' he said, taking up the crease again.

The two captains looked at each other helplessly and Nick walked back to the bowling end. There was nowhere he could look that didn't make him feel sick. As he reached the wicket, a hand gripped him and he turned to see Alexander Rosenheim, his eyes burning with hatred at what he had done.

'I don't know who you are,' he said. 'But if you do that again, I'm taking my team home.' He turned his back and walked away.

Nick stood at the end of his run-up. He saw the fear in Roger's eyes and remembered his happy preparations for the previous ball. He felt the tension stretched across the sunlit pitch; the love directed towards Roger and the disgust towards himself. He pictured rolling the ball to Rosenheim and walking off the field; but that would make it even worse, setting the memory in aspic forever. Trying to block the rest of the white figures from his mind, He jogged up and released a slow drifter. As the ball left his hand, Roger shied and his bat took off the bails. The umpire wearily dismissed him and he walked off the field to cheers. Nick saw the hero's welcome from Dominic and the old artist set about making a fuss of him. He bowled two more balls and returned to the outfield.

When the match broke for tea, Nick ran into Dominic behind the pavilion and felt his arm gripped tightly.

'What the fuck are you doing?' said Dominic, his eyes swelling with anger that Nick had dared to jeopardise his plan. Nick tore his arm away.

'Fuck off, Dominic,' he hissed. 'Just fuck off.'

*

Lady Caroline Ancaster stalked her kitchen garden, thinking of how typical of Dominic it was to bring two people at one day's notice.

'Caro,' had come the rare confirmation phone call. 'Looking forward to Hugh's cricket match.' That at least she knew: with Rosenheim here, wild horses wouldn't keep her brother away. She had waited for whatever was next and his tone had changed on cue. 'Look, I've got two friends I'd love to bring.'

Almost everyone had to move rooms. Emily had gone to stay in the cottage with Dinah; Charlie had gone into her room; and Hugh's poor friends had been squeezed together in Giles' old study. All so these two could breeze into separate rooms and a decent bathroom, probably thinking it all happened on its own. Why couldn't Dominic just take people to Selwood if he wanted to entertain them? Because he didn't want to know their own family's house even existed.

And he had bought a girlfriend who must be at least fifteen years younger. There was no-one in particular to feel embarrassed for, as she imagined such relationships were normal to Rosenheim. But she herself felt it was deeply wrong; not only wrong but typical of her brother's insouciance and the shameless professing of his own pleasure. Yes, he had been the cleverest of them: but what were brains without humility? Without a worldview that meant something? The words came back to her; if you have not love, you have nothing. And she pitied her brother for his life.

Giles didn't care, of course. He and Dominic loved each other. They would sit for hours after dinner and trade sniggering laughs which no-one else understood. It wasn't even polite; let alone that she hated talk without action. That's right, she thought as she leant down to one of the beds. If you want something said, ask a man; if you want something done...

'Ask a bloody woman,' she muttered, and a bunch of carrots came free in an explosion of soil. Giles would love the young blonde too. Her husband was drawn to anything immaterial or subversive. It seemed to spring from some sense of being wronged by life. But how? By inheriting this place? Or by marrying her? He would be a lot happier if he spent more time on the land and less in his study, where he didn't even study anything. But of course saying that would only confirm everything he already thought about her. And then there were Dominic's guests. Nick, another useless one! So what if he could speak Mongolian? He was probably hopeless with animals. And the other one, with his awful clothes and dreadful car. He had actually called her 'sweetie'. When *had* the English started producing such useless men? Twenty for dinner; of course, Dominic, why not make it twenty-two?

She stomped back to the house, a spaniel following nervously behind. Inside, she found the Great Hall of Toadsmoor House dressed for dinner. Silver trees grew from the white tablecloth and the virginal wicks of candles curled above them. Giles had gone into the cellar with recalcitrance and emerged with abandonment, and twelve dusty bottles of wine now huddled on the side. She looked down the long table, wondering if there was any hope of placements with two cricket teams to feed. Alexander's wife had once again not come down from London and it seemed this had set the tone for the rest of his team. They were short of women.

Her weathered eyes darted around the table. Rosenheim would have to have Imogen: she was the best they had, and Emily should be kept away. Giles and Dominic didn't deserve women so they could have each other. She could have the dilettante Nick, as Giles knew the family and he might be a nice change for her. What to do with the Pop Star, who apparently had somehow managed to injure himself? Charlie was always playing terrible music too loudly; he could have him. Hugh and his friends could have the few women Rosenheim had brought, and Emily could be thrown to the wolves of his team. Fine. She quickly distributed the cards around the table then reached into the centre to adjust one of the arrangements. She hoped they hadn't gone over the top for a dinner that wasn't even black tie. Or was it? Caroline realised she had no idea what people would come down in. Another job for her: wear something that goes with everything. She picked a stalk of grass from the tablecloth and went to join Amber in the kitchen.

10

The candles threw dark valleys among the roses and lilies, their thermals lifting slow columns of dust and pollen above the middle of the table. Light flickered on the varnished paintings of the Great Hall and the oak panels warmed to the sounds of dinner. Amber Fotheringhay moved easily around the edge of the table, a stem of flowers trailing from her hair as she removed plates of late asparagus. You'll be enjoying these later, she thought. Drop of turpentine in the bowl deals with that; I wonder if Lady C knows? Amber liked helping Caroline. It wasn't the money: it was just better than being at home, where her husband avoided her eyes.

Imogen saw her coming and wiped the last of the butter from her plate. She picked up a trace of fresh cider as the woman leant over for her plate and recognised the snatch of tune she was humming. I bet you know where the good parties are, she thought. She looked along the table and felt again how different it was from home. Theirs was a farmhouse and Giles Ancaster didn't look much like a farmer, with his watch chain and mocking eyes. But Caroline did, and their conversation earlier had found its way as surely as the rain reaches the sea. When Imogen said which part of Shropshire they farmed, her hostesses' eyes had sparkled with familiarity. I do love it up there, she said, and mentioned the people she knew. Imogen said she didn't know them but her parents did, smiling to hide how infrequently she went home and how far her life was from what Caroline imagined. She could see Caroline's disapproval of her relationship with Dominic but guessed it would lift in a moment if they became engaged. It would be strange to have a sister-in-law who was old enough to be her mother.

She looked across to where Dominic was sitting next to Rosenheim. She hadn't answered his late-night message during week and had enjoyed his silent irritation on the way down in the car. This weekend was too good a fact-finder to miss, as Dominic never spoke about his family. She knew him too well to put it down to self-effacement, which meant it could be a real Achilles Heel. The very fact he had invited her seemed to show some movement; but she didn't know if it was in their relationship or some other game of his.

Already the day had shown her those flashes of hatred in Dinah's eyes when he walked past. Now Caroline Ancaster was releasing a different sort of furious glance towards him, and Imogen had the odd feeling that Dominic had invited her there to protect him. She watched as Alexander Rosenheim turned to speak to him. The more Dominic deployed his charm, the harder it was to notice; and now it went into overdrive. She knew exactly who Rosenheim was and had already introduced herself when Dominic was not around. She had a less clear idea about Roger Curtis, who was sitting next to her and recounting his afternoon to both her and Caroline on his other side.

'First ball,' he said. 'Six! Straight over the rope! And we only won by four runs in the end...' Roger raised his eyebrows meaningfully. It had only sunk in afterwards that he had won the match for them with his one ball.

'Well, we are most grateful for your efforts,' said Caroline. 'They won last year, you know, so you've quite restored our honour. And at some personal cost, I hear? Emily broke a rib last year and the poor thing couldn't ride for weeks!'

Roger smiled but the pain still throbbed in his chest and it hurt each time he reached for his water. He had eventually retired from the fielding and Imogen had taken his place, which he worried had reflected badly on him. Then a nice woman had produced a drawing of him hitting the six. It was up in his room now, and he wondered why she wasn't here.

'Oh no,' he said. 'That was nothing. It was my fault really. I... I didn't move my foot to the right place.'

'Well,' said Caroline, laying a hand on his arm. 'You're the hero of our family.'

Dominic flicked her an appreciative glance, too fast for her to notice.

'Let me get you some wine,' said Caroline.

'Oh no,' said Roger. 'I don't drink!'

Caroline put down the bottle again.

The main course was brought in and the vapours of chicken in white wine and mushrooms filled the table. Roger saw the hungry glances of the other cricketers and worried when he saw the meat. I like these people, he thought. I want to accept something from them: but what? Giles and Hugh rose to their feet and brought bottles of Saint-Émilion from next to the fireplace, and Giles wondered why he still put them there in summer. The full black shapes joined the empty yellow ones of the Burgundy, and the serving dish reached Roger.

'I'm sorry?' said Caroline. Amber smirked behind them, and Caroline looked at her imploringly.

'I'll find something, your ladyship,' said Amber, and Caroline flashed her a bunched-up smile. 'Your ladyship' indeed!

A growl reached the guests and was greeted with cries of encouragement. Timur had been ranging among the legs, sniffing at ankles and the hems of trousers. Now he was confronting the longhaired pointer for an asparagus stem. He won and the other dog retreated under its owner's chair.

Alexander felt her arrive and leant down to scratch the soft head. He was relaxing and was grateful to the Ancasters for inviting him. Social situations made him tense because he often seemed to be at the centre of them. He hated having to distribute his attention between people so carefully. Just talk to me or don't, he wanted to say: we're all the same! Instead, people approached him with this gleaming excitement. Sometimes it was commercial; that at least he could understand. Send me a message, he would say. So they did and his secretary had to deal with even more correspondence. But they often wanted something else; some abstract social thing which he couldn't fulfill as he didn't know what it was. He felt more and more like a piece of public property; passed around and greeted by ever more people, while he still only knew the people he had always known.

He had bought Covington Manor as a place to get away from it; a place where he could get to know fewer people better. But instead the same life had followed him there. Between his wife and the family office, a year's worth of work had happened on the house; a year's worth of decisions, architects, security people, garden people. All of it had resulted in local patronage which he was now loathe to cut off. As soon as it was finished, dinners the size of this one had started to happen every weekend, instigated either by his wife or by his own half-remembered invitations. Now Tamara was bored of the place so the influxes from London had subsided, yet they had left not the peace he had hoped for but emptiness. He was restless in the evenings and the gaunt memory of his sister followed him through the rooms.

Coming to Toadsmoor reminded him of the time before the work started, when his house too had its own smell. His time with the Ancasters usually never touched on anything outside the South Cotswolds, and they felt like the first new real friends he could remember making. It was disappointing that they had placed him next to Bannerman, probably thinking that the country bored him and he would want to talk about business. He would rather have had Dominic's girlfriend, or even Emily. People like Dominic tired him with their endless refracted glimpses and half-open doors. He imagined them always needing to make new friends to replace the ones they had lost, as their greed turned every win-win into a win-lose.

Listening to Dominic's smooth-flowing conversation, the words of his father came to him: these people, their ships will blow apart at the first storm! He remembered Franz Rosenheim's finger pointing into the imaginary rigging and then at him. How can you trust someone beyond doubt? How can you know they will tell you the truth about what they have done, unless they can tell you who they really *are*? Instead Dominic's talk ranged among the people he knew, laying out the namedrops like stepping stones. Yes, thought Alexander wearily; there is probably something in that crowded head of yours which could help us. But I cannot let you onto our ship until you show me what type of man you are. And he realised that the men who do not show themselves are always the wrong ones. It is why Dominic had been so easy to bluff that afternoon: because he expected men to lie and that meant he was probably a liar himself. Yes, he thought, I have learned something this evening. I have learned that we will keep ourselves free of you.

Dominic was asking if Rosenheim Group had any interests in Uzbekistan, and Alexander realised he needed an answer.

'Uzbckistan?' he said. 'I'm not very keen on their human rights record.'

Pain appeared at the back of Dominic's head; a trace, like an architect's line drawn in the ground. A moment of altruism was approaching: with Rosenheim of all people! He looked to the table for something to stop himself but the wine would only fuel it and his plate was already empty. He looked at Rosenheim's just-maturing face. It must be thirty, over ten years younger than him.

'Human rights?' he said. 'You believe in them?'

Alexander looked at him and nodded. This was a strange departure from Bannerman's usual script.

'Yes,' he said.

'Everywhere?' said Dominic.

'Everywhere,' said Alexander.

'As much on a desert island as here in England?' said Dominic. 'They pre-exist, do they? Like the sky?'

Rosenheim was looking at him with interest.

'Yes,' he said steadily. 'They exist on a desert island.'

'But what is to stop me killing you if we're both on a desert island?' said Dominic, feeling the irritation start to colour his face.

'Nothing,' said Alexander. 'But you would still be contravening my rights.'

Dominic stared at the neat, reasonable man beside him. He was starting to feel light and wished he could change the subject but an irresistible gravity was pulling him towards Alexander's mind. The most gifted beings in the universe: why this insatiable desire to lie?

'If you'll forgive me,' he said. 'That's not much good if it actually happens.'

'So what does exist then, which people call rights?' said Alexander carefully. He wanted to hear more, if only to understand the brutal lack of progress that existed in the world; and not only in the world but here in their midst.

'Law, of course,' said Dominic. 'Because it can be enforced. A right without a law behind it is nothing. It's the difference between this little island and that other one.'

'Yes,' said Alexander patiently. 'That's why law is based on human rights.'

'You have it in one,' said Dominic, hot now under his summer jacket. 'Rights used to be based on laws; now laws are based on rights.'

'And what is wrong with that?' said Alexander.

'What is wrong with that,' said Dominic rapidly. 'Is that rights used to be there to *stop* governments doing things; they used to be things that were enforceable on the government by individuals. But now the government has empowered itself to deliver people's rights, which means it has made itself *more* powerful on the pretext of limiting its own power!'

A new religion, he thought; my ideas over yours, because mine come from the universe. The iron hand in the velvet glove, closing tighter around his throat. You will never get me: never. He wished Machiavelli could see this grand amphitheatre of lies clamping down on the very virtù he had loved. Yes, Niccolò had understood rights, true rights; because he himself wanted to be free. Or were human rights just virtù by other means? Pretty. He fleetingly regretted that he had moved himself away from Giles, the only other person at the table who would understand it. Instead, he now saw Rosenheim's confusion take refuge in dislike.

'I think you'll find,' said Alexander as his eyes cooled. 'That rights are there to guarantee people's freedom...'

'Are they,' Dominic cut in. 'Are they really? Freedom used to be bigger than all this. Freedom is what pre-exists. Or used to. But as soon as you label it, it's gone.

Do you think I want a some academic or civil servant telling me what I'm free to do? Or what I'm free from? Write a list of human rights and you stab freedom right through the fucking heart.'

His words rippled across the table and he looked away, the slump of humiliation hard and sudden. What he had said was worse than an anachronism to people like Rosenheim. It had made him into an anathema, a positive evil; and the private lunch he had imagined could never happen now. Dominic stared at the flowers in the middle of the table, ignoring whatever eyes might be on him. He thought of Charlotte and the low gleam of mockery which she carried: *she* would understand. Imogen's blue dress sparkled at the edge of his vision and he realised how the two had already come to exist in parallel. Already? He had only seen Charlotte once.

'Ah,' he heard from Alexander. 'But you would say that there is nothing but law. You're a lawyer!'

Realising that the conversation could never have happened in London, Alexander suddenly felt warmer towards Dominic than he had all evening. Dominic turned to find him filling up their wine glasses with a forgiving smile, and felt pathetically grateful for his good manners. Across the table, Imogen was watching them.

*

Nick was sitting at the foot of the table, next to Dominic's younger nephew Charlie. The boy was wearing a paisley shirt and velvet jacket. Nick was wearing a sports jacket and looked around the table at what others had on. Some were in black tie and the host himself was in a smoking jacket and loose bow tie. Dominic was in a dark summer jacket with an open shirt, yet Roger was closest with a white shirt and something that could pass for a dinner jacket in the candlelight. Nick wondered why he was looking at what people were wearing, and realised that what had happened that afternoon had made him paranoid. It had fractured his relationships in this place before he even had a chance to form them; and was almost certainly why he was down here with the younger generation. Probably the only person with whom it had not fractured his relationship was Roger himself, who seemed to view the event as some kind of bond. He had kept on saying it didn't matter; and each time he said it, it mattered more.

Nick looked up to where he was now captivated by Imogen. She was looking stunning yet relaxed enough not to be overdressed. He had felt a kind of sinking inevitability as he was introduced to her, wondering if there was any way for Dominic to assert his superiority which he had yet to exploit. Across the table from Imogen, he and Rosenheim had now turned to speak to their other neighbours. Do not say anything about the mine in front of Alexander Rosenheim, Dominic had said. Obviously, he had scoffed. Yet he could not remember exactly why Rosenheim was important, aside from thinking that someone he used to know was now associated with him.

The whole top end of the table seemed to be another

world; one from which he had fallen. He felt justified in tucking into the wine instead and Charlie was turning out to be a good companion. During the first course, it transpired that he had already travelled in India and knew some Asian history. Now the boy couldn't get over the fact that Nick's dog was called Timur; and Timur couldn't get over the fact that Charlie couldn't get over his name. Nick tried to appreciate his enthusiasm but the commotion was embarrassing and the name seemed trite when brought to light. When Charlie started pressing him for anecdotes about his travels, he had a vision of himself asking John Streeter the same questions over twenty years before; and felt the same unease which John must have done at being asked to carve war stories from life. He had an uncomfortable premonition of Charlie coming travelling with him, if he ever went again.

The thought took him back to Roger, who was obliviously happy near the head of the table. Dominic's promise that they would speak to him this evening seemed impossible to fulfill in the high-spirited room. The details of the mine were fading under the wine and Nick found himself hoping that the conversation would be postponed; especially given that Roger would be sober. When Charlie said that he had spent the afternoon reading the Upanishads but couldn't remember much, Nick realised that he hadn't been at the cricket. No wonder we like each other, he thought self-pityingly. He poured another glass and leant forwards to hear Charlie's ideas for a music festival in the Toadsmoor Valley.

Giles looked down the table. I used to sit down at that end, he thought. I wonder if Hugh will ever sit up here? Looking at the boy's broad shoulders and checked shirt, he thought: that is probably exactly what you want.

*

The candles burned lower and their updraft caught the plumes of cigarette smoke being blown into the middle of the table. Someone had put on music in the next room and a large oak door had been swung open to let in the night. Abandoned glasses lay scattered across the mottled cloth and people had reformed into knots.

Charlie had disappeared out into the garden and Emily's hair was disarrayed as she giggled at the antics of two suitors. Alexander had moved next to Sir Giles and was probing him on the philanthropic activity of the county. He was wondering if there was anything for the Rosenheim Foundation to do, given that the area did not seem to be long on drug addicts. Giles was instead telling him about building conservation and a classical music festival, but it would be rude to say that those were things which could pay for themselves. Beside them, Imogen listened sedately.

Nick had thrown off his shame and moved up to sit next to Caroline. They were talking about his uncle, with whom Giles had studied, and anything else that came to hand. He found himself enjoying the small talk and thought: if not this, what? They would be as mute as animals, and he had the dim idea that civilisation is really nothing but filling the silence. I am silence, he thought; but listening to Caroline made it difficult to remember where he had heard the phrase, and he realised he was drunk. The memory of the cricket match tugged again. There was no way he could yet join the same conversation as Rosenheim, and he was suddenly grateful for Caroline's unselfconscious attention. But then again, he thought; this is her job. He felt a tap on the shoulder and turned to see Dominic.

'Let's have a cigar,' said Dominic.

'You can smoke in here,' said Caroline. Dominic shook his head minutely at Nick.

'Please excuse me,' said Nick. His hostess gave a thin smile, not even looking at Dominic. One step forward, two steps backward, thought Nick. He got to his feet and Dominic nodded briefly in the direction of Roger.

'Could you collect our friend?' he said. Nick looked towards where Hugh was listening to Roger, then felt Dominic's hand on his arm.

'And remember,' said Dominic, the cool eyes resting in his. 'Don't say anything until he asks.'

Nick doubted Roger would ask about anything, but he nodded. He skirted the table, steadying himself on the hooped backs of the dining chairs, and Roger's face lit up as he approached. Nick saw Dominic drift from the room and wondered what to say.

'Mr Bodyline!' said Roger, clapping a hand on Nick's arm. Hugh gave a slurring laugh, and it turned out he had been explaining cricket tactics to Roger. Nick leant down to Roger.

'Come and join us,' he said, looking towards the door.

Roger looked around the room for Dominic and wondered what was next. He stood and Nick lead him uneasily across the flagstone floor. A black square of night filled the door to the garden and Nick wished he could go there to breathe a little first. He felt Caroline's eyes on them as he further broke up her party. In the passageway, they found Dominic studying a tapestry of a sylvan hunting scene.

Dominic turned to them with a smile, happy to be free of the dinner. He had felt beholden to Alexander for the rest of the evening and even his unfulfilled conversational duties with Giles had become a weight. Seeing that Nick had been drinking, he was filled with the fun of what they were about to do and laid an arm on each of their shoulders.

'Come!' he said, steering them away down the corridor. They passed wall hangings and large pieces of furniture whose purposes had been lost over time. The air was everywhere heavy with the particular smell of the house. Dominic opened a door and Nick saw a small library where three chairs were pulled up around an empty grate. On a side table sat a bottle of spirits, three brandy glasses, and three cigars in plastic sleeves. Very nice, thought Nick, deciding he was ready for another drink. He and Roger sank into deep, dense armchairs. Roger had never felt anything quite like it: the chair felt like it had been sat in every day for a hundred years.

'Let's relax a little,' said Dominic. 'I find these dinners can be a little...' He made a burdened gesture. I know what you mean, thought Roger. Even with the attentions of the family, he had found it hard to relax;

and he was surprised that even Dominic had felt the same. The library was wonderfully quiet after the crowded dining room, and still seemed to belong to the people who looked down calmly from the paintings. There was a quiet snip as Dominic guillotined one of the cigars.

'These,' he said, holding it up. 'Are from the oldest cigar house in Cuba. I bought them down for us.' He passed it to Roger, who cradled it in his hand. Cigars don't count, he thought: this I have to try.

Nick accepted one too, turning the old familiar weight in his hand, and leant across to look at the bottle. Domaine du Tariquet, it read. *Tariq'at,* he thought, hearing the soft sounds of the Persian. A spoke on the wheel; the inner path; a brotherhood seeking truth. The floating chant of the Dervishes came to him and the gentle, insistent sound of the flute. Cantemir's *Book of Science and Music.* Forty one paths under the seven crowns; from the outer path of law to the inner path of meditation; only then maybe certainty, maybe truth. Each morning in Istanbul, he had sought it on a prayer rug as the dawn muezzin rose across the city. How far had he gone? Had he even been on the path at all? And here was the word again, written on a bottle of alcohol. A path, at least! He realised his eyes were closed and hoped they would leave him for a moment longer.

'Not for me,' he heard, and opened his eyes to see Roger refusing a glass.

'One won't hurt,' said Dominic, sliding the brandy balloon onto a table by Roger.

Nick saw him look at it with outlawed longing and

thought: one *will* hurt. Maybe Dominic actually wanted to get Roger drunk to help ease out the money? The look on Dominic's face that afternoon had been almost demonic, and he could still feel where the grip had bitten into his arm. Looking at Dominic's reclining shape and neatly crossed legs, Nick realised that he couldn't wait to be rid of him.

Sweet blue smoke began to gather in the middle of the room, and Roger raised the glass to his nose. The fumes grabbed him and he felt a thin floor beneath him. He lit the cigar instead, sucking the flame into its end. The heavy mouthful of smoke seem to seeped outwards through his whole body, dulling the pain in his chest. The gravity of his life gathered around him and he thought how good things were. The glass in his hand was starting to smell wonderful; a long-lost sibling of the cigar, separated by the Atlantic but reunited here in England. What a country! He looked at the other two, both stretched out straight with their faces toward the ceiling. Nick's eyes were closed again and Dominic was blowing rings of smoke through each other. There was a sound by the door and a dog appeared. It sniffed the heavy air, then curled itself against the front of his chair. His problems had never felt so distant: they were all safely parked outside the estate, where they couldn't touch him.

'Nice to get away, he said.

'Oh sure,' said Dominic. 'Especially with things so busy.'

'Quite,' said Nick, letting go of his moment of pride as he sensed Dominic's opener.

'What sort of things do you get up to?' said Roger, thinking the business of life was a good topic for now. The cigar made him feel like he was looking down on his life from above.

Nick realised that Dominic was leaving the question for him; but they hadn't discussed exactly what to say and now the opening panicked him.

'Various things,' he said, the words thick in his mouth.

'Investments,' said Dominic, balancing the wide glass on his chest. 'Various investments.'

Investments, thought Roger, and all his problems came back into focus. His money only ever went one way, like sand in an hour glass. What had it even been invested in? Funds. Numbers on a page. Securities. Ha, what a name! There had been nothing real; nothing he could touch. What should he have bought instead? Property? But apparently the people who had invested in property ended up worse than anyone. He wondered where Dominic and Nick put their money. They seemed like such opposites, yet there was some intangible thing they had in common. An air of always being right, perhaps. Whereas how much had he got right? From marriages to money, almost nothing.

'I never know what to invest in,' he said, shaking his head.

'Well,' said Dominic. 'That is the big question.'

Dominic watched Roger as the silence settled. The blonde figure sunk in the wide armchair was different from anyone he had dealt with before. He had only ever been among musicians on their own turf in New York nightclubs and backstage at concerts. He knew their money irrigated the markets but also that it was stewarded by quiet men in suits; those wolves dressed as shepherds who held the clients so delicately as the money trickled down their throats. He wondered if anyone was standing behind Roger and if a pair of trained eyes would ever fall on their proposition. He doubted it, as Roger seemed to have all the impetuousness and vanity to do something like this alone. If Nick was wrong about the deposit, he would answer for it; but if he was right, Dominic's options would give him the freedom of movement he needed. He took a satisfied pull on the Larrañaga and let his thoughts slide back towards Charlotte. He would never have guessed that she could kiss in the way she had on that dance floor. Her passivity had vanished and another memory awoken as she pulled her body into his. She had kissed his neck and under his ears, pushing her forehead against his chin and holding herself against him. Her smell became present and he felt an abandonment which he thought must come from the pain of childbirth. He had even worried about Uncle Eric's presence in the corner, expecting a tap on the shoulder as it went on. Then, just as quickly, she had looked at her watch and announced she had to go. She had got into her taxi without a word, leaving such a strong presence that he had walked all the way home.

'What have you got on at the moment?' said Roger finally. 'If you don't mind me asking.'

Nick glanced at Dominic then leant back and looked at Roger, seeing the curiosity in his blue eyes.

'It's quite sensitive,' he said, his voice still distant through the drink and smoke. Roger nodded, gesturing to show he could be trusted. 'But we know where rather a large gold deposit is.'

Gold! thought Roger. What could be more real than that?

'How fortunate,' he said. 'And I bet it's not in your aunt's sock draw!'

'No,' said Dominic with a smile. 'It's in...' Nick raised a finger from his armrest and Dominic stopped. 'It's in the ground,' he said, and saw the flicker of hurt in Roger's eyes.

'How do you know?' said Roger determinedly.

'Intelligence,' said Nick to the ceiling. 'Followed by seismic refraction.'

'Who found it?' said Roger.

'I did,' said Nick, and the memories unfurled. The location given to him by a stranger with an emphysemic cough; an evening drive out to the disused concession; even his unease at the old Soviet explosive which he had used for a surface charge. Then the sight of the computer screen, balanced on the bonnet of his jeep under its sun hood. He had checked and re-checked what he was looking at before slowly collecting the geophones and eradicating what traces he could. Then a slow drive back to Samarkand, his mind turning steadily through the options; then, only six months later, the painful departure to Istanbul. He could still smell the untamed desert and see the white dust hanging in the air from his explosions. And only he had the grid reference. Only he knew.

'I found it,' he repeated quietly, challenging anyone else to speak. He thought of the future; a future which he could almost touch. To be in an old airport again, willingly gripped by the bureaucracy; to speak Dari and hear the dawn muezzin floating down the valleys; to feel the Asian sun and taste the wind of a motorcycle. This time he would write books to last long after he had died. A journey from Lahore to the South China Sea perhaps, or from the Northern Ocean along the Yenesei to Lake Baikal. England would again become what it should be; the doorpost for a thread paid out into the great labyrinth of Asia. And it would all start *now*.

'I could do with a good investment,' said Roger.

Nick leant forwards but Dominic cut him off.

'Very unlikely I'm afraid,' said Dominic. 'The syndicate's closed. Half of London would be biting my arm off otherwise!' He gave a little laugh and tapped his cigar as if seeking Roger's understanding.

Nick released his breath, catching up with the bluff. But it put the schedule back and he felt a surge of anger that he had not been consulted. Dominic rebuffed his look with an innocent smile and Nick was still staring into the empty fireplace when the door clicked open. It was Dominic's nephew, Hugh. He was drunk.

'Ah,' he said. 'There you all are!' He held onto the open door and it swayed lightly. 'Bike polo?'

Nick wanted to tell him to fuck off. Roger wondered what he meant. Dominic thought: actually, that's not bad.

'Why not?' he said, getting to his feet. 'Come on chaps.'

Nick felt Roger's reluctance as he followed Dominic from the room, and hated him even more. Dominic thought he was finessing it but he was just a control freak, and would probably rather it failed than succeeded in any other way than his own. I'll talk to Roger myself, thought Nick; and *then* I'll talk to you. If needs be, I'll tear up your fucking paperwork and start again.

By the time they emerged into a stable yard, he felt a little better. Now Roger was interested, and he was still the only one who knew where to sink the core samples. If he could put Dominic back in his place by finding an excuse to shorten the deal timing, things would be back on track. The rest of the party was gathering and laughter rose into the still night, punctuated by the glowing ends of cigarettes. He pulled on his cigar and looked up to where stars showed between the pale clouds; the same stars which would mark his journey East.

Dominic looked for Imogen so he could kiss her on the neck but found her joking with Rosenheim and some of his friends. Roger stood among them all, thinking how much more fun this was than what people called fun. A chain rattled as Hugh pulled open two wide doors and neon light blinked across the cobblestones. The party gathered closer and saw tens of old bicycles stacked against one wall of the stable, with half-size polo mallets leaning against the other. Nick smiled, remembering drunken mêlées in Fulham many years before. Hugh and his team pulled the bikes free and started ferrying them up to the cricket pitch.

Dominic organised the adults, handing out bunches of mallets and telling them to follow by car. Nick piled some into the open back seats of his car and offered Roger a ride. As they followed the line of cars crawling heavily over the pitted drive, Nick smoked distantly, keen not to return to the conversation and betray his new strategy.

The cars were forming into a circle around the cricket pitch, their headlights lighting the arena. Nick joined it then picked a bike and rode out into the middle. Looking around the circle of lights, he picked out the tired yellow rectangles of his Mercedes beside the high circles of a Land Rover; then the oriental slits of a Maserati and the low, gleaming points of Dominic's BMW. He peddled harder, swinging his mallet with anticipation. Lamps appeared to mark the goals and a fluorescent ball was passed across the field. The two teams formed up again, gaming each other across the wide space, then a gun sounded and they rode towards each other. Wind-milling silhouettes flitted across the lights as the players circled and collided, their eyes busy on the darting sprite of the ball. Imogen lunged for it and felt a mallet connect with her shoulder. It was Rosenheim and, seeing his eyes widen in horror, she quickly hooked the ball away from him. Roger circled at the edge, the place on his chest hurting at the exercise.

Dinah had wandered up from her cottage and was sketching the scene as a dark Guernica with bicycles. The teams shrank as retirements took place and Emily set up a bar for the injured, who returned to the match with new vigour. Giles sprawled in the passenger seat of his wife's car, having driven it up to escape her complaining that Dominic had interfered with the seating plan at dinner. An Strauss recording played from the cheap speakers of the Toyota and he thought: yes, when the house is full, no-one can fault this life.

'Someone has to bloody win this!' shouted Hugh. Calls were made and received in the darkness but no goals had been scored and people were beginning to tire. Nick had made a few plays and was panting, alcohol and blood coursing hotly under his skin. But it had to be him! He wheeled his bike around the outfield, looking for a gap. When Dominic got the ball, Nick shouted to him and began riding diagonally towards the centre. Dominic sent the ball beside him at an acute angle and it met his path fifteen yards from the goal. Nick circled his mallet and drove it fast between the waiting lamps. A cheer went up from the whole field and exhilaration rose through him.

'You should try it on an elephant!' he shouted, feeling acceptance flood out his afternoon of shame.

JULY

11

Rachael and Adam Falk chased each other around the kitchen table, squealing accusations at each other. Charlotte sprung open one of the white panels and took down boxes of cereal then reached for a bowl as the children passed her again. It slipped and her shoulders jumped as it cracked, sending thick shards across the counter top. She closed her eyes.

'Stop it!' she screamed. 'Just bloody *stop it!*'

Rachael started to cry and Adam looked at his mother with hurt. He led his sister to a corner of the room and started plucking pieces of porcelain out of her hair.

'Come back here,' Charlotte snapped. 'Come back here immediately!'

The children hugged each other silently. When Daniel appeared at the door in his gym kit, they scrambled across and grabbed a leg each. Charlotte picked up her phone and slipped it into her pocket.

'Everything alright?' said Daniel, his concerned face scanning the room.

'It's nothing,' said Charlotte. 'Just dropped a bowl.' Daniel pulled the children off and came over, his dark eyes searching her as he pulled her towards him.

'Are you ok?' he said. She felt how tense her body was

in his arms, and produced a smile.

'I'm fine,' she said. 'Just a little tired.' She nodded towards the children. 'I think the china is in their hair.'

Daniel's eyes widened. He released her and sat at the kitchen table, lifting a child onto each knee. With one arm encircling them, he began removing the fragments into a neat pile on the table. Charlotte swept pieces of china from the countertop into the sink, then had to start plucking them out again.

'Isn't that woman coming in today?' said Daniel. Charlotte didn't turn around. 'To paint the kids?'

'Is it today?' she said lightly.

'Yup,' said Daniel. 'Such a great idea! Where did you meet her?'

'At a gallery opening,' said Charlotte, pushing the rest of the broken bowl down the wide plughole of the sink. There was some type of whirring device down there which could take it on later or get broken.

'Ah yes,' said Daniel in a satisfied tone. 'I remember.' She heard him put the children down and felt him come up to her. 'I'm playing squash with Jason,' he said. 'I'll be back for lunch.' He gave her a hug and kissed her on the top of her head. She nodded, reaching for another bowl.

*

Dinah waved an arm at the taxi rank of Paddington Station. She was wearing a heavy cotton poncho with the bag of painting materials resting under one side. Punk's lead extended from the other, holding the terrier up on his hind legs as it barked at a group of tourists. A taxi drew up for her.

'He won't pee in the back, will he?' said the driver.

'No,' said Dinah, climbing in. 'But I might.'

She saw him smile as he pulled out. It had been a wonderful journey up with her Rachmaninoff and her gin. But the trains went too fast these days and the cinema reel of England was over too quickly. Great rhomboid fields sketched on the Wiltshire limestone; a pub sliding by close to the track; then lines of post-war housing, each containing a little universe. She was old and the world was a dangerous place: that journey could be her last! Why should it be cut short by some busybody in the government and a privatised railway firm? There should be one slow train a day, she thought, for *us*.

Paddington always made her think of the farewell with her daughter Anna, and what had happened before. She had been to see her mother at Toadsmoor and they joined a nocturnal picnic with the family down by the stream. When it got late, Dinah had left her there with Dominic and the others. The girl was already in her twenties but something had broken in her that weekend. It was almost too fine to notice; only a mother's eye could see the new incompleteness. But it had still been there when they parted and probably still marked her now, thousands of miles away in Portland, Oregon. The same thing had happened that night which used to happen in these Bayswater squares throughout the Seventies; free love, which didn't turn out to be so free in the end. Anna had once been different and after Dominic she was that little bit more like everyone else.

She hadn't come back from the States yet. Now she had met a man, she probably never would.

Bayswater turned to Notting Hill, an unfamiliar population swirling around the familiar landmarks. On so many corners, a memory. Where Peter had stood for a day, busking on his clarinet with a single note. Can you hear it yet, Dinah? I cannot hear it! The way his voice bit off the two syllables of her name as if he was saying it for the first time. Di-*nah!*

She passed the place where two men had tried to mug them and he had quickly stripped then fallen to his knees on the pavement. 'Take me,' he had cried. 'I am ready to die!' They ran away and Peter ran after them while Dinah wept with laughter. Death, drinking, and nudity; his favourite pastimes. One of his greatest games had been to pose as a corpse on public transport. If no-one came to his aid, he would reanimate himself and castigate the passengers for their inhumanity. Yet if someone did try to help, he would frostily tell them to let him die in peace. If an official tried to remove him, he would, of course, start to weep. Peter had loved to cry. His favourite slogan: strength through weakness! Lachryma Russki!

Yes, she thought, we had a fine time, Pytor Gregorvich. And we could have had it for longer if you hadn't drunk yourself to death. She thought of the hospital and the crushing absence of beauty which had surrounded him at the end. She knew by the movements of his lips and the tilting of his head which pieces were coming to him. Schubert's B-Flat Sonata, Beethoven's A Minor Quartet: those claims to life at death. Then, from nowhere, his eyes had cleared. He focused on her and whispered 'Contessa, perdono'. She still didn't know if he had been giving voice to the duet or trying to tell her something. The thought of him dying unhappy still followed her like a cloud. So what if it meant he had been unfaithful? How could it have mattered then? But he died before she could react.

Then she had cried. Cried on his warm, medicated body. Cried in the dead flat, its spirit departed. Cried among his manuscripts and at the sight of her paintings, their spirits departed too. Then, just as quickly, the tears had stopped. She had children to tell and a funeral to organise. And it was hardly Peter's fault if he had a weak liver. He certainly wasn't a weak liver! She smiled at the pun, thinking how he would have liked it.

The car passed the place where he had done most of the drinking and she remembered the man he had done it with: Felipe, the mad tour guide. And the conversations! The Battle of Borodino; the Varangian League; Ludwig II! Felipe was younger and had survived. Once, with a cold streak of fear, she had seen him drinking with her son Pippin. Still, even unto death, people's lives are their own.

Except Dominic. She felt the familiar tightening in her chest, which she had never felt against anyone else. Here she was, going to see another of his women; or someone soon to become one. And at what cost? The family she was about to meet would soon be just another wreckage sinking in his wake.

Dinah closed her eyes in the warm interior of the cab. Maybe there was something wrong with *her*, to be so sensitive to the damage people do? Who was she to say who was good or bad? Or what Charlotte should do? Or even Anna? When she herself had moved in with Peter then never married him, her own parents had been just as upset. But she had found something with him and followed it; and thank goodness that she had! The thought made her feel lighter and her anger was overtaken by curiosity about Charlotte. And the girl was going to be a customer, which meant she could do what she liked! On which note; materials, my dear, expenses! She had kept the train tickets to submit with her first invoice and needed a canvas, so diverted the taxi in a wide loop down Kensington High St. It pulled up by an art shop with a wide banner that read: 'Let's fill this town with artists.'

'Feckin' get rid of them, more like,' she muttered, and told the taxi to wait.

*

The doorbell rang and Charlotte answered it.

'Hello!' she said.

Dinah Laughlin was standing on the doorstep in a piece of ethnic clothing and a straw hat, with wraparound sunglasses and bright red lipstick. She was supporting a large linen bag, a new canvas and a cigarette; and held a lead which ended in a mistrustful brown terrier.

'Hello, dear,' said Dinah. She saw her host look at the cigarette and stubbed it out on the clean porch.

'Thank you,' said Charlotte, suddenly longing for a

cigarette herself. 'Come in.'

They went into the drawing room and Dinah dropped her things in a pile. She unclipped Punk's lead and he began to circle the hems of the sofas, sniffing each section intently. Don't you dare, she thought.

'Would you like something?' said Charlotte.

'Gin and tonic, dear,' said Dinah, and Charlotte turned towards the kitchen. Eleven o'clock in the morning, she thought.

Dinah perched on the edge of a white sofa. Would you look at this place? It's like a hotel. You couldn't die here, they'd just clear you away like an old meal! And some man pays for it all while the girl runs around town. Seeing Charlotte again, she still didn't seem like the type. Dinah stopped herself. Type? Seventy-four years, Dinah Laughlin, and you haven't learned a thing!

Charlotte came back with two tall glasses, a slice of lemon bobbing in each of them. Dinah recognised one of the painters Charlotte had bought and they discussed the work a little. There's room for more on these walls, she thought; and wondered if she could sell Charlotte another work after the portrait.

'Come to my exhibition next year,' she said. She mentioned the gallery where they had met but Charlotte interrupted.

'Let me introduce you to the children,' she said. 'I'll just go and get them.'

Of course, thought Dinah: she had been at the gallery with Dominic. Its owner Felix was his cousin, and it was Felix who had arranged the cottage at Toadsmoor when her lease finally ran out in Bayswater. Yes, she owed the family a lot. Emptying the old flat to go down to the country, she had seen Peter's traces more clearly than ever. The fragments of a record which he had disliked still gathered in the corner; the guano stains where he had kept hens; the long scar of a sabre along one of the walls. This melancholy always came to her in London and already she was looking forward to being back in her quiet valley. She would play the piano in the pub that evening, and raise a quiet glass to him.

Two children ran in and Punk was on his feet, barking caustically in the perfect room. Rachael took her brother's hand and Dinah swept the dog up onto the sofa. It burrowed in beside her, quivering as it eyed the children.

'Hello my dears!' said Dinah. 'What are your names?'

'I'm Adam,' said the boy. 'This is Rachael. She's my sister.'

Dinah looked at them sceptically.

'Are you sure?' she said, and leant forwards with a frown. 'I thought *you* were Adam and *you* were Rachael?' she said, pointing at each of them in turn.

The children looked at each other and giggled. Rachael dropped her brother's hand and approached Dinah.

'I'm Rachael and he's Adam,' she said. 'I'm *four* and he's *five*.' She held out four short fingers.

'Ah,' said Dinah. 'Well I am Dinah and I'm...' She stopped to count, then held out both hands. 'Seven,' she said hesitantly.

Rachael grabbed her skirt and small knots of material bunched in her fists.

'No, you're not!' she said. 'You're...'

Adam ran up to join them, and a white canine emerged from under one of Punk's trembling black lips.

'A hundred!' he shouted.

'Two hundred!' shouted Rachael.

'Children!' said Charlotte, and the dog's growl became audible. The children trusted dogs because of Timur and she couldn't imagine Daniel's reaction to one of them being bitten. Rachael stopped punching Dinah's legs and tried to climb into her lap. Charlotte put down her drink.

'Ninety hundred!' shouted Rachael, and Adam started battering Dinah's leg.

'A thousand!' he shouted. Punk was on his feet with his front teeth bared. Charlotte started towards them but Dinah swept the dog away and off the sofa. He twisted his muzzle upwards as he fell, then slunk into a corner where he curled up with his back to the room.

'Well,' said Dinah. 'If I *was* ninety hundred, why would I eat these?' She took a sweet out of her bag. Rachael's attention left the dog and she looked at Dinah seriously.

'Can I have one?' she said. Dinah gave the children one each and Adam held his carefully.

'Are you going to paint our picture?' he said.

'I don't know,' said Dinah. 'Why don't we ask mummy?' Adam turned to face Charlotte.

'Mummy,' he said. 'Can we have a picture? It can go right... There!' He pointed to where a large painting hung above the mantelpiece.

'Yes, darling,' said Charlotte. 'That's why we're here.'

Then, to Dinah: 'I thought I'd put you in the garden room where the light is good.'

Dinah followed her through, the question worrying at her like a rat. Why are you doing it? And why with *him*? She had seen houses like this before and knew that the men who owned them didn't appreciate being humiliated. Charlotte's husband looked out of several pictures. Seeing his thick hair and dark eyes, Dinah knew that she and he shared their ancient blood. Maybe he just didn't care? Never presume to know the secrets of a marriage! Or maybe she was wrong about Charlotte and Dominic? No. His instruction for Charlotte to leave the gallery had been too direct, and Charlotte's change of subject when she had mentioned the place was too quick. The very fact that Dominic hadn't been mentioned was proof enough. They passed a framed picture of another man she recognised; thin and tanned, with dark blonde hair swept back from a high forehead. He had been at the cricket match too, and she remembered the silence when he had put that batsman down. Another nasty piece of work; they seemed to be all around Charlotte. Just wait, she thought. You're here now; an answer will come.

Having settled them in the makeshift studio, Charlotte walked quickly to the newsagent and back. She listened for a moment to the distant patter from the garden room before going down to the basement and re-emerging into the communal gardens at the back of the house. In the three weeks since their party, summer had set in and the bright, acrylic green of the lawn was starting to yellow. She picked a bench and looked around before sliding the narrow packet of cigarettes from the pocket of her jeans. The cellophane came off in the same satisfying loop which she remembered, and the unchanged smell of fresh cigarettes reached her on the summer air. She slid one out and ran it under her nose, then lit it and took a long draw. She sat back and looked along the plume of smoke towards the house, then took out her phone and opened the message from Dominic.

12

Roger was watching the late evening light from the terrace of his bedroom. *The Best of Arvo Pärt* was playing inside and he had laid down his book. He was supposed to be at an event but thinking of the noise and semi-acquaintances had kept him at home. He had let go of his housekeeper and the kitchen was turning into a mess. Still, taking charge of it was fun and he liked the new quietness of the house. He left the balcony doors open at night and was planning to go back into his studio soon; maybe even the next day.

He couldn't remember the last time he had been in London over the summer. It felt lighter, like a place left to its own devices. The black paintwork of his Porsche had gathered a relaxed coating of dust from being parked up by the Heath. He drove there each morning to read and sunbathe before cooling off in the ponds. His current book was very good. Be still, it said; experience where you are. He had thought of going back to work on his own book on Truth and had even started putting down some new notes. He had no regrets about missing Croatia and Ibiza. He could never grow in places which belonged to phonies! But this land of England was real; as real as the dust on his car. Irina was coming back soon and he planned to take her out of

London this time, perhaps to the sea. His phone chirped quietly on the table and he picked it up. NICK PAGET, read the screen. Roger felt the easygoing touch of summer, and regretted not having spent it in London more often.

'Hey,' he said. His voice was loud on the terrace and he realised it might have been the first thing that he had said all day.

'Hi,' said the familiar voice. It was high and slightly pinched, as if Nick was always thinking about something else. 'What are you up to?'

Roger looked at the golden cloak of light lying over the crest of Primrose Hill.

'I'm chilling,' he said. 'How are you?'

'Good, thanks,' said Nick. It had been ten days since the cricket match and they caught up. Roger wanted to be invited back to Toadsmoor House with Irina but didn't say so, as he knew it wasn't Nick's invitation to make.

'Come and join me and Dominic this evening,' said Nick. 'There's something we'd like to chat to you about.'

Roger put his feet down and reached for a piece of paper folded between the pages of his book. Their unfinished conversation after dinner had stayed with him, and he thought he had sensed an incompleteness when they parted the next morning.

'Sure,' he said. 'Where?' He wrote down an address which was twenty minutes away in Mayfair, and said he would be there in an hour.

Nick rang off and put his phone down on the café table. He was in the garden of an Iranian restaurant, where sweet smoke and Persian rose among the ornamental trees. He had eaten on the boat and ordered only sweets, coffee and a pipe. The hookah now snaked in his hand, apple tobacco burning richly in its foil-covered cup. The girl he had met at Dominic's club had called earlier and not left a message when he didn't pick up. He didn't regret it: he had to concentrate on the deal now and that meant claiming a bit of free living for himself. He had called Dominic on the Tuesday after getting back to London and said that another consortium was getting interested in the concession. But Dominic was indifferent to the pressure, and Nick had little choice but to resume his unwilling obedience.

'Don't ask him to come,' Dominic had said when he finally called back, naming this evening as the time for the next meeting. '*Tell* him. And tell him there isn't much time. Get it while it's hot: that's how it works.' Nick felt the man's hateful inhumanity and willingness to sacrifice people; the jarring hustle which would have got the door slammed in his face in any civilized country. Still, that's what made Dominic who he was and was how he earned his ten percent. It's what meant it would work this time.

Nick slid the documents back into their sleeve and stood, thanking the waiter in Persian when he brought the bill. Eyes were drawn to him from the pavement tables as he walked south along Edgware Road. The brusque sound of the Arabic only made him think of *his* East; of deserts and mountains far from the shores of the Gulf or the Mediterranean. He would be going there soon to inspect the concession and organise the drilling:

and that meant seeing Samarkand again. He drew a deep breath and tasted wisps of hookah smoke still clinging to his lungs. Samarkand! Yes, he thought, I will see you soon enough my friend.

At the end of Oxford Street, shoppers had settled like tramps on the ledge in front of a department store. He turned off it into a street where rounded gables were marked out against the gloaming sky. The dark brick of Georgian terraces rose in the yellow street light, cupping the sound of his footsteps. He thought how little he wanted to live there; and that he would not let money build a cage for him. He sighed in satisfaction, trying to keep his excitement bound.

Making his final turn, he saw Roger hovering uncertainly by a street light, the blonde head tilted down as he toyed with his phone. Nick exhaled and called to him.

'Nick!' answered Roger. Nick saw the tan and thought how he too would soon be able to make these little hops abroad.

'Is this it?' said Roger, gesturing towards the plain green door of Dominic's club.

'Yes,' said Nick proprietarily. 'It's just a little place we use.' But the exaggeration grated and he realised he should try harder to avoid these little lies.

'Good evening, sir,' said the doorman, and Nick calmly absorbed the recognition. Not bad after one visit, he thought; unless Dominic had somehow planted it there as part of his endless stage management.

'Good evening, Mr Paget,' said a smiling lady behind a low antique table. Nick suppressed a smile and nodded in acknowledgement. 'If you'll just sign in,' she said. 'Mr Bannerman is upstairs for you.'

Roger wrote his name carefully on the cream pages of the visitors book. The place smelled timeless; traces of perfume, sauces and woodsmoke met on the still air. Had it been here a year or a hundred years? And why had he never been? Roger stopped himself: why should he have been? He didn't recognise anyone else or even expect to. The other members were all swathed in the anonymity of power. Their tans were more even and their hair more perfect than anything he had seen: even their spectacles were as tooled as shotguns. A couple waiting for their coats were channelling their impatience into a perfect civility. The most beautiful dog he had ever seen crossed the hall and looked at him. It was like a whippet draped in long nightclothes with dark highlights on its eyes and ears. Roger touched Nick's arm and pointed to it.

Nick beckoned to the Saluki and she walked towards him. Her nose trembled as she traced Timur's scent on his trousers then she looked up at him, the brown eyes searching for meaning. Nick muttered something in a foreign language. He ran the back of his finger along a silken cheek and the feathered tail swayed as if caught by a breeze.

'That's a Persian Greyhound,' he said. 'They have been bred for ten thousand years.'

'Wow,' breathed Roger. He reached out but the dog jinxed sideways and trotted around a corner.

'If you would like to follow me,' said Cesare.

'Of course,' said Nick.

A wide staircase rose to the first floor and they were lead into the spaces that Nick had glimpsed on his previous visit. Roger stopped for a moment so he could look down into an ivy-clad courtyard where girls bared their delicate shoulders around small tables. He wondered if he could become a member and bring Irina here, then realised the others were waiting and hurried to catch up. Each chamber they passed through was a different colour; scarlet, dark yellow, deep green; and the single group of people in each fell silent as they passed. In the final one, they found Dominic.

'My friends,' he said, laying down the newspaper and pushing himself to his feet. They shook hands and Roger settled into another dense armchair. The room was like being inside one the jewel boxes Lily's mother had kept on her side table; studded and perfect. The man who had brought them up took the drinks orders, and Dominic looked at Roger with a smile.

'How's your injury?' he said, and cast a needling glance at Nick.

'Oh fine,' said Roger. 'That's cricket!'

'Yes,' said Dominic, smiling. 'I suppose it is.'

'You did well!' said Roger.

'Oh, it was polite to give the other captain a wicket,' said Dominic. Nick laughed pointedly. He could see Dominic's tactics more clearly this time, and was not going to be overwhelmed by them again.

'Who was the other captain?' said Roger.

'Oh, some neighbour of theirs,' said Dominic. Alexander Rosenheim had been in the Club earlier and had greeted with unexpected warmth.

'I liked the family,' said Nick, and Dominic looked at him with amusement.

'Yes,' he said. 'Giles is alright.'

That's faint praise for your sister, thought Nick, then remembered that he and Charlotte shared the same ambivalence. Siblings are neither good nor bad, he thought; just annoying for being themselves.

'That bike polo was fun!' said Roger. He had never seen so many people willfully injure themselves, and was glad that he had stayed back.

'Wasn't it!' said Nick with a grin.

'Giles's father started it,' said Dominic. 'Now Hugh is obsessed.' Dominic thought of his bluff nephew, sturdily carrying out his duties at some desk in the City. He couldn't even remember what the boy did. The service sector had been overrun by a generic army of Hughs, armed with enough manners to impress their clients and few enough brains to realise how little time they had left. London was already little more than an airport for money. As soon as the Chinese and Indians trusted each other enough not to use the place, it wouldn't even be that. Dominic looked around the impeccable room and thought: at least they will still come here for *this*. Comforted by the thought, he took a sip of whisky and leant forwards with the cigar box.

Nick took one but Roger declined. He had woken at five in the morning after the last one with his heart racing, and his throat had hurt for days. The familiar smell filled the room and Roger wondered if they had forgotten that they had wanted to talk about something. Or changed their minds?

'So,' said Dominic. 'Our little gold deal.'

'Ah yes,' said Roger obliquely. 'Where was it again? Afghanis...'

'Uzbekistan,' said Nick.

'Ah, yes,' said Roger. 'How's that going?'

'Oh, very well,' said Nick.

'You could be in luck,' said Dominic. 'Someone's dropped out.'

'Really,' said Roger distantly. 'Why?'

'The guy took a bath on some tin concession,' said Dominic. 'Doesn't want to do any more mining. I don't blame him!'

'Right!' said Roger with a laugh. 'How much do you need?'

'We don't *need* anything,' said Nick sharply. 'There's a lot of money chasing this deal. We just thought you might be interested before we show it to the rest of them.'

Nick leant back, ignoring Dominic; and Dominic looked at him through narrowed eyes. Fundraising alongside you, he thought, is like shooting next to someone you suspect isn't gun-trained. Seeing Charlotte reflected in Nick's high cheekbones, his annoyance was compounded by the fact he hadn't yet heard back from her. The memory of that kiss was gripping him harder as the weeks went by. I'll try one more time, he thought defiantly.

Roger took a sip of jasmine tea and studied a painting, swinging his foot a little.

'Could be interesting, I suppose,' he said. 'How does it work?'

Nick leant forwards but Dominic spoke first.

'Well, we need to finalise purchase of the concessions,' he said. 'And because of this fuck-up we only have a month left to do it. But Nick already has the seismology reports, which means all we then have to do is drill some core samples, analyse them, and then...' Dominic's hands parted like magician releasing a bird.

'Core samples?' said Roger.

'Get some rock out of the ground,' said Nick, sitting forwards with his elbows on his knees. 'And see how much gold is in it.'

'Why hasn't someone else done it?' said Roger.

'Because they don't know where to look,' said Nick impatiently, and Dominic's smooth voice cut in.

'You're quite right, Roger,' he said. 'People should have done it long ago. But they haven't.'

'And how do you *know* they haven't?' said Roger nimbly. Nick's abruptness had made him notice the centre of gravity shifting towards him, and it was a good feeling. Dominic indicated to Nick, who picked up a brown envelope from beside his chair. He stood and slid some some photographic prints out onto the green baize of a card table. Roger joined him and saw black and white images which looked like the craggy surface of the moon. In one corner of the monochrome landscape, a circle had been drawn in translucent yellow marker pen.

'See anything?' said Nick expectantly.

Roger shook his head, wondering what he was supposed to be seeing. The next print looked the same but had a large yellow rectangle drawn on it with red circles scattered diagonally across. In the centre of the diagonal was a grouping of disused buildings, and he could just see a black square like a missing tooth at their centre.

'This is the concession,' said Nick, running a finger around the yellow rectangle. He pointed to the buildings, then up and down the constellation of red circles. 'And this is where the original mine runs underground.'

Roger imagined dark passages held up by wooden staves, the image of the mine fusing with the passage of rooms through which they had just passed.

'That is where they have been sinking new core samples to look for side seams,' said Nick, tapping his finger on a few of the red circles. Roger looked more closely and saw the land was scarred within each circle.

'Now,' said Nick. He produced one of the pens and began cross-hatching a yellow rectangle close the edge of the concession. 'This is the area that you can see on the first photo, which is the area we're interested in.' He pulled the two prints alongside each other. 'See?' he said, looking up with finality. 'No marks. No core sampling. No-one's looked there. And I think that the new seam lies across like *this*.' He extended the shaded patch in a line across the corner of the concession, then stood up straight. 'It doesn't cross the one other, you see? They didn't know it was there, so whatever is down there is undisturbed.'

The two men looked at each other, and Roger thought for a second.

'And what makes you think it's worth looking there?'

he said. Nick reached for the file and produced a graph readout like a hospital chart.

'This are the results of the seismic refraction survey I did,' he said. 'It is consistent with a different rock seam running across the concession at that point, and the seam is consistent with gold ore.'

'I see,' said Roger. He studied the pictures with their multicoloured overlay and the jagged graph. It seemed to be what he had been praying for. The door opened and the three men looked up.

'We're fine, thank you,' said Dominic.

Cesare heard his tone, saw the photos, and looked at the floor as he withdrew. Roger took the pen from Nick and tapped the new yellow section.

'How much do you think is down there?' he said.

'Well,' said Nick, pointing to the red circles. 'This mine contained an average of five and a half grammes per tonne of ore. It's roughly the same geology. I think it will be about the same.'

'That doesn't sound like much,' said Roger, and Dominic's voice sounded behind them.

'Believe me,' it said contentedly. 'It's plenty.'

'It's strange they didn't find it...' said Roger, then wondered if it wasn't just the voice of Negativity getting a toehold.

'It's not really strange,' said Nick, tapping the red dots again. 'Given that they weren't looking in the right place.' Roger acknowledged this with a sound.

'Couldn't they have tunneled across to get it?' he said suddenly.

'Nope,' said Nick, the wonderful logic clicking into

place as if for the first time. 'The new seam is much shallower, so there would be an open cast mine there if anyone knew.' He took the images from the card table and slid them back into the brown envelope. They retook their seats and Roger let out a thoughtful breath.

'So how much is there left to invest?' he said.

Dominic gave him the figure, which was enough for a decent flat in London. He saw Roger flinch and thought: so you can do it, but only just. There was silence, and Dominic looked at his empty glass.

'Why is that man never here when you need him?' he said, pressing a small button by the fireplace.

*

Roger jogged up The Broad Walk in Regents Park. The deal was perfect! Only six weeks ago he has asked the universe for something new, and here it was. Best of all, it was quick: the core sampling took two weeks and the analysis another two weeks. Then they would be sitting on a goldmine, literally. Five grammes a tonne, and he could own half!

He jogged on the spot at the crossing over Chester Road and checked his heart monitor. Right on target! His personal trainer had used to make him shadow box and try to pull down trees with pieces of elastic rope. But Roger had let him go and now preferred to run on the path, where he could see people and they could see him. The traffic cleared and he carried on. And besides, what else was there? The year before an advertising agency had got in touch with his record company, and it

173

seemed that the Ice Machine back catalogue would start making money again. But the agency had changed its mind and the idea of offering the music to others had made him nervous. Then earlier in the year Fabrice had wanted him to invest in a new club in Juan-Les-Pins. But even that would take two years to start paying back, if there was anything left after the crooks had taken their cut. And he hadn't even gone out there this summer. People had spent the last ten years trying to get him to invest in things; complicated things put together by people he didn't trust. But Nick and Dominic, they were friends. They were friends and they played hardball. Didn't he know? His chest still ached.

But what if Nick was mistaken, or some of the local people swindled them? Nothing was guaranteed, and that meant he should think of the downside. Yet it was hard to imagine Nick and Dominic dropping the ball. Nick had seen the stuff almost with his own eyes and Dominic would hardly let himself be hoodwinked. It was strange for Roger to have spent years in VIP sections and First Class cabins, and yet never to have met someone like him; one of the people who actually ran things. Or maybe it wasn't strange at all? If Dominic was in St Tropez, he probably wouldn't even come ashore. And Nick... Well, Nick was a philosopher. A philosopher and a spy! Roger could hardly picture him on the Côte d'Azur at all. What would he have to talk about there? And would the people even listen?

Roger paused, feeling for a moment that he had wasted his whole life. But at least he was here now, where the action was! More likely would be that he didn't invest and then the gold *was* there. That would be unthinkable: unthinkable and typical. He had already had more than his share of bad luck with money. And it wouldn't only be this deal he would lose, but all the future opportunities which they then wouldn't offer him. He would be losing both money and the chance to make money! Not to mention their respect: after all, half of London would bite their arm off yet still they had come to him.

And when it came off, he could make everything go away. The court case in New York, Lily's mother in Los Angeles, the lawyers everywhere. Snap! The rich pay late: that was the rule. They paid their lawyers and no-one else. However big a boat they offered him, he would turn it down. He would buy a country place here in England. Best of all, he could marry Irina. She was definitely the one for him; with her purring smile, and her *Moy Rogers*, and her kind word for everyone. He trusted her and she would get over her mistrust of Nick and Dominic once the money came in. Yet she didn't seem to spend very much and actually tried to pay for things herself sometimes. He broke his step and almost stopped. What if she knew the money was running out? The lawyers knew, the accountants knew, even the yacht charter company knew. No, it was impossible. But if it did run out, then she would know! Know and be gone.

He stopped and his chest felt heavy in the still air. He couldn't start again with someone else; and he was too old to go back to having lots of girls. This was his last chance to settle down and have another child. Irina could chose the name; Anastasia or Sacha or Ilya. Ilya Curtis! A crazy thought: maybe he should ask her advice about the deal? But who asked their girlfriend about money? And then she would know for sure that there was a problem. No, it would be much better to surprise her. Or not even to mention it at all and just let the money carry on flowing? One little reference, perhaps, to being in business with the others; their little concern was doing rather well.

Roger started running again. The light was green at the next crossing and he continued over the road without breaking step, then threaded his way past people on the narrow bridge over the canal. The giant aviary of London Zoo rose on one side and a floating Chinese restaurant was moored on the other, its red eaves hanging precariously over the water. His paces became heavier as he hit the incline of Primrose Hill and the sound of his breath was louder in his ears. The slope got steeper at the top like some clever torture, and for the first time he thought he wouldn't make it.

He reached the summit and bent down, taking long breaths, then stood and looked out over London. First the West End, then the City, then Canary Wharf rising like the Nordic heaven he had once seen on the back of an opera set. He pitied those people their lives of computer screens and conference calls, as they chased money around these giant invisible companies. Money wasn't made by reports and meetings; it was made by a quiet word between friends, a drink shared, a man's word! Nothing had changed since the old days; real money never left the top, where he had finally arrived.

Roger threw a towel around his shoulders and sat heavily at his desk. He reached for the phone then paused. Irina was somewhere in the house, and he had an image of her snatching the phone and putting it down. He felt for his mobile and took the sheaf of papers outside instead. A small pagoda rose by his water garden, where the round mouths of carp broke the surface of the pond. He settled on the stiff cushions and his pulse quickened at the sound of the long international ring tones.

'Good afternoon,' said a voice, its accent barely belonging to a continent let alone to a country. Not like England, he thought. He gave a series of codes and was put through to the man he had recently been avoiding.

'Mr Curtis,' he heard. Roger thought he could detect a current of unwelcome beneath the smooth surface of his bank manager's voice. He pictured the man's tanned, bald head and his corner office with its view of the Mediterranean. He would change banks when the deal came through, and change countries too. Somewhere more tasteful than Monaco. Geneva perhaps? Or Jersey, where Cantemir Resources was also based? He pictured the company's office in a little white building by the sea, then remembered it was only based there on paper.

'Maurice,' he said. 'I would like you to arrange a transfer.' He gave the recipient bank details and the amount, and there was silence. He heard keys being tapped and a small voice began to sound in his head, like a distant radio station coming through static. He wasn't even sure what it was saying.

'Mr Curtis,' said Maurice. 'May I ask what this is for?' Here they come, thought Roger; the patronising questions and attempts to head him off. He almost said no outright.

'I'm making an investment,' he said. There was another pause and Maurice seemed to be searching for words.

'May I ask what type of investment?' said the banker finally.

'Maurice,' said Roger tolerantly. 'That is confidential.'

'*Mais oui...*' he heard and his impatience started to tick louder. Maurice's tone was different when he spoke again, as if he was trying a new approach to an old problem.

'Mr Curtis,' he said. 'You know how much we appreciate having you as a client of Banque Vallauris...' So that's it, thought Roger with a warm rush: he thinks I'm leaving the bank!

'Maurice,' he said. 'I'm not going anywhere. I just need to invest this money. When the investment...' What was the word? '...yields, I will put it back on deposit with you. And more.' So typical of a banker! What was it they said about banking? You risk a hundred pounds to make one pound. How could Maurice be expected to understand a real investment?

'*Je m'en doute,*' said Maurice, as if he was speaking to himself. 'Mr Curtis, the problem is if I make this transfer...' The voice became suddenly firm. 'Your balance will fall below the level necessary to hold an account at Banque Vallauris.' There was a pause. 'You understand, it will be difficult for me to keep your account open.'

Roger felt a jolt. He had never heard of a bank having a minimum level before. Or was it just a ploy to stop him taking his money out? When a Frenchman said something was difficult it was usually well within their power. Anyway, it would be Maurice's loss if he kicked Roger out. His loss and the gain of some other banker. The Isle of Man was good for tax; maybe he would go there?

'Maurice,' he said. 'I can guarantee you the account will be well within your necessary level again very soon.' And well beyond it, he thought, picturing Maurice's annoyance when he read about the gold strike. Even at the minimum level, the yield on his money was to be several hundred percent in the first year. But there was something else in his mind; a small black door which he didn't want to open. Irina was standing near it. Why would she be telling him not to do this? After all, he needed to make the investment for her sake as much as anything. There was silence and he decided he would not speak again before Maurice.

'Very well,' he heard finally. The voice was cold and tight. 'I make the transfer. But if the account has not recovered in six months, *puis...*'

'Thank you,' said Roger coolly, thinking that he would probably never speak to the man again.

'*Au revoir*, Mr Curtis,' said Maurice, and the line went dead.

13

Sir David McAllister paced his top floor office. The protesters outside United Minerals put him in a black mood. Did they think that he – *he*, David McAllister, who had built one of the greatest mining companies in the word – didn't know that the planet was running out of resources? That he, with access to the finest geological information; the best government relationships; the most highly-paid scientists *in the world*, knew worse than them what was taking place under the earth? Wasn't it obvious that the less stuff remained, the further he went to get it? He spent every day trying to think of solutions to the problem, as one would certainly not be emerging from the people camped in front of the building. Their cause only seemed to bloom in the summer, either to win headlines when the newspapers were empty or just because anarchy wasn't much fun in the rain. They sickened him with their dreadlocks and their violence; their posh girls to screw each day instead of going to work. He almost hated them.

He had snapped out a statement to the Head of Public Affairs that morning, and it had been filtered through the departments until what was replaced on his desk read like cold tea.

'Put your name on this bullshit,' David had said. 'I want a press conference.'

The public affairs head had an insipid accent and a purple tie.

'No,' he said. 'It has to come from you.' David's eyes blazed. He knew what was coming next.

'It's not your company anymore,' said the man. 'It belongs to the shareholders.'

'Well,' said David. 'Let's see what the shareholders bloody well think?' He had pulled the screen of his terminal around and thrust a finger at it. 'What do you want? One week prices? Three months? Five year? Believe me, the shareholders want *you* to do what *I* say.' The man had simply pushed the statement back at him for approval.

David walked back to the screen and looked at it again. There was the stock price, healthy as a baby. People with the brainpower of planets backing *his* plan; voting for *him*. A deep breath escaped him. One of those guys, with their hundred-million pound investment decisions, counted a hundred; no, a thousand times more; no, there was no comparison... But still the anger came. His staff had locked the balcony window, presumably to stop him dropping things on the protestors below. His secretary Jill had taken one look at him and cancelled the morning's activity, which meant he had missed two hours of work already. He knew what to do. Anger channeling, the Americans called it. He jabbed out a message to the Chief Operating Officer, the Finance Director, and the International Director. His three horsemen, he called them.

'Right,' it said. 'Each bring me the worst problem you've got and we're sorting them today. TODAY.'

He slumped back in the chair. He knew what his worst problem was: that wanker in the purple tie. He had tried to fire him once before, and what had he been told? David, we can't fire the Head of Public Affairs or people will think there are problems at United. There is a problem at United, he had answered. It's bloody *him*.

David took off his glasses and rubbed his temples, the St Andrew cufflinks glinting on his white cuffs. He needed to do something until the horsemen arrived. He sat up and swept the pile from his in-tray onto the desk then stared at each piece of paper for five seconds before sweeping it onto the floor. At the fourth one, he stopped.

'UM_Confidential', it read. 'Intel Tashkent Concession #AU638026U Kattakurgan East V acquired by Cantemir Resources Ltd Jersey RC 762943.'

His mind changed register. Kattakurgan had been a minor legend when he was in Asia. People said that the Soviets had dropped their core samples in the wrong places and abandoned the mine too early. But surely no-one actually believed it? His blood started to rise again. Who were Cantemir Resources? Didn't his office know how to find this information? He reached for the phone then stopped, the words 'It's not your company any more' ringing in his ears. We'll see whose company it is, he thought, and pulled out his personal phone.

'Kobus?' he said, and a single deep monosyllable reached him from the other end of the line. 'I want you to look at a Jersey company for me. Cante...' He spelled the name instead and waited as the other man took down the details, picturing his sun-wizened face and the deep eyes which had seen too much. Kobus had escorted him into the interiors of some profoundly lawless countries, dispersing militia checkpoints with his black-magical touch. They were not places a chairman should be and the trips had run up huge 'key man' insurance premiums. When the Accounts Committee complained, David cancelled the policy. Kobus armed with a rucksack of dollar bricks and an assault rifle was the best travel insurance in the world.

'They've just bought an old mine in Uzbekistan,' he said, feeling he should include Kobus with more details. 'And I'm curious. Aye...' he signed off. 'In your own time.' This was a standing joke at United Minerals, and only once had someone taken it literally. He put the phone down and paused. Uzbekistan, the Kattakurgan concession; and he had suddenly thought of Baku, a thousand miles to the west. Why?

The soundproofed door of his office swung open and two of the horsemen quietly entered. A third popped up on the screen from Buenos Aires, finishing the top button of his shirt. Two of them had started as mine managers and could still fix their own vehicles as well as fight their way out of a bar. David felt a thrill of pride and smiled at them broadly.

'Now,' he said. 'Who wants to go first?'

By lunch, his mood had improved considerably. Their main trade finance bank in South Africa had very publicly lost the company's custom forever. Two senior executives had lost their jobs at United Minerals and another been promoted beyond his dreams. A South American mines minister would soon find envelopes of cash turn without warning into envelopes of photographs, addressed not to him but to his wife. As his wife was also the President's cousin, David expected the onward succession of events to happen quickly: the man would be removed and United's mineral concessions would be safe. It was the minister's fault for playing silly buggers, and not only with David but with his own wife. He looked at the photo on his desk, which had been taken in Lourdes the previous year of his wife and four children. He chuckled: nothing could protect him from Aileen if he followed that man's example! David never used people's goodness against them but this was different. The shareholders of United Minerals could come before the minister's job and marriage.

Lunch soon reversed the improvement. It took place in the company's private dining room with young Alexander Rosenheim, who had become the representative of United's largest shareholder when his father Franz had died. David still thought of the old man every day; his thirst to escape the boardroom to remote corners of the world, his love of drinking under canvas, and his anecdotes about prospectors in California in the 1850s or Azerbaijan in the 1920s. The stories always ended in quixotic failure and gales of laughter from the old German. Yes, the money that Rosenheim Group had put into United had changed everything. It had put David on the front foot with the banks and let the company stay private for another three years. They had flown around the world together buying up mines, with Franz always picking the right ones. Then, just as the Chinese became insatiable and every commodity graph was pointed upward, they floated the company. 'United turns to gold dust', read the headlines. The banks had slashed their fees to get the mandate and then funds bid up the stock another twelve percent in the first week. What a month! He had come home each night to find Aileen ever sterner and more unimpressed. You mind yourself, David McAllister! You'll not take it with you! When the Honours Committee called to tell him he was to be knighted, he had taken the news home with more apprehension than excitement. But he saw the pride cross his wife's face before the act started again. They still called each other Sir David and Lady McAllister sometimes.

He and Franz had both known the rise couldn't go on forever; and David had also known there were voices in the other man's ear telling him to sell. The oldest adage in business: there's never a bad day to take a profit. And boy could Franz have taken one on his one fifth of United Minerals! But he didn't. He stuck to it like a soldier at his post, even when the graphs started to dip and his shares with them. Franz had been one of the few who loved business more than money. He had to own mines, and of all the mining interests he could have kept it was his shares in United Minerals. And that twenty percent block voted with the board every time. David's chest tightened as he thought of it. With the Rosenheim dragon asleep on its pile of shares, it *was* still his company!

And then suddenly, painlessly, stubbornly, Franz was gone. The illness had only lasted six months. Close to the end, David had put the three horsemen in charge and flown out to see him in Mexico. Still, the light in his eyes; the talk of the next mine. It was strange for David to wipe away tears on the way back to the airstrip.

Now he had Alexander instead. The boy made sure his family still voted with David, and United in turn held ten percent of Rosenheim Group. The cross-holdings held the titans together like two great cantilevers, protecting them both from takeover. He and Alexander could never drift too far apart, yet still there was something alien about the boy. He had something of Franz's lightness and enthusiasm but his eyes glazed at technicalities. Worse, he was developing a muddled way of looking at the world which seemed to mix business and charity.

As the main courses were brought in, Alexander again suggested that David hire drug addicts from the Rosenheim Foundation's recovery centres. But where could they work? said David. You can't have drug addicts working down mines! What about the ship? he said, using Franz's old phrase. How can you have those people up in the rigging? Alexander seemed not to have thought of this and the mention of his father made him change tack. He started talking about Romania, where his family had bought up tens of thousands of hectares of forested mountain range. Aye, thought David; and the largest gold deposits in Europe too. But the land they had bought seemed to be just that, and whatever might be underneath was out of bounds. I'm a miner, said David with a smile; I can't walk about with my head above ground! Lastly, fatally, Alexander started talking about the protests.

'They're right, you know,' said Alexander, cracking the top of his crème brûlée. 'United does need better governance.'

'And what does that mean?' said David, distancing his wine glass and switching to water. 'Not letting my men get hurt? Why wouldn't I do that already?'

'Ha!' said Alexander. 'Not quite.' Some investment consultants had been to see him recently, and made dark references to the methods which United was rumoured to use.

'You stop accidents by hiring good people,' said David simply. 'Not by making more rules.'

Alexander tilted his head, wondering if David was being disingenuous. The investment consultants were one thing: another was the infinitely delicate approach which the family had received to sell its shares.

'It is really about greater oversight at board level,' he said, deliberately testing the chairman with his bland words.

Sir David thought of his South American plan and forced a smile.

'Come now, Xander,' he said. 'You wouldn't want me fighting with my hands tied behind my back, would you?'

Alexander laughed gamely.

'It's just that shareholders want more transparency in a company these days,' he said, excluding himself from the statement with a gesture.

David concealed a sigh, and again tried to explain the intensity of spying ranged against United Minerals. The slightest leak on their production costs would be unthinkable ammunition in the hands of their rivals. As he said the word, he pictured the faces of their chairmen; the South African, the Texan, the Russian. He could never show them Alexander, with his smooth face and exaggerated politeness to the waiter. The boy had grown up in a world of universities and charity boards and celebrity, being courted almost from birth. He was both the only son his father could have had and yet also not his son. Franz had known it and asked David to take care of the boy after he died. Aye, thought David as he looked across the table, I'll take care of you. And I'll do it by protecting United from your stupid ideas. He pushed away his untouched pudding and looked at his watch.

'Is that the time?' he said. 'I'm so sorry Xander, I'll have to skip coffee.' They stood and shook hands at the end of the long table. And don't you fucking dare talk to those protestors on the way out, thought David.

Back in his office, the gloom deepened. Some government committee wanted to see him about business practices. The minister who had signed the letter virtually owed his job to David, who alone had not opposed the man's stupid pieces of legislation because he thought they were allies. Now because it was a quiet news day and some bottom-ranking news programme had picked up on the protests, the man was pulling him in. And not for a quiet drink but for some kangaroo committee. David could already imagine the minister's quiet, fake apology and his plea that he had to do it for appearance's sake. He had been right there in St James Square for the United Minerals summer party only a month ago. But what could David do? If he didn't invite the man to the next one, it would count as a rift; worse, it would look like an admission of guilt. So the politicians had it both ways while he, who generated the taxes and funded the party, was humiliated at will!

He sat low in his chair, thinking about the time before these tidal waves of hypocrisy had engulfed the world. When his phone rang, Kobus's flat voice brought him back to himself. At least there were some places in the world where you could still take your chances! An American rival had lost their Uzbek concessions purely on the whim of the government. That's what transparency buys you, he thought; and found himself envying this oddly-named minnow of a company which had bought up the Kattakurgan mine. At least some people could still make the running without bureaucrats and activists hanging from their arms. But there was no point in dragging Kobus down.

'So Kobus,' he said brightly. 'Who's behind this new rival of mine then?'

David laughed with joy when he heard the names. Nick Paget, never one to let something die! David shook his head as he remembered, even fifteen years before, the man's interest in the Kattakurgan mine. He had seen Nick at the Club a few months before and thought he recognised the other man; Daniel Bannerman, that posh lawyer from across the square. His intuition had tried to make the connection with Nick when the mine had first landed in his in-tray: he was getting slow. So Nick and Bannerman were having another go at Kattakurgan! With whose money? Some private investor called Roger Curtis. The sheer incredulity of it cheered him up. He looked out of the window, stroking the acne scars on either side of his chin. Nick was easily lead astray yet there must be real basis for him to be doing this; some tip off or ground survey. But even if there was any truth to the old wives' tale, would the mine actually be worth having?

He turned to his screen and pulled up the three year gold price. Then he found the grid references of the concession and entered them into the company's geological database. Four grammes a tonne local average, which gave him plenty of leeway on extractions costs. If there was enough of it, even at two grammes he could just wait till the next price spike. They were never far off with the world in such a mess, as the smart money always came home to gold! His mind flicked onwards. He didn't know enough and he wasn't going to chase fairy tales, but finding out was worth a little extra investment. He picked up the phone and called back.
'Kobus,' he said. 'I'd like you to keep a little eye on this one for me.'

14

Dominic showed the tickets and they were guided into a shorter side queue. The venue was a converted theatre in Kentish Town and the tickets for a famous band, already decades into its history. People of all ages crowded the pavement and he hoped he wouldn't run into anyone he knew. He didn't tell many people that he came to rock concerts, yet he loved feeling the bursts of sound ripple across a fervent crowd. The chopping guitars and the rounded punches of the bass opened the pores of humanity, with the whole crawling anarchy roped in by silent security staff. How could he be anywhere else?

And the gig had proved to be a perfect choice. His previous messages had been well spaced and casual yet still they had not raised a response. It was easy to imagine her having subsided back into her daily life, and that her sortie with him had been a one-off. Or, it if it wasn't, that she always did it with someone different. The thought annoyed him and he vengefully saw more of Imogen, yet doing so had only thrown their relationship into uncomfortable relief. Thinking of what it lacked only brought his mind back to Charlotte and the unplumbed depths which their evening seemed to conceal. Convincing himself there was something in it beyond his own stubbornness, and aware he had only one more message to expend, he had scanned the schedules for the right event. String quartets, theatres and film premieres were all too obvious and self-conscious; too confirming the same existence. He needed something that would scratch her and draw blood from the pale surface of her life. When he saw the gig advertised, his intuition clicked. He sent her a message saying he had tickets. Her reply arrived the same day, as lightly-worded as if they had never been out of touch.

In the car on the way up through Camden, all her talk had been of the band; and he took pleasure from her flushed face and stories of younger days. Even her body seemed to have shed the memory of children. She was slimmer in jeans and a simple top, with no handbag and heavy cowboy boots. An old gig-going outfit from the past, he guessed. Her head and hands moved pointedly as she spoke, but her look slid out of the window more often than towards him. He wondered if she was nervous or just unselfconscious: perhaps she would be the same with anyone? Either way, her excitement about the music was useful as it smoothed the time and gave him little to say; like at dinner, he remembered. Choosing the band was another of those little coincidences which attended his life, like the song which had come on in Uncle Eric's night club. He thought of them seeded together at the moment of the Big Bang: yes, a random universe also has its gifts. He had put on a dark shirt so his jacket didn't stand out and was also wearing jeans and cowhide boots. As they reached the front of the queue, he realised they looked like they had dressed together and wondered if she had noticed.

Charlotte entered the neon lit foyer and struck out towards a pair of large doors which lead into the auditorium. The place smelled of use and she wanted to be in the bestial mass of a crowd again, shouting to be heard. Fingertips appeared on her elbow and she realised Dominic was guiding her away and towards a stairwell. They mounted it together and passed old event posters streaked onto the yellow walls. Strips of grey silicone glinted on each wide step and the leather soles of her boots dug into them hungrily. She couldn't remember the last time she had been in a truly public building. Everywhere she went these days was designed for small numbers of people but here every corner was a stress point; every crowd a risk. Yet somehow Dominic didn't look out of place, even as the linen jacket gripped his back on the way up the stairs. She was surprised that he had invited her to something like this, and reminded herself that she had said yes not because of him but because of what it was.

They reached the top and crossed a landing to another door. Dominic showed the tickets again and green paper bands were clipped together around their wrists, and the door opened to show a deep balcony overlooking the crowd. A half-knowing smile played on Dominic's lips as he ushered her into a different sort of space, where each person's gravity was intact rather than dissipated into a crowd. They held their drinks straight and spoke assertively, the women leaning back like models. Charlotte was disappointed. As they moved towards a sponsored bar, she peered over the railing and thought: I'm going down there later.

Dominic lifted a glass of champagne from the clean surface of the bar and she thought of the young people downstairs, probably queuing for expensive drinks. Whoever has shall be given more; who said that? Dominic raised his glass and the grey eyes rested in hers for a second.

'Cheers,' he said.

'Yes,' she said, thrown by his direct look. Charlotte was finding these moments of energy hard to absorb. Leaving a car or entering a doorway, she would feel his guiding touch on her body. She looked away to take in the venue better and it made her think of Nick. Hadn't he liked this band before he became such a snob about music? And what if Daniel were here too? She pictured his polite attention while his mind strayed onto the next day at work. He would subconsciously find his way to someone on the balcony worth meeting and have a structured conversation before producing the inevitable business card. His business cards appeared wherever they went, like little white bullets. She hadn't lied to him, of course, but simply said she was going to a concert and would be back later. He didn't go out on week nights so it hardly mattered where she was going. Her going to a concert was the same as him going to play squash or visit his mother: wherever they went, they always came back.

Torn between guilt and annoyance, she followed

Dominic to the balcony rail. Two columns of speakers were suspended above a crowd stained blue and purple by the wandering stage lights. A cheer erupted as the band filed onto the stage and other VIPs crowded in behind them. The band leader's dreadlocks were held back by a white bandana and his amplified voice swept across the space: 'Hello London!' Her pulse jumped. It was him! The very flesh and blood whose voice had been on all those recordings, and who had created the songs from nothing. She felt Dominic next to her and looked at him.

'This is amazing!' she said.

'Isn't it?' said Dominic. Her eyes were glowing and he nearly put an arm around her waist. Why do it? he thought. Why marry a girl and leave her bored? London was full of these diligent, lifeless men driving their wives into the arms of others. A huge instrumental build up was taking place on the stage below them, spreading a smile across his face. He raised the champagne and took a still-cold sip. Charlotte was moving next to him and he hoped she noticed how well he had secured their space at the front.

At the fourth song, she turned to him.

'I have to go down there,' she said, and his eyes widened. But it was her evening: that was the whole point.

'Of course,' he said. He took a last look over the rail before moving back and letting the gap close. The black door swung open again and they emerged into the different smell of the public area, where groups of youngsters moved purposefully holding plastic glasses.

Charlotte skipped down the yellow staircase between two lines of people and Dominic followed with difficulty. Some girls tumbled past him and a laugh went up. He moved his wallet and phone to his inner pockets, the current of unease growing stronger. The foyer separated the pulsating gig from the summer night like an airlock punctuated by the yellow vests of the bouncers. Dominic pushed the big double doors and sound waves hit them from the speaker stacks. There were people dancing in the narrow margin before the crowd started and it was hard to see further. We are too close, he thought.

Charlotte breathed in hungrily, her student memory taking over. She started along a side wall and Dominic followed, keeping his eyes on her expensive hair and narrow shoulders as they plunged into ever smaller gaps. His arm was suddenly wet and a sharp word cut through the noise, then he felt a deliberate contact and his body tightened.

Charlotte had become a terrier. Her eyes burrowed ahead, picking the spaces to widen and slip through. Her mind's eye was on the stage, upper right of her senses, and the music was getting louder. She wanted to be front and centre with sight and sound converging. She hit a dead end behind two large forms and a strange hand explored her waist but she snaked away. The voices she left in her wake were getting angrier. She had to keep moving to let each gap close or she would be wedged between the people she had pushed aside. Finally the singer was above her with his band spread out like wings on either side. The song came to a crashing finish and screaming erupted in the blackness. Long hair flew and her face was sprayed with sweat, and an elbow struck her head. She reached up to cover her temples and staggered but there was no place to fall. The gigantic weight of the crowd was around her, almost lifting her as it flowed in different directions. She tried to breathe but her chest was too weak to push against the damp mass of bodies and the air was dense as if the oxygen had already been sucked from it. Her breath was quickening and the people blurred around her. She pushed outwards and felt other hands pushing back. 'Who the fuck is this?' she heard. 'She wasn't here before.' Someone pushed her from behind then she felt a pain in her breast as someone else pushed her back. The lights came up, blinding her like white suns as they were pointed into the crowd. A tidal wave of noise broke over her, sucking her downwards as the floor started to move. She felt a scream but heard nothing then the crowd lurched again and she started slipping down into the stampede.

A hand reached her, then an arm. Its soft material encircled her back and found a way under her arm. She was lifted and felt the weight on her feet again.

'Look who it is,' shouted a voice. 'Hello cunt,' said another.

Dominic turned Charlotte away from the stage and pulled her towards him, forcing his free arm between people as he tried to make a path for them.

'Who the fuck are you?' said a voice and plastic crumpled into his side. 'That should have been glass,' it hissed. He drew Charlotte closer and felt her hair against his cheek as she gripped him. His eyes bored into each face until the crowd finally began to part and the pressure around them eased.

They reached the side wall and Charlotte turned herself into his front, breathing in damp cotton and a trace of aftershave as his arm encircled her shoulders. His other hand lifted the hair above her ear and stroked her temple, then cupped the back of her head. He closed his eyes and breathed the scent of her hair then lifted her chin. Her eyes were wide and broken as they searched his. The music hit a new crescendo and he turned towards the foyer with one arm still around her.

There was sudden quiet as the doors swung closed behind them. The neon light fell brightly on Charlotte, and Dominic didn't know where to look. She wiped quickly under each eye.

'Sorry about that,' she said, and he gave a light laugh.

'It's alright,' he said. 'Nothing wrong with being gutsy.'

'Stupid, you mean,' she said. She should go to the ladies but their acrid smell reached out into the foyer and the same people might be in there. Her breath was still light and she realised her shoulders were shaking. Dominic saw the uncertainty and thought of going back to the balcony. But it would be unfair to re-enter the auditorium anywhere, and he touched his phone to get the car outside.

'Shall we go?' he said. Charlotte nodded, trying not to show her gratitude as the shame started to creep up on her. He guided her back through security and onto the wide pavement, where the night hung still and lights from the venue's awning washed over empty crowd barriers. Charlotte felt air on her side and realised her top had been filleted up one of its seams.

'I can't go home like this,' she said to herself.

'No,' said Dominic, trying not to look at her too closely. The fear had gone and kind of ready physicality settled in its place, like someone who had just returned from a hike. So this is you, he thought. He wanted to hold the strewn hair back from her face and be close to her again. Then he had an idea: a perfect one.

'I know where to go,' he said.

'Oh yes?' said Charlotte, pretending to re-arrange her hair.

'Yes... Somewhere cleansing,' he said, immediately regretting how awful it sounded. She raised an eyebrow and he felt an unexpected rush of happiness that her confidence was back. The chirp of a horn reached them and his driver pulled up with a quick pulse on the headlights. The door was opened and Charlotte climbed gratefully into the car's still interior. This is the smell of your life, she thought; grow into it. She pulled a powder compact from her jeans and looked into its round mirror. Her face was lit by the passing headlights, rising from the shadows then sinking back into darkness. It was lightly streaked with dirt and her eyes reminded her of someone in a Western film. She snapped the mirror shut. Dominic's door closed heavily, cutting off the night, and the car pressed silently forwards.

'Music, please,' said Dominic. The sound of a piano trickled around them and a fragile peace settled. Through the ringing in her ears, Charlotte listened as the communal notes built a slow, unbearable tension; then dispersed it into the air.

'Is this Bach?' she said.

Dominic made a distant sound.

'Sort of,' he said. 'It's a transcription. The pianist was dying when he played it.'

As the cadences of the music again began to tighten around her, Charlotte almost reached out for his hand. The car slowed and swung left into a narrow turning, then the houses disappeared on one side and a dark space opened beside the lane. She lowered the window and a thick smell of foliage blew into the car.

'What's out there?' she said.

'Hampstead Heath,' said Dominic.

'Oh well,' she said resignedly. 'Just give me a decent burial.' Dominic looked at her and gave a rippling laugh which she hadn't heard before.

'Spade's in the back!' he said. Then, to the driver: 'Here, please.'

When the car slowed and fell silent, Charlotte opened the door for herself and stepped out with a deep breath. The land was releasing its scent into the cooling air and she drank in the deep silence which flowed off the Heath. The parkland was pale under a clear sky and an expanse of water showed black at the bottom of the slope. A larger hill rose from the other shore, crowned by the distant shapes of trees. Behind it, a dark orange aurora hung over the city.

The other door opened and Dominic was standing beside her. He started walking down the embankment and she followed, their boots crunching lightly on the dirt path. He opened a low wooden gate at the bottom and they passed through into a dark tunnel of trees. The night air painted tiny currents on her shoulders and she wondered if she should be feeling scared. She smelled water and they emerged onto the shore of a small lake, encircled by the dark undersides of trees. The bank dropped away vertically and she made out a corrugated metal sheet holding back the earth. Dominic's eyes found hers in the moonlight.

'Freshen up,' he said.

'I haven't got a costume,' said Charlotte.

'I wouldn't have expected anything so bourgeois,' he said.

Charlotte chuckled, thinking of night swims with her cousins when she was young. They sat down and started to pull off their shoes. Dominic was soon ready and dropped into the water. His torso rose like a statue in the corner of the pond, sending ripples across the reflected sky.

Dominic heard the slip of fabric behind him then the long sound of jeans being pulled off, and looked across the water towards where a heron had awoken.

'You alright getting in?' he said over his shoulder.

'Yes,' said Charlotte quickly. She laid her clothes apart from his, the black underwear invisible on top of the pile. Feeling the air on her skin, she wondered how warm the lake was and knew Dominic wouldn't have flinched. She sat on the high bank and reached down with a toe, parting water which was warmer than the air. She dropped in and quickly crouched to her neck, feeling the silt around her feet.

'Well done!' said Dominic, and they began to swim. A bow wave gathered like a soft choker around Charlotte's throat as the water sheathed her body below. Its still surface was flecked with tail feathers and pieces of blossom, and she was careful not to break it with her hands. The series of notes she had heard in the car rose again in her head, tightening and releasing across the dark water.

Dominic's even breaststroke was carrying him ahead. He wanted to turn over and face the sky but submerged instead, pulling himself downwards with the blackness soft on his eyes. He imagined himself in the deep ocean, passing frilled sharks and pellucid squids. This place will be here when we are gone, he thought. His lungs sent their first signal, a bluff. On the third stoke, they started to burn. His ears rang with the pressure and adrenalin was released. His chest started to buck and he had to fight to keep his mouth closed. Water or carbon dioxide, he thought; you can't make up your mind, can you? A darker darkness appeared at the edge of his vision and he imagined staying there forever. He kicked upwards but the carbon dioxide was heavy inside him then pulled harder but the pressure in his ears remained and he realised how deep he was. Then in a gathering rush it began to release. He broke the surface and sweet air flooded his lungs.

Charlotte swam over to him. All her hair was wet and her large eyes were touched with annoyance.

'Where have you been?' she said.

'Having a look around,' he panted.

'Find anything?' she said.

'Nothing I could mention,' he said.

'Dark secrets?' she said, raising her eyebrows behind the damp veil of hair, and he smiled.

'Here,' he said, swimming towards the diving board.

Charlotte hovered, beating her arms like a jellyfish as she watched Dominic pull himself up the steps. The water glinted as it streamed down his flat back, running across a scar on one shoulder blade. There was something Florentine about his lower body and she was surprised by his good condition. His shape fixed itself in her mind as he mounted the diving board, which bowed deeply then rattled as it fell back into place. His body described a long arc and entered the water in a straight line, the head tucked in low between the arms. A tall bird stood up and flapped its wings on the bank.

'Go on then!' called Dominic from where he had surfaced. She swam to the ladder and put her hands on the cold metal. The water unsheathed her and the air tingled on her skin as it flowed around her limbs. She saw Dominic's wet footstep on the concrete, and the silicate tongue of the diving board hung gleaming over the black water. She stepped onto its end and stood for a moment, pushing back her hair with both hands. Then she skipped forwards and landed stiff-legged at the end, and it released her upwards into the air. She jack-knifed at the zenith and disappeared silently into the water. Dominic started swimming back to the board and she resurfaced close to him.

'That was good,' he said.

'Did it at school,' she said.

'Let's have a competition,' he said, swimming back to

203

the ladder. He climbed it then turned and extended a hand to Charlotte. She took it as she reached the top and turned herself into his arms. They stood together, the water running down the channels where their bodies met. Dominic ran a hand under her hair and down her spine. He moved her gently onto the board and she lay back with her head towards the water, her body glowing pale in the moonlight. He knelt on the concrete and ran the back of his hand down her side, then the front down her front. He saw a noiseless sigh and blew drops of water across her chest; then touched her side with his lips, trying to find her aroma under the water. He kissed her skin and felt it drying under the warmth of his breath. Fingers ran through his hair and he touched her with both hands. Charlotte saw that clouds had come in and made out dim stars between them. She gasped.

AUGUST

15

Nick lay on his bed in the business hotel, enjoying the air-conditioned silence. He had forgotten what it felt like to stay at the expense of a company or government, with room service and a fridge full of drinks. He was grateful for this promontory of the West, where he was neither tourist nor anything else; and where, he thought, the staff had almost begun to respect him.

He had been in Tashkent for three days. From the moment he stepped into the terminal, he knew that he had gone soft. The border guard's eyes had rested on him for several unexplained moments before he was let through and he thought: is it that obvious? The receptionist at the hotel gave him the same lingering look before handing his passport back. Out in the city, it was worse. His skin was too pale and he had not had time to renew his Uzbek. The few phrases he tried stuttered and crashed, attracting not warmth but contempt. In the old days, he had learned to channel his excitement into a kind of humility, which would be reciprocated and draw him together with the people. Now he couldn't dig below the mistrust to find anything at all.

Maybe it had all been a self-deceiving fantasy? He remembered Tolstoy's story *The Cossacks*, the hero of which rides away from his local friends immediately to be forgotten. But he had lived here for years and done everything with these people; he had studied their buildings and their faith, and nearly married one. Now all that seemed impossible; and all he could do was try to build his wall of inscrutability higher than theirs. The markets smelled the same but were crowded with tourists and the stallholders greeted him as one of them. He no longer knew which pieces were good and could not picture haggling with so little of the language. They would probably refuse point blank and he would be humiliated. Only one café was just as he recalled it; but they remembered him politely and without warmth. The figure of the man in Death in Venice haunted him and he realised that he too was unrequited and aping a younger self. Then the cascade of references itself became an embarrassment, as he had never made comparisons when he was here before. Importing this grotesque sentimentality is making me into even more of a stranger, he thought as he drank his tea.

For two days, he had moved around Tashkent meeting sampling companies. They were more professional than he remembered and he thought that the corruption he feared might have receded. When they handed him business cards and he did not have one to hand back, he felt like the weak link. When one of them knew the mine, he seized up and quickly left. He had finally appointed one almost at random, signing them to confidentiality in their tall offices. Even so, he hesitated before giving them the coordinates where he wanted the samples taken. They noted the information silently and he remembered what was said of the Gold Rush: it was the men who sold the buckets and spades who got rich. He looked around the office and thought: you make your money whatever happens. Catching sight of his sunburned face in a mirrored wall, he thought of how many men had sat there before him. He had somehow expected they would travel out to the mine together, but instead he was given a time schedule and the meeting was closed. Air-conditioning whirred in the ceiling and the man opposite was wearing a suit: there was no need to bump along any tracks.

He shifted on the hotel bed and closed his eyes. There was a patch of desert out there, beyond this sealed room and Westernised city. The place had been engraved in his memory for years but now he could not picture it. As he drifted into sleep, his ideas of what to spend the money on were as distant as ever. He found himself missing Timur instead, and hoping that he was happy.

*

Dry heather scuffed Dominic's cords as he pushed on towards the top of the ridge, followed by one of his brother's dogs. He was annoyed at the animal for coming, as it was a cloying satellite of the house and a perfect reminder of Richard. It was typical of his brother's vigilantism to have invited him before the grouse shooting; almost certainly punishment for some transgression which Richard had discovered. Dominic had brought his guns anyway and they were sitting in accusatory isolation in the boot room.

The Hebridean wind hit him as he crested the hill. The Isle of Jura came into view across the wide sound with Islay beyond it, like the backs of two giant whales breaching the North Atlantic. He turned to look back along the sea loch, its still basin cupped between two variegated wings of land. His family's hunting lodge was half-hidden by its garrison of pines, the round drive populated with a few cars. There were hardly any other guests as the shooting hadn't started yet, and little was expected of him other than to be there. Each morning, he swam in the loch then went with one of his nieces to pull up empty lobster pots. As the only childless one, he was often passed the jobs of the younger generation; collecting wood for the barbeque or cleaning mussels in a bucket.

The days had changed little since he was a boy and this annual gathering had become a morbid reminder of childhood. Yet the three girls seemed to enjoy it as much as he had hated it. They were only a few years apart, sporting their blonde hair and ridiculous prefixes through good schools and bad universities. He was strangely popular with them; he, who would snatch their futures away. Uncle Dominic, invariably, with a hand on his sleeve and eyes flashing under tousled hair. Maybe the way he was spoken of in their house lent him a wayward glamour, or they saw him pictured in the same magazines where they looked for themselves. Perhaps they were just hedging for a future where he held the purse strings; or the keys to the house at least, as the purse itself was largely empty. But they couldn't know how their conversation exhausted him as it jumped between topics, each thought a new sensation. The adults didn't have much more to offer, of course. Each evening, Richard and his guests relentlessly described what they had caught or sighted that day. No wonder my class has to kill things, he thought; it's the closest thing they have to sex.

His father had tried to teach him to fish thirty years before. Even as a child, he had recognised love and duty mingling in the man's attempt to spend time with him. When at the age of eighteen he had gone to Italy for the summer instead of coming here, he had expected to return to cold disappointment. But instead Dominic had seen a new glimmer of respect; a vicarious pleasure, even, in the freedoms which his son had begun to enjoy. It began to dawn on him that being a younger son was a brilliant escape. As the eldest, Richard could never avoid going to Scotland; or being schooled in the arcane procedures of Selwood Park; or living the life he now lived. Not that it would ever occur to him to want to do anything different. People like him obeyed precedent in their every thought, ending up powerless to live their lives. No, freedom meant living on your own terms. It was witnessing this that made his siblings hate him so much; and all the more because they could sense it but not comprehend it.

Since it had become clear that Dominic not Richard would command the family's future, the impotence had only fanned their anger more. Yet while he could not fail to appreciate the foiling of his brother's sturdy progress through life, it also made him angry. Richard was older by twelve years and the spotlight of blame was already trained on Dominic. When Richard died, it would blaze into light. The psychology was so clever; it must have outflanked hundreds before him. The poorer you are, the more you struggle to keep the whole thing going; the richer you are, the less excuse you have to let it go. Which meant that as soon as Richard died, nothing that was Dominic's would be his any more. Even if Nick did strike gold in Uzbekistan, his share would soon be sucked into the pit of his alleged responsibilities. Worse, he would be fêted for restoring the family fortunes, which meant the same as spending as little as possible on himself. They would expect it to go on maintaining a decrepit old house, the only real use of which was as a film set; more importantly, on allowing as many future generations as possible to do nothing but luxuriate in their own self-obsession. And yet after his brother died, making his own money would also become impossible! Half his clients would look on him with awe and the other half with ridicule. He didn't know which would be more embarrassing.

He had often stood there with his father and looked at this same view. If only the man had lived long enough to find out that Richard and his wife would not be charging further down their blonde avenue of procreation. But he hadn't and neither had he been willing to pre-empt the future of Richard's family; and so had never given his second son that touch of approbation which might have diffused things to this day. Even so, Dominic was sure that in the unspoken hinterland of his father's being, he had been loved for his freedom. But now his siblings had him on a leash. Richard and Caroline were both desperate for him to marry and condemn some wriggling baby to go next, when the one thing Dominic liked about children was the Rousseauean openness of their lives. To create one with a predestined future seemed like a kind of death; the same death which was now lined up for *him*.

He sat on a rock and the dog plumped itself down, the wind lifting the spittle from its tongue. Always, the same thoughts when he came to Scotland. The old house with its smell of gas, his brother's lumpen dynasty of Labradors, even the yellow-lichened rocks beside this path; they had all become simulacra for the same problem. The problem of his future. Caroline would already have sized up Imogen as a perfect Lady Warminster; cornerstone of charity committees, darling of the press, mother to another blonde tribe. Imogen, who never put a foot wrong; who talked the right amount and was so quick to intuit when she was showing inexperience. The girl to whom men's eyes were helplessly drawn, and to whom they helplessly returned.

Even in the sharp Atlantic air, he could imagine her smell. He thought of her hips, just heavy enough not to be boyish, and of the perfect density of her breasts; and of her slow crescendos, exploratory and helpless. Yes, the material energy of mankind flowed down those limbs with unedited strength. But that was also the problem. He had begun to think of her as a kind of apotheosis rather than a real person. Her consciousness seemed to have found a home in her body, whereas his found only a prison. It was her very adjustment to life that had betrayed it, as he realised that even her rebellions were not rebellions but celebrations. She would never understand that truly to love life, you must first be able to reject it completely; to forgo every physical calling, even survival itself. Only on that blank canvas can the shapes of true appreciation begin to form. The realisation had been gradual and unwilling, seeming to lead to the mortification of religion rather than anything that made sense. But even so, it had recently hardened to certainty.

He rested an elbow on one knee and circled his cheeks with thumb and forefinger. Perhaps this was the hold that Charlotte had over him? That something in her manner sailed close to the rim of truth. The hollow laugh and one paw resting on a string ball of depression; the Schubertian fall he had twice seen in her eyes; her wanton, adolescent refusal just to *be*. When she spoke, he had a sense of her words being a line drawn around nothingness. But in that nothingness, he wanted to say, was also inexpressible truth; in it was the beginning of everything. Now she was separated from that part of herself and instead of searching for it again, she was burying it. Maybe that was just growing up; the growing up which she had done and he refused to? The thought of her two children was embedded like an anchor, its unbreakable chain of responsibility meaning she could never be his future. Yet her kiss in the nightclub had felt like a rebellion against that very same thing.

Then at the ponds, he had seen something different again. She had been wide-eyed and silent as she ran her arms and legs around him, breathing deeply as she plough her nose along his chest. She had shuddered silently under his touch, searching him with her eyes and hands. Yet still they had not made love. This waiting was something new. It was not nervousness or self-denial but a kind of suspension; a strange, non-linear path to fulfillment. He felt it even now. It was as if each time he saw her, the previous time was still present and unresolved, and he wanted to be in it again before going on to the next.

What next time? He hadn't spoken to her after the ponds and now she was probably on holiday with her family; probably spending the afternoon with her husband, following the deep pathways of the marriage bed. That was real life.

And what was it for him? More dates with Imogen; more tiring conversations about the world; an eventual proposal, if only to give her what she wanted. He took a deep breath of the Argyll air, and realised that for once he wanted to stay in Scotland longer. Not just for the grouse but long after the other guests had gone. He could grow another beard and take his gun out onto the moor, then read through the long northern dusk. All the family wanted him to do was live and wait, so he may as well do it here as a hermit.

Two fishing boats were ploughing along the sound, their wakes marking the dark sea. There had been half a dozen when he used to come up here twenty years before; now only these two travelled up the loch to their tiny home. He stood and slowly followed the dog down the long path to the lodge.

Half an hour later, they entered the stable yard and its tail wagged heavily as it lumbered towards an open door. Inside, Dominic found his brother in shirt sleeves shucking oysters from a bucket.

'Hello Purdey,' said Richard, then looked up at Dominic. 'Nice walk, Dom?'

'Yes,' said Dominic. 'Blowing a bit up there.'

'By the way,' said the earl. 'John Conyngham called. He can't make it for the grouse; something about their place in Spain. Would you like to take the gun?'

Dominic looked at him.

'Thanks Rich,' he said. 'I would.'

*

Leaves hung like giant hands from the oak outside Toadsmoor Cottage. A breeze rustled them and passed into the kitchen through the open door. It was the first of the afternoon.

Dinah squeezed some Burnt Sienna onto her palette, deciding Rachael's hair was going to be lighter in the painting than it was in reality. She didn't think a strong corona suited the girl's character and it would unbalance the picture against her brother's dark curls. Anyway, children's hair often darkened when they grew up and that is when the painting would count. They could just remember her as an auburn-haired child. A trace of sadness had also entered her face, which was nothing to do with Rachael but might be the future reflected onto her. Dinah regretted it but wasn't that how it had always worked? Artists simply know things first. After all, Picasso had split his atoms a full ten years before the scientists did.

She stepped back, hoping this particular atom would remain un-split at least till the children were older. Did Charlotte even knew what she was holding in her hands? Her whole generation were so careless, fighting pretend battles to maintain their children's innocence then sweeping it casually to the floor. She had watched in her very own lifetime as people stopped being able to think beyond themselves. It was as if a switch had been flicked and the engines of the human spirit gone into reverse, pulling the world into a vortex of selfishness. If I'm not taking, someone else is taking from me; if I give, I will end up with nothing. But how can you love without giving? How else can you find out that there is always more? The frenzy of mistrust fascinated her as it would so obviously end in disaster. I'll not be there to see it, she thought as she looked at the portrait. But you two will.

How could Charlotte do it to them? And to her husband? Daniel Falk had come home while she was making her sketches and Dinah had liked him. He was a warm and generous man who had welcomed her even as Punk bared his teeth. She had seen Charlotte's look of distant love before her eyes went elsewhere. What's the big mystery? Here you are together; make love! If only she could to sit down with Charlotte and hear about it straight.

Not for the first time, Dinah wondered when she had become such a nosy old woman. The night-time Guernica she had begun during the bicycle polo lay

219

propped against a wall, waiting to be turned into a painting. She had found it painful handing over the sketch of the injured batsman without charging him: without adding invoice to injury! She chuckled. You're a terrible woman, Dinah Laughlin! And then the tall, thin one whose picture hung in Charlotte's hall for a reason Dinah still couldn't understand.

She changed brushes and started working on Adam's hair, which was thick and black like his father's. Daniel Falk would make a good subject for a portrait, and not a commercial piece but a real one. Thinking of him pulled her thoughts back to Dominic, the great destroyer; so jealous of being slighted even as he ploughed these ruts through other people's lives.

The old heaviness settled and she put down the brush with a sigh. The mug of tea was more cold than warm but she took it to the open door. The sides of the valley curved away like scoops of butter and the tower of Toadsmoor Church rose quietly from a fold in the hills. She had only met Charlotte twice: who was she to know what was best for the girl? And for the children? Thousands of people had been happier for their divorces and probably thousands of their children too. She felt low at this new willingness to dictate other people's lives for them. It seemed brutal to hold the world to the deep standard of love which she had been given with Peter.

She wondered when she had changed and her eye rested on the river before it passed out of sight into the gardens of the manor house. It was Dominic, of course. If Charlotte had been involved with anyone else, she wouldn't have cared: she would probably say go and be with him. But the thought of Dominic getting what he wanted cast a darkness over the whole world. Something gave way and she felt a new warmth trickling into her chest. This time she would do something.

*

The airliner banked and Nick woke up. He was grateful for the sleep, even if the slowing heave of the aeroplane meant they were already over Britain. He looked down to where the lights of towns and roads were clotted together in one lymphatic mass. Breeding light out of the dead ground, he thought; the place is too fertile, it will die.

It was painful to be back so soon. He had arrived at Tashkent airport alert and himself, bidding the place no special farewell as he would be back when the drilling results came in. Yet already his departure was a faded memory and it seemed that only the country below was real. The plane touched down and his fellow travellers were diluted then lost as they walked through the terminal; the last trace of Asia, gone. Meanings invaded him from posters and announcements, and he had the usual feeling of being a stranger in this country where he understood everything. He saw the hunted look of British families when they travel, and walked through the customs hall with the unavoidable frisson of the innocent.

The Mercedes was parked high in a concrete pen, its sky blue body and cream hood lying among fungible modern saloons. The smell of the interior was the smell of his life and he was excited to be back as he settled into the cold leather. It was still early but he would pick up Timur on the way home. He snaked out of the airport and joined sleepwalking lines of motorway traffic which hardly belonged to the same world as the virile driving of Tashkent. The large script of the number plates and bright road signs signified a country rationalised into nothingness. Arriving in London, he turned south into the narrow, red-brick streets of Fulham. The car pitched as he accelerated then braked down short identical streets, his temper fraying as he searched for the house. He had been in England for two hours and already the peace was gone.

Samantha answered the door in a white bathrobe and flushed when she saw Nick, sunburned in his summer jacket.

'Hi!' she said, somehow finding two syllables in the word. Timur ran between her legs letting out involuntary barks, and Nick picked him up but didn't want to make too much of a fuss in front of Samantha. She leant up and gave him a peck on the cheek.

'How was your secret mission?' she said.

'Just that,' said Nick. He put the dog down and it started sniffing his trousers intently. He knew that Samantha would have spoiled him with too much attention and that his behaviour would have begun to turn. Nick hated ransoming part of his life to her and wondered if he should have bought back a present; but that would only personalise things even more.

'How was he?' he said.

'Oh, fine,' she said. 'He's a dreamboat! You just off

the flight? Want a coffee?'

'Yes,' said Nick. 'I mean, yes, I've come from the airport.'

'Ok,' said Samantha with good-humoured resignation. 'Off you go then.' Her hand closed around the lapel of his jacket and he smelt shampoo as she kissed him goodbye. She had been surprised when he dropped off Timur without any paraphernalia; and now he was glad not to have to go into the clean kitchen and collect anything.

'Say goodbye to mummy,' she said to Timur, then looked up at Nick with an embarrassed laugh.

Albert Bridge shone white in the morning sun as he parked across the road from his houseboat. Timur jumped down from the car, smelling the river and home. In the boot, Nick's travel bay lay beside a rug rolled into a spiral of Uzbek Airlines packing tape. As he tucked the rug under an arm and reached up to close the boot, he heard the rasp of tyres and two car horns. He turned around to see a delivery van stopped in its turn off the bridge with its door opening. By its front wheel, a small white form lay on the tarmac. The world went silent and the bag came loose from his hand. He ran into the middle of the junction and knelt, touching Timur with both hands. The tail twitched in recognition and he tried to raise his head. Sunlight glinted on his nose and his breathing was light and fast. Both front legs were broken and splayed onto the road, and Nick could see where his ribcage had collapsed. He put a hand under the head and smoothed down one of the soft ears.

'Timmy,' he whispered. The pink tip of Timur's

tongue appeared at the end of his muzzle, then his eyes widened and froze. Nick knelt in a ball, burying his face in the dog's coat and breathing in the warm hearth of its smell. Thick tears leaked into the fur and he heard cars close to him. He felt the sun on his back and wanted to stay in that blackness forever. He rocked back, gathering the body in his arms. The van driver was standing in front of him, his face creased.

'He was trying to go home,' said Nick.

SEPTEMBER

16

Roger stopped at the edge of the park. Blond dogs bounded among young families and expensive pushchairs stood abandoned as parents followed their children's first steps. It was not a place he could be after all.

He turned right instead, climbing a steep pavement under oaks with full heads of leaves. He had a vision of them in a few months' time, bare and whipped by the winter rain, and realised he could not be in England when that happened. He turned into a gently sloping road, where low tenements faced the familiar terraces of Primrose Hill. He felt lighter for a moment before realising it was only the easing of his step down the hill. The road joined another in a broad confluence, its space and quiet suggesting a peaceful future. Then the houses stopped and a gaping space opened above the railway line. Its tracks flowing like a river straight into the centre of London, and the moment crumbled.

He stopped again by the wide pedestrian bridge. Its metal sides were hemmed with amateur art which he had watched change over the years. Tourists carrying bags from Camden Market crossed towards him in a slow trickle, navigating uncertainly towards the Hill. The hump of the bridge created a low horizon, beyond which the way sunk into a dark thicket of trees. He had used to take morning walks on the other side, up towards the Heath and down towards the Market. Maybe he could go to there and lose himself? But his new fact would follow him everywhere. He could walk to the other side of London or get on a plane to France and it would be waiting there, probably looming higher where he was a stranger and would be alone with it. He would be alone everywhere now.

Roger realised he was stationary on the threshold of the bridge. He felt attached to his house as if by an invisible line, like when they had drawn circles at school using a pencil and a piece of string. It was carrying him along the edge of the neighbourhood, which was still scuffed by the invisible presence of the railway just as it had been when he moved there sixteen years before. It seemed impossible for so much to have changed in a day. He didn't know how long it had been since the phone call but the sound of his shouting still echoed in his head. He couldn't remember the last time he had raised his voice. It was probably deep in the days which he couldn't remember; but now this snarling, helpless anger felt like it would be a part of him forever.

The fact came at him again, swooping down from a new angle. All the rest of his money had turned into things; travel, property, cars. But this money had gone just gone; not hidden, or saved, or used to buy something, or even lent. Just disappeared, like something in a magic trick. He sat down on some steps and closed his eyes. It was him, Roger, here in his neighbourhood; two minutes' walk from home with his car keys in his pocket. But there was also someone else who he didn't know at all. He didn't know what this person did, where he shopped or ate, or who he saw. How he *survived*. The idea pulled at the pit of his stomach and a new coldness took hold as the bank manager's words came back to him. We will have to close your account.

He pushed the sunglasses up and covered his eyes with his palms. His fingertips trembled on his forehead but the scent of his hands was warm and close. An elbow rested with even pressure on each knee as his chest rose and fell in the centre. His breathing deepened, the passage of air becoming a cool balancing point between the two sides of his body, and a kind of stillness emerged. His mind started to empty and for a moment he forgot why he was there. He opened his eyes and shapes dazzled him; a flat triangle at the top of a house, an ornamental tree, the bumper of a car. His breath lightened again and the shaking returned to his hands: it was real, like a raven beating its wings above his head.

He walked on into a future that opened like a huge, breathing pit. The heavy air was making his shirt stick to his back and a new tightness was entering his chest. It was nothing he had asked for; nothing he had sought out. The smell of cigar smoke came back to him, sweet and sickening; then the overbearing tone of the banker as he told Roger not to do it. Someone else had said the same thing. But who? He had never told Irina about it or discussed it with anyone else, so it must have been a voice from within himself. And he had been right.

Whereas not once had the other two warned him that the deal could go wrong: not once. He stopped and a woman manoeuvred her pushchair around him. Maybe the whole thing was a lie? Just a cheap concoction of papers and 'satellite photos'? Those photos could have been taken anywhere: he even thought they looked like the moon.

He was moving again, and aware of figures standing like giants just out of his vision. Lily; her mother; her mother's attorney, with that brutal look in his eye. She had changed lawyers the previous year and put this one on a percentage of the kill. The woman was making millions but he knew that her friends would be goading her on, threatening to withdraw their respect unless she drove him ever further into the ground. Lily's anger too he now saw more clearly: it was like a grenade with its firing pin tied to a tripwire of money. He remembered the time in Paris when he had made the merest suggestion of a cheaper dress. Within seconds, the shop had been split apart by her bolts of punishment.

'You fucking hit mum!' she screamed. 'You took whores home and fucked them in her bed, you fucking sick pervert! I'm surprised you didn't fuck me too! My shrink's not happy with some of the things that happened! You think you can get away with that? Huh? Who do you wanna know first, the courts or the Inquirer? You think I fucking care about this?' She held the dress up and threw it in his face. 'You think that means anything to me? That is *nothing* after what you did!'

She had walked out, leaving the dress crumpled

around his feet and Parisian shoppers frozen around him. He followed dumbly and found her calmly making another pile of clothes in the next shop. He had paid in silence and taken her to lunch at Maxim's.

What would happen when the news reached their lawyers? The panic dropped from his chest and he felt a ripple of nausea. Would it be enough for them to take his house and car? Or were there longer forms of punishment? He didn't know how much of the house he even owned as the financial structure around it was so complicated. And there was a letter waiting at home about the apartment in New York, which meant that would probably soon be taken. His parents were gone and he had sold their house in North Oxford without thinking ten years before. If only he still had it, something solid and not connected to the last thirty years; something that was actually *his*. How would it even start? This had never happened to anyone he knew. He couldn't call anyone in his address book, any more than he would want them to call him if this happened.

Beyond the sickness, he could already feel a black silence covering the rest of his life. For thirty years, he had not been alone; and now the only person he could talk to was the person he could least afford to tell. He had waited until Irina was out of the house before calling Nick, then immediately left in order not to be there when she came back. Now his throat as well as his chest were tight. Since coming back to London, she had taken the garden in hand and discovered where to buy plants from a superstore off the Finchley Road. He had enjoyed walking through the sliding doors into the DIY warehouse: the place made him feel like a householder and a man with responsibilities. Irina would rummage single-mindedly and they would load the back of the convertible with plants, their tall green fronds swaying on the way home. When she had finished gardening, he drove her to Hampstead to cool off in the bathing pond. She could be happy there for hours; diving and sunbathing, unaware that anyone was looking at her. Dogs always attracted her attention, making her coo and talk in Russian. He had been going to get her one for her birthday, as he knew that having a dog here would make her stay in England. He had even been to Bond St to look for a ring but sensibly decided to wait. Until when? Until now, when he heard news.

He had reached another corner where two wide streets crossed in an empty, sun-bleached junction. One on corner stood a pub, its large windows divided by black woodwork and topped with gold lettering. He had always pictured it as his local, and each summer felt the old pull when he saw people spilling onto the street. He crossed the street and went in.

*

Nick looked at his phone. Dominic again. He didn't pick up. It had been years since money was at stake, and Roger had already torn open the world to show the fury that it put in people. Now all he could think of were the vengeances extracted by Russians who had come to Baku and lost their investment. It was like the Law of

Conservation of Energy. The money could disappear but its energy could not: it had to be returned if only as revenge. A pound of flesh and more; bodies entangled in shrimp nets.

The thoughts were mixing with the humidity and felt like they were choking him. The drilling report had arrived the day before and he had read it and re-read it, trying somehow to puncture the neat rows of figures. The percentages were far below the economies needed to produce gold. The geology itself was hardly even like the seam of the main mine. He couldn't bring himself to compare it with the seismology report. The grid references on the core samples were given to eight decimal places: there was no chance they had been taken in the wrong place.

That night, the humidity seemed worse than ever. Struggling to find oxygen, he had left his bedroom and lain flat on the deck. The pregnant clouds sagged like purple and orange bruises in the glow of the city. Comforted by them, he let himself wonder if the failure would really affect him. His name was on all the paperwork; but other investments went wrong and life went on. After all, it was not only Roger's money that had been lost but his own. *He* had nothing left but the boat he lay on, whereas Roger probably still had plenty to spare. He put his hands by his sides on the warm metal, then went back to bed and slept fitfully. In the nightmare, he was lost on the streets; the panic rising. He knew that Timur was safely back on the boat but he couldn't find it as he searched among the traffic, until a van bore down and he woke with a cry.

In the long wait until morning, he replayed the rest of that day. He had carried Timur on board and stroked the cooling fur as he held the body in his lap. There was no blood as his thick coat had withstood the impact, and he didn't want to invade the dog's spirit by probing his broken parts. There is no rite for mourning an animal so he just sat remembering for an unknown amount of time. On the drive back from collecting him, the puppy had sniffed all around the footwell then curled up with his eyes on Nick. He had prepared the boat by running a roll of chicken wire along the deck rails: it was still there, browning and curling after its six winters.

He didn't imagine if things had been different. It had happened, that was all. Yes, Charlotte always nagged him about using a lead but that didn't make a difference now. Perhaps it had been his fault; perhaps the driver's; perhaps no-one's. Yet he couldn't help thinking whether the dog would have been better off with another owner entirely. Jack Russells live to fifteen and beyond: he had only been six.

He stood finally and wrapped the body in the fragment of Indian rug on which Timur had slept. The tears were strangely cold on his cheeks as he closed the last fold of material around the small head. He looked for something to weight it and found a length of chain in the fo'castle, which he wrapped around before securing the whole thing with duct tape. It was a strange looking package which he took down into the dingy; like something from a smuggler, either very valuable or worthless.

He cradled it in his lap and started downstream. But if he did it by Battersea Power Station, he would think of Timur whenever he saw the building. He carried on but the anonymous banks of Pimlico were also wrong and beyond Vauxhall Bridge the river only became even more desolate. Millbank Tower faced massive cuboids on the other bank, which bore no human imprint at all. He held the little cylinder in his lap, thinking how his weakness was betraying Timur even in death; then finally dimmed the motor and let the incoming tide carry them back upstream. Finally both banks turned to green where Hurlingham House faced the oak avenues of Wandsworth Park: England. He turned the boat into the stream and pressed the coarse package against his forehead. A made-up prayer passed through his head, then he took a long breath of Thames air and released the casket into the water. It sank quickly and he was strangely pleased with his preparations.

Back on the *Roxanne*, things seemed different. For the first time he noticed dust lying on the window sills and the loose tassel of a sword hanging on the wall. He was used to imagining, in the moment before he opened the door, that his home would bear the imprint of someone else's presence; a sensation which he thought was common to all who lived alone. But this was different. There seemed to have been a minute reorientation of things on the deck; some earth spilled from one of the pots perhaps, then cleared away.

The thought came back to him in the early morning and he realised it must have been seagulls; or just him noticing more because his attention wasn't earthed to the dog. He finally got up and drove through the dawn to Hyde Park. London was still and he wished the grey early light could hold back the day forever. The Serpentine was empty and he swam for an hour, trying to push his tiredness and the news out through his pores into the cool water. Walking back to the car, he passed dogs being walked and the accident hung like a fishing sinker attached to his heart.

Soon after he arrived back on the boat, his phone rang. It was Roger and his breath lightened as he saw the name. Roger too must have been awake the previous night, daydreaming about his future. The empty space in Nick's chest got bigger with each ring and he finally picked up. Roger greeted him cheerfully and didn't even ask the question. They had spent an evening together socially since Nick arrived back, and now Roger didn't betray a hint of his expectation. His face appeared next to Timur's and Nick thought: if only neither of you had met me. The conversation reached a pause and he sat down on the piano stool. In the moment before he started to speak, he knew what every doctor feels.

'I've got some bad news, I'm afraid,' he said. There was silence. 'There was nothing there.' He could hear the hum of the phone signal as he waited for Roger to speak.

'What do you mean, nothing?' said Roger finally.

Nick took a breath.

'Nothing,' he said. 'No ore.'

'But you took the readings yourself?' he heard.

'That was a long time ago,' said Nick in a weak voice. He could hear Roger's breath deepening at the other end of the phone.

'Are you trying to tell me it grew legs and fucking walked off?' said Roger.

There was silence.

'I'm sorry, Roger,' he said. 'I was wrong.'

And then it started. Hell came out of Roger's mouth. Nick closed his eyes. He couldn't interrupt as he had nothing to say and he couldn't hang up. So he put a hand to his forehead and just listened, realising with mounting grief how much he had come to like Roger. The man's optimism, his ability to raise a laugh, even his odd self-serving spiritual appetite; they were all things which were unique to him. Roger had called soon after he got back from Tashkent, and he had invited him down to the boat. His guest bought a good bottle of wine and Nick was touched when he refused any, realising it had been a selfless gift. Roger innocently asked after Timur and the sympathy which followed was surprisingly real. He spoke about losing his own dog as a boy, and nothing he said was misplaced or irritating. Nick felt a glow of humanity and the conversation turned to Sufism. Roger had listened intently and Nick remembered what one of his teachers had said. Do not judge a man by what he has or what he knows, for in these things he had no choice; judge him only by what he values.

That evening, he had begun to think of Roger as someone who valued the right things even if he struggled to practice them. When they started talking about music, Roger sat at the piano and self-deprecatingly picked out the riffs from some of his old hits. Nick joined him, improvising on the treble notes until they were embarrassed and stopped. Nick instead showed him how some of the metaphysical ideas he had mentioned appeared in music. But Roger gripped the concepts too hard and they disintegrated in his hands. They finally sat together in silence as the music of Dimitrie Cantemir drifted out into the night; Cantemir, whose name Nick had crassly given to the failed company.

Thinking of the evening as Roger's words came down the phone, a fissure opened in Nick's heart. There had been not a trace of this in Roger's character before. He, Nick, had unearthed it singlehandedly. It was not difficult to love people: it was hatred that took work, and he was becoming someone who people hated. He was trembling at the idea.

Roger was asking how much money he could get back and he couldn't answer. His own extended trip had eaten up some of the margin they had worked into the figures and Dominic would claim the remainder in fees. The only hope was selling the rights to the mine but they would be worth nothing after another failed exploration. He offered to find out, and with a final swift blow Roger ended the conversation.

Now the phone was flashing Dominic's name with each insistent ring. Nick had thought of calling him as soon as he received the report, hoping he might have a way out or be willing to tell Roger himself. But now it was too late: Dominic had found out from Roger and was calling with his own fury. For him it would not be a question of money as he not invested any. It was more than that; the time, the reputation, the very fact he had believed Nick in the first place. Nick couldn't even imagine him being angry; and he certainly couldn't have another conversation like the one with Roger. When the phone finally stopped, he immediately thought how long it would be before it rang again.

He turned it off and sat down. It was becoming more and more difficult to breathe. Opening the doors had just let in thick air laced with distant traffic fumes. The nausea was worse and a stream of sweat was thickening down his spine. Chills started and he saw himself from above, bent on the piano stool. Oh Jesus, he thought; not now. But fighting the panic attack only chased the air further from his lungs and he felt himself starting to shake. The rattle of traffic became muffled and blackness gathered at the edge of his vision. First Timur then me, he thought. First Timur, then me.

17

Charlotte pulled the small blazer from its cellophane and ran her hand over the wool. It had been new two weeks before and already it was back from the dry cleaners. Another child had apparently thrown their lunch at Adam. He complained about wearing the jacket in the heat but she told him to keep it on when the other children had theirs on. Now for three days he had gone in without it.

Already she could see new uncertainties arising as his forcefulness was curbed by school. She hoped he would come out neither a bully nor bullied but a leader. Hopefully it would just pop out of his genes when he needed it, like seeds germinating in springtime. Daniel seemed to have it. Or have had it. He had changed in the weeks since they came back from holiday and now came returned from the office withdrawn. Some grain had got under his skin; probably the sort of imperfection she had always looked for in him and missed, yet now she was worrying herself about it. But she knew better than to ask what it was; after all, it had taken her years to train him not to ask her how she was feeling.

At first she thought it was Dominic. But the cloud seem to lift when he came home in the evenings and he still looked for comfort in her. She saw him looking at the children not with his old satisfaction but with a kind of hopeless pathos, as if counting the threats to them. He did not make love to her and she would find him awake at night, curled on his side. Leaving the house in the mornings, the cloud would lower and his old determination be replaced by uncertainty. At least the children had not noticed him changing; him, the only immutable thing in their lives.

A long cry came down the stairs, its desolation blowing against her heart. Rachael was at home with an ear infection. Charlotte had tried and failed to explain to her the pain would leave finally. 'But make it go *now* mummy,' Rachael would say, gripping her hand in panic. Daniel had looked on encouragingly as the doctor prescribed ever stronger painkillers and Charlotte saw the fear that illness struck in him; the deep worry that money and science still could not chase it from their door. News of Rachael's illness had quickly spread through Daniel's family, and his sister Tabitha had volunteered to come and sit with her for the coming night. Rachael's pain had kept Charlotte up through the early morning and each step was heavy as she climbed the stairs. At some point earlier in her thirties, the batteries needed to miss a night's sleep had vanished completely.

She sat on Rachael's bed and the girl's arms closed on hers. Charlotte held her head, smoothing the curls and catching the tears that fell on her soft cheeks. She pulled the cover over her legs and Rachael burrowed into her side. It had been a strange time since arriving back from holiday. They had left the area for the weekend of the Notting Hill Carnival and gone to stay with Daniel's cousins in Hampstead. When they went for a walk on Hampstead Heath and passed the swimming ponds, a bodily tingle started in her. The children wanted to go in but Daniel worried the water wasn't clean and Charlotte quickly agreed. Taking Adam to his new school, the same physiological secret whirred inside and she wondered if any of the other parents had their own. She had realised that she was actually enjoying the density of it; the feeling that she was no longer suspended helplessly in the air with all the weight on Daniel's side of the marriage.

She had arrived back in London deliberately agnostic about Dominic, having decided to do nothing to encourage him. But a head of annoyance soon started to build that he hadn't called, and she realised the hypocrisy of trying to wash her hands of the decision. His call finally came in the middle of the afternoon, when her conjugal life was at its ebb. They spoke of their holidays and he knew the places she had been in the South of France. She had a silent flush of envy when he mentioned Tuscany; less so for Scotland. When he said he had been delayed there, she thought she detected a hint of apology. He suggested dinner and she found herself assenting neutrally. There was a moment when the ruffling of diaries could have taken place but Dominic said he would send some dates instead. She was busy on the first two evenings he suggested: a dinner party with Samantha, to which Nick was also invited; and a work function of Daniel's, where even she detected a cooling of his relationships. The rest of her evenings were quite free but she was pleased at the inadvertent wall of resistance. His messages stopped for two days, then came the suggestion of a Friday lunch somewhere on Curzon St. It was after the beginning of term, and she said yes.

She wore a dark red day dress, her pendant and no earrings, as if it were a lunch with anyone; and put together some errands to do beforehand. A trip to the Tredegar Gallery to pick up a catalogue of Dinah's last exhibition, where the owner waylaid her with a coffee; then a visit to the bookshop on Curzon St. By the time she arrived at the address Dominic had given, she had a small collection of bags and a nicely busy air. Even her light sweat gave the impression of just lunching with a friend.

A white-haired doorman swung open the heavy door and she entered cool, marbled air. A hand appeared for her shopping bags and she released them into it. The atmosphere was beautifully dry after the outside and she drew long discreet breaths, conscious of her damp skin. A fish tank was set in one wall and she stopped in front of it to cool off. Blue and yellow fish moved in the darkly lit interior, first wide then narrow as they turned to look at her. She refocused on her reflection and saw a ghost of herself, both present and not.

The place was a casino, its small spaces accentuated by incontinently grand Roccoco decor. Gilded cornices and curved picture lights encroached from the walls, but the dark oil paintings were not strong enough to fight back their surroundings. They passed rooms where roulette wheels clicked and Charlotte wondered if they would see Dominic at one, feeding a closet addiction in the minutes before lunch. She was annoyed at the prurient thought: what was it to her? She asked for the bathroom and was shown into a similarly pregnant space. Her naked ears seemed like a child's against the gold decor so she let her hair down, picking up a tortoiseshell brush which lay beside the marble basin. She turned away and leant back on its cool edge, the silence pressing in on her. She could leave now and send Dominic one of a hundred rock-solid excuses related to the children.

But the man had waited for her outside. He led her between narrow pillars and up a spiral staircase which looked like it had been shrunk from a Loire chateau. At the top of a second flight, she saw daylight and they stepped out onto a roof terrace. Dominic was sitting sideways at a table laid with a white cloth, reading a magazine with its name printed in heavy red capitals. He was wearing a pastel blue linen jacket and three buttons were undone on his shirt, with a pair of sunglasses hooked over the fourth. The tan was deeper and an orange drink sat before him in a long glass. She stifled a smile; he had obviously brought his holidays home, or rather decided to let the ongoing holiday of his life break the surface. He looked up and smiled, and held her elbow lightly as his lips brushed her cheek. The chair was moved out for her and the waiter nodded appreciatively when she ordered a white wine spritzer.

Dominic's eyes settled on her with that intimate force which she had forgotten, and she looked down at the menu. They ordered sea trout and talked about the summer, too casually at first. But at least he knew the stretch of coast where she had stayed in France and many of the places she had visited. She realised she was saying 'I' not 'we' about the trip but it was too late to change without being obvious. In any case, she had been alone during the parts of the holiday she mentioned. Dominic acknowledged the art collections with an undertow of obligation, as if they trespassed on the real purpose of the South of France. She remembered Daniel's look of strained anticipation as they took a speedboat around to the beach club on the end of the St Tropez peninsular, and thought Dominic was the very archetype of the sort of person he had hoped to meet.

He talked about Scotland with mock hatred, saying his brother had deliberately inveigled him there early; and it was hard not to laugh when he impersonated his nieces with their wandering attention. But he spoke the word family with a hiatus between the first two syllables, and she could feel his weariness. He finally fell silent, his jaw setting like a teenager as he looked over the roof tops. She found herself talking about the children; Adam's encounter with the new school and Rachael's unexpected, lateral observations on life. She knew children harboured their thoughts for months before voicing them, and it worried her when people spoke unguardedly in front of them. Dominic listened with an academic kind of interest. Children are like dogs, he said simply. They want power but it will only make them unhappy; so the fewer choices they have, the happier they will be.

The words came back to her now, with Rachael shivering quietly under her arm. She had nodded even as Dominic's hard tone belied how little he knew. It was difficult to imagine him as a father, trying to put that Victorian austerity into action on his own flesh and blood. People had done it once, even in her own lifetime. She had once been put on a plane to France at the age of ten, only to find she had to complete the journey to her friend's house using the railways. Her mother's face had darkened when she told her; but her grandmother had shrieked with delight.

The terrace had still been empty when the main course was cleared, and she wondered if he had somehow booked the whole place. She was on undiluted Soave and had started to feel enjoyably sybaritic. Dominic offered her a zabaglione and ordered two before she could refuse. They arrived with a sweet sparkling wine. The warm deserts disappeared quickly and the conversation found its way to Italy as they lingered over the wine. He said he had escaped there for a weekend and she wondered if he had gone on his own. She listened to the details of Siena and Assisi, probing him hungrily on different churches until he gave up with a laugh. Her head felt only slightly light but her joints were heavy and relaxed. They stood next to each other at the edge of the terrace, pointing out landmarks to the south. She had never seen Mayfair from above. Air conditioning units clung to the brickwork and bamboo screens suggested other terraces nestling far above the traffic. She saw a space where the buildings stopped and knew that Green Park opened there in a wide sweep down to Buckingham Palace. Her hand touched his and they both stilled. He turned to face her and stood motionless with one hand on her arm, his lips brushing her hairline. She closed her eyes, hearing the distant sounds of lunch being cleared. It had been nice not to think for those moments.

Rachael's pain seemed to be subsiding and Charlotte knew that if she stayed all afternoon, she would have to stay all night. She gently released herself and got down from the bed, tucking the duvet higher and promising to come back later. She looked back before closing the door and saw Rachael's eyes following her with quiet abandonment. At the bottom of the stairs, she stopped with a hand resting on the end of the banister. She had replayed the lunch almost every day. It was hard to imagine not seeing him again but they had not made another plan or spoken explicitly at all. Was this an affair or just a friendship which had once slipped into indiscretion? Was he having the same thoughts? Or had he compartmentalised her away from the rest of his life?

A cold idea struck her: men like him probably wanted their lovers married, as it so neatly sidestepped the future. It was impossible to imagine him wanting her to leave Daniel and introduce two children into his life. Their faces came to her, confused and frightened when she had shouted at them in the kitchen. She imagined seeing him without Daniel knowing and felt a twinge of nausea. And then what? Either it would stop or the storm would break, hitting Daniel out of the blue. The ranks of his family would snap shut and 'I told you so' be whispered across North London. What would he do? What would they all do? A crushing divorce settlement probably, giving her only enough money for the children if she was allowed to see them at all. Daniel's family would quickly resettle him with a girl of their choice and she would become as an unwanted nub from his old life. The family would be faced with an impossible situation as the children grew up; unable completely to forgive her or to condemn her. Yet she sensed that she could stop Dominic easily. Even the slightest implication would bruise his pride enough for him to back off. And what would follow? Life would continue on the same rails as it had done for the past six years. For how long? She could picture a kind of middle age with Daniel but old age was a blank.

She carried on and stopped in front of Nick's picture. It was the author picture from his book on Turkey and showed him weathered and looking away from the camera. He still thought he was that person, even though he had barely left the country for years. He had arrived at Samantha's dinner without Timur, saying he didn't want to take the dog somewhere it had recently boarded. Only as they said goodbye outside did he tell her what had happened; and she had just stopped herself before asking why he wasn't on a lead. He seemed to think the world was bound together by some invisible force which would keep his dog beside him. The same careless faith had marked him since they were children. She touched the silver picture frame. Timur would be a long heartbreak, stubborn and silent. She reached the kitchen and dialled his number, and it rang six rings before he answered.

'Charlie?' she heard. He sounded strangled and she frowned.

'Nicky..?' she said.

'Charlie,' breathed Nick. He was lying on his bed and the boat seemed to be moving. His head was thick and his voice sounded like a whisper.

'I'm not well. I think it's...' His arm felt like lead and he could barely hold the phone. Maybe a tick bite from the trip, or false malaria? The figures of Dominic and Roger swirled outside the boat and he thought he heard Timur barking on the pontoon. His eyes closed and the buzzing came back to his ears, and he wished he could speak.

'Nicky, my God,' he heard. 'I'll come straight away.'

'Wait,' he breathed. 'See Bruce. Get Dox...' The names of the drugs were imprinted on his memory from many self-prescriptions but seemed impossibly long to say.

'Doxycycline,' he said in a burst. 'Chloroquinine. And tonic.'

Charlotte wrote the words phonetically on a message pad. Bruce Dickinson was an expedition doctor and the only person her brother would use. His surgery was on the way and they had tonic left over from the party.

'Nicky, stay put,' she said. 'I'll be there in half an hour.'

Nick's eyes closed again. Stay put, he thought; I can't move. He didn't know if he said 'Thanks Charlie' or just thought it. The line went dead and he dropped his arm onto the damp sheet.

'Fuck,' said Charlotte. She dialled another number and Daniel's sister Tabitha picked up straight away.

Charlotte explained and asked if she could come and look after Rachael now instead of that evening. Tabitha said yes immediately, as illness was the ultimate call to arms. Yet Charlotte sensed her sister-in-law's disapproval that the she was putting an adult before a child; perhaps also that Nick had no-one else to look after him. She felt the usual kick of annoyance that everything ran so perfectly in their world and pointed out that whereas Rachael was diagnosed, Nick was alone and could have anything. Tabitha gushed her approval, saying she would come at once.

Charlotte rang off and looked for Bruce Dickinson's number. Nick's aversion to organised healthcare was another of his great fantasies of self-sufficiency. He would be furious if she turned up with an ambulance or a strange doctor, and that wouldn't help if he was as weak as he sounded. Bruce's receptionist picked up and said he was away but as it was Nick she would speak to him to authorise a prescription.

Charlotte put down the phone and realised how quiet the house was. She ran from the kitchen and up the stairs then quietly opened the bedroom door. Rachael was asleep, her brow knotted against the dreams.

18

Cesare was smoking outside the staff entrance of the Club when he realised someone was approaching. She was a tall girl with blond hair piled above a strong chin: Mr Bannerman's friend. He stood on his cigarette and instinctively straightened his jacket.

'Cesare,' she said, seeming relieved to see him. 'Have you seen Dominic?'

The lines of her forehead were crumpled and her eyes rimmed with tears. *Carina*, he thought, you have had a fight. He had high hopes for them and always checked her hand for a new ring when they came to the club. She reminded him of his own daughter, widowed at twenty two and patiently living out her years under holy orders. It pained him that people struck themselves apart so easily when the world was so ready to do it for them.

'No, *amore*,' he said, wanting to take the trembling hand. Her eyes veered to the side and a tremor crossed her lips. She stepped forwards and pressed a card on him, and he held her hand for a moment.

'Will you send me a message if you see him?' she said. 'Please?'

'*Si*... Yes,' he said, and touched her arm.

*

Afternoon light glowed through the gaps in the venetian blinds of Roger's music room. The door was locked and a whisky bottle sat on one of the consoles. He had pushed Irina out of the way and come here to listen to music; but it had just distracted him and now he sat in silence. The tumbler was warm in his hand and he raised it mechanically every few minutes, his breath deep and steady.

He remembered when he first saw Nick, leaning against his car and facing the distant hills. Why were their cars parked next to each other? He remembered a lunch in the sun then making love to Irina beside a hedge. His lip curled as he thought of her trying to take the bottle from him then trying to stop him coming in here; always trying to stop him. What right had she to plead when she was no better than any of the others? They had made a fool of him in front of her by leaving him standing outside that party as the door girl got his name wrong. When who was inside exactly? Bankers and nobodies. Nick's sister had floated over full of air kisses and fake compliments but he had seen her eyes slide down to his shoes with a smirk. Posh people set their rules in secret yet still you feel grateful when they forgive you for breaking them. Him, grateful to them?

He remembered the cricket match and the sight of Nick's cold eyes as he ran up to bowl. He had thought he was going to die when that ball came towards him. Nick had not done it to anyone else yet still he had run up with his fake apologies. Then he had made Roger turn himself into a fool by getting himself out with the bat, and even that had only earned him more fake cheers. That old woman who had drawn the picture of him; they were all so *fake*. At dinner, another smirk from Lady Caroline because he didn't eat meat. He, who had travelled in India and the Himalayas; who had studied in monasteries; who had followed a path for five years, embarrassed in front a stuck-up bitch who had probably never read a book in her life? When what did they all actually do? Nothing. Nothing but talk about themselves and complain. The smaller the problem, the greater their self-pity. Poor Emily can't ride today; *poor Emily can't ride today!* She had actually said it! And what had her husband said to him? 'Oh, you're a musician. Are you in an orchestra?' Roger looked up at the gold and silver discs on his wall. No, he should have said; I've had three top ten hits in the UK and one in America. Yet instead he had just laughed and said: 'Oh, I wish I was good enough for an orchestra!' And so they won again. They did nothing, thought nothing, achieved *nothing*; and always won.

And Dominic, breathing superiority over everyone, his eye flickering minutely when Roger made another invisible mistake. For what exactly? Because he had a nice suit and an office in Mayfair? The meeting room where they had signed the deal was the smallest Roger had ever seen. The fronds of the potted palms even brushed his back as he made his way around the edge of the chairs. They had probably rented it by the hour. The room had not been air conditioned and it had felt like he was sleepwalking through the meeting. His signature seemed to go down on the endless documents from someone else's hand; and his writing got worse as he gripped the pen harder against his dyslexia. That quiet voice of resistance – *his* voice – had been obliterated by their greed. He had walked home light-headed as excitement and fear mixed in the pit of his stomach. That same circling worry that had gone with him all summer, coming back every night and morning; what if they were wrong?

Now everywhere he looked, he saw only lies. Five grammes an ounce; the spy photographs covered in children's felt-tip; the 'other investor' who had pulled out. Hadn't he even heard Nick laugh when Dominic said that? That club where he had felt underdressed; the beautiful dog that would not even let him stroke it; Dominic folding his newspaper, one expensive shoe suspended above the other. No, there was nothing left to believe. No wonder Roger had never met Dominic before. There was nothing to meet.

Worst of all was the evening he had spent on the boat with Nick. Trying to follow the meaningless descriptions of what he believed and never once being asked what *he*, Roger, had found out. Of course Nick didn't care what he believed: he was just waiting for the moment when he could keep his money and be rid of him. They had probably even agreed that Dominic wouldn't even have to see him again. Roger's breathing deepened further in the still room. What a mistake they had made. He had been in London for thirty years. He was older than them; he knew more people; he had more respect. His face hardened and he almost felt sorry for them. Or might feel sorry, afterwards.

He picked up his phone.

*

Eric Dodds' brow furrowed as he looked at his phone. Light gleamed on his narrow cranium from neon strips hung on the warehouse ceiling, and his ears rose in pointed tips. The hooded eyes were expressionless and burned with energy.

Roger Curtis, that blonde fool from Ice Machine, was calling him. Curtis, who had started buying him drinks in his own club; who clapped him on the back in front of the wrong people; who finally had one of their girls all weekend then not paid. Eric couldn't remember why he had let the debt go: probably because the man was so pathetic. He would never have done it in the old days and neither would his father. But now he found it too demoralising to go after minnows. It was a risk for the organisation and he preferred to save his attention for where it was needed. So instead he had paid for the girl himself, along with a doctor and a new dress. He couldn't even remember having sent Curtis a warning.

Eric sighed. He could hardly complain if people forgot who he was when he was doing the same himself. Maybe Curtis had been reminded somehow and was calling to settle up? It would be fair to give him the chance at least. Eric laughed at himself even as he had the thought: since when was a second chance fair on anyone? Yes, he was changing too much for things to end well for the firm. More likely Curtis was calling to ask for drugs, or for a gig in one of the clubs, or just accidentally from his pocket. Eric had discovered extraordinary things from those calls and people's carelessness amazed him. He realised that he had to pick up, if only from curiosity and to stop Curtis calling anyone else to get to him.

'Eric?' he heard. The voice was molten and slow. He had heard that Curtis had gone dry but it was no surprise that he had fallen off. They all do.

Roger was looking across his mixers and computer screens, thinking that his power was rooted in them and in the people he knew. There was silence at the other end of the line then he heard the old voice. It was dense and flat, like a lake frozen all the way to the bottom.

'Who is this?' said Eric. Roger was looking at the framed discs again.

'Roger Curtis,' he said weightily.

'And what does Roger Curtis want?' said Eric.

Roger told him.

'And I want to be there,' he finished. Eric made a neutral sound. It was more incredible than any of the things which he had guessed: Curtis actually wanted another favour. He was too surprised to think of an answer.

'Wait by your phone,' he said.

Eric looked along the line of freezers, amazed at the distant realities in which some people lived. Curtis seemed to think that if you were rich, things happened for free; and that they kept on happening regardless of what you did. The idea itself was good, funny even, and Curtis wanted to be there. Well perhaps some things do happen for free. He turned to someone behind him.

'Get Speed Dog to come in,' he said.

*

Dominic paced the empty upper bar of the Club. He should not be this angry. Nothing Nick tried to do now could make a difference to the deal. His options were in place and he could use them to take control of the mine tomorrow if he wanted. Still, his jaw was locked dangerously tight over his crowns. Another wave passed through him, higher than the building. His muscles tightened further under the double-breasted jacket. This is how people fight, he thought. This is how we fight.

Nick Paget was going to war with him. Nick Paget. In not one of Dominic's memories of school did Paget feature properly; none of the things they were caught for and none of the things they got away with. Where had he been instead? Not playing sports or bedding girls, that was for sure. Probably sucking on a joint somewhere and playing the guitar. And what had he done since? Nothing. Wandered around Asia and lived on a boat. The man was not a doer, which is why he was a nobody. Now, finally, he was rolling the dice; and he had chosen to roll them against Dominic.

An echo of comedy came to him, mocking not only Nick Paget but his own anger. How could he be wasting it on this? Did Nick even understand who walked through the doors of this club? What the top of the pyramid actually looked like? Or that it even existed? He tried to imagine Paget's life with him as an enemy and realised it was impossible for doors to be closed to

Nick as none were even open. The man was too irrelevant even to provide him with the tools for revenge! He shook his head but the chattering cycle of laughter only grew louder. Someone would have to be very big or very small to set themselves up against him: no-one in the middle could have thought of it. Yet the smile had spread itself across tendons thick with anger. It was his own fault for even entering into partnership with someone so naive. He had known at the time it was a mistake to leave Nick with fifteen percent of the deal. Just do it properly next time.

He ran through the situation again, disturbing the waters even as he looked for calm. The drilling results had arrived and now Paget had ignored three of his calls, which meant the results were positive and he was trying to take over the mine. But the options which Dominic had written made that impossible. Everything pointed to the fact that at the stroke of a pen, he could now own eighty-five percent of an undiscovered gold seam. Anger was the very opposite of what he should be feeling! And yet still his breath was coming in quivering scoops, each one stoking the fission in his chest.

The only other possibility was that the deal had failed. Yet why would Paget then ignore him? None of his money had even been on the table and Nick Paget probably lived on failed deals: why react differently now? No. Nick Paget, financially and legally illiterate, in his old suit, was trying to rip him off. There was no point in calling Roger Curtis. Either he would also be on the receiving end of Paget's quixotic little attempt – that's right, thought Dominic, go to war with *him* – or an accomplice in it. The idea of them conspiring together was even more embarrassing than Nick trying it on his own, and he felt even more belittled by his anger.

He rotated the empty tumbler in his hand and tried harder to look for calm. If it was not the outcome that had done this to him, it must be the attempt itself. Yes, finally the glint of reason. If he let it pass this time, next time it would be worse, until soon it reached someone big enough to count. So this anger was not completely vain or illogical, it was actually showing him something important: that he had to go to some ridiculous little barge to stop the loss. In person, this evening. It had to be something Paget would never forget, and he pictured stopping at his flat to pick up a shotgun.

Cesare watched him from the shadow of a curtain, his hands cupped together on his chest. He had never spoken to a member about his life before, and the room had never felt so small. How could he tell Mr Bannerman that she did love him and she wanted to see him? But he had to try. He closed his eyes and prayed for a moment then stepped into the light. Dominic looked at him and Cesare drew breath.

'Whisky. Ardbeg. Double. Thank you,' said Dominic.

He turned back to the bar, and Cesare nodded then withdrew.

*

Butch was parked in Vauxhall, across from the Houses of Parliament. He looked across the river at the

261

last of the evening light washing the side of Big Ben. The black sleeves of his tee shirt stretched over his biceps as he steadily gripped the wheel then released it. Parliament only made him think back to the hostel. One day all of them were going to get it. Not just the ones this evening. All of them.

Speed Dog was slumped against the window in the passenger seat. A rolled cigarette sat between pale lips and the colourless hair was gathered in a ponytail. His small eyes moved in a lined face and a tank top hung from his narrow shoulders. Butch had never seen him eat: he lived off other things. Two men passed the van, going to one of the bars.

'You like it down here, don't you Butch?' said Speed Dog. 'Your kind of area, isn't it?'

Butch looked away, feeling the thin smile and torturing eyes, and his large face flushed under the shaven head. The holdalls were in the back. One day.

*

Timur stood above him with legs the size of pillars. The giant muzzle lowered like a black sun and Nick smelt the suffocating breath, all oxygen drawn from it by the giant lungs. Timur prodded him and he rolled, the voice crushed from his chest. He heard the other's thoughts: 'I do not know you,' they said. The eyes narrowed and the markings around them became long and oriental. He saw a round helmet and thin beard trailing from the chin, and his blood ran cold. The Emperor Timur. His captor's eyes darkened as they looked at him, then darkened again. 'I do not know you,' they said. 'Why have you been near my buildings?'

Punishments were taking place all around and Nick's chest was heavy with another pain. The path, he tried to say; I am on it, we are the same. Silent words came to him, not from the Emperor's mind but from his own. 'Everything you have loved has hated you.' Thank you, he thought; finally a glimpse of the truth. If it is too late for my own people to have me, then let me love nothing and die.

His sister was near. She was there because of him but would only be enslaved and prostituted by the Emperor. He tried to shout to her but darkness gathered and only Timur's curling smile remained. He was falling and thick unoxygenated air rushed between rough walls. There were bones in them and creatures that lived in solid earth. He turned slowly but his limbs did not glance from the sides and he realised this was a new torture; the seemingly endless fall followed by a crushing impact. He heard a trickle of laughter and knew the Emperor was near the opening of the mine. But the laughter was not for him, who had already been forgotten. It was for someone next to Timur; a favourite from the court. A single mocking note reached him from the *ney*. It was Prince Cantemir. You should not have abandoned me, went the Prince's thoughts; for now I have abandoned you.

Forgive me, thought Nick, his face wet with sweat or tears. The walls were tightening and his limbs were no longer free but held tight against his sides. He was bound by a chain and rough fabric gagged his face. The water of the Thames was around him, first seeping through then driven by cold pressure. The river was as deep as a trench, its surface narrowing to a line as the city folded out of sight. I'm sorry Timur; he thought: I would not have put you here if I had known. The line disappeared and blackness filled his lungs.

Nick's arm struck Charlotte's hand as she tried to reach his brow. He had been awake when she arrived, his face drawn and fearful, and taken the antibiotics automatically. The tonic had flowed from the sides of his mouth like an invalid as she held the bottle for him. 'No doctors,' he had said, his eyes not focusing on her. 'Only Bruce.' Soon after, he had slipped back into unconsciousness and started to twitch before his visions. Words half formed on his lips; a long name beginning with K, then Dominic's name; then Timur's, which he seemed to speak with terror. Then her own. She gave him her hand and first he gripped it tightly then snatched his away.

She had seen him like this before and knew it would lift eventually. The strain made him look even more like their father. For years the same lines had been forming across his forehead as the strong cheeks and curved nose became more pronounced. She wanted to lie down next to him while he was weak and could not resist. For years she had tamed her love in order to give him what he wanted, which was to be left alone. It is why she wanted him to have Samantha; not for the sake of it but because then at least he would be loved. He talked all the time about love but for him it seemed only to be a force in the universe or a philosophical idea, never an experience. That vain separation would keep him alone until the end of his life, and she couldn't bear the thought of him haunting his cafes and libraries as an old man.

She felt the familiar bell of hypocrisy. What had she to say about love? Here she was, loved but not loving; and castigating Nick for not doing the same. When she had married, it was Nick who had given her away. Afterwards, he had been warm with Daniel but silent with her; probably because he didn't want to disturb his quiet relief. If she bolted from David now, he would be furious. And what kind of conversation would he be able to have with Dominic afterwards?

She looked out of the porthole window to where dusk clung heavily to the shore. The thoughts exhausted her; the past and future condensing impossibly into the moment. She thought of Rachael's illness, and the way Adam had quietly adopted his father's worry for her, and Daniel's hourly messages from work, and Tabitha's swift arrival with food sealed neatly into Tupperware. Just for this night, she could be adrift from it all here on the boat. Nick had stilled into a deeper sleep. At the sound of his even breaths, the floor of her own tiredness started to give way. She looked at him for a last time, then went into the main cabin and lay down on the hide-covered sofa.

*

When Imogen's phone buzzed for the second time, she shut down her computer screen and hurried across the

265

empty office. Cesare's first message, saying Dominic was at the club, had made her smile with ignoble satisfaction. But she soon realised the illicit knowledge was useless on its own. So what if he was at the Club? If she went over, it would be no different from being there normally; except for his surprise and likely irritation. So she had taken another chance and written back: 'Please tell me when he goes... I must see him alone. Thank you Chesare xxx'.

There followed an uneasy silence and she felt a glimmer of worry about herself. It was one thing to manipulate people using sex, or greed, or their dislike of someone; but something else to do it using their goodness. Yet it was an iota compared to what Dominic probably did, and worth it to see something from behind the facade of his life. It could be anything, even him going to the gym or buying food on the way home. A sight like that might be mundane enough to put her off or real enough to make him lovable. Or she might see something that hinted at a deeper eccentricity which drew her in further. She had seen something new break through at Toadsmoor House, when he had dealt out peevish contempt to Alexander Rosenheim before fleeing to his wine glass. Yet it had been strangely reassuring to see the chameleon change so helplessly into the colour of his caste, and she had found herself wanting to hug him. Maybe there wasn't anything new to know? Maybe he was just a busy, successful man who didn't see her more often for fear of trespassing on her younger life? She felt a flush of tenderness at the idea.

But when Cesare's second message said Dominic was

getting ready to leave, the equivocal thrill returned. She was hungry for a result; even the sight of infidelity, if that was even what to call it. As the lift doors closed, she wondered if she would ever tell him about having done this. What if she just ran straight into him outside the Club? He would greet her casually and fix the next date, his life once again impervious.

The outside air was damp and heavy after the dry office, and a passing taxi braked sharply as she hailed it. She got in and told the driver to join the rank across the street from the Club. It was only a hundred yards away and she didn't have long to catch him. When they rounded the corner and stopped, an odd silence settled. She pretended to use her phone but knew the driver could see her eyes flicking to the unmarked green door. Dominic never left quickly as there were always greetings to be made on the way out. But when the driver finally cut the engine, she was sure she had missed him.

The door opened and Dominic's small shape was framed against the warm interior light. Her heartbeat accelerated. When he stepped out into the darkening street, she sat back sharply. His lips were tightly pursed and his eyes wide and unblinking. There was no pleasantly or tip for the doorman and the owner's dog stood ignored inside the doorway. He had become a different man. Even at work when the fund crashed, she had never seen anyone look like that. She could usually see through people's anger to the powerlessness beneath it. But Dominic didn't look powerless: he looked like he was about to do something. She remembered the cowhand who her father had once stopped from driving to the village with a loaded shotgun. But that man had been on fire, and even from here she could see the ice in Dominic's eyes. His head turned slowly towards the cab rank and she shrank into the seat. Maybe he wasn't angry at all? Maybe this was just *him*?

Go home, she thought. Go home now. But she imagined being scared the next time she saw him and not knowing why. He was crossing to the front of the cab rank and she leant forwards to the driver.

'Follow that taxi,' she said, clearing her throat when her voice stumbled on the words. The driver raised his eyebrows and she wondered if he had ever heard those words before or if they had ever even been spoken in London. They emerged onto Park Lane and she sat back with her eyes on Dominic's taxi, which eerily prefigured the manoeuvres of her own. They passed the high wall of Buckingham Palace gardens crowned with razor wire then kinked around Victoria Station onto Vauxhall Bridge Road. On the straight mile leading down to the river, she imagined Dominic's cab swerving to a stop and him jumping out to confront her. She didn't know whether he was scaring her or she was scaring herself. It was a relief when the other car moved right to turn along the river, as at least she wouldn't be pulled across the bridge into some unknown hinterland of South London. Her taxi pulled up behind Dominic's and she saw his head leaning sideways on outstretched fingers. Her driver looked impassively out of his window as the motor idled and she wondered what he was thinking: probably that this was a new craze or some obscure sex game. The lights changed and the two cars swung right across the wide junction and onto the Embankment.

She closed her eyes and felt the embarrassment rising on her cheeks. This was Pimlico, where he lived! He was simply going home and would probably see her drive past when he got there. As the other car indicated into Dominic's street, she leant forward to give the driver her own address. But the indicator on the other taxi died as she was about to speak. She froze then slumped back as her car accelerated after it along the river.

Suddenly she was too exhausted to care where Dominic was going, or about anything that happened in London. She was tired of the city and this paranoid person she had become; and thought instead of her brother at home, dividing his time neatly between the farm and the pub. She decided to take her car on when Dominic stopped then just call him. They would see each other and talk like normal people. She would find out what had made him angry and they would talk about the future, if there was one. Right now, it didn't really matter: anything would be better than this. She felt better as they glided along the river in the last of the twilight. Then the car ahead braked and began to pull in near the end of a bridge. The driver looked at her expectantly, and the trap of curiosity snapped shut.

'Turn right and stop,' she heard herself say. Dominic had got out and was paying his taxi as she slid anonymously past. Her car pulled in at the end of the street which came off the bridge and she looked over its curved roof as she paid the driver. Dominic was walking towards a large gate which gave onto the river. She had the crazy thought he was going to drown himself, and remembered thinking when he was at that garden party that he could do anything without surprising her. Only now was it actually true.

Her taxi pulled away and there was nothing between them but a wide road junction. She crossed the road quickly and mounted Albert Bridge, then crossed the road it carried and looked carefully around one of the white metal pillars. Dominic's progress had been stopped by a large metal grille, behind which a covered walkway led down to two lines of houseboats. Moored on either side of a floating pontoon, they looked like a giant bracelet unclipped and laid on the water. Electric bulbs on the suspension lines of the bridge lit up polished wooden masts and white metalwork, and she saw white foam where the outgoing tide parted around the boats.

Dominic had posted himself by the gate and was smoking casually. A couple in black tie emerged from one of the boats and walked arm in arm along the floating pier. She saw him notice and distance himself a little from the gate. When the couple reached it, he looked up from his phone in apparent surprise. Words were exchanged and they let him through. Her fear came back sharply as his shape invaded the private space and started to descend the long ramp. She stood closer to the metal pillar and felt the day's heat radiating from it. Dominic reached the pier and started walking slowly along it, checking the names of the boats against something in his hand. He reached the last boat and stared at it, his grey shape motionless against the dark water.

She ran off the bridge and along the embankment, stopping level with the final boat. The lights were on and curtains drawn across the windows of the main cabin. She could see Dominic moving on the deck and her fear voiced itself with an unwelcome clarity. What if he did something bad? No, she couldn't just leave and let things to take their course. At the very least that would mean being eaten up by curiosity next time she saw him, and every time after that. She took a breath of the Thames air and looked for anyone else who might be converging on the gate, and caught herself expecting someone in a captain's hat or sporting a tattoo of an anchor. When a women left one of the houseboats, Imogen stationed herself by the gate and started toying with her phone as Dominic had done. When the gate swung open, she looked up.

'I'm so sorry,' she said. 'I'm late for something and my friend isn't answering.' She held up her phone apologetically and the woman's lips twitched in amusement.

'And which boat would you be visiting?' she said.

'Last on the left,' said Imogen, pointing to the one that Dominic had boarded. The woman looked her up and down with her hand on the gate.

'It would be,' she said dryly.

Imogen gathered herself and walked through with icy thanks, noting where the exit button stood like a green mushroom inside the gate. She smelled the river below and felt the long drop as she descended the narrow walkway. What if Dominic had turned around and she walked straight into him? She would have to pretend to know someone on another boat, probably implying it was a man to make him go away. She stepped onto the pontoon and felt the swirling water beneath, then slowed as she walked towards its end. The less space that remained, the less excuse she had for being there; and Dominic's reaction was unimaginable.

She approached the final boat, placing one foot silently in front of the other. It was smaller than the others and the wooden superstructure needed work. The roof was scattered with unkempt pots of herbs and some washing hung from a side rail. She just made out the name *Roxanne* on the stern. Long windows ran down each side and the lights were on inside. If Dominic was outside, he was on the bow or crouched on the far side of the cabin. If he was inside, the lit interior would stop him seeing out. She placed a hand on the pontoon rail and slowly lowered herself so the whole cabin came into view.

Dominic was sitting on a piano stool, leaning forwards and staring at a sleeping woman. The rug had slipped down to cover her lower half and one arm was raised behind her head. Imogen could see where the heavy linen dress had shifted unnaturally and the bra would be digging in. The women was older than her, with pale blonde hair that fell across an uncomplicated face. Her eyes seemed to be large under the pale lids and Imogen thought she was probably beautiful. So this is who had dragged Dominic into that furious pit of intent. It was hard to imagine him being angry with a woman: or perhaps only a woman could have done it? She saw the anger still carved deeply into his tanned face and knew in an instant that she could never raise such emotion in him. The eyebrows were creased in confusion and his eyes had widened. Finding her asleep seemed to have opened something else in him, and now he was frozen.

Imogen leant back a little and caught herself on the rail of the pontoon. Sitting at her desk an hour earlier, she could never have imagined something like this. Yes, there was more; but it was not a more she wanted to know. She should go. Yet that would mean this scene being imprinted on her mind forever; seeing it and forever not knowing who the woman was or what happened when she awoke. A fight, or sex, or something else.

A boat creaked and her shoulders twitched. What if a neighbour found her like this? Dominic and the woman would soon be outside confronting her. She tried to picture herself leaving now, slipping back through the gates into her normal life carrying this jagged new secret. Impossible. She slipped off her shoes and put them in her bag, then moved sideways onto the *Roxanne*'s gangplank. The warm metal took her weight silently and she could just see Dominic through the rear window of the cabin. The boat rolled minutely as she placed a foot on the deck but he did not move. She moved along the perimeter of the stern with one hand on the rail, then silently along the blind side of the cabin. She heard the distant traffic on the riverbank and imagined the curtains being swept aside in front of her. When the woman woke up, Imogen promised herself that she would melt away again onto the pontoon. She reached the bow and a new perspective came into view through the front window. She saw the pale surface of a grand piano; then Dominic's suit stretched over his shoulders; then the woman peacefully facing them both. She lowered herself onto the bow and cupped her chin in her hands.

19

Dominic felt more deeply than anything that Charlotte did not belong there. He looked at the small mouth which had sought his; the strong neck which he had kissed; the pale underside of her arm. One breast was pushed upwards under the linen dress and the hair which had fallen across her face was being parted by each breath. His eyes followed her legs under the covering to where her strong, small feet emerged. He had noticed them before with their high arches and pearly nails.

How could she be the sister of the person who lived here? The atavistic shapes of the room crowded down on her, plucking at her silver pendant and unmarked skin. Coloured Arabic characters were framed on the walls and the surfaces were covered with black wood carvings. A smell of carpets and stale incense hung in the air. What drove Nick Paget to want to be something other than himself? Men like that ended up as halflings, rejecting their own and rejected by those they wanted to be like. They became nothing.

At least Charlotte could never live in this pastiche of someone else's culture. He thought of her dark humour and casual knowledge at their lunch two weeks before. The alcohol flush had risen on those pale cheeks and she had started to look at him with knowing, suppressed eroticism. Why hadn't he kissed her afterwards? The strange suspension which he had recognised in Scotland was stronger than ever. It was a kind of realisation through unrealisation; a bringing forward of the future into the present; a waiting. But waiting for what? For her to leave her life and for him to lose his? Or for now? He imagined her waking and smiling, then drawing him onto the sofa with her. Seeing her was like an antibody to all his anger and now he could neither leave nor wake her. Her sleep was too perfect: it was the life they all wanted. The wrongness which had swirled around him all day was the same wrongness which she had felt for all her years of marriage. Those compromises had broken in on them both, adulterating them and turning life into something less. But now, finally, was the chance to un-compromise their lives and be together. He stood and started moving towards her.

White light punched his retinas from the windows. He raised an arm but the sight of Charlotte stumbling from the sofa already left a trail. They met and he took her shoulders as her own blinded eyes tried to focus on him.

'Dominic?' she said, her voice heavy with sleep and fear. He held her for a moment then laid her back on the sofa. A hissing sound had filled the boat and sparks were falling across the windows.

'Stay here,' said Dominic, feeling the unruly kick of his heartbeat. He moved out onto the stern but white patches like supernovas moved across his sight, hiding parts of the bridge. He turned to see two bright jets of heat pointed into the gap between the boat and the pontoon. An industrial burning filled the air and molten metal hissed into the water below. One of the torches changed its angle, cutting a shower of orange as it passed the metal railing of the boat. It was being pointed towards him. He raised his arm but a rush of airless heat gripped him and bright light appeared behind his eyelids. He felt the skin of his face tighten and the hair singe from his eyebrows, and realised he was falling.

Butch looked away as Speed Dog lowered the oxyacetylene cutter. A delirious grin split Roger's face behind the welding mask. Alcohol fumes were gathering behind it and he couldn't see much through the darkened glass. A smell like a volcano rose around him; lava, gas and melting plastic. The more he breathed, the more powerful he was in his knight's helmet. Hardware; the right tools for the job! Uncle Eric had sent two men immediately: the old London, still answering his call. The men had picked him up behind Sloane Square then driven here purposeful and silent. One was small and looked like a builder, the other large and silent beneath a shaved head. The builder had walked up onto the bridge with some binoculars when they arrived. 'One minute,' he said when he got back. 'We're running the torches for one minute, then thirty seconds back to the van. Anyone left, we don't know you.' His small eyes had rested for a moment on Roger, then his associate nodded and lifted the equipment out of the van. They had penetrated the gate easily and Roger lead them to the boat. And now it was happening! There was a heavy splash as one of the moorings gave. One of the torches died and the gap between the pier and the bow started to grow. He craned forwards to see the other one go and made out a figure crawling in the back of the boat. Suddenly his arms seemed trapped and he thought they must be tangled in the railings of the pontoon. But now they seemed to be pinned behind him and he was being moved towards the gangplank.

He shouted but the sound deafened him inside the damp metal casket. It was lifted brutally from his head and the boat was white again without the dark glass. He saw it was Dominic at the back and realised that he too could now be recognised. His arms were free again and he was about to turn when a boot gripped the small of his back and hurled him down the gangplank. He hit the deck as the metal walkway detached and fell behind him, leaving one leg suspended over the water. He pulled himself up and turned to see the space widening between the boat and the pier. A white power cable rose into a straight line then detached and splashed into the water. He gripped and pulled himself away from the edge, his eyes wide. The men had gone and the pier was already five yards away. He looked over his shoulder and saw the trees and headlights of London slipping away.

An animal scream tore the night, hurting his lungs after the heavy chemical vapours. Even his own people had betrayed him! Dominic must have paid them; or Neil, nursing his grudge from the band; or Irina and her Russian friends. So what if he had hit her? She shouldn't have tried to stop him coming here to take what was his. But he didn't need any of them now. Not Eric and his sleaze, or Irina, or those lawyers and charlatans. Nothing that happened on those banks mattered because what he wanted was here. He stood. This was his boat now. The figure at the back was trying to get up, and Roger saw the wide lapels and disturbed hair. He pulled himself quickly along the side of the boat, grabbed the lapels and threw Dominic back to the floor.

'*You cunt!*' he screamed, landing a foot in the soft stomach. 'Where is my fucking money?'

Dominic had just begun to breathe again after the rush of carbon monoxide but the kick pushed this new air from his lungs. A figure rose above him, the cabin light falling on blond hair and enlarged eyes.

'Roger?' he whispered. The bilge was cold against his head again and he knew the burned smell was coming from himself. Darkness was closing around him and he had to get air. 'Roger,' he whispered. 'Help me.'

Roger leant down and started pulling Dominic towards the cabin by his tie. The knot tightened around his neck and he struggled along the floor, trying to stop the noose biting deeper. They reached the cabin door and its metal lip scored him as he was dragged over it. Charlotte, help me, he thought. But when he stretched his eyes around the cabin floor he found it empty. He felt a foot under him. It turned him over then rested heavily on his throat and he saw Roger's blue eyes smiling down at him.

Charlotte trembled as she held Nick's head, cupping each temple in her hands.

'Wake up,' she whispered through the tears. '*Wake up.*'

Nick's eyelids flickered. Charlotte, he thought, back from Timur's soldiers. He tried to reach her but she dissolved. I'm sorry Dad, he thought.

Roger stood over Dominic with one foot on his windpipe. He had dragged the man effortlessly. I am strong, he thought.

'You *know...*' he said. He bent forwards and the pressure on Dominic's throat became critical. 'You know where my money is. Now give it back to me.'

Dominic registered the words and Roger's stupidity released adrenalin in him. He tried to move but his face glowed with pain.

'I don't fucking know,' he whispered with breath drawn from somewhere. He conned me too, he tried to say. Roger bent lower over him.

'I don't believe you, you *ponce,*' he breathed, and brought a hand backwards across Dominic's face. The damaged nerves felt nothing at first then a deep pain began below the surface. Dominic closed his eyes. Don't hit me again, he thought. The boat titled and something touched his right hand. His fingers closed on smooth wood and he brought the object up hard against the side of Roger's knee. The pressure disappeared from his neck and he sucked in the air, pulling himself away with the weapon still in his hand. It was some kind of phallus, carved from dark wood. The blood stung as it coursed under his cheeks and he pulled himself up on the piano stool then turned to face Roger.

Imogen's fingers shook as she tried to operate her phone. She had flattened herself against the other side when three men formed out of the darkness then heard a terrible scream as the boat started to move. A crack of thunder split the sky and she almost dropped the phone. She held it to hear ear and heard distant ringing.

'Which service do you require,' said a female voice.

'Police,' she said, hearing the fear in her voice. They were passing under a bridge and she thought for a moment that she would lose reception. A male voice came on the line.

'Go ahead,' it said, and Imogen composed herself.

'I am on a houseboat on the Thames,' she said as calmly as she could. 'It has been cut loose and hijacked by a man named Roger Curtis. He used to have a band... I think he's famous.'

'Which band?' said the voice, and Imogen searched for the name.

'The Ice Machine,' she said. She could see another bridge approaching, the current dividing fast around unforgiving stone pillars. She had no idea the river moved so fast.

'I know them,' said the man. There was a pause. 'You are saying that Roger Curtis of Ice Machine has hijacked your houseboat?' The air was cooling and Imogen's jacket was damp. Another crack of thunder sounded and a heavy raindrop broke on her head.

'It's not my boat,' she said. 'But yes.'

'Do you have the name of the owner of the boat?' said the man.

'I don't fucking know!' she said, fighting the rising panic. 'But can I tell you where we are?'

'Oh, I know where you are,' said the man lightly. 'You've been taken hostage by an Eighties music legend.

On a houseboat, was it? Just one more question...'
Imogen blinked and a new fear started to close around
her. 'Is Elvis with you too?' he said. She heard a
suppressed laugh then the tone changed. 'Listen, young
lady,' said the man. 'I have your number here. Do you
realise that wasting police time is an offence?'

'How fucking *dare* you?' she hissed. 'Just do your
fucking job and get some people here!' The line went
dead and Imogen looked at the screen of the phone. Its
battery was almost dead and tears pricked at her eyes.
Next time sound scared, she thought; as scared as you
really are. She wiped her face and looked back through
the window to see the woman had reappeared.

'*Stop it,*' screamed Charlotte from the hatch leading
to the bedroom. Her shoulders were shaking and the
breath coming in uneven gulps. Dominic met her eyes
and saw they were full of tears. 'Just fucking *stop!*'

She swept the contents of a window ledge on to the
floor then slid down the wall. Dominic went to her and
crouched down. Her mouth was stretched wide and her
eyes moving under their film of tears. 'Please stop,' she
whispered, holding Dominic's arm. 'What's happening?'

Dominic smoothed her hair with his other arm
around her shoulders.

'Where's Nick?' he said, and Charlotte closed her
eyes.

'He's downstairs,' she said. 'Please don't hurt him.'
Her chin was shaking. She touched his face and he
couldn't feel it. 'What's happened to your face?' she said.

Dominic felt a cold point at the back of his neck. He
slowly let go of Charlotte and turned to see the long

blade of a sword extended towards him. It was not like the ceremonial swords with which he had grown up but was sharpened with Oriental cruelty. Roger's blonde head hovered behind the hilt. His eyes wore a wide, fixed look and a giggling smile played on his lips. Jesus, thought Dominic. You're drunk.

'*Stand and deliver!*' sung Roger gleefully. 'You're money or your *life!*' He brought the point of the sword up under Dominic's chin and made a sound like a hunting horn. He closed his eyes and took a breath.

'Roger,' he said, his lips cracking as he spoke. 'I'm hurt. Nick's ill. Charlotte hasn't done anything. We have to get off this boat. *Please stop.*' Charlotte's hand found his and he held it tightly.

'He's here, is he?' said Roger. 'How interesting. And where might that be?'

Dominic tried to shake his head but Roger was tapping the flat tip upwards on his chin, and Dominic could see his legs unsteadily compensating for the movement of the boat.

'Don't know, do we?' said Roger. 'Well, maybe Captain Roger should go and have a little look?' His hand was searching for something behind him, and Charlotte whispered in Dominic's ear.

'My phone,' she said. 'It's in my bag.' Dominic inclined his head slightly. He thought he could still feel his own phone inside his jacket. Roger had found a roll of duct tape and looped it onto the sword, sliding it down the blade so it fell in front of Dominic.

'Now, old chap,' said Roger. He had stopped humming and adopted an old-fashioned English accent.

Dominic wanted to kill him.

'I would be much *obliged*,' said Roger, gesturing first to Charlotte then to the piano. 'If you would tie that there *lady* to that there piano *leg*.' His gestures with the sword were getting wider and passing closer to them, and Dominic tried not to look at his leering face. The lights of the shore were passing quickly outside and rain had started to drum on the roof.

'Roger,' he said slowly, and Roger raised his eyebrows in surprise at being addressed. 'Can you please explain what you think has happened?'

'Now a very great man once said,' said Roger, stepping forwards. 'That some people rob you with a fountain *pen*.' He brought the sword across in a diagonal slash and Dominic heard the blade pass in front of face. He could smell the alcohol now. He knew of dry drunks serving long prison sentences for things they had done during a binge. Charlotte was moving behind him and he willed her to stop.

'I tell you what,' said Roger obsequiously. 'Perhaps *madame* would care to secure *sir* first?' He pointed the blade towards where the roll of tape lay on the floor, then towards the piano. Dominic nodded. The police must arrive soon, he thought; we're in the middle of a city.

'Do it,' he said over his shoulder to Charlotte. He started crawling slowly towards the piano with Charlotte following. Halfway across the room, she reached towards her bag. Roger turned and brought the sword down in a long arc on her arm. She screamed and Dominic's heart stopped. Outside, Imogen dropped her phone and it slid off the metal deck. The side of the blade slapped onto Charlotte's forearm and she collapsed. Dominic quickly gathered her under the piano. Roger picked up her handbag and emptied the contents over the rug.

'If you'd pick up that *telepho-o-ne!*' he sung, separating the phone from the other contents with his foot. He brought his heel down in a chopping motion and the screen splintered. 'Ground control to Major Tom,' he sung. 'You're circuit's dead there's something *wrong!*'

He approached the piano. Charlotte was shaking under Dominic's arm and a thin line of blood was rising on her forearm. Roger bent over theatrically and prodded under the piano towards Dominic.

'Seaman,' he said. 'This is your captain speaking. Give up your ship to shore, sir! We're going upriver. Cambodia. And that means....' He drew a finger across his lips. '*Radio silence.*'

Dominic didn't move and the blade flew into one of the piano legs, cutting a weald of pale wood in the varnished surface.

'*Your radio, sir!*' screamed Roger. Dominic pulled out his phone and pushed it across the floor. Roger brought the sword down and the phone cracked.

'Radio gaga, wouldn't you say?' he said, cocking his head with a throwaway laugh. He kicked the duct tape towards them. 'Now, if you please? Gentlemen first!'

Charlotte reached out for it, her hand shaking. Dominic listened to the rain as she wound the wide tape around his wrists. It was landing hard on the metal roof and painting the windows in thick rivers. He didn't know how far they had already come, and thought of the widening estuary that ran into the North Sea.

'Roger,' he said, his arms now trussed behind him. 'Whatever has happened, it can't be fixed out here. We need our phones. We need to get to shore. Then we can get you your money. Otherwise...' He remembered Charlotte behind him but carried on. 'We are all going to die,' he said. She let out a wounded cry and her sobs deepened.

The shore! thought Roger. They would be all lined up on it, waiting for him. Neil, still waving his pieces of paper; his ex-wife and Lily; Maurice the banker, waiting to close his account; that traitor Eric Dodds. All of them surrounded by hundreds of lawyers and probably the police. He was the victim but now everything would be pinned on him! They would lead *him* away not these shysters or that gangster Dodds. And to where? He had no house, no friends, no money. And Irina was gone. No. He would not go to the shore without his money; without the life they had stolen.

'We're all going to die, are we?' he said bending down to Dominic's face. 'Or are you trying to frame me? It *was* your little scheme, wasn't it?'

Roger turned to tie up Charlotte and Dominic felt bubbles rising in his bloodstream. You are going to die on this boat, he thought. Because as soon as I am free, I am going to kill you.

Nick sensed the boat moving. It had been running away from him, becoming smaller and smaller; but now he was on it and somehow it was moving. He saw the wooden ceiling and heard rain outside. Charlotte had gone and he was alone. The boat would be his bier, carrying him away like Timmy. The thought relieved him and his breath came more naturally as he slipped back into sleep. Or death, he thought; that infinite sleep.

The rain fell in thick curtains between Imogen and the bank, wrapping itself around her and flowing down inside her clothes. When her phone slipped into the water, her heart had lurched. But still she had moved onto the roof to start signalling. Now they were out in middle stream passing the South Bank, where she made out the shapes of people hurrying with their heads turned down against the water. She wanted to shout but the rain sounded like hail on the surface of the water and she would only be heard in the cabin. She turned the other way towards the Savoy but it seemed even further. The trees looked like ghosts behind the sheets of rain and the noise hid the sound of the traffic. She sank to her knees and felt tears rising again. The sight of the blade falling on that woman's arm kept coming back, and she had gone cold inside.

She wiped the water from her eyes and slid down on the blind side of the cabin, her bare feet landing numbly on the metal, then reached the forward window and crept in front of it. The nausea came back stronger. Dominic and the woman were now sitting on the floor tied to the piano. Curtis was pouring a drink on the side and the sword hanging from his hand. Dominic was looking at him with death in his eyes; a wild, hot hatred that she had not seen before. Beside him, the woman had stopped crying and was trembling with her eyes closed. Imogen rolled back against the side window. Another bridge was approaching but she couldn't even see over its lip to anyone on the pavement. The boat passed under it and the rain stopped. She looked at the beautiful curved underside and imagined the echo it would give, then herself jumping off and trying to hold onto the sheer stone.

The rain reappeared on her head and she looked pleadingly at the edge of the bridge as it slipped away. The roof of a passing bus was visible over the side wall and something in the familiar sight released a flat, warm feeling. Thoughts of home appeared; her brothers, the farm, her school friends who had stayed in the county. Her parents would be going to bed now and she wondered if they had this weather too; then what a good thing it was that her brother was taking over the farm and not her. The sound of the rain retreated and she saw the view from her home. The plastic-wrapped bales of silage looked like giant stones dotted across the fields and the water ran on their shining surfaces. It was a world that she was glad to have shared. She had the drowsy thought that this must be what lost mountaineers feel before they go to sleep in the snow. No. Not now. She crouched again to look into the cabin. You've only got one chance at this Immie, she thought.

Nick woke again. This time he felt the layers of unconsciousness beneath and knew he had to fight them. The boat was moving and he had to do something. He lifted himself on a weak arm and slid his legs over the edge of the bed. The floor was moving terribly and the sound of falling water drummed in his ears. I'm in the tropics, he thought; no wonder the malaria came up. He began moving slowly towards the steps, holding onto the side of the cabin. The roof of the main room came into view through the hatch and he lifted himself onto the first step. There was a man he recognised standing over his drinks tray. Nick knew him; and not from the dreams but from recently. The man turned towards him with a smile.

'Nick,' he said broadly, and started walking towards him. 'My old friend.'

Noises reached Nick from the piano. Its legs had turned into people who were shouting at him. No, he thought; no more visions, I am awake now.

'Roger,' he breathed. 'Thank you for coming. I'm... I'm sorry.' He couldn't remember what he was sorry for but at least Roger had come to help him. Roger the vegetarian, who had brought him the nice wine. He of all people had come. Thank you, he thought; and it gave him the energy to get up another step. Roger was coming towards him and the voices from the piano were getting louder. No, he thought: I am well now, I will not hear you! I am well and we are reconciled. He reached out and Roger reached back, his arm long and shining.

Imogen walked swiftly across the cabin, picking up a stone carving. Roger heard and turned but she was still too far. She threw it and it broke the window above Nick. Glass fell on him and he slipped back down the stairs. Roger stared at her, the sword held wide. Dominic blinked. Imogen bent forwards and ran. Her shoulder connected at the meeting of Roger's rib cage.

She felt the air go out and heard the weapon fall from his hands as they pitched down the short steps. She thought Roger's head was struck as they went down, then she heard a cry as someone else took the impact below. She stood quickly with a foot on Roger's stomach and ran back up the steps. The sword lay on the floor and she stamped on it near the hilt but the metal rebounded. She picked it up and took it to the piano, where Dominic was looking at her like a child. His face was red and his eyebrows were gone, and she remembered the scream earlier.

'Imogen,' he said. 'What are you..?'

'What are any of us doing here, you mean?' she snapped. 'I don't know.'

The woman was looking her with a kind of miraculous joy.

'Hello!' said Charlotte. The sword was too long to cut the tape easily so Imogen ran the blade inside the binding and sawed backwards. The tape sprang open and Dominic pulled himself free with a tear then leant forwards, rubbing his wrists. Imogen moved across to the woman, steadied her wrists away with one hand, and cut her free.

'Thank you,' she said in a small voice. It was somehow the last thing Imogen had expected to hear. The two women looked at each other. 'Who are you?' said Charlotte. She sounded like a young girl. Imogen indicated Dominic.

'I know him,' she said.

'Watch out,' said Dominic. Imogen turned to see Roger had emerged from the stairs and was crossing the cabin, his face crazed and terrified. She swung around but he ran past and out into the back of the boat. Dominic was on his feet beside her. He helped up the woman, who quickly made her way towards the front hatch, then turned to Imogen.

'What are you *doing* here?' he said, and she felt something wearing thin. Here he was; helpless, disfigured, his life saved, and he still wanted to be in control.

'I followed you,' she said coldly.

'Why?' he said, and the old look gleamed from under his naked brows.

'Because I don't trust you,' she said, pushing away his arm and turning back to the door.

'But how did you know where I was?' said Dominic.

Imogen spun around.

'Because,' she spat. 'Cesare told me.'

Dominic raised his head minutely.

'I see,' he said.

'Or would you rather I hadn't?' she said. 'Look at you, you fucking prat! What is happening here anyway?'

Dominic's eyes narrowed.

'I don't know,' he said. 'Something of Nick Paget's went wrong. I was here to help him.' Nick Paget, she thought; that is who had been behind Curtis. Surely this wasn't all about a cricket match?

'And what exactly went wrong?' she said. The rain was blowing through the doorway and she knew Roger was out there: but this might be the only chance to hear.

'I think he lost some of the other guy's money,' said Dominic.

291

'How much?' said Imogen.

Dominic told her. Imogen blinked.

'You are out here for *that*?' she said. 'Do you even live in the real world?'

She looked at him contemptuously then turned away, and Dominic followed her out into the storm. The rain was intensifying and there was no other traffic on the river. Roger was standing by the stern rail, his hair already plastered to his head. He was holding something over the back of the boat. Imogen approached and saw it was his phone. Behind him, the tall shape of the Tate Modern rose like an obelisk into the night.

'Roger,' she shouted. 'I am nothing to do with this. I am here by accident. Please may I borrow your phone?' She saw a flicker of recognition cross his face, then Dominic stepped past her. His voice rose above the rain as he raised his arm.

'How dare you, *dare you*, threaten me?' he said. His fist rounded in a high circle and came down onto the corner of Roger's brow. It was the punch he had been waiting to deliver all his life; back knuckles, powered from the shoulder, connecting above the eye. The phone fell from Roger's hands and he crumpled into the deck. Imogen turned and grabbed Dominic.

'You fucking *prick*,' she screamed. 'You think I want to die on this fucking boat?' She slapped him but the rain was cooling his face and he looked at her defiantly. The railings formed a gate behind where Roger lay. Dominic lifted the latch and kicked it open, but Imogen was already gripping one of Roger's hands.

'Come on,' she shouted. Dominic looked at Roger

coldly then pointed to the river bank.

'Shouldn't we signal for help instead?' he said.

'I've fucking *tried*,' said Imogen. 'We need to make a plan not just wave our fucking arms about!'

Dominic took Roger's other hand and they dragged him over the lip of the door and back into the cabin. Charlotte was helping Nick slowly up the steps and he flinched when he saw Dominic, who tried to offer him a calming look. They dragged Roger into the centre of the rug and sank to the floor on either side of him. Charlotte reached the sofa with Nick, lowered him carefully and sat close into his side.

'What's happening?' said Nick weakly and Charlotte squeezed his hand. Imogen closed her eyes. Dominic looked at him.

'Nick,' he said. 'Can you please explain what has happened to Roger's money?'

Nick told him.

*

Dominic came back into the cabin, a dark shawl of rainwater across the shoulders of his suit.

'It's gone,' he said. The rope to which the dingy had been attached was burned through. He had wanted to wake Roger and find out how it had happened but Imogen had intervened, saying they were better off down to one problem.

'Nick,' said Imogen. 'Does this thing have an engine?' He shook his head. It had barely worked when he bought it, before eight years of decline. He knew the next question.

'Radio?' He shook his head again. The radio had been fun for a year before it died too.

'Flares?' she said, and he had the surreal feeling of failing as a host even though he still didn't know why they were all here. He was starting to feel a new type of sickness gathering on top of the seeping aftermath of the fever.

'It's a static houseboat now,' he said. 'It's not designed for this.' Water was flowing into the cabin from the stern and soaking the steps below the broken window. He knew the lights would go soon, if not from a short circuit then from the battery dying. The storm had become a solid downpour and he remembered the days of humidity which had gone before.

Charlotte was shivering next to him. Every time she closed her eyes, she saw the children. Daniel must be looking for her. He would come. He must.

Dominic wiped one of the windows and saw they were coming into the Square Mile. He was a strong swimmer and had made it across the sea loch that summer. But in a tidal current, it would be suicide. He turned to face them.

'The police must come,' he said. 'They've got London under a microscope. How can they miss this?'

'I called them,' said Imogen. 'They said I was wasting their time.'

'*What*?' said Charlotte, and Imogen looked at her sympathetically.

'I know,' she said.

'They still have the call logged,' said Dominic. 'And

the location. Where is your phone, anyway?'

'I dropped it,' she said, and he looked at her with the old look of disappointment. 'When I thought Charlotte was about to lose an arm,' she snapped.

Charlotte had forgotten the moment and took a sharp intake of breath. I'm sorry for saying that, thought Imogen. But her anger at Dominic was growing. No-one seemed to understand that she had just saved their lives. Instead, he seemed to be absorbing the credit; as if she was some sort of permanent bodyguard of his.

'Where's your *phone*, Nicky?' said Charlotte.

Nick shook his head.

'I can't find it,' he said. 'I think he grabbed it from my room.'

They all looked at the black form with its blonde head, and Dominic found himself admiring the man's crazed efficiency.

'But why was he on the boat?' he said.

'He must have been coming to see me,' said Nick emptily, remembering their phone call.

'Then who cut the moorings?' said Dominic. They all looked at Imogen, who had said she was on the boat when it happened.

'I don't know,' she said, pointing to Roger. 'But he arrived at the same time.'

'How many enemies *do* you have?' said Dominic to Nick.

'Fuck off,' said Charlotte.

Imogen stood up and walked the edge of the cabin. They had already tried signalling from the roof again and unseizing the rudder. She had even thought of

295

opening and closing the curtains to signal but knew no-one on the shore would notice. It seemed incredible to be so helpless.

'How long till we get to the sea?' she said.

The rugs were dark with water and Nick raised his eyes from the floor.

'That's not the problem,' he said, looking at them painfully.

'What is the problem?' said Dominic. His anger was returning in gusts and soon one would take hold.

'The problem is hitting something,' said Nick. 'We must have been under four bridges already. It's a miracle we haven't hit one.' He heard Charlotte's quiet tears start again beside him and tightened his arm around her. 'And when the battery goes, we will have no lights,' he said. 'Which makes it likely we will be hit by another boat.' Charlotte let out a quiet moan. Dominic was staring at him, the eyes wide in his scalded face.

'How long does the battery last?' he said.

'I don't know,' said Nick, and Imogen stepped towards him.

'You don't know how long your own power supply lasts?' she said.

'*Please*,' said Charlotte. 'I have children.'

'I'm sorry,' Imogen said to her. 'Anyway, that means we need a look-out.' She looked at Dominic.

'Fine,' he said. He knew it was a useless job. They had already asked for a torch to signal to other boats and been answered by Nick shaking his head. But at least if he was outside he could act first, and it also meant he would be away from Imogen. Charlotte seemed to have forgotten him and was becoming more catatonic between her outbursts. He wished he could comfort her but it would only horrify her more; her, and the others too. He glanced at her one more time then wrapped himself in one of Nick's coats and went outside.

The rain was cool on his face and puckered the surface of river. The boat had started to rotate in the current and the City of London passed in a slow panorama. He lay back and thought of his last whisky in the Club. It had been served by Cesare, who it turned out had been lingering in the shadows to spy on him. He would complain to Conrad de Salis about that in the morning. Then the stupid flight to the river and almost stopping to arm himself at the flat, which might only have got him killed. Still, it was impossible to believe they were in real danger. It was too absurd to be held hostage this close to civilization, let alone by Roger. Danger was the launch cutting out off Argyll and being caught in the whirlpool. This just felt like a holiday that had gone wrong.

Except for his face. He raised a hand and gingerly touched it. The skin was soft and hurt if he moved it too much. There was no mirror in the cabin and it hadn't seemed right to go and look for one, and part of him didn't even want to see. But the body had its warning systems and he was sure that a serious burn would hurt more. He touched his eyebrows and felt stubble like a burned-off wheat field. Neither of the women had cared; only Charlotte, in the brief moment when she noticed.

He took a deep breath and pulled the old coat closer around him. Whatever had left them out here must be something to do with Roger, and he felt the heavy ball of anger starting to grow again. It was directed against himself as much as the other two. How had he been so blind? He had chosen to partner with them; and then instead of walking away, he had come here. That meant he was no better than them: it meant he was *one* of them. When he got off the boat, he would let it all go. No police, no compensation, no recriminations. Just hand over whatever money was left and go somewhere alone to recover. Finally, a use for the house in Scotland. When he came back to London, he would start again slowly. He would head off the outbursts, make better choices, and find his Stoicism again. And Charlotte? He closed his eyes. For now, he just had to give himself up to the current and wait. It was an odd feeling to be so free. He lay back and closed his eyes, feeling the rain on his eyelids.

*

Roger's head was hurting in two places; a tender throb above his eye and a sharp pain, dug in like an anchor above the top of his spine. Another morning on the floor, which meant it was probably a hotel room. He wondered where and what he had done. The uncertainty was worse than usual and he felt the deep chime of something having gone very wrong. The room was probably wrecked with a girl asleep somewhere. But there was something else too, something bigger. If only he could go back to sleep but the floor was moving, which meant he would have to be sick soon. He opened his eyes and saw wooden walls with small round windows. A ski chalet? Switzerland? He realised he was cold and there was water around him. Wrecked plumbing: an even bigger bill.

'He's awake,' said a female voice.

'I'll get Dominic,' said a man.

'Don't,' said a younger voice.

Dominic, he thought with familiarity. They were discussing him as if he was in hospital. His body did feel heavy. Gravity weighed on each limb and even pulled on the slow beating of his heart. He tried to move and the pain in the back of his head exploded like a nail gun. A girl was standing over him with wet blonde hair falling over a torn business suit. She was stunning, and she was holding knife.

'Please,' he mumbled. 'I haven't done anything.' He pulled himself backwards to the edge of the room. It wasn't even a room; more of a tipping, ruined wooden capsule. Everything was wet and he saw two more people, sitting next to each other.

'Nick,' he said to himself, and started to remember how his life had changed. He had been in Primrose Hill and his money had gone. Irina, the one he had wanted to keep; she had gone too. He had been in touch with Eric Dodds and now his life wasn't going to be his any more. The churning in his stomach and his memory were becoming one. The more he remembered, the sicker he felt. He put his face in his hands then looked up.

'Where are we?' he said.

Nick stood over him.

'Really?' he said.

'Please,' said Roger.

'Not sure I buy that,' said Imogen.

'You tried to kill us,' said Nick.

'No,' said Roger.

'Yes,' said Charlotte. Her eyes were burning on the wet sofa. 'And you still might succeed.'

Roger was touching his scalp with his fingertips as if looking for a break.

'I don't drink,' he said. 'I can't drink. Things happen.'

'Well you did,' said Nick. 'And they have.'

'What things?' said Roger, and Nick heard the fear breaking his voice. He squatted down and felt a sharp pain where Roger had landed on his ribs. But at least his head was clear, which meant the fever had passed or been buried by adrenalin. The sight of Roger's hunted face made him oddly happy that at least Roger didn't hate him any more. He could see Imogen's cynicism was wrong. This wasn't a man who could lie. His forcefulness had gone and been replaced by a gulf of fear and self-hatred: he was more scared of himself now than of them. *Jihad an-nafs*, thought Nick; the war against the self. You were winning it and now you have lost it again, because of me. He touched Roger's shoulder.

'Roger,' he said gently. 'Try to tell us what happened. Who helped you?'

Roger rested an arm across his knees and buried his head inside the elbow. He took a deep breath and the words came out slowly from behind his sleeve. Charlotte came over to listen with a blanket gathered over her shoulders.

'I wanted to warn you... To show you all I was serious,' said Roger. 'So I arranged for the boat to be cut loose. I didn't know who was on it... I didn't want to hurt anyone. I'm sorry.' He was crying quietly into his sleeve and the listeners leaned closer. Nick put a hand on his other shoulder.

'Roger,' he said. 'It's alright. No-one has been hurt.' He thought of Dominic's scalded face. 'But who did it for you? Can you contact them?' And why are you *here*? he thought.

'I can't tell you,' said Roger. 'I really can't. It doesn't work that way.' Nick raised Roger's head and looked into the tear-streaked blue eyes.

'Roger,' he said. 'You must tell us. They are the only people who know we are out here.'

Roger looked into his Nick's eyes and saw the innocence. Nick didn't even know people like Eric Dodds existed. He shook his head again.

'Who is it?' said Nick.

'Please don't tell anyone,' said Roger, and a new fear appeared on his face. Imogen shifted impatiently and Charlotte put a hand on her arm. Nick nodded gently.

'Eric Dodds,' said Roger, and Nick looked blank. 'Uncle Eric,' said Roger. 'If you don't know him, you're lucky.'

Uncle Eric, thought Charlotte; where have I heard that name?

'Will he come back, your uncle?' said Nick. Roger shook his head, and more tears brimmed then escaped.

'They pushed me onto the fucking boat,' he said.

'Why?' said Nick.

'I don't know,' said Roger, wiping an eye. 'I don't fucking know.'

There was a deep crumpling sound and Nick fell forwards onto Roger. Charlotte let out a long, whooping cry of panic. Imogen tried to catch herself on the piano but her hand slid off the wet wood. The rest of Nick's possessions fell and made trails in the wet rugs as they rolled across the floor. There was an electrical noise, and they were in darkness.

'Oh Jesus,' said Nick. 'We've hit something.'

The windows cast pale panels of light which moved across the cabin as the boat turned around its point of impact, showing the piano, then the wet hide on the sofa, then Charlotte and Imogen trying to stand. The floor seemed to be listing already and Nick saw its contents roll towards one end. He raised himself on the window ledge and saw the stone pier of a bridge approaching for the second time.

'Dominic!' said Charlotte.

'Stay here,' said Nick. 'Just stay in the middle.'

The stern was unexpectedly dry in the lee of the bridge, and Nick quickly pulled himself along the side rails to the bow. It was empty. The downbeat of road traffic pulsed from the metal underside of the bridge and echoed between the piers. The shallow ledges which pointed upstream were empty and shining with water.

'Dominic!' he shouted, searching the dark water. '*Dominic!*'

Nick heard a sound and saw hands gripping a down rail between two fenders. He lowered himself and held onto the central mainstay as he reached out. He touched one of the hands and it let go of the metal to grip him. The stone wall was approaching for a second time, and the fenders weren't deep enough to keep a man from the impact. Nick put a foot against the bottom of a railing and pulled. As Dominic found the deck, the boat hit again and Nick lost his hand. Dominic slid to the edge but his feet found the stone wall and he pushed himself back. Nick dragged him into the centre. He was hyperventilating and looked around wildly.

'I nearly died!' he said. The boat passed out from under the bridge and the air was thick with rain again. Tower Bridge rose above them, light glowing from its yellow sandstone and blue metalwork. Nick stood and shouted and waved both arms, but the bridge was too high and slipped away too quickly. He had never seen the river move so quickly and realised the storm drains were emptying into it.

'Dominic,' he shouted. 'I need to look at the boat. Hold onto me.' He flattened himself on the deck and looked over the edge. The hull had crumpled and white splinters of fibreglass showed through the paintwork. Even in the swell, he could see air bubbling from them. He pulled himself back in.

'It's fucked!' he shouted. 'We're sinking!' Fear covered Dominic's face. 'Come on,' said Nick. 'We need to get to the others.' They entered the cabin and Dominic started when he saw Roger awake but Nick stilled him with a hand. Imogen was rapidly emptying the cupboards.

'Do you have any life jackets?' she shouted.

'Of course I don't!' Nick shouted back. 'Or else you'd

be wearing them!'

'What happened to the lookout?' said Imogen.

'Does it fucking matter?' said Nick. 'This boat is going to sink. We have to get off.'

'How?' said Roger, pulling himself to his feet.

'We have to swim,' said Nick. Someone grabbed his arm. It was Charlotte, close into him. She looked at him with breaking eyes.

'Please don't make me do it, Nicky,' she said. 'I can't swim in that. Please.' She buried herself in his front and he put his arms around her shaking body. Roger was in front of him.

'She's right,' said Roger. 'Swimming in that is suicide.'

It is for Charlie, thought Nick as he held her head, which means it is for me too. But Imogen was young and confident. Maybe she or Dominic could make it and get help? The water was already around their ankles and the sight of the crushed bow came back to him.

'Dominic,' he shouted. 'What do you think?' Dominic's eyes flicked across the two women and Nick nodded minutely.

'Ok,' said Nick. 'We're going to stick it out. It should stay afloat till someone comes. It can't be long.'

Charlotte's hand crept up his chest to thank him.

'How many hulls does it have?' said Imogen, and Nick looked at her.

'I don't fucking know how many *hulls* it has,' he said.

Imogen took a breath and looked across the dark, rutted water. I know I can make it, she thought. The River Wye had strong current, which just meant you just ended up swimming across in a diagonal. She thought of a map of London and remembered that the river got wider as it went on. She looked around the group and imagined leaving them.

'If we're going to end up swimming, we should do it now,' she said. 'The river is wider downstream so we're less likely to make it. Otherwise we're betting this thing will stay afloat forever.'

Charlotte shook her head against Nick's chest and his eyes blazed at Imogen.

'Go if you want,' he said. 'I'm staying.' Imogen looked at Dominic, and he looked at Charlotte.

'Imogen,' shouted Dominic. 'I can't let you go on your own. And I can't come with you. We have to stay.'

'What do you mean you can't *let* me?' she shouted. 'Where the fuck would you be without me?'

Roger stepped into the middle of the group and extended both his arms.

'Wait,' he said. 'Just wait. There must be something we can make a raft from.'

They all looked at him.

'Fenders,' said Nick.

'What else?' said Imogen.

Dominic waded to the piano and lifted the lid.

'Are you fucking joking?' said Imogen.

'Do these things float?' said Dominic.

'Fuck knows,' said Nick. 'But it'll float for longer than the boat if we tie the fenders to it. Two people inside and the others can kick it to the shore.' He handed Charlotte to Imogen and waded towards the galley.

Imogen closed her eyes. The water around her feet made her more and more sure she could make it. It was only swimming. Please, she thought; just let me go.

Nick returned with two kitchen knives.

'Dominic,' he said. 'Come with me.'

Charlotte straightened up beside Imogen.

'Stop, Nicky,' she said clearly, and Nick turned back. 'I've changed my mind,' she said. 'You should swim. You should all go. I'll be fine.' She gestured away from herself. 'Just go,' she said. Nick's eyes widened and Dominic's face fell. Nick handed the knives to him and moved towards Charlotte. He held her and she looked up at him.

'Nick,' she said. 'I don't want you to die. I know you can swim it. You love swimming...' She put her arms around him and let out a sigh, then looked up at him and smiled. 'Just be a good uncle,' she said.

Nick's face was frozen. He handed her to Roger and looked into his eyes.

'Don't let go of her,' he said. Roger nodded and chastely took hold of Charlotte.

'We need to get the piano out onto the rear deck,' said Nick. 'Otherwise it'll go down with the cabin. Dominic, put the knives inside the lid. Imogen, get the other corner.'

Nick counted them in and pushed it towards the rear doors, then lifted each leg over the metal lip. Rain drummed on its walnut top and Dominic just made out the name *Bösendorfer* in gold on the front. Nick opened the lid and handed him a knife.

'The ropes will be too wet to untie,' Nick shouted. 'Cut them but keep as much rope as possible.' Dominic nodded.

'Imogen?' said Nick and she leaned across the wooden surface. 'We'll hand you the fenders,' he said. 'Tie one at the top of each leg. More if we have them. Ok?'

Imogen nodded and the two men slid away down the side of the boat. The banks were dark and distant, and she felt a deep sadness. It came to her that her parents had paid out their love like a rope; never too much, never too little. She would have liked to call them now; not to tell them where she was but just so they could hear her voice. A moment before, it had not even occurred to her that she was going to die. She saw the tip of a skyscraper and thought of her job at the investment fund. Another analyst had died the previous year in a car accident and they had replaced him in a week. She thought of the things she would never know; of how marriage finally happened, and with whom; and the children she could have raised as her parents had raised her; and of not seeing the farm again or the Welsh coast. Someone handed her an orange buoy and she concentrated on the job, pulling the blue rope in a tight bowline; but her hands seemed like someone else's.

Charlotte looked at the thing they were building for her and started to laugh, first quietly then hysterically. She clapped raucously with Roger's hand still on her arm.

'We're going to sea in a piano.' She giggled and turned to him. 'Not in a pea-green boat, in a *piano!* I do hope you can play?'

Roger watched the raft taking shape and thought:

what a gift is life! They would keep it and he would be different afterwards. Irina would leave him and the house would be sold but it didn't matter. This was the start.

Dominic's trips along the boat were getting more dangerous as it listed lower. He sat astride a down-rail and started sawing at the nylon rope, his shoes filling with water as they submerged over the edge. It was cold and there were no lights on the southern bank now, just dark industrial shapes. He had a vision of the boat from above, with buoys like party balloons tied around the clef shape of the piano. He was sure it was going to work, otherwise they wouldn't have thought of it. The knife stopped in his hand. He had never thought anything like that before. Why now? Then he had the overwhelming urge to live, and sawed harder.

The tears flowed down Nick's nose and fell warmly on his hand among the raindrops. I don't want *you* to die, Charlotte had said; that still tone matched by the stillness of her body. Then she had actually smiled. He never wanted to think of that moment or to neglect her again. He would push the raft himself: if someone was to die it would be *him*. The water blurred his eyes and he sawed at the big front fender. The orange globe seemed to be getting bigger and brighter. Light was surrounding him and his ears were beginning to roar. Not yet, he thought. I must do this first! He got the buoy free and started along the side of the boat. The stern was bathed in white light and he saw the four figures frozen like statues. Spray kicked up in a circle around the boat and a shattering noise had appeared. He looked up into the wind and saw a dark shape growing in the sky. A halo of rotors was sketched behind the long black body and a spotlight twitched in its underside. Something was hanging from it and disturbing the light: a wide loop on a winch, swaying in the downdraft. He dropped the fender and waded quickly to the stern.

20

The padded ring gripped with mechanical force under Charlotte's shoulders and the weight left her feet. In the moment before it happened, she had thought that the process might be under her control; but instead she was lifted like a doll through the roaring air. The river widened beneath her with the helpless boat at its centre, where four people shaded their faces against the light. She saw her brother and reached down to him, then the wire was pulled sideways and she was manhandled through an opening. The ring disappeared from her shoulders and she was pushed sharply away from the doors towards a row of seats. She scrambled onto one and pulled the seatbelt automatically across her front. Her eyes closed against the noise and industrial smell of the cabin. Don't go last Nicky, she thought; just come here.

Imogen went next. She closed her eyes as her feet left the deck and her lungs filled with relief. Her future was back. As she reached the helicopter, a man in a jump suit and round helmet pulled her through the entrance. It seemed like hours had passed since her emergency call and she thought with satisfaction of the man who had answered it. Then Charlotte's eyes greeted her from the row of seats, and their hands found each other.

The three men looked at each other. The cold water was up to their waists and the piano floated between them. The orange ring appeared again and Roger pushed it towards Nick. He paused then nodded briefly and fitted it under his arms. It tightened and he was airborne. Below him, only the white roof and outer rails of the boat were visible above the water, with the stern rail encircling the shape of the piano. Dominic and Roger had climbed onto the roof and were gripping each other against the downdraft. He was passed through the opening and took a seat by Charlotte, who released her belt and lay sideways across his lap. Exhaustion closed in on him and he remembered that he had been ill. He closed his eyes and folded his sister's arms in his.

The ring reappeared as the boat started tipping onto its bow and belching air from its hull. Dominic and Roger looked at each other, and Roger pushed it towards Dominic.

'Go,' Roger shouted, and Dominic's hairless face looked back at him through the spray.

'Roger,' Dominic shouted back. 'Take it!' The boat lurched and they both grabbed the ring. The helicopter rolled above them and a lifejacket slid out of the door. It fell into the water by Dominic and was pushed away from them by the downdraft.

'They want us to go one by one,' shouted Dominic.

'No!' shouted Roger. 'We'll go together.' The stern breached the surface as the boat turned onto its bow, wrenching the piano out of the water. The railing struck their legs and Dominic felt a moment of deadly downward force before pulling his foot free.

'Ok,' he shouted. 'Together!' They entwined their arms tighter around the ring and each other, and Dominic closed his eyes as the winch slowly started to move. His shoulder and leg were aching, and the ascent seemed to be taking longer than for the others. His arm slipped and he felt Roger's grip tighten around him. Then hands appeared, pulling them over the cold ledge of the helicopter floor. He glimpsed a pockmarked face giving orders as they crawled into the cabin. The winch was swung in and the sliding door slammed shut along its runners. The throttle increased and the aircraft started to climb, turning on its axis to point down the river. Reaching a seat, he looked through a round window and saw the banks of the river accelerating past.

Roger couldn't take his eyes off the two men seated either side of the cockpit door. They were wearing blue flight suits and radio microphones extended from the chin of their white helmets. He closed his eyes and the future crowded in: witness statements, prosecution, a criminal case on top of bankruptcy, trying to cover up for Uncle Eric. But why should he cover up for Eric? It was Eric's men who had pushed him onto the boat! But now he felt an intense, almost painful gratitude that they had. Thank God he was here with the others, not waking in a panic with no news of them. And, of course, being a victim would also be a much better defence. Which would mean what? Testifying against Eric? What if they offered him a plea bargain, like in a mafia film? That would mean a lifetime of hiding from Eric. He put a numb hand to his face, feeling the wrinkled fingertips.

The only people who could help him were the people he was now with. But why should they? He looked sideways at Dominic, whose head was turned away towards the window. Roger could sense him disowning the situation and becoming a stranger again. Could he even talk to him? But they would probably be separated after they landed and the distance between them only grow. He touched the arm and Dominic turned to look at him. Roger felt a stroke of horror seeing his face again, and now remembered the moment when the accident happened.

'Dominic,' he said. 'What are we going to say?'

Dominic looked at the wide, begging face and saw broken skin where his punch had connected above the eyebrow. He remembered his decision on the boat: walk away. But from what? He still didn't have any answers himself.

'Roger,' he said coolly. 'I still don't know what happened.'

Roger frowned then remembered that Dominic had been out on the deck when he explained to the others. He took a breath.

'I was my fault,' said Roger. 'I planned it. But then I was pushed on too.'

'Why?' said Dominic, and Roger's eyes flinched.

'I don't know,' he said despairingly.

'But why did you plan it at all?' said Dominic.

'Because I thought you had cheated me,' he said. 'All of you.'

Yes, thought Dominic, so did I. And he felt uncomfortably close to Roger for a moment.

313

'I see,' he said. 'And who did you get to do it?'

Roger told him and Dominic's eyes widened.

'Eric Dodds?' he said. 'Who owns...' He named the club where he had first kissed Charlotte, and Roger nodded.

'Jesus,' said Dominic, and his scorched brow knotted. 'You realise how dangerous that man is?'

Roger shrugged. He only half knew anything about Uncle Eric; only that he had clubs and drugs and girls.

'I wanted to show you I was serious,' he said. 'About getting the money back.'

Dominic closed his eyes and pictured Dodds standing like a bald goblin in his club that night. He remembered his relief that Dodds didn't know who he was. Now that was probably no longer even true, yet he was too exhausted to be angry with Roger.

'If you involve Eric Dodds in something,' he said. 'Any money will end up with him.' He paused. 'Is that why he pushed you on? Had you already paid him?'

Something twitched in Roger's memory. He had stopped calling Eric at some point: why? He shook his head.

'I don't know why,' he said. 'Maybe it was his idea of a joke?' Yes, thought Dominic, that sounds like him. Roger leant towards him again. 'Do you see?' he said with low urgency. 'What are we going to *say*?'

Dominic remembered what he knew of Dodds, head of one of the last old London families. They had fought off everyone; the Old Grey Fox at Scotland Yard, the Jamaicans, the Russians. The latest had been the Albanians, and even the Chinese in Soho had done a deal. The world had changed too much for him to last another decade, yet he still had some of the very same interests started by his father fifty years before. Dominic knew someone who had been at old Paul Dodds' funeral. Twenty creeping Daimlers; broken noses on bowed faces; Covent Garden flower market all but emptied. It's a funny thing, his contact had said, but gangsters love flowers. And Dominic realised that his instinct to walk away had been even more right than he realised.

'We?' he said, and saw the fear flashing across Roger's face. 'I don't care what you do,' he said. 'But I have nothing to say. I'm disinterested. And I would be grateful if you circumscribed yourself from mentioning me at all.' Roger's face fell in relief and Dominic realised that in his mind this counted as a favour.

'Thank you,' said Roger earnestly, and he looked back out of the window.

Roger looked over his shoulder. Nick had his eyes closed and Charlotte was gripping his hand. Roger could see his shallow breathing. Imogen was looking out of the window. Her eyes flicked to him and back. He turned back to Dominic.

'Will you tell the others?' he said, and Dominic gave him a sideways look.

'What they say is up to them,' he said. 'Nick may feel differently. He doesn't have anywhere to live now.'

'But what shall *I* say?' said Roger.

Through his tiredness, Dominic realised that he was about to give some free advice. The time alone in Scotland could not come too soon.

'Don't say anything,' he said. 'You don't have to say anything. If Nick agrees, just say you were on the boat. Or, if he doesn't, just say you were arriving to see him. Let the police do the work. If it was who you say it was, they won't have left any evidence.'

Roger digested this.

'But I told Nick it was me,' he said. And the two women, he thought.

Dominic sighed, thinking that answering stupid questions was the reason lawyers put in bills.

'So what?' he said. 'Unsay it. Say he made it up or misheard. The guy was ill anyway. Or say you were fantasising, or joking.'

Roger was listening intently.

'Do you think I'll have to?' he said.

Dominic closed his eyes. He wanted to be at home. He wanted to be at the wheel of his car, listening to Bach and driving to Scotland. He would give the shortest statement possible then leave. He took a breath and met the other man's eyes.

'Roger,' he said. 'I appreciate that we have been through a lot. I appreciate that you claim to have acted under diminished responsibility and didn't really mean it. I understand that you don't want to go to prison. But the honest truth is: I just don't care. The most I can do is nothing. If it's not enough, too bad. It's nothing personal but it's your fight now. Ok?'

'Ok,' said Roger after a pause. 'Thank you.'

And *stop* saying thank you, thought Dominic. He turned back to the window to see the lights of London had thinned and they were still heading east. He felt uncertainty rising through his tiredness. Battersea Heliport was the other way, and only two miles away. London City Airport was even closer. He closed his eyes against the unanswered question as it only made sleep more distant. Maybe it was a coastguard helicopter? That would mean a long drive back to London in some uncomfortable ambulance. But the inside of the cabin seemed too bare for the coastguard. The elasticated stowage nets on the walls were empty save for some tools and the only medical equipment was a tiny green first aid kit. And yet no-one had yet offered him first aid even with that.

Dominic unstrapped his belt and moved past Roger towards the front of the cabin. He crouched down in front of the older man, who had overseen the rescue. The edge of grey, close-cropped hair was visible beneath the raised visor: a military cut. The man's eyes were set deep in a lined face and looked ahead as if Dominic was invisible.

'Where are we going?' he shouted, searching for insignias on the man's flight suit. 'Are you the coastguard?'

The black eyes moved to meet his.

'Sit down,' he said. The vowels were flat and forceful: the sound of the old South Africa.

'Where are we going?' shouted Dominic. 'Why are we not flying into London?'

The man stood up and Dominic's cry sounded across the cabin. His arm was being held at an excruciating angle. Nick and Charlotte opened their eyes, and Roger's heart went into freefall.

'Sit *down*,' barked the man, pushing Dominic to the floor. He got back to his feet to see four frightened faces raised towards him. Charlotte's lip was shaking and her eyes were begging him for this not to be happening. He moved back towards them, holding onto the top of the seats.

'This is not a police helicopter,' he said, his voice quivering. That grip had come out of nowhere and now he could hardly move his arm.

Grow up, thought Imogen. Of course it's the police. You got them out of bed when your stupid feud got out of hand then nagged them with questions: I'm not surprised they bent your arm. She was looking forward to giving the authorities a once over for ignoring her call. And being free of Dominic. And going to bed. She needed to get a message to the office this evening so she could sleep in the next day, otherwise a car would turn up at nine thirty with a coffee and a note summoning her. She looked back out of the window to see the rain had slackened and the outskirts of the city beginning to pass.

'What's he saying?' said Charlotte, gripping Nick again. 'Of course it's the police! They came to rescue us!'

Nick frowned. The chopper suddenly didn't look like government property: there were no safety notices or rescue equipment, and the men weren't in uniform.

'Don't worry, Charlie,' he said. 'I'm sure it is.' He unclipped his belt to move up by Dominic, so the three men sat in a row.

'I think Dominic may be right,' he said in a low voice. 'This looks like a private chopper.'

Roger felt a glimmer of relief mixing with the fear.

'Who is it then?' he said, staving off the answer. They both looked at him. 'No,' he said, his eyes widening 'It can't be... Why would he?'

'You involved him,' said Nick. 'Who else could it be? Who else knew we were there?'

Dominic closed his eyes.

'Are you fucking joking?' he said. 'Are you really suggesting Eric Dodds had a change of heart and sent a helicopter to pick us up?'

'Well,' said Roger weakly. 'At least we're safe.'

They both looked at him.

'Are we?' said Nick. He had the insane thought that it was the Uzbek secret service. They had had it in for him once. 'Look,' he said. 'We're tired and we're losing it. Of course it's the government. No-one else can fly over London like this. Maybe it's Special Branch or even Six...' He stopped. It wasn't impossible. His old contacts at the Foreign Office knew where he lived, but why would they even do it? They didn't owe him anything and he hadn't even parted on very good terms. 'Or someone else,' he said. 'But I'd rather be up here than down there.' And for the first time, he realised he had nowhere to live. The helicopter banked to the left and they all looked out of the small window. Dominic spoke tiredly.

'We're flying around the edge of the London airspace,' he said. He had been flown into it once by someone on the way back from a party and they had rapidly been escorted out again. 'Which means we are not in the hands of the government,' he said, then

319

looked   at Nick narrowly. 'Unless you know a department that's too secret to use its own fucking airspace?'

Nick felt his breath lightening. No, he thought. I cannot afford another panic attack now. He remembered the advice: let it come, don't fight it. He went back to his seat and Charlotte looked at him searchingly. He took her hand and closed his eyes. Fine, he thought. Have a panic attack if you want to; you've done nothing wrong and you're alive. And it passed.

Roger felt the circle closing around him again. Eric; the lawyers; the bank; the lost money; Lily's mother; Irina; and now this. He closed his eyes and prayed. I'll do anything, he thought; just take me away from this.

Dominic was starting to breathe more heavily. Imogen had looked at him with renewed contempt as he came back from the front of the cabin nursing his arm. Now a new ball of anger was forming at the intolerable thought of still not being free. Yet as his blood rose, his face only hurt more.

Charlotte turned and whispered to Imogen.

'What's going on?' she said. Imogen smiled into her scared face and put a hand on her arm.

'Nothing,' she said. 'Just men and their fantasies. We're safe now.'

Charlotte smiled. Imogen was wonderful.

'You must come to lunch,' she said involuntarily. Imogen looked at her as if she was mad then softened, recognising the hysteria.

'Thank you,' she said. 'I'd love to.'

Charlotte closed her eyes, feeling a sea of tears

waiting to break inside her. It felt like she would never see the children again. She had gone to look after Nick when Rachael was ill. What if Rachael had gone into hospital and no-one could contact her? It was her own fault for starting an affair with Dominic. That is what had got her here; separated from her family and sitting next to someone who was probably his girlfriend. She felt the first lurch of humiliation and knew it would only deepen. And here she was asking people to lunch. She opened her eyes again.

'I'm sorry,' she said, her voice cracking as the tears rose again. 'I just don't know what's happening.'

Imogen took her head and laid it on her shoulder, stroking the blond hair. It was paler than hers and straighter, and she remembered when she had first seen Charlotte asleep through the boat window. That look still came to Dominic's face when his eyes rested on her; a kind of intense, petulant interest. So something had happened between them. Not that it mattered now, and she felt a new flood of relief that she would never have to see him again.

'Come out and stay on our farm,' she said. 'You'll like it there.'

Charlotte looked up at her.

'Really?' she said. 'Can I bring the children.'

'Yes,' said Imogen. 'We'll take them to see the lambs.'

The tears rolled down Charlotte's face and she let out a small breath.

'Thank you,' she said.

*

Their unease lapsed into silence beneath the heavy drone of the rotors. The heating warmed their damp clothes and even Dominic's anger finally paled into abandonment. When the helicopter made a wide turn and started losing altitude, attention again rustled through the seats.

Dominic looked through the window and saw dark hills. A motorway passed through them in a wide chalk cutting and he recognised the Chilterns hills, forty miles from London. He glimpsed a floodlit building in the centre of a clearing and heard the noise change as the helicopter slowed. It tilted backwards and the landing lights showed a lawn and waves of air being pushed across the bordering trees. He saw early autumn leaves being shaken free and felt the noise being reflected back in the small clearing. The rear wheels made contact then the front, and the rotors began to slow with a steady whine. They stayed in their seats with their eyes on the crew men. When one opened the door and the other gestured towards it, they all stood at the same time.

'I don't suggest anyone tries to run,' said Dominic quietly.

Nick nodded. He had fallen asleep for a few moments on the flight and woken in a kind of hell. His home was gone and his only money had gone. He had stumbled out of bed with nothing and was with people he no longer trusted; except for Charlotte, whom he had dragged into all this danger when she had only wanted to take care of him. All for a fantasy gold deposit, which people had been telling him for years didn't exist. Now the story itself would last for years, and he could already feel the ignominy spreading. He could hardly be angry with Roger, whom he had targeted from the moment they met. It had cost Roger more than it had cost him; and sure enough Roger had now cost him the rest. Living with Charlotte for more than a few nights was unthinkable, which meant he had to borrow or earn the money for a plane ticket as quickly as possible. To where? It hardly mattered. He stepped out of the helicopter and saw the grounds of a country house. Lawns guttered with shadows curved between box hedges and a floodlit Eighteenth Century house rose in the centre of the park. As he helped Charlotte down, the lights went out behind them.

'What's there?' said Charlotte.

'A country house,' said Nick.

'Nicky, I'm scared,' she said, standing close to him. Nick searched for something to say.

'Hopefully we'll be warm soon,' he said. And hopefully they will let you go, he thought.

Raindrops still hung on the trees and Imogen shivered under the draft from the slowing rotors. Already it felt like the girl who had gleefully planned to follow Dominic was someone else; some discontented child looking for thrills. She turned and saw Roger stepping down with a defiant look, like someone walking to the gallows; then she saw Charlotte's drawn face in the moonlight and Nick's, both looking like they would sacrifice anything to go home. Dominic lingered at the back of the group, his suit stained and hanging open as he looked towards the dark mass of the house.

She felt apart from them all, and hoped their captives would see it.

Their feet sank into dense grass as they walked across the lawn, flanked by the two crewmen. The box hedges gave way to paved parterres where rainwater had pooled on the even stonework. They passed a square pond with a carved fountain in its centre and Charlotte noticed the handles of a submerged grille for lifting out weeds. Their escorts turned them away from the main house towards a low wing with large windows, and she recognised an old orangery. One of the crewmen opened a white door and she smelt eucalyptus. They passed through and lights came up on the aquamarine water of an indoor swimming pool, its surface level with the white floor. Mirrors filled high arches on the back walls and a large Jacuzzi bubbled quietly near the shallow end. In the corner was a small marble bar, finished with a brass rail. The crewmen's helmets had been left in the helicopter and now they saw the old scarred face of the one who had given the orders. He surveyed the room briefly then spoke.

'Get warm, have a drink,' he said. 'It won't be long.'

The door closed behind him and locked with a click. They looked at each other and Charlotte sank onto a low wooden bench. Imogen laughed nervously.

'Where are we?' said Roger, and the others looked at him silently. Dominic went to the bar and found a silver tray supporting a bottle of whisky, a silver vacuum jug, a sugar bowl, and a plate of lemon slices studded with cloves. Steam rose when he lifted the lid of the vacuum jug. He blinked, then poured a whisky and drank it.

Nick let out a slow breath as he slid into the Jacuzzi. The temperature had been turned up and eucalyptus steam filled his nose. He breathed it deeply then slid under the surface and the soft, warm water chased away the cold Thames. He resurfaced and rested his head on the padded lip, his eyelids falling and reopening. Charlotte's dress crumpled to the floor and she got in next to him. On the far side, Roger gingerly stepped down; then Imogen, still wearing her business shirt. Dominic walked around the edge with a tray of hot whiskies, then dropped his clothes and the hot aerated water wrapped around his aching limbs. Only the gentle rising of the water broke the silence. Each cupped the hot tumbler on their chest, letting its sweet fumes mix with the steam. They slept, then awoke, then slept again.

An inner door opened silently and they all started when a maid appeared. She lifted the glasses and carried them back to the bar then returned with a pile of bathrobes. They climbed out slowly and slipped into them, tying large knots at the front. She offered them white towelling slippers and lead them towards a different door. Charlotte cast a glance back to where their clothes sat, each damp pile disfiguring the floor; and nearly laughed at the thought of them swaddled like babies and held prisoner by a maid. They passed through corridors which had the perfect finish of a hotel, then arrived in a wood-panelled room where a fire burned. Translucent green lampshades hung from curved bronze table lamps and the leather spines of books lined the walls. They gathered their robes and sank into deep sofas and armchairs, looking into the fire. A teaspoon clicked on glass as the maid attended to an identical bar.

A door opened and Sir David McAllister sprung into the room. He was wearing a polo shirt and plimsolls, his black hair neatly combed above the metal glasses.

'Nick!' he said, approaching Nick's sofa. Nick stared at him and his hand was lifeless as David grasped it. 'Glad to see you in one piece after all your adventures!' said David.

'And Daniel,' he said, turning to Dominic brightly. 'Been in the wars I see!' He squinted at Dominic's face, then picked up a phone from the side table.

'Aileen, my love. Can we borrow your nursing skills in the library?' He put down the phone and turned to Roger.

'And you must be Roger! Well you're a bloody minded sod, aren't you?' He clapped both hands around Roger's with a smile. 'David McAllister. Nice to meet you.' He greeted the ladies with a courtly gesture then poured himself a whisky and settled into an armchair with a sigh. 'What a day,' he said. 'What a day!' He shook his head and looked into the fire.

'David,' said Nick finally.

'Aye,' said David. 'How have you been? Fine old time we had in Baku... Mind you, not a word to the wife!'

The door opened and they were joined by a short woman carrying a large first aid box. She clucked when she saw Dominic and produced a tube of salve. He raised a hand but she started applying it to his face, continuing until only his eyes were visible. Aileen

McAllister giggled and patted him on the head.

'All you need now is some slices of cucumber!' she said, and Imogen found herself smiling. Lady McAllister stood up and closed the box. 'Now don't you all keep David up too late!' she said, giving David a stern look as she left the room.

Imogen leant over and extended a hand to Sir David, holding her robe closed with the other.

'Imogen Somerville,' she said. David kissed her hand lightly.

'David McAllister,' he said.

'I may need to use a phone at some point,' said Imogen.

'Of course, of course!' said Sir David, and she could see that he meant any time other than now.

'This is Charlotte,' Imogen said. 'Nick's sister.'

Charlotte was still staring at Sir David as if he had just appeared.

'How rude of me,' said David, springing up again.

'David McAllister,' he said and Charlotte took his hand silently. 'Your brother and I knew each other in Azerbaijan,' he said David, before turning to face the room. 'Quite a place, Baku! You know they make their own country music? Fifty years of Communism and all they want to do is sing country and western... Terrible stuff mind!' He laughed and settled back into his chair.

'This is a surprise,' said Dominic slowly, the mask of face cream undulating as he spoke.

'Aye,' said David. 'Shame about the weather too. Looks like summer's gone!'

Nick couldn't stop himself staring at a man he hadn't

seen for fifteen years. The boardroom had done nothing to smooth the long boxer's face and pitted cheeks. From Glasgow via the East End, it was no surprise that David was still looking for bigger fights to win. His eyes sparkled with the same playfulness and Nick could see he wasn't going to let on too easily.

'David,' he said finally.

'Aye,' said David, looking at him encouragingly.

'Was that one of your helicopters?' he said.

'Aye,' said David with a dutiful nod. 'At your service.' Nick leant forwards.

'But how did you know?' he said. 'And... why?'

'Ah, Nick,' said David expansively. 'Anything for a friend!' And he directed a small smile into the fire.

'Well, thank you,' said Nick weakly, remembering how he had felt responsible for the others on the boat.

Dominic sunk back into his char. He was enjoying the cool outer skin on his face and knew he didn't have to speak, as McAllister would give Nick the facts if he was going to give them to anyone. He thought of the United Minerals headquarters across St James Square from his office. Sir David must have had Nick's mining concession on some kind of watch list.

'I would quite like to know what I am doing here,' said Charlotte in a clear voice.

'Well,' said Sir David defensively. 'We could hardly leave you on that boat could we?'

Charlotte put down her glass and looked at him coldly.

'David, whoever you are, I have children at home. I would like to go and see them. Before I go, I would like to know what is behind all this.'

David gave her a contrite look.

'Well, that depends on how much you know about what these three have been up to,' he said. Nick and Roger leaned forwards, and Sir David gave them a wink. 'The three musketeers!' he said.

Charlotte remembered meeting Roger at her garden party and guessing there was something going on.

'I had no idea they were up to anything,' she said levelly.

Imogen had retreated into the shadow of her chair, her eyes traversing between the faces of the men. Roger had shrunk into his bathrobe and was trying not to move. Sir David stood and rested an elbow on the tall mantelpiece so the firelight lit him from below.

'These three lads,' he said. 'Have been on the gold sands. I should know! I've been on them myself for year.' He paused. 'But they'll drive you mad before they make you rich... especially if you go picking a mine without any of the stuff in it!' A smile played on his shadowed face, then he leant forwards into the light and raised his eyebrows. 'Now,' he said. 'I could have told you that! That Kattakurgan mine is an old wives' tale. It always has been!'

Dominic and Roger's eyes swivelled towards Nick, who looked away into the fire.

'However,' said Sir David, raising himself a little on the balls of his feet. 'I'm the first to admit that nothing in this world is completely certain. In fact, things wouldn't be much fun if we knew everything! So...'

He coughed lightly and looked around their

expectant faces, like his children when he had read to them before bed. He hadn't thought of exactly what to say yet. Surely they knew how things worked? But talk could be expensive, especially with a pack of backstabbing civil servants after him.

'Excuse me for a second,' he said. He went to the corner of the room, sprung open a draw and returned with five sheets of paper, then shuffled them into order and handed them around.

Nick looked at the heading. Non-Circumvention Non-Disclosure Agreement, it read. It was an affidavit of secrecy, with his name and the address of the houseboat printed at the top. *Roxanne, Cadogan Pier, London SW3*. He turned the sheet over and closed his eyes.

Dominic's was headed with his name and the address of his office in St James Square. He read it quickly. It was all very standard, although the punitive clauses for them breaking it were heavy. He had wanted all this to go away and if David McAllister wanted the same thing, that meant it would happen. But it was still worth pushing a little while he could.

'Sir David,' said Dominic. 'What is all this about?'

Sir David? thought Imogen, and the wheels of understanding began to turn. David McAllister. Sir David McAllister. She closed her eyes. Of course: the chairman of United Minerals! The fund she worked for owned a lot of their stock and here she was in his house, the last to catch on. She must get quicker. The sheet of paper in her hand had a space for her name and address, which meant he didn't know who she was yet. And the very need for a secrecy agreement meant she had a bargaining chip. She laid aside the document, planning what to say.

Roger's blood had run cold when he saw his name at the top of the document, but now he was looking around for a pen. If this man wanted things kept quiet, he was happy to oblige! And maybe if he signed this, he could use it as an excuse not to testify anywhere else? Beside Nick, Charlotte was looking at her sheet with contempt.

Sir David addressed himself to Dominic's question.

'Well, Daniel,' he said.

'Dominic,' said Dominic. His name was correct on the document, so David was obviously doing it to rile him.

'Dominic,' said Sir David. 'The purpose of these wee pieces of paper is to allow me to tell you what it's all about.' He went back to the desk and returned with a blotter and a fountain pen, which he handed first to Dominic.

Dominic paused for show then signed. The last thing he wanted was anyone to know he had been involved in this charade. He handed the pen and padded leather panel to Roger, who did the same. Nick paused when he received them. Yet David usually had a good reason for doing things; and Nick wanted to hear what he had to say; and there was nothing left to lose as the mine was empty. He signed and Charlotte took the blotter from him scornfully.

'It's alright,' he said quietly. 'He's an old friend. It's just a formality.'

Charlotte scrawled a signature, leaving the other

spaces for someone else to fill in. She passed it to Imogen, who wrote on her sheet. Sir David collected them in a like a school master and looked at them one by one.

'Imogen Summertown,' he read slowly. '28 Battersea Rise, London SW12.' He raised his eyes to Imogen. 'Somerville, Summertown,' he said thoughtfully. 'Not much in it...' He dropped the piece of paper in the fire.

Imogen saw Dominic's eyes burning with irritation through the round clearings in his sea of face cream. She looked levelly at Sir David.

'I work for Samartian Capital,' she said.

Really, thought Dominic; you actually want to do this?

David raised his eyebrows in mock interest.

'Good for you,' he said. 'Tony Samartian is a good man. And a good friend. Tell him anything you want.'

Sir David's face was tightening as he looked at Imogen and she understood what it meant: that Tony Samartian would much rather liquidate her job than his investment in David's company. Sir David returned to the desk and handed her a new sheet.

'Somerville,' he said. 'Which, unless I'm mistaken, is spelled S-O-M-E-R-V-I-L-L-E.'

Imogen felt herself flushing deeply and quickly wrote her details. She had never even met Tony Samartian. Sir David took the sheet and looked at it.

'Thank you,' he said, and his eyes rested coldly on her for a moment. 'Ladbroke Grove, how nice.' He walked back to the desk and they heard it lock. The short click unnerved Dominic and he suddenly regretted signing the paper. Sir David took his seat again.

'Now,' he said. 'Where were we?'

'Kattakurgan,' said Nick. 'You knew about it. How?'

Their host smiled at him.

'Come now, Nick,' he said. 'If you'll excuse the cliché, it is my job to know these things.' The Uzbek state register, thought Nick; always was leaky as a sieve.

'But if the mine was empty, why the interest?' he said.

Sir David spread his arms.

'I wanted to be sure!' he said. 'I mean, which of us really knows anything?' He raised his eyebrows in wonderment. 'Maybe all those drinks you used to buy in Tashkent had got you some good information after all.' He winked at Nick, and Nick almost smiled.

'So?' said Nick.

'So I...' Sir David's eyes swivelled to the side and he cleared his throat again. 'I took the liberty of keeping a little eye on your boat... Or a little ear, rather.'

Roger's eyes widened. Charlotte shook her head. Dominic smiled. Imogen thought of the affidavits. Nick leaned forwards, remembering his intuition that someone had been onboard while he was away.

'You *bugged* my boat?' he said.

'Nick,' said David sharply. 'That is not a word I like!'

The glass hung forgotten in Nick's hands.

'But *why*?' he said. 'We had the concession. What was the point?'

'Nick...' said David, the sound lengthening as if what he was about to say was obvious. 'You're not going to dig the stuff out of the ground yourself, are you? You would have needed a partner!' He gestured towards himself. 'Who better than your old pal?'

Nick was taking lighter breaths. Didn't David trust him enough just to call him? It was true that joint venturing with United Minerals would have been a good solution, although it was not one that had occurred to him.

'But David,' said Nick. 'I would have called you.'

'Would you...' said David dryly. 'Would you really?'

Dominic leant forwards impatiently.

'All that makes sense,' he said, and Sir David acknowledged the realism with a little nod. 'But why send out the chopper? If you wanted to rescue us – and thank you, by the way – why not just call the police?'

David looked thoughtful, then glanced at Roger with a smile.

'Well,' he said. 'It's true I hadn't counted on our friend here!' Roger looked away and he looked back to Dominic. 'Come now, Dan ...Dominic,' he said. 'You're a lawyer. Can you imagine what a terrible lot of questions they would have asked? I mean how could I, an old man out here in the middle of nowhere, possibly have known what was happening on your boat? And even if I did, United isn't *my* company anymore. It belongs to the shareholders. It's amazing the boxes you have to tick to run a simple mining company these days! Not to mention the trouble dear Roger would have faced.'

He winked at Roger, and Roger had the feeling that David might really be on his side.

'No,' said David, shaking his head. 'If you want a job done, do it yourself.' Dominic nodded, quietly amazed that he had taken such a risk for them.

Nick felt his anger subside. It was characteristic of the man to go out of the way on a point of principle. David had once called him in Baku and asked him to close off an account at a bar; and when he did it turned out only to have seven dollars on it.

Charlotte looked at Nick then the angular Scotsman. Had he really saved her life?

'Thank you, David' she said simply, and he looked up at her in surprise.

'Oh,' he said. 'No bother. We all do what we can.'

He stood with finality.

'Well, ladies and gents,' he said. 'It's getting late. Can I offer you all a bed for the night?'

The word acted on them all. Their skin was clean and scented from the Jacuzzi, and their blood warmed by the whiskies. And they had no clothes. I should go and see the children, thought Charlotte wearily. Roger didn't want to see his house yet. Dominic thought of his small, distant flat. Maybe he could wake early enough to leave before the others? Nick remembered the sight of his boat as he was winched off it; his books, his collections, his music, everything. He couldn't remember if it was even insured, as the correspondence was all in an unopened pile on the boat itself. He could hardly say no to a bed anywhere.

'Thank you, Sir David,' said Imogen carefully. 'But I still need to use your phone, if I may.'

He picked it up and handed it to her.

'But no buggering about,' he said with a thin smile, and Imogen nodded in embarrassment. She dialled work and left a short message saying she was ill.

'Well, aren't you a fine little fibber?' said Sir David.

*

They were lead to separate bedrooms and sank into deep white sheets. Imogen ploughed herself into the bedclothes and slept immediately. Nick thought of his times with David; and finally it seemed as if they had been in Baku that day and only come back here to sleep. Dominic drifted, his consciousness hanging from the single thread. There was a discord somewhere in McAllister's neat explanations, but the effort of reaching it only blew it further away. The thread snapped, and he slept.

In Roger's sleep, he saw Irina. Flowers were arranged around her for a wedding, and she laughed and whispered in his ear. He turned around and she was crying, running from him and pleading more the further she got. He awoke with a start and looked for her next to him, then remembered. She had tried to push him back down the hall as he left to join Eric's men, and cried more in alarm than hurt when he bought his hand across her face. He remembered her smell and her *Moy Roger*, and their gardening trips and swims on the Heath. The bottle won't share you, his therapist had said: it will be your only master if you go near it again. He reached out and put his arms around the pillow, and started to cry.

Charlotte lay awake. Her reverse telescope had grown and the house in Notting Hill seemed smaller than ever.

A doll's house lived in by a doll Charlotte. Even the events of the last few hours were more real; and the four men she had just left seemed more familiar than her own husband. Every time their host had called Dominic by Daniel's name, it had jarred her with supernatural precision. Both she and Nick would now be dependent on Daniel for a home, and she knew how deeply living under their roof would scald her brother's pride. She thought of Dominic, feuding with Imogen while also staring at her as if she had done something wrong. At least the evening had shown her the truth about *that* situation. She thought with a shudder of their teenage night out; little Charlotte Bovary on her diving board. Nick must never know. And then Roger, destabilised and maddened by one of her brother's schemes. She never wanted to see him again.

She tried to think of the next day. Would this man have them driven to London? What would she say when she arrived? That she had slept on the boat, which was now at the bottom of the Thames? There had to be a reason for Nick coming to stay but she could let him chose it; and she thought again of those insulting contracts they had been made to sign. But at least she would see the children. Rachael would be better or worse, and Adam would need attention having given way to his sister during her illness. As she hadn't come back, her sister-in-law Tabitha would still be there, radiating disapproval. And in the centre of it all was Daniel. But it wasn't Daniel. It was a space called Daniel. As sleep closed over her, she couldn't even see his face. I'm sorry, she thought. I don't love you.

21

Sir David was up late in his study, examining a core sample from Nick's mine. He was in high spirits and there was no point in attempting sleep yet, although he must try soon or else he would need those little pills to keep going the following afternoon. Sex used to be the only thing that really tired him out but now that would be unfair on Aileen. He didn't know what to do about the problem. There was a single quiet knock on the door, signalling who it was.

'Come in,' he said, and Kobus silently entered the room. 'Ah!' he said, then stood and went to his drinks tray. 'Drink?'

Kobus nodded and sat by the fireplace. David handed him a tumbler and sat opposite.

'Sorry about all the drama,' said David, his eyes twinkling. Kobus knew Sir David lived for 'the drama'. He had ex-colleagues running other private security companies and knew the work was only as good as your clients let it be. Sir David was one of the best, even if he did take odd decisions sometimes.

'Who did the boat then?' said Sir David, then cocked his head. 'It wasn't you, was it?'

Kobus allowed himself a smile. He shook his head

and looked around the room. He had designed the house's security himself and his men had been over it the previous month. It was probably alright to talk.

'Eric Dodds,' he said. 'London crime family, one of the old school. Looks like Curtis called in a favour and it went wrong.'

Sir David leant back with a satisfied sigh.

'What a bloody minded bastard!' he said 'I should give him a job.'

Kobus's eyebrow lifted minutely and Sir David winked. He went to his desk and picked up the rock sample from Uzbekistan.

'All for this!' he said. He tossed it to Kobus, who held it up to the firelight. 'What do you think?' he said.

'Could be,' said Kobus, running his fingers along the stone. Some kind of ore sparkled in it, maybe bauxite. He put it on a side table. 'About this evening...' he said.

David retook his seat attentively. It was a rare thing for Kobus to volunteer information.

'Air traffic control went crazy,' said Kobus. 'We had to identify ourselves. They were about to put up some jets.'

David inclined his head slowly.

'Bureaucrats with fighter planes,' he said. 'Who would have thought it?' He paused. 'So we'll be getting a rap on the knuckles from someone. Who?'

'Probably the Home Office,' said Kobus. 'Maybe the Ministry of Defence.'

David shook his head. When Kobus told him the boat was loose, he had immediately thought of the offshore transport helicopter sitting on his lawn outside.

Yet surely they wouldn't be adrift for long? When Kobus then intercepted Imogen's failed emergency call, the idea came back stronger. Sure enough, the government had failed in its most basic task; whereas he had the means to save them without turning to anyone. Still the voice of so-called reason objected, reminding him of the questions he was now having to face. And then something bigger intervened, majestically sweeping it all aside. Of course he couldn't risk having five souls on his conscience, including that of a friend! David ordered the chopper up and commandeered a hotel helipad for it to pick up Kobus from his lair in Maidenhead. He had quietly objected, saying there was nothing to gain from the mission and offering to set up a scrambled emergency call instead. David refused, offering his personal guarantee to the pilot. He stationed them outside London and, when the boat lost power, ordered them in. The operation had saved five lives and several hundred thousand pounds of government money, yet instead of a medal he would be getting a fine. But thank God he had done it. Thank God!

'Fine,' he said. 'I'll deal with it.'

Kobus caught his eye.

'Aye,' said David wearily. Of course Kobus hadn't been there. The man was never anywhere! But David wanted him there while he thought through this new problem of the government, and filled up their glasses. He sat heavily and rubbed his temples. He knew the Home Secretary. A year earlier, he could have picked up the phone and made it go away. Now he wasn't so sure, not after that mean-minded summons to the committee hearing. The government's mendacity couldn't hide the obvious gathering of knives for him and putting in a call like that would only make it worse. It had to come from someone else; someone with cleaner hands who would also add a little extra weight. He thought of the right man and opened his eyes. But the need to ask for basic favours was humiliating and he would have to give something in return. He usually had a drawerful of information to swap, and began to sift through it.

'Kobus,' he said, and saw the other man's annoyance at hearing his name spoken. Well, thought David; you debugged this place yourself so if it's not safe to talk here, I'd better get another security chief! But he didn't say it. He liked Kobus, and the man had earned his peccadilloes.

'How is the South American thing going?' he said.

Kobus thought for a moment.

'Looks like it's going to happen,' he said, and David raised his eyebrows. Their attempt to blackmail the South American mines minister who was threatening his concessions had backfired spectacularly. The minister had concluded that the compromising photographs of him which his wife had received were sent not by United Minerals but by the President of the country, who was also his wife's cousin. It then turned out that the minister had better friends in the military than David and Kobus had realized; and that his wife was more interested in power than her husband's fidelity. Instead of backing down, the man was now swiftly moving to take over the government. That would almost certainly cost United its concessions, which would be a body blow that the company could hardly afford. The obvious solution was to get a message to the current President. But the man didn't have a reason to trust David any more than he had a reason to trust the minster; worse, it would associate United with the coup attempt. David had found little choice but to ride it out and pray the coup would fail, but now Kobus said that was unlikely. He sighed. This new problem at home was a trifle compared to losing his tin mines: yet knowing that the President was about to be replaced might also be the bargaining chip he needed to solve it.

'Thank you,' he said. 'We're going to need to think about that one.' He clapped his hands on the side of the armchair and stood up. 'Well,' he said. 'Round up the bill for this and send it to the usual place.' The usual place was a long way from the British Isles. Kobus nodded and left silently.

David looked at the clock on his mantelpiece. He would not usually call this late but it was better than first thing tomorrow, when some corner of Whitehall would already be clucking over his mercy mission. He picked up the phone.

*

In his flat above the Club, Conrad de Salis's phone lay beside the backgammon board. He picked it up and looked at the name on the screen. Unusual; still, there must be a reason. He gave his opponent an excusing look and let it ring two more times before answering.

'David,' he said. 'You're up late.' His voice was

retiring to the point of being apologetic. I cannot help it, it said: I am simply here.

'Evening, Conrad,' said David. 'Hope I'm not disturbing you?' He could feel the embarrassment rising that he could no longer sort out his own problems when once he had been able to sort out other people's.

'Not at all,' said Conrad. He looked at the woman on the other side of the board and thought: later, perhaps, you might have been. The stakes on the game were high.

'I had one of my whirlybirds over London tonight,' said David.

'I'm sad you didn't give me a ride,' said Conrad, smiling at his companion.

'The Home Office is going to have the hump tomorrow,' said David. 'Can you put in a word?'

Conrad frowned. It was a strange thing for David McAllister to ask. They had both been shooting with the Home Secretary the previous year. Why didn't McAllister call him himself? People asked these things when the wind was starting to blow against them, and Conrad could see from the newspapers that this was happening to David. Yet it was only worth helping him if he was also going to save himself, properly and fully. Knowing McAllister, he almost certainly would. People's return favours were also disproportionally large when they felt threatened, and David was not a bad person to have at the end of the phone. But he would still think a little longer before deciding whether to put in the call.

'Of course, David,' he said. Anything for a Member.'

David could hear the grain of mockery, glinting like a coin at the bottom of a river.

'Aye,' he said. 'By the way, do you have any members from...' He named the Latin American country.

Conrad looked past the woman towards the window.

'One or two,' he said absently. 'I've barely heard of the place.'

'Well,' said David. 'Looks like the President's out. One day next week. I'm not happy about it but it looks like it's going to be...' And he named his enemy, the mines minister.

Conrad gave a dry laugh.

'How Sullivanesque!' he said. 'Good night, David.'

*

They were woken by the sound of the helicopter engine firing and the accelerative beat of the rotors. Their bodies ached and disordered memories found form. Dominic and Imogen got up briskly in their separate rooms, drawing the curtains and hunting for something to wear. Charlotte sat up and drew her knees in under her arms. Nick and Roger both lay motionless with their eyes open. When each of them quietly opened their bedroom door, they found the right pile of clothes lying laundered outside. They separately descended a wide staircase and the followed the smell of breakfast into a high-ceilinged room overlooking the park. The lawn extended to a gap in the woods, beyond which the plain of South Oxfordshire extended under the morning haze. They ate in silence, watching as the low sun dispersed the mist.

Outside, two identical black cars waited on the

gravel. Charlotte and Imogen wordlessly got into one. Dominic and Nick shook hands briefly, and Roger offered Nick a bear hug. Nick got into the car beside his sister and Roger joined Dominic in the other. The cars pulled out together, crunching across gravel then through automated gates and out onto a lane. They drove through a village then crossed the motorway which Dominic had seen the previous night before looping back to join it, and soon lost each other in the morning rush hour.

Dominic and Roger's journey passed in silence, and Dominic got out as soon as they entered London. As the car skirted Regents Park towards his house, Roger started to feel a steady drip of fear. Who would be there? Police? Bailiffs? Or Eric Dodds' two silent employees? But the driver already knew where he lived and he somehow couldn't emulate Dominic by stopping the car. Anyway, going anywhere else would be worse, leaving him prey to his imagination. Or maybe the lawyers at least would leave him alone now that his money was gone? And he realised that all he wanted was the house. If he could keep the house, he could make a new start. He even had an idea of how.

Passing the grand villas of the Outer Circle, he remembered doing this drive in the opposite direction on the way to Charlotte's party. Irina had worn her hair up and held his hand in hers, and the driver had opened the door as if they were royalty. He took a slow breath and the neutral smell of the company car filled his nose. He would have to package everything about her into the space she had left; her laugh, her smell, and the way that everyone liked her. Just seal it in and forget. But he had learned a lot this summer and life is a zero-sum game; so it wasn't surprising that he had lost a lot too. He suddenly felt very close to the hardness of life, and tried not to show it in front of Sir David's driver.

They rounded the final corner and the familiar shape of his house appeared. The climbing rose he had planted was in flower and the paintwork by the door had its familiar web of cracks. He paused then quietly slid the key into the lock. The heavy purple door swung open to show the hall with its mirrored wall and black sculpture. The lawyer's letter from New York still lay on the side. He picked it up and moved through to the living room, his heels clicking loudly on the chequered marble; and he felt the beginnings of relief. There was a noise upstairs and his heart was suddenly fast. Of course he would not be left alone: how could he be? He took a few long breaths and positioned himself with an arm on the mantelpiece. At least they couldn't put a price on dignity.

Irina appeared in the doorway. She was wearing the headscarf which she wore to pray, and there was a plaster on one cheek.

'Roger!' she said, and Roger stared at her.

'Irina,' he said. 'You're here!'

'Of course I am here,' she said. 'Where are you?' He walked over to hug her but she held him away with one hand and pointed to her face. The plaster sat on a shallow mound, darkening to grey with the red spots of broken vessels. Roger couldn't keep his eyes on it.

'I'm sorry,' he said, then remembered the headscarf

and thought of her praying to her portable icon. 'Forgive me,' he said. Her eyes narrowed.

'Is not me,' she said. 'Is...' And she pointed towards the ceiling. Yes, thought Roger: but how? Then he remembered his last desolate moments before falling asleep, and thought it would be enough if she alone forgave him.

'I'm so happy you're still here!' he said. He reached out but Irina looked at him with frank eyes and cut him off.

'Roger,' she said. 'No...' She made a drinking gesture. 'And no...' She pointed to her face.

Roger shook his head. It had been five years, and one day had almost cost him everything.

'Never again,' he said. But her arm was still straight and her brown eyes were still moving minutely, as if searching for something.

'Promise,' she said.

'I promise,' he said. Her arm slackened and Roger buried his nose in the scented red hair. He held the back of her head and let out a deeper sigh, feeling his fears dissolve; then drew back and looked for happiness in her face. But the mask of bravery had fallen only to be replaced by fear. She gripped his hands tightly.

'Roger,' she said. 'I was scared.... Not for I, but for *everyone*. I don't know what you might do!' Her eyes were searching him again and he lead her back to the sofa, gathering her in his lap and stroking the smooth temples. The lawyer's envelope was still beside him, and it felt like he could face anything now. He gently removed a hand from Irina, slid it open and read it over her head.

I am pleased to inform you that the Civil Branch of the Supreme Court of the State of New York, New York County, has decided in your favour in the case of Curtis v Manheim, it read. He blinked and carried on. *The Court has awarded you legal costs, which you will find detailed with this letter. Please apprise us of any additional costs, such as travel, which you have incurred due this to lawsuit. Please also inform us if you wish to counter-sue for damages. Such damages may include but not be limited to stress, reputational damage and loss of earnings.*

It was signed with the name of a partner in his law firm. He moved Irina off his lap and felt the air flood into his lungs. Travel? He had been to New York four times! Stress? It was virtually all he had thought about for a year! Reputational damage? They had withdrawn his yacht charter account because of this! Irina was looking up at him in puzzlement and he put his arm back around her.

'Irina,' he said. 'Will you marry me?'

'Roger...' she said, and looked at him silently.

*

Imogen was sitting in the front. The world seemed unusually bright and detailed, the way it used to look after she had stayed up all night at a party. She knew she would only ever see Dominic again by chance. It was an odd new beginning, which she was looking forward to contemplating while lying on the roof terrace of her flat.

It felt dangerous to be without a phone: she would have to get the support people at work to send her a new one on the quiet. Until then, she could just lie in the blustery sun and listen as emails pinged into her laptop. Something made her wish she could turn on the impassive stereo of the company Mercedes: turn it on, and turn it up.

Behind her, Nick sat uneasily. It was difficult to hold the normal pose of a passenger with no home to go to. The pyjamas he had been sleeping in the previous evening now smelled of expensive detergent and were covered by an old raincoat. He hoped that Charlotte realised he was coming home with her, as he didn't want to say it in front of Imogen. The new car was incredibly quiet and he thought of his own car, which was now almost all he now owned. He wanted to go back to Charlotte's and sleep; anything rather than starting to scale the administrative mountain before him. Losing everything used to leave you with nothing but the future; now it locked you inexorably into the past with a hundred tiny bureaucratic hooks. If only he could take this car on to an airport and leave. But he didn't even have a passport, let alone any money. He closed his eyes and tried not to think.

Charlotte occupied a deeper silence beside him. She felt a new traction on the world, as if some hidden ballast had reappeared within her. Things seemed denser and her thoughts once again had a special valency all of their own. She needed to steward it, carrying it back into her life and drawing on it until her task was done. Or else it would be gone again; in weeks, in days, in hours. She drew the back of her hand slowly across glass of the window.

The car stopped at Imogen's flat first. She turned around and said goodbye to Charlotte. Half-remembering a moment of kindness from her on the helicopter, Charlotte suggested they keep in touch and the driver produced a note pad. Then Imogen looked at Nick, and said 'bye' with an uncertain laugh.

'Come swimming in the Serpentine,' he said unthinkingly. But it would be a shame to lose touch with her, and that was now the only place he could meet people. Charlotte gave him a sideways look.

'Wild swimming?' said Imogen. 'I'd love that! Charlotte's got my number.' She got out and the door closed, then the car passed under a railway bridge and started to climb Notting Hill.

'Charlie...' said Nick, and she quickly extended a hand to him.

'I know,' she said. 'Come to our house.'

They entered Westbourne Grove and familiar shops started passing, then the car made one more turn and pulled up outside the house. She looked at it through the window and thought: that's the *other* Charlotte's house. She had decided to write a letter for Daniel and let him find it when he got home. That at least would give him some room to absorb it before having to see her. But how would Nick react? Intuition told her not to say anything to him for as long as possible. Yet now he would be in the house! She smiled at the absurdity and bit her lip to stop a laugh; then realised with horror that it might look as if she had brought Nick to help her, or to protect her even. No: she would not be one of the women who let the man blame himself for what had all been her own fault.

The heavy car door swung open and the white gateposts were brighter without the tinted glass. She got out and Nick emerged on the other side of the car. When the driver asked if they had everything, Nick gave Charlotte an ironic smile and said they did. The man touched his cap and the long car rolled away.

Nick looked at his sister. Her brow had knotted lightly, the way it used to when she was working on something as a child.

'Nicky,' she said. 'Let me just go in and see if everything's alright. Rachael was ill yesterday.'

'Of course,' he said. Her absence the night before and his presence now were not easy to explain, and they hadn't even discussed what to say.

'Just pop down to the corner and have a coffee,' said Charlotte.

Nick gestured to his empty pockets then Charlotte did the same. They looked at each other and burst out laughing, then came together and hugged.

'Thank you,' she said. 'Thank you for looking after me. I'm sorry about your boat.'

'It's ok,' he said, and kissed the top of her head. They stood for a moment then she gave him a squeeze and released him, gesturing towards the cafe.

'Don't worry,' she said. 'They'll look after you.'

Nick turned away, striding off in the old overcoat. She smiled, thinking that his purposeful figure had never been more at odds with his life; then mounted the steps and stood before the tall door. The buzzer sounded different from outside and she thought how appropriate it was to have to ring. She took a single long breath, feeling that precious weight which had been with her all morning. Steps appeared on the other side and a figure clouded the glass; and she started when Daniel opened the door. It was a weekday but he was at home, unshaven in his dressing gown.

'Baby,' he said, and put his arms around her. There was a packing case in the hall, and she had the strange thought that he had pre-empted her. She gently released him.

'What's this?' she said. Daniel shook his head and looked at her, then took her hand and led her to the kitchen. The children's breakfast was uncleared and a bottle of spirits stood open next to a glass, dirty from the previous night. Some files sat on the side.

'How's your brother?' said Daniel. His voice sounded hollow, as if he was repeating lines from memory. She looked at him blankly before remembering why she had gone to the boat. It was unusual of him not to notice the dress was ruined and her handbag was gone. She thought of Nick, trying to get a free coffee down the road in his pyjamas.

'He's better,' she said. 'How is Rachael?'

The name seemed to jog Daniel's memory.

'She's improved,' he said. 'Tabitha stayed. She's outside with Adam.' He was speaking automatically and looking at her with searching pity, as if someone had died.

'Daniel,' she said. 'What has happened?' He came to

where she was sitting and squatted with his hands in her lap, then leant into her for a moment before looking up.

'It's gone,' he said. 'The bank fired me yesterday.'

Charlotte looked at him in confusion.

'Why?' she said. He shook his head and she stroked the thick black hair.

'Some information got out about a deal and they decided it was me,' he said, and took a shuddering breath. 'Gross misconduct. No notice, no payoff.' He buried himself deeper in her lap and let out a long sigh.

Charlotte looked away across the kitchen.

22

Sir David stood in his office facing his Wall of Fame. It comprised rows of fist-sized chunks of rock, each one mounted on a plastic stand with the name of its mine made out in black and gold. He arranged them with ore content on the vertical axis and production volume on the horizontal, so when production dropped at a mine which was an old friend he could simply move it to the left rather than remove it completely. The top right sample had been there for two years. She was his princess, a Malaysian tin mine which was the envy of the sector. He could picture the geography there and smell the air, and still spoke to the manager every week.

He had visited every mine on the wall and could name the manager of each one. He had used to have these mini-samples flown to England as a safeguard against fraud by local sampling companies. It had been an imperfect defence, yet he had valued the signal it sent. Now he had his own testing facilities on three continents but he still called in the nuggets out of habit. He had got used to holding the rock from a new mine and trying to guess its ore content by comparing it with the Wall of Fame.

David held up the sample from Nick's mine and

turned it slowly in the morning light. Something glittered. He took down a sample from an old mine further down the Zervashan Valley and the two rocks sat impassively in his hands. They looked like they may as well have come from opposite sides of the world. Maybe the geologists were right and he was just a sentimental old witchdoctor? Still, science would tell him soon enough! He didn't know what to expect from the results. Most likely nothing; but even so he wouldn't regret having taken a little punt on the mine. Some of his best acquisitions had come from these little poaching operations. The cheapest way was actually to go to a concession while it was being drilled and pay the team to move the drilling rig. But you needed good men on the ground for that, and they didn't have any in Uzbekistan.

Instead Kobus had to call the management of the sampling company and acquire the core samples on behalf of United Minerals; and then pay the company to extract more samples elsewhere and analyse them for Nick's benefit. The original samples had been freighted out of the country to David's own testing yard in Romania. After all, which local drilling firm would say no to a company like United? And the incentive they had been given contained a healthy margin over what the State Committee would have paid. More importantly, he had provided the firm with a cast-iron guarantee of secrecy. Nick probably hadn't even offered that in the first place; yet without it the drilling company would have had little choice but to send any positive results into their own government.

David smiled. Here was the whole point! If there was any gold in this little piece of rock, there was no chance the Uzbeks would let it pass into the hands of a foreigner. Least of all Nick, who had spied on them! David had worried about him going there at all: it was out of the question that they would also let him walk off with the rights to a new gold seam. They had already kicked out a company even larger than United, which had been their own joint-venture partner. Nick wouldn't have stood a chance: so whatever existed below the ground, the three musketeers would end up empty-handed! No: if the results came back positive, David knew that he alone could outflank the government.

He would start by using a tiny front company quietly to relieve Nick and his friends of the mineral rights. The lads would probably be desperate to get some money back by selling them, although it wouldn't be much after the negative set of drilling results which David had provided. Then he would put together a consortium with some Russians, making it too uncomfortable for the Uzbeks to mess them around and make enemies on both sides. Then, pop, transfer the rights to the consortium, register his drilling results, and down we go! He, David McAllister, would have saved the mine for Britain! He looked at the rock sample and laughed. If those lads wanted to be miners, they should have stayed at home and bought his shares. It's what they were there for! And once again, he was struck by the sheer rightness of the world.

Yet he was still bothered by the thought of Nick, who would have unwittingly brought him the mine. If it made money for United, he had to do something for Nick. A simple pay-off wouldn't work when the man wrongly believed the whole mine should be his. He could save Nick's blushes by owning it through a distant subsidiary. But it didn't solve the problem of sending him a slice of the cake, and doing so in a wrapper that he wouldn't recognise. The poor man would need it even more now that he was homeless. David walked slowly back to his desk. Listening to the intercepts and phone traffic between the three partners had pained him. They shared such a sad, self-defeating humanity: Nick with his unchanging dream; Bannerman playing on everyone's greed while blind to his own; and poor Roger Curtis, way out of his depth even in the shallows.

Maybe he could find Nick a job in the company, somewhere out of the way? But he thought of the men he trusted to run his mines and then he thought of Nick. He remembered Franz Rosenheim's maxim: keep dangerous hands where you can see them. No, he owed better to the shareholders than to send Nick overseas. If it came to it, the job would have to be something close to home; preferably something which you did best when you did nothing at all! But he would only do it if the company had hit gold using Nick's coordinates: if not, the man could fend for himself.

David's desk phone rang. Affection and apprehension mixed when he saw who was calling. These calls were never time well spent, even if they were with his largest shareholder.

'Hi David,' said Alexander Rosenheim. It was the first time he had been back to his country house at

Covington since his cricketing defeat against the Ancasters in the summer. He remembered the weekend warmly and his previous telephone call had been to invite them to drinks on Saturday. As he waited for David to pick up, he was wondering if Emily would have left for university yet.

'Ahoy Xander!' said David. He could hear a dog barking in the background of the call. It was the middle of a weekday morning and he thought: of course, why not be at home? He looked at his watch then out of the window: five minutes for the young playboy, no more.

Alexander said he wanted to bring him up to date on his Foundation's activities in Romania. He was going to open some rehabilitation centres there and give the attendees work on his land conservation projects. David assented, saying United would do what it could and he would personally contribute. It occurred to him that Alexander's foundation was probably a place where Nick couldn't do much harm. But he didn't want to owe Alexander any more favours; and least of all by sending him a loose cannon. There was a shareholder vote coming up and he needed Alexander on side.

'Oh, David,' said Alexander, and David thought he heard a hint of mischief. 'I hear you've been flying around over London recently?'

There was a pause.

'Just a wee bit of bother,' said David. 'Nothing to worry about.'

'Doesn't bother me,' said Alexander. 'But they're breathing down our neck about this sort of thing. It's not the world it used to be.'

'Aye,' said David tersely. The boy was thirty years younger than him. He put down the phone and stared at it. How did Alexander know about the helicopter flight? David thought that he had a spy somewhere in the company but it would hardly be in Logistics. Aside from them and Kobus, the only other people who knew were the passengers themselves.

David's face tensed as he pulled the five signed affidavits from a drawer and stared at each one. Dominic Bannerman was the one most likely to know Rosenheim. Yet it would be out of character when Bannerman had nothing to prove or gain by telling him. He put the sheet to one side. Nick would not have done it in a million years; and David had seen the relief on Roger Curtis's face as he signed his document. He more than anyone needed to keep everything secret. Nick's sister had interrogated the room with a certain brio but he couldn't picture her wanting to contact Rosenheim. He stared at the final name and the room contracted around him. He had warned that girl once and now, the very next day, she was throwing her weight around again. Weight? She was younger than his own daughter. But he had to do something; and do it quickly before the anger overtook him even more. He dialled Tony Samartian.

'Tony! David McAllister here,' he said. The sound came out in a brisk burst and he hoped Tony couldn't hear the fury in his voice.

'David,' said Tony in his broad New York tone. 'What have you got for me?' David usually called with information Samartian could use to start shorts on

359

United's rivals, and today's topic seemed petty by comparison. But he owed it to the girl as much as anyone to let her know she shouldn't try this sort of thing, and it was better than invoking the Non-Disclosure Agreement against her. And there was no way he was going to spend lunch this angry.

'One of your analysts got a wee bit out of line with me recently,' he said.

There silence at the other end. Blood ran thicker than water with Tony, the only fund manager to buy David's stock on nothing more than his word; and David wondered if he was doing the right thing. The girl had balls at least, and Aileen would kill him if she found out. When Tony Samartian spoke, his cool tone was a hemisphere away from what it had been before.

'David,' he said. 'I'm sorry to hear that. Who was it?'

David reluctantly gave him the name.

'What do you want me to do, Mac?' said Tony. It was clear from his tone that David could say almost anything, and he realised that his anger against Imogen Somerville had disappeared completely.

'Oh,' he said mildly. 'Don't break her legs, Tony. Just make me feel better.'

'Sure thing,' said Tony. 'Consider yourself feeling better.' They caught up a little on business and the South American situation played on David's mind: he should really mention it as Tony almost certainly had interests in the country. But Tony also had an interest in United and would immediately see the implications for the company of a change of government. My silence is a sin of omission, he thought; I'll just have to play surprised if the coup happens. But he had already told Conrad de Salis! And David wondered what was happening to him.

'Don't you dare raise your dividend!' Tony was saying. 'Fuck those pension funds! Just get out there and buy more mines!'

David chuckled and said goodbye. At least Tony didn't care about protestors, or government committees, or anything other than the investors in his titanic hedge fund. He put down the phone and slid the affidavits back into the drawer, feeling a little lighter about the situation. The documents were better here than with Legal, his least favourite department. He looked up to see the Head of Public Affairs standing by the glass partition outside his office. Least favourite department but one, he thought.

'Ok,' he said to his secretary. 'But put through a call in five minutes.' Jill chuckled knowingly on the intercom.

The Head of Public Affairs entered his office, wearing a suit with a single button and tapered trousers. David imagined sending him out to Western Australia and wondered if he would even come back. He started counting the minutes until Jill's call.

'Sir David,' said his visitor. 'May I sit down?'

No, thought Sir David.

'Yes,' he said.

'Sir David,' he heard, and briefly had to close his eyes. The only man who called him that was the one who hated him most. 'We had a call from the Home Office this morning. Apparently one of the company's aircraft was in restricted airspace recently. The London Control Zone, to be precise. They want an explanation.'

David stared at him and felt the room begin to close around them. He concealed a deep breath and walked quickly over to open the balcony doors. You fucking little shit, he thought. You fucking traitorous little shit. Is that what you call transparency? His breath was deepening and he could feel his eyes growing. There was no way he could last five minutes with the man now. And then what? An employment tribunal, more fuel for this man's campaign to destroy the company that he worked for. David wanted to lock him in a room with Kobus for a few hours.

'Oh, it was nothing,' he said lightly, still facing out of the open doors. 'Just a personal matter.'

'Sir David,' said the man. 'I have told you before, you cannot use company resources for personal means. Or personal leverage for corporate ends.' Don't tell me, thought David: you know about South America and you'll be bleating to Rosenheim about that next.

'Aye,' said David, stepping back to his desk. 'I know, it doesn't do right by the shareholders.' He sent a message to Jill. 'ASAP,' it read.

'And what explanation shall I give the Home Office?' said the man accusingly. 'Or shall we just pay the fine? It will show up in next year's report.'

'Don't worry,' said David lightly. 'I'm dealing with it.' The phone rang and he picked it up.

'Hello Minister,' he said. 'Thank you for calling back.'

He made a gesture of apology to the Head of Public Affairs and the man got up to leave. When the door closed, David thanked Jill and hung up. He stepped out onto the wide balcony, where the air was cool and damp after the previous night's storm. Uneven clouds moved across the sky, and small gusts of wind got up and disappeared. Perfect weather. He took another ten breaths then returned to his desk to find a message from South America, where it was still early morning. He called Kobus.

'Is this really true?' he said.

'Ja,' said Kobus with a chuckle. The mines minister; his wife, who was the president's cousin; two generals and three colonels had all been rounded up that night.

'Well what do you know!' said David, leaning back in his chair. 'Do we know who the new mining minister will be yet?' he said.

'You know, Sir David...' said Kobus, and David sensed a joke coming on. 'I don't think that is uppermost in the President's mind!' said Kobus, and David laughed.

'Kobus,' he said teasingly. 'It wasn't you was it?'

Kobus chuckled again. The news seemed to have put him in a good mood. Probably because he had invested his pension in United stock; unlike those three jackaroos they had pulled off the boat the previous night.

'No, sir,' said Kobus. 'Not this time.'

'Kobus,' said David. 'Do us a favour and get a shortlist for the minister job, then show it to International.'

'Ja,' said Kobus, and the line went dead.

Sir David replaced the phone and shook his head. What a day! He didn't believe it was possible to destabilise a country: countries were either stable or they weren't, and sometimes the ones that weren't just swung back your way. What next? The old minister's fall-out with United was well known. Now the President would see his threat to redistribute the mineral rights as a prelude to the attempt on government: which meant whoever the new minister was, he would be too scared to touch them for years! David felt a lightness in his chest but stopped himself before it grew. What if the men were all shot? Well, there was every chance they had been planning the coup before Kobus had sent off those photos. And even if they hadn't, the photos were hardly an invitation to take over the government. He stopped again. They had been rounded up only hours after he had told de Salis.

Impossible, surely? It was much more likely the information had got out in the country itself. Sir David knew from experience that security around these coups was paper thin. Still, the possibility was there; which would mean that far from being a late night indiscretion, telling Conrad had actually been what saved him! Yet he had traded that information for a good word with the Home Office; and it seemed from the officious visit he had just received that none had been given. Unless Conrad had tried and failed, which was very possible given the disloyalty of politicians these days. He let out a sigh. He would know the truth when he looked Conrad in the eye, which at least meant he now knew where he was having lunch.

Who should he invite to the Club with him? Short notice counted for nothing: he knew twenty people who would cancel their lunch plans to come and join him.

Sinking a bottle of wine with Tony Samartian would be fun, but sadly it really was too short notice for him. David fleetingly realised that now that girl Imogen would get it in the neck for nothing. Well, not quite for nothing: she had still tried to falsify a document right under his nose the previous night.

'Ah, stuff business,' he muttered and picked up the phone to his London house. 'Can I speak with Lady McAllister? he said.

'I'll just get her,' said a voice. He smiled then his wife came back on the line. 'Lady McAllister here,' she said.

'It's Sir David McAllister here,' he said. 'Would her ladyship care to join me for lunch?'

An hour later, they were shown to a table in the Club. Aileen McAllister had noticed her husband's good spirits and was looking at him suspiciously. De Salis passed at the other end of the room, his eyes making their invisible sweep. David caught them and Conrad drifted over, a smile glimmering on his lips. David lifted his eyebrows questioningly and Conrad's shoulders rose in a tiny shrug.

'I tried,' he said, as if all he had ever done was try. I believe you, thought David; and I don't blame you for failing with those two-faced snakes in Westminster.

'And the other thing?' he said, fixing Conrad with a suggestive look, which the green eyes easily absorbed.

'Do try the rabbit,' said Conrad, the word coming out with a long first vowel. 'The rabbit's excellent.' David tried to suppress a smile as Conrad left, and Aileen looked at him sharply.

'David McAllister!' she said. 'Have you been up to no

good?'

David raised his champagne glass and looked her in the eye.

'Only good, my dear,' he said. 'Only good.'

*

Cesare paused on the landing to check his tie. Everything had been just right that day: the smell of mustard sauce from the kitchen; the swift, calm movements of his colleagues; the generous tip from Sir David. Mr de Salis had walked around the Club as usual and hadn't found a single wrong detail. Cesare felt that they were two of a kind, caring deeply and equally for all the guests. And now Mr de Salis was finally about to show it. At the top of the next short flight, he knocked lightly at the door of the apartment.

'Come in,' said the familiar voice. The Saluki lifted her head and then sank back in recognition. The only time Cesare had ever been reprimanded was for stroking her while on duty.

Conrad looked up and his green eyes settled on the figure. It froze his heart to think of what the man had done. He was lucky it had cost nothing more than a petulant phone call: it could easily have been a member shot dead on the pavement outside.

'Cesare,' said Conrad. 'Did you send a message yesterday giving the whereabouts of a Member?'

Blood rushed to Cesare's face and his eyes widened. He felt the owner's eyes on him and saw the eyebrows rise accusingly. The seated figure with its crossed legs and high, old-fashioned socks became huge then tiny. Cesare tried to speak then looked away to the cigar ashtrays and neat piles of books.

'Cesare,' said Conrad. 'If you'll forgive me, that is all the answer I need. Please empty your locker.'

Conrad reached for his cigar and looked back to the newspaper in his lap. Cesare opened his hands and raised them slightly. Conrad looked up and spoke patiently.

'Don't worry, Cesare,' he said. 'You are still a good waiter. You will receive two week's pay and a good reference, on condition that you never tell anyone what you have done. Understood?'

Cesare nodded. He looked at the dog for a last time then withdrew, fixing his eyes to the floor as he walked down the stairs.

23

The rain storm had leavened the waters of the Serpentine. They were cooler and cleaner, and had started the long descent to winter cold. Nick pulled away from the bank, leaving the girl to take her time.

It had been a strange few days, living in Charlotte's house while the place sat under a heavy miasma. His sister moved around mutely attending to the children while Daniel brooded. He left once to meet with a contact and then returned withdrawn. He had eventually asked Nick about Dominic but received few answers. Nick tried to absent himself during the day, entering and leaving by the garden square. There, at least, he could find a place of his own. He pushed through the water, wondering if it was too soon after his illness to be swimming again. He thought he knew which microbe had reappeared during the week, and was waiting for the results of the blood tests to come back.

A long administrative road opened towards getting his life back; and he had already taken the first weary steps. He had gone out with cash borrowed from Charlotte to buy some new clothes from the charity shops on Westbourne Grove. Then he went down to the pier and borrowed an angle grinder from the pier master to cut loose his bicycle. The man looked at him with irritation and Nick saw that the gate had also been damaged during the night. Most of his former neighbours passed by in silence, as if the disfiguring gap left at the end of the pier was somehow his fault. To those that stopped, he pleaded vandalism. Some looked on with sympathy while others were transparently fearful for their own boats.

With the bike free, he rode over to his garage and the man there agreed to help him unlock the car. Nick stood by awkwardly and offered to give him something later: the man waved him away and he realised how obvious his situation must be. He found his driving licence in the glove box then spent a long afternoon answering questions in a bank branch until they agreed to order him new cards. As late as he could leave it, he finally called Chelsea police station. They insisted on meeting him at the pier, and when he returned there it was to find two constables with their notebooks flapping in the breeze. One officer lifted the scorched end of a rope and looked at it sceptically.

'Vandalism?' said the other, his voice shot through with sarcasm. 'Can you think of anyone who might have a reason to harm you?'

'No,' said Nick neutrally.

'Were you on the boat at the time?' said the constable.

'No,' said Nick.

They issued him with a reference number and said they would be in touch with any developments. Maybe the boat would be found.

'Thank you,' said Nick, trying to lace his voice with hope. At least he would be able to claim the insurance, if the boat turned out to be covered. Failing that, the mooring itself was probably worth something. Perched on a stool in a mobile phone shop, he was taken through the long process of transferring his number onto the temporary phone they had given him. On the way back to Charlotte's, he stopped in Kensington Gardens and listened to the messages that appeared. There were fewer than he expected.

One was from the editor of *Sufi Journal*, who was still waiting for his Cantemir article. Nick sent one back, telling him the work had been lost and he would not be delivering it. One was from Samantha, suggesting a trip to Battersea Dogs Home to find him another dog. It was a strange reminder of Timur; and Nick realised that without the boat his memory had already faded. The third message was from Roger Curtis. Nick had been startled to hear the voice again so soon; and not only so soon but rejuvenated and unscarred. Roger said that he was starting a residential meditation centre at his house in Primrose Hill, and he wanted to offer Nick a room for as long as he needed it. He shook his head when he heard the name Roger had chosen and a terrible picture formed of the new commune. But by the time he arrived back in Notting Hill, Nick realised that he probably had to take up the offer. It was embarrassing staying at Charlotte's, and the place was probably going to be sold now that Daniel had lost his job.

He heard a splash and looked back to see that

Imogen had launched herself into the lake. She was swimming towards him, her brown eyes sparkling as the pile of blonde hair quivered in the cold. It was Charlotte who had encouraged him to follow up his parting invitation to her, and now he found himself regretting not having watched her approach the water.

'This is great!' she called. "Thank you!'

Splashing into the lake had elated Imogen. She often saw lines of bathing caps in the mornings but only Nick's suggestion had made her think she could join them. The sharp water reminded her of swimming in the rivers at home rather than the antiseptic pool of her gym. On the other bank, dust rose where two riders walked their horses; and even from the surface of the water she could see the London Eye in the distance. She stopped and trod water, admiring the low arches of a bridge across the lake.

Being free of Dominic for the past two days made her realise how he had occupied her thoughts while giving nothing back. The only thing that had really left a mark was the awful confrontation at work the day before. Halfway through the morning, a senior partner had appeared by her desk. He was someone with whom she had spent two years building a relationship. She gave her usual smile then saw his face and stopped: he was looking at her as if she was worse than a stranger.

'I don't know what you've been up to,' he snapped. 'But the next time you throw the name of this firm around, you're out.' He was gone before she could speak. Her face burned as she looked back at her screen, feeling the satisfied eyes of the other analysts. She had sat in Grosvenor Square at lunchtime with only anger holding back the tears. Her bonus had just disappeared and possibly also the chance of the fund backing another of her stocks. It felt like Dominic, swiping at her for having escaped; and she remembered the annoyance which had shown through his facepack that night at McAllister's house. Either that or it was Sir David himself, although a petty reprisal seemed out of character for him. Still, she had gone back to the office and sent him a note and a present thanking him for the overnight stay. If it had been him, he would know she had got the message; if not, it couldn't hurt.

She had taken home the fund's internal report on United Minerals and quickly saw how the company was a projection of its chairman's character. It had grown quickly and was brutally well run yet seemed to belong in a different era. The regulators were circling and there were rumours it was vulnerable to takeover, especially if the Rosenheim shareholding slipped. Alexander Rosenheim had been there with them in the Cotswolds and she wondered if there was a connection. They must have taken Roger Curtis there to tickle the money out of him and she could barely believe people still tried to work in that way. She now realized it was exactly the sort of exotic and nebulous thing in which Dominic would be involved.

She looked towards where Nick Paget stroked evenly along the inside of the swimming pen. It was partly curiosity that had brought her this morning, as it seemed that on some undiscovered level he was worth knowing. Why else would he know both Dominic and

McAllister? The chairman had greeted him like an old friend; and it seemed that without that relationship, they really might have had to swim to the banks of the Thames. She remembered her moment of warm surrender on the boat and let everything go as she turned over to face the autumn sky.

Nick turned into another length, replaying the previous morning's call from David McAllister. He had been lying in the bath waiting for the children to go to school when the replacement mobile rang. He picked it up expecting someone from a call centre wanting him to jump through another bureaucratic hoop, but instead the wide-awake Scottish voice leapt from the phone.

'How are you, Nick?' said David.

'Fine,' said Nick, sitting up and trying to conceal the echo of the bathroom.

'So sorry about your boat Nick,' said David sincerely. 'I hope you're keeping dry somewhere.'

'Oh yes,' said Nick lightly. 'No need to worry about that.'

'Now,' said David, his voice changing key. 'How do you fancy coming to join me? We've an opening here at United.'

Nick had stared across the bathroom then asked what the job was. David told him and Nick asked what it involved then immediately regretted it, as he should already know that if he was to be in with a chance. But David brushed off the question, saying he would send over some details. Nick had no idea what to say. He felt sure David was doing him a favour, yet he had never had a full-time job in London or wanted one. He said thank you and David firmly suggested that he should think about it. Later that day, some documents arrived from United Minerals. Nick started wading through paragraphs of jargon but soon forget them when he saw the salary. He had no idea what people earned these days but the figure seemed massive by any standards. He stared at it, trying to translate it into his life.

He had re-read the document that morning before coming to meet Imogen. 'Head of Public Affairs' felt like a contradiction in an industry as secretive as mining. The description had something to do with government relations, although the corporate language made it sound quite abstract. Like everything, it could only become real in practice. Anyway hadn't he once advised the Uzbek government? And he knew parts of the British government very well indeed. Laying aside the details, the very novelty of having an office and a business card started to appeal to him.

Riding to the park that morning, he tried to put the whole thing together. He could live initially at Roger's in Primrose Hill and walk through Regents Park to the office in St James' Square. He wouldn't be able to have another dog but he would have money instead; money for suits, lunches and holidays. The work itself was only a distant part of the picture although even David himself had been vague about it. 'To be honest,' he had said, 'the less you do the better. Just do as I say.' That meant becoming David's confidant, which would be a strong position in the company; and there would probably be travel too. He had until the following week to decide and was beginning to realise that he would probably have to accept.

With the boat and his savings gone, he had less now than at any time in the past twenty years. Hard though it was to admit, the job offer was a lifeline. But it was also more than a lifeline. It was the signal for a new kind of life, in which he stood level with people instead of aside from them; a life which let him see this city from the inside. And it would give him a focus beyond mopping up the embarrassing remnants of the mining deal. At least it was Saturday and the tense conversation could not take place until next week. But of course! Having a new job would give him something to say! Joining David would restore his credibility at a stroke. He should accept as soon as possible; certainly before seeing Dominic and Roger again. He stopped swimming and took a long breath of morning air.

Someone ducked under the row of buoys near him and he saw it was Imogen, the hair dark and wet on the back of her neck. She swam out ahead, her long legs beating like a water boatman, and he turned to follow.

*

The phone rang and Charlotte picked it up.

'Hello my dear,' said a familiar voice. 'It's ready!'

Charlotte tucked an arm across her waist and propped an elbow on it. The money in her bank account wasn't enough to pay Dinah for the painting, and she couldn't ask Daniel now. He had walked her outside the day before and pointed to the upper windows of the house. 'We own from there up to the roof,' he had said.

'All the rest, the bank owns. And when I can't pay each month, they are going to want it back.' She had heard the sickness in his voice. He wasn't a simple materialist yet money was his yardstick for pride and success. It turned out that he had been spending because he felt he had to, which meant there was little saved or invested. The thought was disorientating to the point of nausea, as she had thought that she was spending to keep *him* happy.

'What do other people do when this happens?' she had said.

'Get other jobs,' said Daniel distantly.

'Can't you?' she said carefully, and he gave her an empty look.

'No,' he said. 'Not on gross misconduct.' It seemed that whatever happened had turned the other banks against his old employer and now they were finding it hard to get shared business. And as the scandal spread, it carried his name with it.

'And *was* it you?' she asked gently. Daniel looked away, as if making up his mind about something.

'No,' he said, shaking his head. 'Impossible.'

She hadn't wanted to push him further when he seemed so convinced his career was over. Either way, it was unlikely she was going to be able to pay Dinah.

'That's good,' she said into the phone. 'Are you pleased with it?'

Dinah heard the flatness in her voice and frowned. It was almost impossible to please a client with a portrait: but they were usually excited on hearing that it was finished then reserved when they saw it. She hoped this time it would be the other way round. It was an excellent commercial painting and someone with Charlotte's eye couldn't fail to be impressed. Even in the grey light of a Cotswold rain storm, the canvas in front of her commanded the room.

'I am pleased,' she said. 'I think you will be too.'

'Dinah,' said Charlotte, knowing she was about to commit one of the worse solecisms in the art world. She thought momentarily of selling something else to pay for the painting and realised that eventually all her other paintings would be sold. But that would take time, and Daniel would probably need the money. She cleared her throat.

'Dinah,' she said again. 'I've got bad news. My husband has lost his job. We may not be able to take it.'

Dinah blinked and looked around the cottage. No-one had ever spoken those words to her before. She had fallen in love with the painting and spent far too long on it but at least it was going to pay the bills next month. She looked at the two children; one moving hopefully forwards, the other in repose. There was a touch of Rembrandt in the delicate curls and dark background. She didn't know a single other painter who could turn out something like it. Yet she could hear the shame in Charlotte's voice and knew the girl was both serious and realised the seriousness of what she was doing. Dinah would happily have swapped it for one of the paintings on Charlotte's walls; but it wouldn't do to take advantage of the situation. She didn't know what to say, and took a shallow breath.

'Just take it anyway,' she said. 'Pay for it when you

can.' Pay for it when I'm dead, she thought. She had imbued the portrait with all of her hopes for the family: maybe having it in the house would help keep them together.

'Really?' she heard Charlotte say in a small voice.

'Of course,' said Dinah. 'It's no use to me!' No use indeed, she thought. The piece would have flown into the Royal Academy Summer Exhibition and sold for plenty. But that's not why I painted it, she thought; and already she liked her decision.

'Thank you,' said Charlotte. 'You don't have to.'

It sounded to Dinah like the first piece of kindness the girl had ever received. She remembered their first meeting at the gallery and then the other reason she had called. She lit a cigarette and settled on the edge of an arm chair.

'Charlotte,' she said. 'There is one thing you could do. Should do, perhaps.'

'Anything,' said Charlotte, hearing the weakness in her voice. Dinah had become the last thread connecting her to herself, and she didn't want to put the phone down.

Dinah took a breath and tried to soften her tone but the words came out hard.

'Don't do it,' she said.

Charlotte sat down on the edge of her bed and looked around the empty room. How did Dinah know, of all people? She realised with a chill how obvious things must have been at the gallery; and how mad she had nearly been.

'Do what?' she said quietly.

Dinah closed her eyes. She had never done anything like this before. She opened them again and looked down at the chipped edge of her mug.

'Get involved with our mutual friend,' she said.

Charlotte leaned across and pushed the bedroom door closed then turned towards the windows.

'I know,' she said in a low voice. The clumsy series of messages she had received from Dominic in the last two days had only made her see how easily led she had been before. 'I realise now,' she said, and heard the other woman draw on a cigarette.

'Good for you,' said Dinah. 'Sorry for butting in.'

'No,' said Charlotte. 'Thank you.' She could feel tears pricking her eyes. She didn't want Dinah to go. 'But Dinah. I can't, I don't...' She wiped the dampness away with the ball of her hand.

'I know, sweetheart,' said Dinah. 'I can see that. But you know what you know. That's a lot for the time being. It's enough, I promise.'

'Really?' said Charlotte. She was suddenly crying hard and holding the phone with both hands.

'Really,' said Dinah. Things were getting easier. 'Just take your time. You'll be pleased you did later.'

Charlotte lifted the corner of the duvet and wiped her face with it. A space had opened inside her for the first time since arriving back.

'Thank you,' she said. 'I will.' Dinah heard the change and something lifted in her chest.

'Now,' she said brightly. 'What will we do with this painting? Would you like to come and pick it up? The weather's terrible down here this time of year!' She gave an dry laugh.

'Oh yes, I'd love that!' said Charlotte. 'Can I come today, as its Saturday?'

Dinah looked around the small cottage and heard Charlotte sniff. Maybe Caroline would put her up in the main house?

'Of course, my dear,' she said. 'Just call me from the station and I'll pick you up.'

'Thank you,' said Charlotte. She put down the phone and lay back on the wide bed.

*

Dominic replaced the phone and stared at it. Charlotte hadn't picked up again and he could not call a third time. He hadn't even planned what to say; platitudes, probably, which tried to reach back to when they had been friends. It seemed impossible that their lunch had passed so completely into history. She hadn't even looked at him before getting into the other car, and the memory of her turning away had stayed with him ever since. He could still feel the anticipation which had been with him all summer, although now it would never be resolved. It was a strange, lopsided feeling.

He paused as a slow fugue from the Well-Tempered Clavier walked through the air. His suitcase for Scotland was open on the bed. Only a month before he had been certain he would not go back after his double-length stay in the summer; yet already he was folding in clothes which still smelled of cordite and the moor. He smiled at the irony and winced as the movement hurt his skin.

It had turned out to be only lightly blistered and he probably could have laughed it off, as the eyebrows particularly looked like a drunken prank.

No, it wasn't his face that was sending him away. It was everything else. The fact that he had involved himself in something so amateurish; then jumped so readily to the wrong conclusions; and then, worse, acted on them. Words spoken about him were reappearing uncomfortably close; that he was hot-headed, selfish and proud. At least the story shouldn't go too far around London with David McAllister clamping down on it. Yet thinking of McAllister's only made his disquiet about the man's neat explanations resurface.

He had spent the previous morning reading United Minerals' press coverage. Half the pressure groups in Europe were after the company, writing to the big shareholders demanding that they sell the stock. There were rumours that even Rosenheim Group was starting to waver. If that happened, a takeover of United would be almost inevitable. The banks would start circling, spreading bid talk while they put together their own proposals; then in a sudden frenzy the company would be gone. The charities that were attacking United Minerals probably had no idea that they weakening it as a takeover target, let alone that they would only drive it into far harsher hands than David McAllister's. Chinese or Russians owners would make his era look like group therapy. Not that the campaigners cared, of course. Once the company was out of their reach, they would simply look for another European firm to harry until it was pulled to the ground by less scrupulous jaws.

Dominic sighed. He didn't want to go away wrapped in depression at Europe's cancerous determination to destroy itself. But David McAllister knew the situation and for him to take such extravagant risks under the circumstances seemed insane. Dominic had seen hubris do for bigger companies than United Minerals but not to the extent of pursuing a failed deal to such a dramatic conclusion. And then there was the odd camaraderie with Nick: had they really not seen each other for so long?

He had run through it too many times to expect anything new, and must instead let the questions rest in his subconscious while he was in Scotland. He thought of the early autumn leaves and the sea loch with its remaining hint of summer warmth. He would swim there in the mornings then walk the moor with his gun before drawing an evening bath and drifting for hours between a book and the whisky. Nothing could change while he was away. His options on the mine were still in place, which meant he could easily block a sale until he was satisfied. And a purchase offer might just nudge his thoughts about Sir David out into the light.

He closed his eyes. Would this chattering commercial monologue never stop? He needed the silence of Scotland; that speaking silence of nature, marked only by the trickle of his consciousness. He wanted the trickle to become a flood and for each moment to grip him again. This new hunger made him almost grateful for the weeks that had passed; if only Charlotte had not been picked up and crushed by them. It felt stupid to be focusing on her now when he had never acted at the time, instead letting his thoughts be blockaded by the innocent presence of her children. Now it seemed like nothing could be less important. Selwood Park had plenty of space and step-children were a small price to pay for someone who would make the place bearable, even fun. He looked down at the patchwork of wool and tweed in his suitcase. Perhaps he would stay in Scotland indefinitely, going deliberately feral in preparation for his term as head of the family? Dominic Bannerman, 10th Earl of Warminster: the words that would one day be branded on him.

The future made him think of his sister. Caroline would greet him that evening him with a look of tolerant disappointment, as if his singed face confirmed everything that she expected of him. It was annoying that the gamekeeper in Scotland was away and he had to drive to Toadsmoor first for the keys. At least they would invite him to stay the night and he could do the long drive north on Sunday. Dominic clipped shut the suitcase and went to check his guns.

***

To be continued

Printed in Great Britain
by Amazon